HEERA WATSON AND THE RISE OF THE DARK KING

KAM VERDEE

I dedicate this book to my family, especially my mum, Manjeet, who has truly been my rock.

CHAPTER 1

Behind the Locked Door

I wandered into my bedroom while I went on listening to Emma Grove, my best friend, telling me what Laura Foster had said about me at school earlier that day.

My mobile had been glued to my ear for half an hour already, and my arm was beginning to ache. I shut the bedroom door behind me and leant up against the radiator by the window. Mum had only just turned the heating on, and my legs and lower back only now began to feel the welcome warmth.

I lifted the curtain and peeked outside. With the help of the street lamps, I could see frost starting to cover the pavement on its way to the cars down the street. It was another freezing Monday evening in Birmingham, in the English Midlands. The weather was typical for the first week of December, and it was only going to get colder.

As Emma revealed the horrible details, I could feel my cheeks growing warm just as my legs and back were. I couldn't help but feel embarrassed about myself. How could Laura be so cruel? I tried my best to brush aside the comments Laura had made about me by shaking my head, as if I was trying to empty it of the cruel words she'd used to describe me.

'Honestly,' I said to Emma, 'I really don't care what Laura Foster and her sidekicks said about me. Nothing they say is going to make me change who I am.'

'What? Are you serious?' Emma asked. 'Laura called you a pathetic geek, and she's been telling everyone she's going to drop you like a lead balloon as soon as the Chemistry project's over. Are you honestly telling me you don't care she said all this about you?'

'I couldn't care less, Emma. Laura isn't worth my time.'

I walked across the room and stood in front of my memo board on the wall covered with photos of my family. Seeing myself in the pictures made me wonder why I was so weak. Why didn't I stick up for myself? I never really remembered a time when I'd been confident in social situations. Instead, I let people walk all over me.

In nearly every photo, my long, straight, black hair partially covered my blue eyes. My usual olive complexion had given way to a pale grey colour, complete with blushing pink cheeks and an awkward smile. I always ended up looking like this when I felt uncomfortable or vulnerable. I wanted to hide and protect myself from the outside world.

Being regarded as a 'high achiever', whatever that was supposed to mean exactly, by my parents, classmates and my teachers did nothing for my social life. I was fifteen years old, and my classmates' perception of me hadn't changed since I'd joined St Claire's school four years ago. They still openly called me a nerd, a bookworm, and the most hurtful of all, a loser.

I was basically a normal teenager, who enjoyed music, films and even a little Reality TV on a Saturday night, yet I was still treated differently and constantly bullied. Laura Foster was the main bully. She was the most popular girl at St Claire's, and if she didn't like you, she'd let you and everyone else know about it.

Laura prided herself on having the perfect figure, and she was very quick to judge you on what you ate during break or lunch. She would always make sarky comments about how much weight someone had gained. I certainly didn't have the perfect figure and neither did I want to take her advice and try the latest fad diets. I was comfortable with the way I carried myself, and I tried not to feel insecure about my appearance.

Laura and her friends were always making comments about how I should wear makeup to 'glam up', as they called it. They recommended I use a particular lip gloss brand to make my lips appear fuller and to use eye shadow to make my blue eyes 'pop' against my olive skin. There was nothing unique about Laura's or her friends' style or appearance. They all looked about the same and I didn't want to be like them, not one bit.

'That's not it though, Heera, there's more, and as your friend, I have to tell you what else Laura said about you,' Emma continued.

'Go on then, tell me.' I knew Laura would have plenty of mean comments to make about me. Whether it be to my face, behind my back or even through social media, she was clearly on a mission to slate me as best as she could.

I wasn't completely alone because I always had Emma to talk to and confide in. We were inseparable. She always stood up for me, and even though she was considerably shorter than me and others in our year, she was able to boss everyone around without any problem. Although we were best friends, we were so different. Emma was outgoing, sporty and sociable, whereas I was reserved, quiet and took pleasure in learning.

'Basically, Heera, she said you're the only one not going to the school Christmas party, and even if you were, you wouldn't have anything nice or special to wear. She laughed because you don't wear makeup and at your owl earrings. She even called the necklace your grandmother gave you, plain and ugly. Can you believe that, Heera? Now, don't you think you need to put her in her place?'

'No, there's no need. Her words don't have any influence on me,' I replied, knowing I was lying to both Emma and myself.

The truth was, I didn't have the courage to stand up to Laura, and I was deeply hurt at what she'd said about me.

Thinking about what Laura had said about my necklace and earrings made me angry. Using my right hand, I began to fiddle with my owl-shaped earrings to make sure they were firmly in place, and then I clutched the necklace my grandmother had given me. I loved the owl earrings my parents had bought me and I adored my necklace; I couldn't care less if Laura had laughed at my jewellery. Who did Laura think she was to say this about me? I never said anything about what she wore? Then again, I didn't judge anyone on what they wore or didn't wear.

'WHAT? ARE YOU COMPLETELY INSANE?' Emma shouted. 'If you don't say anything, I will. I was about to have a right go at her until Mr Ford began to hand out detentions left, right and centre in class, and as soon as the bell rang, Laura was straight out the door. Heera, you need to stick up for yourself. I know you pretend people's opinions of you don't matter when I know they do. I can tell when your feelings are hurt.'

I was glad I wasn't in Maths today when Laura had said this; I was picked up early from school by my mum to go to a dentist appointment. Even if I had been present, I probably would've kept quiet and listened to her bitter words and tried to block them out.

'What exactly do you want me to do?' I asked. 'No matter what I do or say at school, everyone will still see me as me.'

'Come with me to the school Christmas party.'

'I don't want to go to the party, Emma… you know it's not my kind of thing.'

'Heera, you need to step out of your comfort zone and show everyone at school you can have fun and let your hair down instead of studying all the time. Heera, I'm your best friend and I'm just trying to help you.'

'Why should I have to show them anything?' I asked her.

'Just to get them off your back. Don't you think it hurts me when I have to hear them slagging you off? There's only so much I can say to stick up for you. Heera, you need to stand up to them too and it seems like I'm fighting your battles.'

'Emma, I don't expect you to do or say anything to them. I'll handle it myself,' knowing I'd let Laura get away with it.

'Heera, I didn't mean it like that… of course, I'm going to stick up for you because that's what friends do. Please just come to the party… do it for me. It can be my Christmas present.'

There was a moment's silence. I used the time to gather my thoughts.

Why couldn't people see the real me? I was a good person and so what if I liked to learn and do well at school. Why did I have to conform to their ideals to be noticed and to be liked?

'Ems, I really don't want to go,' I said.

'Oh come on! It's going to be so much fun,' Emma continued. 'I can do your hair, makeup and I have the perfect dress for you. All you need to do is get the accessories. You will look like a whole new person… they won't even recognise it's you.'

'I really don't know, Ems.'

Dressing up, doing hair and makeup were of no interest to me. I laughed to myself at the way Emma was selling the idea to me. It was as if she was describing an ideal scene from an American teen flick, where the nerdy bookworm transforms into a gorgeous girl, and the whole school stands and stares at her beauty. Finally, the girl is seen as an equal and becomes the 'It' girl. I couldn't think of anything worse than being the centre of anyone's attention, and there was no way on this planet I was going to let myself become an 'It' girl.

'Please, do it for me? Don't make me beg like this, Heera.'

I had to stand my ground. I hated being put in these awkward positions when all I wanted to do was flat out refuse to go.

Emma was waiting patiently for me to answer. OK, Heera, I said to myself, it's just two letters… N… O… just say NO.

'Emma, you see, I erm… YES, I'll go,' I said, punching the air in frustration at how my own mouth had deceived me. Emma screamed in delight on the other end of the line. The school Christmas party was on the fourteenth of this month, and I only had ten days to prepare myself for it.

'You promise?'

'Yeah, I promise,' I reluctantly said.

'Do you promise you'll say something to Laura as well?'

'Like what though?'

'Tell her exactly how you feel about what she said about you, or she'll keep doing it over and over again. Laura thinks she's better than everyone else with her bright, dyed blonde hair and blue eyes. She's nothing more than an arrogant bully. Now promise you'll say something or else I will, and you know how I can make a scene, Heera.'

What on earth was I going to say to Laura? I simply couldn't confront her. For now though, I agreed with Emma just to get her off the phone.

'I promise,' I said.

'Good, it's about time she gets what's coming to her. Shoes… oh, wait… I've got these gorgeous shoes you can wear. You're going to look fabulous. You'll wipe the smile of Laura's face and show the whole school a different side to you. I can't wait! The dress is silver, so you need to get the jewellery to match, and I'm not talking about cheap plastic jewellery either, Heera. Ask your mum to lend you some of her accessories… she always wears nice things.'

'OK, I'll ask her. I have to go now because I need to finish my English homework. I'll see you tomorrow,' I said, desperately trying to figure out how I could get out of having to go to this dreadful party, where everyone was going to act fake to each other's faces and pretend they were all best friends.

'Go ask your mum about the jewellery straightaway, Heera. Also, don't forget to take pictures on your phone and show me what you've found tomorrow.'

'OK,' I said.

'It's going to be so much fun!'

'Yeah… I'll speak to you tomorrow, Ems.'

'See ya!'

I turned the phone off and put it on charge.

It had been three hours since the conversation with Emma and I was completely stressing out. Not only was I worrying about the party and having to come face to face with Laura Foster tomorrow, but my mum had outright refused to let me borrow any of her jewellery.

The only jewellery we owned had belonged to my grandmother, my dad's mother, who we called Mamma. The jewellery was kept in a safe that was hidden in my dad's locked office down the landing.

I wasn't irresponsible. I was annoyed with my mum for refusing to lend me the jewellery, even though I knew some of the heirlooms were intended for me. As soon as Mamma had passed away, Mum had placed everything we'd inherited away in the safe, and she rarely let any of us go into the office.

As I stood waiting in my room for my parents to go to bed, I knew I'd made a big mistake in agreeing to go to the party. The promise I'd made to Emma was forcing me to go behind my parents' back to open Dad's locked office and to search through the safe for the perfect jewellery to match my outfit.

I gripped the pendant around my neck. This too had belonged to Mamma, and she'd given it to me on my birthday, seven years ago, on the fourteenth of January. The very next day, she'd passed away in her sleep. It was a simple gold cylinder with a round, clear stone in the centre, and every time I was nervous, I held onto it tightly. I was very close to Mamma and I believed the pendant gave me strength somehow. Moreover, the pendant was a constant reminder she was always looking out for me.

In my other hand, I held the keys to the safe and the locked door. I'd found the keys an hour ago in my parents' bedroom and I'd hidden them. I felt so ashamed and guilty, but turning back now would mean backing out of my promise to Emma.

No, enough was enough. I'd made up my mind.

If going to this party would show everyone at school a different side to me and help me to fit in at school, then I was willing to take the risk of being caught by my parents. As for Laura, she'd made my life difficult with her sarcastic comments about me, and every time I chose to ignore her, where did it get me? Nowhere.

What was I thinking? Who cared what they thought? I wasn't brought up to just fit in. I was always told by my parents and Mamma to do what I wanted to do and to not follow the crowd. I had to be true to myself. I'd tell Emma tomorrow that I wasn't going to the party. I lay down in bed with the duvet over me and tried to switch my mind off.

How I hated my own thoughts. It was a constant internal struggle to do what was right, and no matter what, I couldn't stop the two voices in my head competing with each other.

The promise, Heera... you promised Emma you'd go to the party and now you're letting your best friend down. No, I couldn't do that to her. I threw the duvet off with great annoyance at the mess I'd found myself in and sat waiting with my heart racing for my parents to go to bed.

I had to follow the plan through.

At exactly eleven o' clock, the light on the landing went out. I carefully opened my bedroom door and crept slowly to the office door. I glimpsed behind me to make sure I was alone in the dark. I inserted the key into the lock, inhaled deeply, steadied myself and turned the key. I pushed the handle, slipped into the room and closed the door behind me.

I stood in the dark, clutching my pendant to my chest. I reached out gently to the sides of the walls trying to find the light switch; I didn't want to drop anything to wake my parents. Eventually, I found the switch and turned the light on. I found myself standing in the middle of a crammed, yet tidy, space with a dark mahogany desk directly in front of me.

I didn't waste any time. I hurriedly began to rummage in the drawers of the desk and the several cabinets around the room; however, all I could find were piles and piles of old paperwork.

I tried desperately to remember where the safe was hidden. It had been several years since I'd been in the office, and the memories I had of the room were vague.

I was about to give up and return to my bedroom when I saw something out of the corner of my eye. There was a large, standing cabinet of books on the left hand side of the room. My love of reading made me walk over to the cabinet and pick up one of the books. However, this was no ordinary book. I found it to be made of hollow cardboard and in fact they all were. This was a clever disguise by my parents to hide something important. Why else would they need a cabinet full of pretend books? I knew the safe had to be somewhere close. I moved the cabinet away from the wall slightly and the grey safe came into view.

My heart bumped with excitement.

I opened the safe to find the upper and lower section crammed with envelopes and packages varying in size. Frantically, I began to open all the packed boxes in the lower section, and I came across an assortment of jewellery, which would be perfect for the dress Emma had picked out for me. There were earrings, necklaces and I even saw Mamma's old brooches.

I picked out a pair of dazzling silver earrings and a necklace, glittered with tiny oval crystals, to go with Emma's dress. I realised these were expensive items of jewellery, but I would be ever so careful with them.

Only one rectangular shaped box was left in the back of the safe. I reached for it and found it to be covered in soft black velvet with odd red symbols carefully embroidered into the material. I opened the package to find three purple, velvet pouches embroidered with the same symbols as the box, and within each pouch, I found a crystal, differing in size and colour.

The only similarity between the crystals was their oblong, rugged shape. I wondered if they were ornamental pieces because they could've been placed on their side on a shelf or a mantelpiece for decoration. I tried to think whether I'd seen these when I was younger at Mamma's house, but if I had, I would've remembered them due to their distinctive colours.

The blue crystal was slightly smaller than the yellow one. I left them both within their pouches. The third crystal was a vivid green, at least five inches long and was larger than the other two. I couldn't resist touching the stone. I put my hand inside the pouch and gripped the crystal. It was cold to the touch and quite bulky. I admired the crystal as it rested in the palm of my right hand.

Instantaneously, I felt a tug around my neck. The gold pendant I was wearing lifted itself away from my chest with such force that I felt the chain tighten and dig deep into the back of my neck.

I was struck with fear. I wanted to scream and run away but I couldn't move my body. What on earth was happening to me?

The pendant hovered over the crystal in my hand and I heard a voice vibrate from the pendant. A calm male voice whispered my name, '*Heera Watson*,' and the crystals began to glow.

The light escaping the green crystal was blinding. The other crystals were equally bright with the light beaming out of their pouches, and I could hardly see in front of me. When I gained some feeling in my body and felt my fingers twitch, I dropped the green crystal on the floor, and the intensity of the light from each crystal simmered down slightly.

I couldn't believe what I'd seen and heard. I was terrified. I began to panic again. Why did the crystals react in this way? Whose voice did I hear? Did my parents hear it too? Questions were racing through my mind but nothing I'd seen or heard could be explained.

Maybe I'd imagined everything? After all, this was the first time I'd rebelled against Mum by taking jewellery without her knowing, and I was feeling extremely anxious about coming face to face with Laura tomorrow. I blamed it on my nerves. They were distorting my reality. I tried to push all thoughts to the back of my mind for now and focus on what I was doing, and the sooner I could leave this room, the better.

I put the items back into the safe as I'd found them, except for the green crystal, which was still lying on the floor pulsating with white light. I decided to take the crystal back to my room and use my computer to research what I'd seen. It was possible that the crystals were novelty items and there was some sort of trick making them glow the way they did.

I noticed a dusty gold book, partly concealed under brown envelopes, in the top section of the safe. The book was well-worn and the front and back covers were falling apart in my hand. I carefully turned the pages of the book and uncovered hand drawn pictures of people, including names and dates written in fine faded writing below each illustration.

Their clothes were uniquely different. Many were wearing outfits relating to their professions such as farmers, soldiers and judges, while women wore long elegant dresses. The pictures could have easily belonged in an old history book. There were over a hundred drawings of people, and yet each drawing was distinctive and detailed. I didn't recognise any of the names.

I flicked through the last few remaining pages, and my eyes were immediately drawn to a sketch of a young woman. Below her sketch, I saw her name, *Hayden Parker*, beside the date of *December 1901*. I wasn't sure of the relevance of the date. It could've been the date of when the sketch was drawn, or when Hayden was born, or even when she passed away. I noticed Hayden was wearing an identical pendant around her neck as mine, and I wondered whether she was an ancestor of our family.

Hayden was not wearing a dress like the other women I came across in the book. She was holding a sword in one hand, a shield in the other and her body was covered in silver armour. This intriguing woman had a look of sheer determination on her pretty face. We both had long, straight black hair and piercing eyes, although hers were brown and mine were blue. She too had high cheek bones like me, giving her sharp facial features, and it was good to see that she wasn't plastered with makeup.

I was fascinated at what I'd seen of Hayden and decided to take the book with me to my room. Whilst, I didn't know anything about her, I admired the fact she was different to the other women in the book, and I wanted to find out more about her.

I placed everything away and left the safe as I'd found it. I picked up the green crystal, and it began to glow brightly again, but not as intensely as before. I returned the crystal to its pouch. I tucked the book under my arm, turned off the lights, locked the office door and crept back to my bedroom with the jewellery and crystal.

I hid Mamma's earrings, necklace and crystal in the pocket of an old black coat in my cupboard. I placed the book under my bed, determining that when I returned home from school tomorrow afternoon, I'd research information on the crystal and on Hayden Parker.

I lay in bed thinking about what I'd experienced. Why did my pendant react that way? Had I just imagined it? No, how could I have imagined something so vivid?

I closed my eyes but sleep didn't come for hours. I kept worrying about what I'd done behind my parents' back and about the promise I'd made to Emma. In time, I drifted off into a deep sleep.

I found myself climbing a steep mountain. The peak loomed above me and I steadied myself, determined to reach the top. After what seemed like hours, I stood at the peak, gazing down at the barely recognisable land below me.

Suddenly, something stirred behind me. I spun around to find a monstrous figure towering over me with his blood red eyes fixated on mine, and his gaunt, distorted face shook with sheer hate and anger directed at me.

I screamed. It seemed time had slowed down and I was suffocating, while desperately trying to gasp for air. The hatred in his face terrified me and he raised his arm to strike me. I closed my eyes in fear.

What was I doing? What was I thinking? I couldn't stop him from hurting me and thoughts of my family filled my head. A kind voice whispered my name in my ear: '*Heera... you're so close... find the crystals. They are your only way of defeating him. Let him guide you... be brave.*'

The woman's voice I heard was soothing but I didn't know who it belonged to.

I awoke and sat up straight in my bed, panting as sweat poured down my face. My hand immediately closed around my pendant and I checked the alarm clock. It was six o'clock in the morning and I only had half an hour in bed left before I had to get ready for school.

I couldn't stop thinking about the vivid red eyes of the figure in my nightmare. I shuddered when I recalled the look on his face. Who was he? And why was the mysterious voice asking me to find the crystals? Could it be because I'd found three crystals in the safe the night before? I convinced myself my mind was playing tricks on me and now my thoughts shifted elsewhere.

Knowing I would have to see Laura and her gang hit me hard again, and I felt as if my heart was going to drop to my stomach. I was dreading having to see and speak to them. I had to say something to Laura, or Emma would step in and make the situation worse.

After half an hour of tossing and turning, I dragged myself out of bed to get into my school uniform. I wore a white shirt, a red jumper and a red blazer with black trousers rather than a black skirt because it was so cold.

I remembered Emma wanted me to take pictures of the jewellery, and I snapped a few shots on my phone before I returned the office key back into my parents' room.

I went down to the kitchen to find my parents and two younger brothers eating their breakfast.

'Morning everyone,' I said.

'Morning,' they all replied in unison.

'Here, have some toast,' Mum said, getting up to butter some toast from the toaster.

'No, I'm not hungry,' I replied.

'Have something at least,' Dad said. His soft blue eyes turned to me with deep concern, and the lines around them appeared more noticeable than usual. He worked as a General Manager at a car dealership, and although he enjoyed his demanding career, the stress had aged him considerably.

'Samuel, I know what's wrong,' Mum said. 'Heera, I know you're upset about me not letting you borrow Mamma's jewellery for the party, but I promise I'll take you shopping on Saturday. As it is, it's my first Saturday off in months and we'll have a proper girl's day out at the shops.'

I felt a pang of guilt but kept a straight face. I didn't want to give my deceit away. Hearing her talk about having a girl's day out was weird because we never really did those types of things.

Mum was very outspoken and confident, and if she saw someone doing something wrong, she'd confront them, even though she was five foot one. We only had our straight black hair in common. Dad always said she was too fiery, saying it was her Indian Sikh Punjabi roots coming through.

I was more like my dad. He was reserved, didn't like confrontation and always backed away from arguments with Mum. I had my dad's blue eyes and I'd inherited his tall gene, making me one of the tallest pupils in the year, and of course, the class took full advantage of this by calling me a geeky giraffe behind my back. I just laughed it off, as per usual, as this was my only way of hiding my feelings.

'OK, Mum, honestly though I'm really not hungry and I'm running late. I best get going,' I replied.

'Mani, give her some toast to take with her,' Dad said. Mum passed me toast wrapped in foil, which I gratefully took.

'Heera,' Mum said, before continuing, 'we also have to find you an Indian outfit to wear to your cousin, Seema's Mehndi evening before her big wedding. Don't give me that look, Heera. It's important for you to be there and to learn about your Indian roots too.'

'Mum, it's not that I don't want to learn, but Seema never includes me in anything.'

'That's because you don't take an interest in what any of your cousins on my side of the family have to say, even though they follow both Indian and Western cultures,' Mum continued.

I glanced at Dad to help me out but he simply smirked at me. It had nothing to do with culture. I loved my Indian roots and my Western roots too, and I was proud to be a mix of both. What Mum didn't understand was all my cousins ever talked about were the same type of things Laura did.

Practically, all my cousins ever spoke about was Bollywood actresses and other celebrities and how to copy their styles. What was the point of that? I didn't join in their conversations because I wasn't interested in glamour, fashion and celebrity life. I'd rather have learnt something new or read a book to escape from the real world for a while.

Still, I knew I had to go to the Mehndi celebration; it was going to be an evening of girls and women gossiping whilst applying henna tattoos to their arms and legs. What fun... or not. The girls talking secretly about their forbidden boyfriends and secret night outs, and the older women condemning the younger British Asian generation for being too modern and losing their culture. Mum didn't see this side though.

'Mum, it's getting late,' I said.

'OK, fine,' Mum said.

I said my goodbyes. My brothers, Dillon, who was five years old, and Taj, who was seven, waved me off. I left the house and made my way to school.

My brothers also attended St Claire's school and were in the Primary department. They started school an hour later than me, and Mum dropped them both off before she headed to her shift at the maternity ward in our local hospital.

It was a bitterly cold Tuesday morning. I walked through Sutton Coldfield town centre to get to St Claire's, considered by many people to be one of the finest schools in Birmingham. The high street was busy with children and teenagers making their way to schools in the local area, and shop owners were rushing to open their business for the day.

My head was filled with hundreds of thoughts about the Christmas party as well as facing Laura. Soon enough, I found myself staring up at the gates of St Claire's school and sheer dread filled me from head to toe.

Hayden Parker's name and picture flashed in front of me eyes. The way Hayden held her sword and shield and, of course, the way her body was covered with shiny silver armour made it obvious she was a fighter, a brave, heroic female warrior. I imagined myself in her shoes. She didn't seem like she could've been easily bullied or would shy away from confrontation.

If we were related to each other, and how I wished we were, maybe I had it in me to fight back. Feeling thrilled and full of a new confidence about the possibility of being related to such an amazing woman, I marched into St Claire's, feeling full of determination and ready to face whatever the day would bring.

CHAPTER 2
The Newbies

I made my way to the first class of the day; it was double History with Mr Powers. I stood in the corridor alone, hesitating to go into class. I wondered if Laura was already in there and all my insecurities flared up again. I even found myself shielding myself from view by allowing my long black hair to cover my face.

'Morning!' a familiar voice said from behind me.

My heart sank. I turned around to find Laura smiling at me from ear to ear, showing her perfect, straight, white teeth. She flicked her long blonde locks away from her face and put her mobile phone away in her school bag.

'Hi,' I said glancing at the floor.

'How are you? You know me and the girls were saying how lucky we are to be working with you on the Chemistry project,' Laura said. 'You're so clever!'

'I'm fine and thanks,' I replied.

The way she stood smiling at me, as if she was my best friend, really infuriated me. How dare she pretend to like me? I'd never done anything to her and I wanted to wipe the smile off her face. My hands closed into fists with the anger running through my body.

'There's this new makeup cream out you should try, Heera. It'll make your high cheek bones pop and you'll look so different.'

'No thanks,' I replied.

'Heera, are you sure you're OK?' Laura continued.

I remained silent, trying to stop myself from reaching boiling point. I was going to put her in her place, and I had no idea where my internal strength and sudden courage came from. I was no longer scared, and I stared straight into her eyes as I moved closer to her.

'Well actually, Laura, I'll tell you what's wrong with me...' I said, but I was interrupted by the appearance of Mrs Oak rushing towards us.

Mrs Oak was the Headmistress at St Claire's and was disliked by the majority of the students because she was overly strict and gave out far more detentions than was necessary. I'd always been on friendly terms with Mrs Oak as she'd been close friends with Mamma.

Mrs Agatha Oak had moved to Birmingham from London and had taken up a position at the school straight after Mamma had passed away. The relationship which had existed between my grandmother and Mrs Oak transferred over to my parents, and she frequented our house on many occasions.

Mrs Oak was a middle-aged woman, tall, slim, and wore colourful, floral skirt suits. I'd never seen her wear anything else and her greying hair was always tied in a tight neat bun.

Mrs Oak usually smiled when she saw me, however, this morning she seemed worried and tired. Her eyes were watery and puffy, and her hair was tied up in a bun rather roughly. Several wispy strands of hair flew across her face, giving her a rather dishevelled appearance.

What was unusual about Mrs Oak was that she had different coloured eyes. One being light brown and the other bluish grey, and I always found myself staring at them.

'Heera, can I have a word, please?' Mrs Oak asked sternly, as she stared down at me through the round glasses perched on her long pointed nose. I saw Mrs Oak stare at my pendant briefly before looking away.

'Morning, Mrs Oak!' Laura beamed at her.

'Morning, Laura, you can carry on and head into class. I need a word with Heera.'

'OK, see you in a bit, Heera,' Laura said, hugging me before she entered the classroom and I flinched inwardly. I didn't want her to touch me. Thankfully, Mrs Oak didn't notice my reaction.

'Have I done something wrong, Mrs Oak?' I asked. She simply stared at me with deep concern. I felt as though she wanted to tell me something, and every time she opened her mouth, she hesitated and glimpsed at my pendant before returning her gaze to my face.

'No, of course you haven't. I need you to do something for me though. We have two new students waiting in my office, and I want you to show them around the school.'

'Oh… OK, yeah that's fine. I'll just go tell Mr Powers I won't be attending his class,' I said, breathing a sigh of relief.

'No… I'll tell him. Go to my office and you'll find them waiting there. Their names are Kal and Lena,' Mrs Oak said reluctantly.

'Mrs Oak, is everything OK?'

Mrs Oak took a deep breath and stood tall. 'Yes… yes… everything is absolutely fine…' I turned to go to her office and she called me from behind, 'Heera?'

'Yes.'

'Kal and Lena… well… you see they are… different… no… what I mean to say is… take care of them. They will be nervous as it's their first day,' Mrs Oak said, managing to smile a little.

'I will, Mrs Oak.' I gave her a reassuring smile and made my way to her office.

St Claire's was in an ancient building and there were hundreds of stairs and dark corridors leading to different floors. Recently, the school had added a newer extension onto the original building, and all my lessons were now held in newly-built classrooms. Mrs Oak's office, however, was in the original section of the building, and pupils referred to the shadowy rooms and offices in this part of the school as prison cells or dungeons.

I went through a cavernous empty hall, leading to a narrow corridor with tiny offices belonging to the school staff on either side of me. As I headed down the steep steps leading to the dimly-lit corridor where Mrs Oak's office was, I contemplated what Lena and Kal would be like. I knew they'd be nervous because first day of school was the same for everyone, and I did wonder what Mrs Oak meant when she said they were different.

I could hear faint whispering from behind the solid wood door to Mrs Oak's office. I knocked before I entered and immediately the whispering ceased. I found Kal and Lena sitting in two chairs in front of Mrs Oak's desk and they turned around to face me. Lena smiled at me, while Kal stared at me curiously.

'Hi, I'm Heera,' I said whilst pulling up a chair to sit with them. I wanted to get to know a bit about them before taking them around St Claire's to meet the teachers and pupils.

'I'm Lena and this is Kal,' Lena said and Kal slightly nodded his head at me.

Lena had a small, pretty button nose. Her face was covered in light brown freckles. She had intense hazel eyes and her hair, which was blonder than Laura's, was tied up in a long ponytail.

Lena was dressed rather casually wearing jeans and a jumper, whereas Kal was wearing a high-collared blue shirt with black trousers, which made him appear older than he actually was. Kal's gangly legs and thin frame made him look like a stick insect, and his dark hair was a stark contrast to his pale face.

His sharp, cold grey eyes stared at me, making me feel rather uncomfortable.

'Which school did you go to before you came here?' I asked both of them.

'We were home schooled,' Lena said.

'Is this the first time you've been in a school then?'

'Yes, this is all new to us,' Lena replied, glancing at Kal, who still remained silent.

'Let's make a move then. There's so much for you to see,' I said standing up and they followed me out of the office.

The tour of the school lasted a couple of hours including meeting a few of the teachers and pupils. Lena and Kal didn't ask many questions and only spoke when questioned.

I understood what Mrs Oak had meant now, when she'd said they were different. Home schooling may have left them shy, especially when they weren't around other teenagers and teachers in a school environment.

The bell rang signalling break time. We had a fifteen-minute breather before we made our way to the next lesson. I led Kal and Lena out to the school grounds. The grass was frosty and the pavement rather slippery.

Several groups of students were huddled together eating crisps and chocolate bars and drinking cans of pop while chattering away. They ignored our presence. I glanced back at the school building from the grounds and saw Mrs Oak staring at us from the hall window. I waved at her and she smiled before walking away.

'Heera, where've you been? Mrs Mead wants to speak to you immediately in her office,' Emma said, sprinting over to me. Emma's curly short brown hair was bouncing around her shoulders as she rushed towards me.

'Why? What's wrong?'

'She didn't say. She wants you to go and see her right now though!' Emma replied.

'OK, Emma. This is Kal and Lena. They are new to the school. Can you look after them while I go see Mrs Mead?'

'Hi guys… how you finding it so far? Has your school uniform not arrived yet?' I heard Emma ask them as I sped off to find Mrs Mead.

Mrs Mead was my Chemistry teacher. She was a plump lady who always wore long pleated skirts, bright shirts and buckled black shoes. Her choice in clothes and footwear, usually a few sizes too small, made her look as if she would burst at the seams, and her rather swollen ankles spilled out of her shoes.

Yesterday morning, when Mrs Mead had set the Chemistry group project and was going round each of the groups, she was rather concerned with the lack of contribution from Laura, Rebecca and Victoria, and she'd reprimanded them in class. I wondered if this was the reason why she wanted to see me.

Soon enough, I was outside Mrs Mead's office. I knocked on the door and waited.

'Come in, Heera,' Mrs Mead said.

I opened the door and found Mrs Mead sitting in a chair behind her desk, peering out of the window overlooking the school grounds with her back towards me.

'Hi, Mrs Mead. Emma said you wanted to see me?'

'Heera, take a seat,' Mrs Mead said. I sat down and waited for her to turn around.

'Am I in trouble?' I asked.

'Well you see, you have something that belongs to me and I want it returned,' Mrs Mead said. I was confused. I hadn't borrowed anything from her and all the Chemistry text books I had were my own. Mrs Mead sounded different. Her usually sweet voice was stand offish and she still hadn't turned to look at me.

'I'm sorry, Mrs Mead… I don't know what you mean,' I said politely. A high pitched cackle filled the silent room and I shuddered as Mrs Mead began to laugh hysterically. Something was not right.

'Heera… leave now!' a strong female voice behind me said. I jumped and searched around but no-one was there. Without warning, my pendant began to move up and down violently.

I didn't understand what was happening. My heart began to race and terror consumed me. I held onto the pendant to stop it from moving but it was still jolting forcefully in my hand. Mrs Mead stood up and spun around to face me, and the person who stood before me was far from the teacher I knew. Her face became severely contorted as her eyes flashed scarlet, and her cheeks were hollow instead of the bright red chubby cheeks I knew Mrs Mead to have.

'Mrs Mead, what's wrong with you?' I asked backing away towards the office door with both my arms behind my back, ready to open the door quickly. She simply glared at me before grinning and the voice that came from her was not hers. It was almost inhuman.

'GIVE ME WHAT I NEED!' Mrs Mead bellowed and thumped the table in front of her, eyeing the pendant, which was vibrating vigorously against my chest. 'You… are the one. You… are… the one who commands them. Give it to me and come with me.'

'No! I don't know what you mean! Leave me alone,' I turned around to open the office door, and luckily, my form teacher was standing there with a concerned look on his face. He was a short, balding man and he stepped into the office and closed the door behind him. 'MR POWERS, HELP ME PLEASE. THAT'S NOT MRS MEAD!' I shouted.

'Calm down, Heera,' Mr Powers said placing his hand on my shoulder. 'Let's go sit down and sort this out.'

'NO! That's not Mrs Mead... something's wrong with her. Look at her eyes!' How could he not see the scarlet eyes transfixed on me? I tried to pull away from him so I could run out of the office, and it was only then I saw his eyes flash red.

'You're quite right, Heera. Mrs Mead is not really here, and I am not actually, Mr Powers... he is somewhat indisposed,' he grinned. He grabbed my hand and wouldn't let me go, while his other hand was placed firmly over my mouth. I could feel him pushing me towards Mrs Mead, who was now leering at me.

Within seconds, I felt a cold rush of air surrounding me, and in the next moment, I dropped to the floor with the sheer force of something hitting me. I slid away from Mr Powers, who lay knocked out cold on the office floor. Lena and Kal were standing over him.

Lena was holding a wand. It was dark brown, carved and appeared to be smooth, and the tip, although blunt, was drawing smoke. Could it have been a spell that hit me? It couldn't be... I mean what was I thinking? Kal helped me up. I blinked several times trying to fathom out what was going on because I had only seen wands in movies and read about them in books, and I knew what I was seeing couldn't be real. I had to be dreaming.

'HOW DARE YOU?' Mrs Mead shouted with her eyes transfixed on Lena's wand, which at this very moment was directly pointing at her chest.

'Not so powerful in this world, are you?' Lena said. I could hear Lena muttering a few incomprehensible words and her wand, which was still directed at Mrs Mead, emitted green sparks. Mrs Mead's eyes glowed briefly and she fell to the ground with a loud thump. 'Kal, let's take her to Agatha's office now! We have no idea how many Fire Blades are walking around disguised as teachers. Heera, are you OK? We will explain everything and don't worry. We're here to help you.'

'I... what's happening to me? And what are Fire Blades?' I asked. I was so confused. I stumbled before Kal steadied me and directed me towards the door.

'We'll tell you everything but now is not the time. It's not safe,' Lena said, holding her wand tightly.

Kal stood still before leaving the office and closed his eyes; his arm was still holding me up. 'The coast is clear,' Kal said, 'and I can't sense any new danger. I had no idea they would come over so quickly... I have nothing to defend myself with.'

'Kal, it was you who had the instinct to follow Heera, and if it wasn't for you, she could've been seriously hurt,' Lena said. 'Let's hurry... I have no idea how long that spell will hold for before they wake up.'

Lena closed the office door behind her and mumbled under her breath with her wand pointed towards the lock. Immediately, the lock made a clicking sound and she led the way onwards.

'Fine but I don't think I can hold her up for long... she's draining my power. Something isn't right with her,' Kal said.

'Keep moving. It won't be too long now,' Lena said.

I felt I was going to faint. What could Mrs Mead and Mr Powers possibly want from me? Lena had a wand and Kal was simply strange. Who exactly were these new students?

The corridors were clear. Pupils were back to class after the short break, and within a few minutes, I found myself staggering towards Mrs Oak's office. Before Lena had a chance to knock, Mrs Oak opened the door and I collapsed into her arms.

I slowly opened my eyes to find Mrs Oak whispering under her breath with a wand in her hand, and she was moving it directly over my body. I could feel my tense body ease, and although the sensation was relaxing, I sat up straight and pushed her hand away. I was terrified to see her with a wand in her hand, muttering words I couldn't understand.

'Mrs Oak, what's going on?' I asked as tears flooded my eyes. Either I was going insane or something bad was going on at St Claire's.

'Heera, it's not good I'm afraid. Something terrible has happened,' Mrs Oak said.

The room fell silent.

CHAPTER 3
The Dark King

Mrs Oak poured a glass of water from a jug on her desk and handed it to me. I didn't even have the energy to lift the glass to my lips. Lena pulled up a chair and seated herself beside me, and Kal leant up against the wall directly opposite me.

Mrs Oak seated herself behind her desk and glanced at my pendant before setting her eyes firmly on me, clearly deep in thought.

Deafening silence filled the room.

'Heera, did you come across three crystals at home?' Mrs Oak asked me directly.

'How do you know?' I asked rather abruptly. I had no idea how she would know this. Had my parents found out I'd been through the safe at home?

'Those crystals have set off a chain reaction and your life is in danger,' Mrs Oak said.

'What do you mean?' I asked. Nothing Mrs Oak was saying was making any sense.

'We have very little time, but I'll give you enough information for you to start your training,' Mrs Oak continued.

'*What training?*' I asked. This had to be some kind of a joke. By the looks on each of the faces staring at me, it seemed I'd committed a crime, but I still had no idea what I'd done that was so bad.

'I'm not of this world, neither are Lena and Kal. We come from a place called Fallowmere. It's a kingdom of witches, warlocks and many other creatures. Fallowmere is full of magic, both good and bad. I travelled to this world to protect

Hayden Parker's family for generations to come after her death in December, 1901. I'd promised her myself I'd always be here to protect her ancestors and the crystals that were passed down to them. Hayden Parker was your ancestor and it seems you have been chosen to face true evil as she had to. Have you come across her name, Heera?'

'Yes, I came across a drawing of her in a book last night, 'I replied whilst trying to fathom out how it could be that Mrs Oak knew Hayden.The date of December 1901, written in the book beside Hayden's name, which I now knew was the month she died, would mean Mrs Oak was over a hundred years old. It seemed Mrs Oak knew exactly what I was thinking because she smiled before continuing to speak.

'Fallowmere is another world, Heera,' Mrs Oak said, 'where age and time are different. I wouldn't be alive if I'd been born in this world. Kal and Lena are the same age as you. They've been sent here directly from Fallowmere to warn me that Bulzaar, most commonly known as the Dark King, who reigns over the kingdom, has come to know your family have the three crystals. Bulzaar's been searching for these crystals for decades and he wants them back. Furthermore, he wants the one who can command the crystals to be brought to him. He wants you, Heera.'

'Why me?' I asked and before Mrs Oak could answer me, I continued, 'I did see the crystals last night, but how did this random person from another world know my family have the crystals?'

'Did something happen when you saw the crystals?' Lena asked. Kal listened carefully to the conversation, and he stared at me intently before looking away when I made eye contact with him.

'Yes, something did happen...'

'What *exactly* happened?' Mrs Oak asked.

'There were three crystals in a box and I picked one up… and they all began to glow, and something happened to my pendant. I also heard a male voice saying my name. I returned two crystals back in the safe and hid the green one in my room. I thought I'd search for information about the crystals online.'

Lena and Mrs Oak glanced at each other.

'Those crystals were created by a powerful God, named Amunah, many centuries ago. There were five crystals in total and Amunah used them to protect his followers from evil,' Mrs Oak continued. 'When Amunah waged war against his brother, Raven, they both vanished, leaving the crystals behind, and over the years, the crystals became misplaced or hidden from generation to generation.

'Each crystal is unique. They absorb and radiate energy, and when combined, they have the same power as Amunah himself. The crystals are both a force of good and evil. If you decide to use them for good, they will grant the beholder protection from evil; however, if used to cause harm and mayhem as Raven intended, evil itself will slowly start to manipulate the beholder. There is another price the beholder must pay if they are going to use the power to do evil, which is that they will not be able to touch the crystals directly without being burned.'

Mrs Oak sipped some water from the glass on the table and cleared her throat.

'As for Bulzaar, he came across all five crystals over a century ago and each day he grew darker,' Mrs Oak continued to explain. 'He would go to battle without reason, and he started to enjoy the violence he inflicted on his enemies, bringing out his brutality on his friends and the entire kingdom.

'He rounded up all the humans in the kingdom, believing they were weak as they had no powers and transformed them into an army of monsters. He called them the Fire Blades and they'd kill without reason and followed Bulzaar's commands. He controlled his army by using the power of the crystals.

'Bulzaar didn't stop at the Fire Blades. He created several new species of creature, making them vicious in order to use them in battle against anyone who dared stand up to him.'

I felt I was listening to an old fairy tale or something completely out of this world. Just how crazy was Mrs Oak? How could this place she mentioned possibly exist? I was in my own world, lost in my own thoughts until Mrs Oak called my name.

'Heera?' Mrs Oak asked. 'I know it's too much to take in but I must continue as we are running out of time.'

I nodded for her to carry on.

'Bulzaar didn't stop at bringing evil to Fallowmere. His next purpose was to bring Raven, Amunah's wicked brother, back to the kingdom. Just as Amunah brought light and peace to the kingdom, Raven was the opposite and only believed in terror and destruction. Bulzaar wanted to use the five crystals to open a portal to the Realm of the Shadows, where Raven dwells, to allow his return to Fallowmere.

'Bulzaar's plan was thwarted when Hayden managed to take three crystals from him and hid them before she was killed by him. Since then, Bulzaar has been waiting for the crystals to resurface, and yesterday, when your name was called by the mysterious voice, he heard it too… and that's why he's sent his Fire Blades after you.'

Mrs Oak finished speaking with a concerned look on her face.

'He heard my name? How is that possible, Mrs Oak?' I asked, utterly bewildered.

'As Bulzaar also has crystals in his possession, he too would have heard your name being called out because the voice belongs to Amunah himself,' Mrs Oak replied. 'The great

God, who created the crystals, named you as the one who can command them and reap their full power just as he'd chosen Hayden Parker before you. And you too wear the very pendant Hayden wore, and I think Amunah is trying to communicate with you through it.

'Amunah only chooses those who can touch the crystals without wanting to misuse their power, and it seems Amunah wants you to bring all five crystals together and to safety. If you find all five crystals, Heera, you will have the same power as Amunah himself, and you will be able to do anything you want with them because the crystals will obey your every command.

'But what you also have to understand is that anyone can find the crystals and utilise their power, but there is a limit to how much power they can use.'

'Why did Amunah choose me? I'm a human. I'm not magical or powerful and I know nothing about Fallowmere or Bulzaar. I don't see what he would want with me.'

I noticed Kal rolling his eyes at me before shaking his head and smirking. I had no idea why he was acting this way, and frankly, I didn't care because I already had enough to think about. Lena put her hand on my arm, I assumed in an attempt to comfort me, but I didn't want to be comforted.

I gazed intently at Mrs Oak, waiting for her to continue.

'Hayden was a human and she stopped Bulzaar. It isn't about magic and power, Heera. Amunah sees something in you and as for Bulzaar...' Mrs Oak said. 'Well he wants you because...'

'Why, Mrs Oak?' I asked seeing her well up.

'He wants to kill you,' Kal said simply. Lena and Mrs Oak glared back at Kal and the blunt way he said the words hit me hard. I felt completely numb.

'What? Why? Kill... me... why?' I stuttered. I didn't even know Bulzaar, and if he wanted the crystals, he could take them. Why drag me into all this? A million thoughts ran through my mind, and I couldn't even hear Mrs Oak talking to me. I could only see her mouth moving.

'We haven't got enough time, Agatha, to drag this conversation out. She has to know the truth quickly… her family are in danger,' Kal said roughly.

'Kal, please can you be quiet!' Lena shouted at him.

'Heera, I know this is hard to understand but I promise you I'll do everything I can to help you,' Mrs Oak said.

'My family are in danger?' I asked, hoping I'd misheard Kal.

'They've been taken by the Fire Blades and they've also found the crystals,' Mrs Oak said. My poor family were suffering for my mistake and I broke down.

'*Will they kill my family?*' I asked, in complete shock.

'Bulzaar will turn them into Fire Blades… a fate worse than death and he will control their every move,' Mrs Oak said.

I could hear my ears ringing with the silence in the room and I grasped the pendant tightly in my hand. My family were gone and I was completely alone. Thoughts of my family consumed me, and it took a great deal of effort to continue to speak.

'But why… why does he want me dead, Mrs Oak?' I finally asked.

'You are the chosen warrior, Heera, and only you can touch the crystals without being burned and only you can access their full power,' Mrs Oak replied. 'If Bulzaar can get all five crystals, he can still cause a lot of harm with them. But in order for him to open up a portal for someone like Raven to come through, Bulzaar will require complete power over the crystals, and that means killing you.

'You see, the only way he can steal the power Amunah has given you is if he first takes possession of all five crystals and then kills you. It is vital to collect the crystals before killing the chosen warrior to ensure Amunah won't be able to find someone else to command the crystals. Of course, Bulzaar knows perfectly well that the chosen warrior will want to possess all five crystals and bring them to safety, and there's no way Bulzaar will contemplate giving up the crystals he has in his own possession.'

'But you said he killed Hayden, so doesn't that mean he already has power over the crystals?' I asked.

'No, Heera,' Mrs Oak said. 'Yes it's true Bulzaar killed Hayden but it was only after he killed her that he realised three crystals were missing from his castle. Therefore, he didn't have complete power over the crystals since he no longer had all five crystals in his possession. Hayden had managed to take three crystals and gave them to her ancestors who fled to the human world before he killed her. Bulzaar didn't have the power to travel between worlds to search for the lost crystals or Hayden's ancestors. Since then, Bulzaar's been patiently waiting for Amunah to choose the next warrior, allowing him to know the exact location of the crystals and the chosen warrior's name.

'If Bulzaar collects all five crystals and kills you, Heera, the crystals will answer to him forever, and he will be as powerful as Amunah. Bulzaar won't allow another soul to touch the crystals, meaning Amunah will never find another warrior to save the crystals from this monster. Remember, Heera, Amunah can only judge someone once they touch the crystals because it's the only way he knows whether you can be trusted as his warrior.'

I took a moment to take in all the information Mrs Oak had given me. I stood up and paced the room, trying to clear my head before taking a seat again. A thousand questions and thoughts were swimming away in my head. Mrs Oak again offered me some water, which I refused.

'Why does Bulzaar want Raven to enter Fallowmere? If Bulzaar does kill me and becomes as powerful as Amunah, why would he need Raven?' I asked.

'Bulzaar worships Raven and wants his true God to return home to Fallowmere,' Mrs Oak replied. 'Furthermore, Bulzaar also thinks that Raven is far more powerful than Amunah and his crystals, and I personally feel that Bulzaar hopes to be rewarded by Raven with even more power than he could ever imagine. Bulzaar believes by working together with Raven, they will be able to destroy Amunah and his followers and rule over the kingdom side by side without any opposition. And now that Bulzaar has all five crystals, he will be unstoppable with the destruction he will cause to the kingdom.'

'He doesn't have all of them yet, remember, I hid one in my room. Mrs Mead also said I had something which belonged to her... I don't think they found the third crystal,' I said, hoping it was still where I'd left it.

'Agatha, we need to check the house for the crystal,' Lena suggested.

'My family will be safe then?' I asked.

'Heera, we can't guarantee anything, but if we have one crystal, and of course you, there is a greater chance of stopping Bulzaar and saving your family,' Mrs Oak said. 'It won't be easy, although it's not entirely impossible. We may be able to use the crystal to bargain with Bulzaar to release your family. Ultimately, it's you and the crystal he wants and it may work. We'll come up with a solid plan to defeat him once and for all, Heera.'

'Mrs Oak, I've heard a woman's voice trying to warn me as well. Do you think it's Mamma?' I asked. I hoped it was my grandmother. We'd been so close, and I always felt she was looking down on me and helping me through my struggles at school.

'No, if the warnings have only started since you found the crystals then I do not think the voice will be hers,' Mrs Oak replied. 'Whoever they are, they don't seem to be a threat and I wouldn't worry about it too much.'

'Time is running out... let's make a move,' Kal said.

'Can I let Emma know what's happened, Mrs Oak?' I asked. I wanted to speak to her and say goodbye. I probably would never see her again.

'No, Heera. It's not safe for her to know everything. Bulzaar can use your friends and family against you, and he may harm her if he finds out she is close to you.'

I understood where Mrs Oak was coming from, and I didn't want anything to happen to Emma. Why did I have to find the crystals? If I had not opened that stupid safe, I would still have my family with me. Everything was my fault.

'Someone's coming,' Kal said pointing at the door. Lena shot up out of her chair and pointed her wand at the door.

'Quick, take Heera to her house and see if you can find the crystal. I will meet you there as soon as I can. If I don't come within twenty minutes, go to Fallowmere without me,' Mrs Oak explained, roughly pulling me out of my chair and towards Lena, who held out her hand to grasp mine.

I didn't comprehend how we were going to leave the office without being seen if someone was at the door.

There was a loud knock on the door. Silence fell in the room. 'It's the Fire Blades. I can sense the same negative energy as before,' Kal whispered.

'Lena, use the same portal I opened for you and Kal. Hurry!' Mrs Oak said.

Lena pulled me towards the wall, which Kal was leaning against moments before. Mrs Oak touched the wall whilst uttering undistinguishable words under her breath. I blinked and the wall vanished, leaving only a small wooden door before us. I was stunned. I mean how could a wall vanish and leave a door in its place. I blinked a few more times to make sure I wasn't imagining this.

The door still remained before us and was not supported by anything; it appeared to float in sheer darkness. Lena pushed the door open, and thick white smoke erupted from inside and escaped into the office engulfing our feet.

Instinctively, I tried to back away from the door. It was daunting having to go through it. Lena held onto my hand and grabbed Kal's before we stepped forward into the smoke. I took a deep breath quickly because I didn't want to suffocate with the amount of smoke surrounding my face.

Just as the door closed behind us, I heard Mrs Oak say, 'Please come in.'

The white smoke disappeared plunging us in complete darkness. A tiny door lit up in the distance and Lena ran towards it, still holding my hand. The further we ran, the more the door seemed to be moving away from us.

Luminous streaks of blue and red flashed on either side of us. I could hear voices in my ear, voices of my family, Emma and Mrs Oak. I glimpsed up at the door and it was now moving closer to us.

Instantaneously, an unseen force stopped me from running. I could feel my feet being pulled down and I came to a sudden halt. Lena and Kal stopped running at the same time, and when I glanced ahead, I found the door was only a few metres from us.

'Go ahead, Heera, open it. The door will open to wherever you want it to open,' Lena said. I took a step forward and wished for the door to open inside my house. I turned the golden knob, pushed open the door and we stepped, once again, into thick white smoke on the other side.

The door closed behind us before evaporating into thin air, and once the white smoke had cleared, I found myself standing in my lounge, except, it wasn't how I'd left it in the morning. Things had been thrown across the room. The lamp was shattered on the floor, the coffee table was split in half, and the sofas were on their side.

I couldn't believe my eyes. How was it I was in Mrs Oak's office, mere seconds ago, and now I stood in my house, staring at the devastation that lay before me? I couldn't comprehend what was happening. When I left the house this morning, everything was normal. I was secretly hoping all this time, Mrs Oak was lying to me, nevertheless, the evidence was to the contrary.

Kal and Lena stood examining the room. I saw my brothers' school bags in the corner of the room, and a sharp pain bolted straight to my heart; they had gone. What had I done?

I found bowls full of uneaten cereal on the dining table that'd now turned to mush, and a carton of orange juice had spilled onto the floor. Lena followed me into the kitchen and put her hand on my shoulder.

'Heera, I'm sorry this has happened to you,' Lena said gently. I didn't know how to respond. I mustered as much courage as I could and made my way up to my bedroom, with Kal and Lena following closely behind. The same devastation lay before me.

The landing was littered with clothes, jewellery, pillows, bedding and towels strewn across the carpet. All doors to the bedrooms were smashed or thrown off their hinges to one side. I headed straight for Dad's office and found the safe emptied.

I had a quick glance in my parents' and brothers' rooms in case my family were somehow left behind. There was no sign of them and I felt my blood run cold. The rooms were turned upside down and seeing my family's belongings thrown like rubbish over the floor made me angry.

I rushed to my room. Everything I owned was either on the floor or over my bed, and my laptop was smashed. My eyes were scouring the room for the coat in which I'd hidden the crystal, and I rummaged through all the clothes I could see. Kal didn't attempt to help me in any way; instead, he kept glancing around impatiently.

'Heera, can I help?' Lena asked.

'Yes please. We need to find an old black coat… I hid the crystal in there,' I said.

'Stand back… let me try something,' Lena said. I stepped back. Lena stood in the middle of my bedroom and moved her wand in a swift motion while muttering away under her breath. I felt a gush of wind engulf the room, and my clothes, books and toiletries swirled in mid-air around us. It was complete mayhem. I ducked a couple of times as my school books darted towards my face. Finally, I saw the sleeve of my black coat protruding from under my bed.

I ran towards it and retrieved it, desperately searching the pockets. I could feel the jewellery I had placed in there last night, and whilst digging into the second pocket, my fingers grabbed an object. I removed the crystal from the pouch and it rested in the palm of my hand, glowing intermittently. I almost leapt with joy.

Lena rushed over to me and all my belongings, moving in mid-air around the room, dropped to the ground.

'Heera, do you know what this means? We may be able to save your family with the crystal,' Lena said, smiling at me.

'Don't give false hope, Lena,' Kal huffed. 'We don't even know if we will be able to save her family… Bulzaar may have already turned them.'

Lena was furious and I could hear them bickering away. I didn't want to argue and I left them to it. I busied myself by collecting clothes and toiletries to take with me to the new world. I managed to find a rucksack under the piles of clothes discarded over the floor and filled it with the chosen items. A photograph I had of my family on my dresser caught my eye. I couldn't bear to look at their smiling faces staring at me. They had simply vanished and I was anxious to see them again.

I grabbed the photograph in one hand and I felt under my bed with the other hand for the gold book, containing Hayden's drawing, which I'd hidden the night before. Thankfully, the book was still there and I added it to the rucksack, along with the photograph.

I held the crystal tight in my hand and started to wonder what my family were doing this very moment. I had spent so much time worrying about how others felt about me, and only this morning, I was worrying about facing Laura, all of which seemed pathetic and irrelevant to my life at this point in time.

No-one had the right to touch my family, and I'd face whatever I had to face. There was no way I was going to let Bulzaar get away with what he'd done to them. I had no clue where this unexpected courage came from, but all that mattered to me was saving my loved ones, and I couldn't care less what happened to me.

CHAPTER 4

The Kingdom of Fallowmere

Once Lena and Kal had stopped arguing with each other, Lena entered my room and stood by my bedroom window, peering into the back garden, and Kal paced back and forth between my room and the landing.

'I think it's best if you change into something warm, Heera,' Lena said. 'The snow's deep in Fallowmere.' I'd forgotten I was still wearing my school uniform. I changed into a jumper and jeans in my parents' bedroom and put on my winter boots.

'Heera! Kal! Lena!' Mrs Oak shouted from downstairs. We all rushed to find her standing at the foot of the stairs smiling up at us. 'It would seem very suspicious if these were left behind and you'd disappeared,' Mrs Oak said, holding up my coat and school bag.

'Agatha, who was at the door?' Kal asked.

'Mr Powers and Mrs Mead paid me a visit. They demanded to know where Heera was and to hand her over to them,' Mrs Oak said. 'Of course, they didn't get very far. I managed to trick the Fire Blades back through the portal to Fallowmere by releasing their hold on Mr Powers and Mrs Mead... fortunately for us, they don't remember anything. I told them you won't be present at school over the next few days due to a family emergency.'

'I found the crystal,' I said, showing Mrs Oak.

'Excellent! Let's make a move, immediately,' Mrs Oak said, climbing the stairs and handing over my coat and bag. I rummaged through the bag and found my mobile phone, and I rang my parents' numbers in case they picked up; unfortunately though, both numbers went straight to their answer phone.

Mrs Oak walked into each of the rooms upstairs, examining the damage left behind, and Kal impatiently followed her around. Lena was closely inspecting her wand deep in thought. I approached her.

'Lena, what's it like in Fallowmere?' I asked. Lena took a few moments to reply.

'It's very different, Heera. You'll be staying with my family in Kendolen and we'll watch out for you. You may not know who has your best interest at heart and that's why you need to listen to Agatha, with her you have the chance to save your family, yourself and the kingdom.'

I was grateful I could talk to Lena. Kal on the other hand was the complete opposite and not at all approachable.

'I'm going to create a portal through Heera's bedroom door,' Mrs Oak said, returning back from checking the other rooms.

I put on my coat, placed the crystal in my rucksack and stood facing my closed bedroom door with the others. Mrs Oak pointed her wand directly at the handle and muttered unusual words under her breath.

The door began to shake and gold light filtered through the sides of the door and through the keyhole. The handle rattled and glowed red.

The door shot open with great force, and we jolted backwards into the wall behind us. My bedroom had vanished into thin air. Beyond the door, I could see a carpet of soft snow and towering trees.

It was incredible.

Mrs Oak stepped forward through the door first, followed by Kal and Lena. Instinctively, I held onto my pendant tightly. I didn't know where this journey was going to take me; I only knew that once I'd stepped into Fallowmere, there was no turning back.

I stepped into this new world, and as the cold air hit my face, I took a deep breath to calm my nerves. The break of dawn was approaching and fiery rays of sunlight began to filter down to the ground through the tall snow laden trees. All was eerily quiet.

I was surprised at what I saw and I stared around me with my mouth slightly ajar. I, honestly, didn't know what to expect to find in a kingdom run by a maniac king, but it wasn't this perfect setting. I thought there would be chaos everywhere, and Bulzaar's army stationed at every entry into Fallowmere to capture me. This new world was spectacular.

'Each of you stay close,' Mrs Oak whispered, leading us onwards. 'Heera, these woods are called Gentley Woods, and we have to make our way through here to reach Kendolen.'

I stayed close to Lena, who had her wand pointing forward like Mrs Oak. Kal was peering around attentively. I was the only one who couldn't defend myself. I felt vulnerable and knew I had to rely on the other three to help me if something was to happen.

We trudged through the snow for a while until Mrs Oak led us towards a dense patch of trees.

'What's wrong, Agatha?' Kal whispered.

'I've lost my way because it's been so long since I was last here. I didn't expect the portal to open so far from Kendolen,' Mrs Oak replied.

'Sorry we can't help, Agatha. We've never been allowed in these woods,' Lena said.

'Don't worry, I'll figure a way out,' Mrs Oak replied.

Lena, Kal and Mrs Oak began to discuss which way to go, while I enjoyed the tranquillity of this new kingdom.

A light breeze swept through the calm woodland, triggering snow dust to fall from the trees. I saw a fox emerging from shrubbery on the opposite side of where we were standing.

The fox stopped still. His ears were alert and ready to catch the sound of danger, and his eyes focused sharply on the environment around him. He sniffed the air before moving onwards into the midst of a clearing enclosed by trees and came to a standstill before the remnants of a campfire.

I was drawn to this timid creature and found myself moving away from the group and inching towards the clearing, several meters away. The fox whimpered hopelessly and fell back onto his hind legs, feeling sorry for himself.

I could hear rustling from beyond the trees, in close perimeter to the fox, and within seconds, the fox was crouching low because he too had heard the rustling. He was watching and ready to pounce on whatever or whoever was coming towards him.

My heart was racing. It could be anyone or anything, and I immediately backed away. For a moment, I'd forgotten I wasn't at home. What if I was in danger? I was completely immobilised with terror.

A hare appeared, hopping absent-mindedly through the clearing, and the fox's beady eyes were transfixed on the approaching animal. I knew what was coming. I moved forwards to stop the fox from pouncing on the hare, but I was swiftly pulled back and a hand covered my mouth so my screams wouldn't be heard.

'Keep still,' Kal whispered in my ear. Mrs Oak and Lena moved to the front, staring at the fox and the hare. I couldn't understand why Kal reacted like this upon seeing these animals, but I knew something was not right with the way Mrs Oak was pushing Lena back towards Kal and me.

By the time the hare had noticed the fox, the latter in a whirlwind of black and red, twisted and turned, transforming himself swiftly into a figure of a man. He was now approaching the frightened hare with his right arm stretched out.

I couldn't believe what I was seeing. How could a fox possibly turn into a man? Was he even a man? Mrs Oak had mentioned the kingdom was full of magical creatures and this surely was one of them, but if something as innocent as a fox was dangerous, I had to be very careful.

I couldn't trust anyone because nothing was as it seemed. Mere moments ago, I was stunned to find myself in a safe tranquil environment and in a flash this had changed. I remained gripped with bated breath at what was going on before me.

The figure closed his hand and lifted his arm towards the lightening sky, and an unseen force flung the hare upwards into the ice-cold air. As he hurtled towards the ground, the hare was thrown with sheer force towards a nearby tree.

A high-pitched cry shot through the woods and several birds fluttered high above the trees.

The characteristics of the fox were long gone, instead the mysterious figure, dressed in layers of black clothing, began to pace back and forth hurriedly.

A grey mask with conveniently placed holes over his eyes and mouth obstructed his face, making it impossible to see his features, and his oversized boots seemed out of place compared to the size of his light frame.

The figure peered into the trees around him and began to mutter under his breath in a low and muffled voice. He was glancing towards where we were standing; however, he couldn't see us because of the sheer density of the trees, and their intertwined, thick branches gave us a safe hiding place.

'No… I can't but if I don't… they will kill me. My family will suffer if I don't obey them,' he whispered to himself, still pacing and rubbing his hands in an attempt to keep them warm.

The figure hesitated and seemed to be contemplating running from the scene, when a loud jeer from behind caught him off guard, and he fell to the ground.

The figure sat up and turned to face the heavy thud of footsteps approaching him. He opened his mouth in terror and forced his eyes shut, clearly unable to stand the sight of what was coming towards him.

My pendant jolted again. I knew it was trying to warn me of danger, yet I couldn't help but look on.

I eventually saw what had made the figure fall to the ground, and I wanted to scream. I placed my own hand over my mouth and took deep shuddering breaths to steady myself. Lena and Kal moved me further back into the trees; however, Mrs Oak remained rooted to the spot watching the scene before her. Mrs Oak wasn't frightened but the same couldn't be said for Kal and Lena; they too, like me, were shaken with the presence of the new arrivals.

The last thing I wanted was to alert the two beasts that came towards the figure on the ground, wielding weapons large enough to crush him. Their armour, although old, seemed tough and their spiked boots clanked as they trudged through the snow. They came to a stop and sneered down at the trembling figure.

The wind blew their matted hair, which partially covered their grotesque faces. They flared their half-bitten, mutilated nostrils and bared their crooked, rotten teeth at him.

The figure slid back in terror towards the old campfire, and the vivid yellow, unblinking cat's eyes of the monsters stared at him and followed him closely.

They laughed hysterically at the plight of their victim, revealing their black tongues moving like serpents inside their mouths, and they shook their misshapen heads in disbelief at the victim's attempt to get away from them.

The taller of the two carried a sword, whilst the other carried an old heavy axe. Both the weapons were similar in that the blades had the image of a dragon's vicious face carved into them; the dragon's mouth was closed and its sharp teeth protruded at the sides.

Mrs Oak turned to us and whispered, 'They can't see us because we're on the other side of the magical barrier. They are Fire Blades.' I couldn't see any barrier between them and us. I even tried squinting to see if I could see anything, but to no avail.

'Yeah, sure that makes it easier to watch then,' Kal whispered to Lena sarcastically.

Mrs Oak had said the Fire Blades were once human but they were far from it now. Bulzaar had destroyed them completely, from their outward appearance to their very souls.

The fiends turned to the campfire, pointed their weapons at the burnt twigs and branches and muttered a few incomprehensible words in unison, and the dragon's outline on the weapons turned crimson in a split second. Suddenly, the dragon's mouth opened wide, and orange and yellow flames flew from the weapons, engulfing the remnants of the fire and melting away any traces of snow instantly. A fire lit up on the ground, and the scared figure rolled away, desperately trying to get away from the flames.

The taller of the two pointed his sword at the dead hare lying in the corner, and the animal rose into the air and was thrown upon the fire. 'That's breakfast arranged,' he said roughly, glancing at his friend.

They each placed a foot on their victim's chest, pushing him down flat on the ground. Again, the taller beast spoke to the frightened face staring up at him, 'Look at what we have here, not so gutless after all. Thought you wouldn't show up, being the coward you're so well known to be.' He laughed as he spoke and his foot bore down harder on the figure's chest. 'What do you think, Morog?'

'That would be a stupid move to make on his part, Bastian,' the Fire Blade named Morog sneered. 'Our little friend here knows what we would do to him if he didn't show his face. Everyone knows the dire consequences of not obeying our orders and nobody can hide from us or even think of betraying us. To disobey the orders of the Fire Blades would mean betraying the Dark King himself.' Bastian kicked the figure and he began to sob.

'Get up, NOW!' Morog shouted and the weeping figure, timidly stood up, unable to look at the Fire Blades. The figure kept his head bowed down and took short, sharp breaths.

Morog, unlike Bastian had a serious look on his face and glared down at his victim before speaking, 'We know you want to help Bulzaar, otherwise you wouldn't have risked coming here to meet us.'

'How is my dear friend, Bulzaar?' the figure said.

'He is weak, but with your help, we can restore him to power,' Morog said. 'You do have the opportunity to redeem yourself in his eyes... you were after all his best friend and trusted adviser. This leads us to the question I must ask you.' Morog paused and towered over the scared figure. 'Do you promise you'll do everything you can to help Bulzaar, your rightful King, take full control over the throne and lead Fallowmere into a new era?'

'Yes, of course I'll help Bulzaar get his kingdom back,' the figure replied. 'The Elders pretend we're all equal, but they do not trust our kind and never will. Moreover, they do not see us for who we truly are. All these years, I've managed to keep my real identity hidden from them, and they only see what I want them to see. I've kept my family hidden well and even the Elders don't know they exist.'

Elders? Who were they? There was so much I had to learn of this world, for now I simply listened. Kal stepped on a branch on the ground and it snapped in half; there was a resounding crunch, loud enough for everyone in close proximity to here.

We all froze.

The mysterious figure stopped speaking and peered around. Mrs Oak raised her wand. I began to tremble. We were going to get caught any minute now, and it dawned on me I was never going to see my family ever again.

'What is it?' Bastian asked lifting his sword.

'It's nothing. I thought I heard something,' the figure made sure they were alone before continuing. 'In my defence, once the Elders had protected Kendolen, it was impossible to leave the town without being caught. I will help Bulzaar but why has it taken him up until now to contact me?' The figure peeked up at the Fire Blades, and he seemed to grow in confidence and straightened himself up a little.

'All except two crystals were left behind when Hayden's ancestors had managed to flee with the other three, meaning he didn't have enough power to do as he wished. He became weak and was unable to travel far distances,' Morog explained. 'These woods are well protected, and our spies could never see anyone from Kendolen. It was only by luck we managed to see you that night in your true form outside the barrier.'

'Oh yes,' the figure said, 'I have to let my skin breathe from time to time, and I was on duty protecting the barrier by myself that night. I walked outside the protected wall before changing to my true image in case someone from Kendolen saw me. I won't let you down.'

'Bulzaar has waited long enough for the moment to reign over Fallowmere again and to allow Raven's return,' Morog explained very carefully. 'The only way he can make this happen is to take back all the crystals and kill Amunah's chosen warrior. Only then will Bulzaar be as powerful as Amunah and our Dark King will be able to wield the power of the crystals as he wishes without any restrictions. We know Heera Watson will come to Kendolen and she'll have a crystal with her. We need you to find the crystal and the girl and hand both over to us. Agatha Oak will surely be guiding her, so you must be careful.'

However, the figure seemed to be losing the confidence he had gained a few moments ago. Bastian was now staring at the hare on the fire, deep in thought.

Lena put her arm around me. It was strange hearing the Fire Blades say my name, and it truly terrified me.

The figure was taking in every last word Morog had said, shortly he hesitated and stuttered, 'I... I can't do that! If the... E... Elders come to find out it was me who betrayed their trust by handing over the chosen one and the crystal... they will... k... kill me. I can't do this. It's impossible... surely there must be another way without using the final crystal.'

'I knew you didn't have it in you. A few minutes ago you promised you'd do whatever it takes to help Bulzaar, and now you're turning your back on him,' whispered Morog threateningly. 'You dare call yourself Bulzaar's friend! You know the importance of Heera Watson and the crystal.

'Do you know what happens when you fail to deliver on your promise?' asked Morog. When he had no response, he answered the question for their victim, 'You pay... you pay with your life.' Morog was the one who now cackled, closely followed by Bastian, who was copying him, and their victim fell to his knees.

'I can't do it… please don't make me. I will do anything just not this,' the figure on the ground pleaded.

'The only way out for you is by giving us Heera Watson and the last remaining crystal. You will have to act swiftly and try not to cause attention to yourself,' Morog sneered.

'Will Bulzaar come for them in Kendolen once the protection has lifted?' the figure asked.

'Once he uses the crystals to gain strength, he will come to take control over the town himself. I hope I'm here when he comes, much blood will be shed. Thankfully, the crystals will make him powerful enough to threaten and maim every being in Fallowmere without having to kill the girl straightaway,' Morog smiled.

The two brutal creatures laughed and Morog addressed Bastian, 'We're getting closer, Bastian… as soon as Bulzaar has the last crystal and the girl is killed, it will be like the good old days but even better. Every creature will serve their purpose for Bulzaar, and we'll have plenty of creatures that'll need to be put in their place.

'If only we could get the crystal and the girl for him instead of relying on this good for nothing waste of space. Nevertheless, Kendolen is protected for now, and we won't even be able to cross the border without shattering into pieces. Our time for greatness will come very soon.'

'Yes, Morog, the Fire Blades will once again rise to defend the great and mighty Dark King, and the whole of Fallowmere will once again bow down to us,' Bastian said. 'Bulzaar made the right decision in choosing you to guide us through our bloodiest battle.'

'Now let's eat before we make our way back… we have a long journey ahead of us and the King will be waiting for us,'

Morog said while Bastian with his bare hands pulled the meat from the hare and handed a piece to his leader.

'You best not let us down, otherwise say goodbye to this world,' Morog addressed the whimpering figure on the ground.

Morog glanced towards the fire and took a long deep breath and opened his mouth; it seemed as if he was going to attempt to blow out the flames, but instead, the fire rose from the ground and Morog inhaled the entire contents into his mouth. The open mouth of the dragon glowed on the axe momentarily before it slowly closed, and the colour of the axe returned to silver.

The figure was silent and was rocking back and forth, clearly distressed. He didn't even notice or care that the Fire Blades were walking away from him, sniggering at the predicament they had left him in.

Gentley Woods, once again, returned to its tranquil setting, until the figure fell forwards onto his front and wept into the snow.

CHAPTER 5

The Elders

Mrs Oak swiftly led us further into the trees, hurrying to get to Kendolen without being detected. Although, the path we were following through the trees was very slippery, we kept on moving onwards for some time. Mrs Oak, now and again, stopped and had a good look around before she gave us the go ahead to continue. The path began to narrow, and a set of ancient corrugated iron gates could be seen up ahead.

'We've reached Kendolen,' Mrs Oak said. 'Lena, please lead us to your home. We'll be much safer there with the protection spells your parents have surrounding the house.'

Without a word, Lena led the way.

Once, we'd left the gates to Gentley Woods behind us, the snow leading onwards into Kendolen was turning to slush with the sheer volume of footprints leading to and from the woods. Not a single soul was to be seen.

Houses and cottages shortly came into view, and as we trudged further into Kendolen, the houses we passed were not only becoming more secluded but were older and substantially larger.

There was still no-one in sight. Lena led us towards an isolated pathway between two detached houses, and a fine set of wrought iron gates with sharp, golden spikes protruding from the edges of the bars could be seen up ahead.

As we moved closer to the gates, a single, menacing mansion was revealed behind them. Its exterior was forbidding with green and black vines covering the entire face of the house.

Two gargoyle sculptures, which I found cute, sat on either side of the black door, grinning sinisterly at us.

The house could've been easily mistaken for a haunted mansion seen in the many horror movies I'd watched over the years, and Lena was leading us straight to its door.

When Lena stepped towards the iron gates, they creaked open as if they sensed she was coming. We followed her up the narrow steps to the black door, and the stone gargoyles, immediately sprang to life and began to laugh. Their mouths opened to reveal jagged stone teeth, and their blank stone eyes stared at Lena.

I was taken aback. I blinked several times to make sure I wasn't imaging the sculptures moving and sniggering.

'Look she's back! Welcome home, Lena!' the sculpture on the left said in a deep male voice.

'And she's brought the warrior with her! Well done, Lena!' the female gargoyle on the right exclaimed. 'Oh Geoffrey, look at her blue eyes and long black hair… she's so pretty!'

'Hey there cutie,' Geoffrey said to me. The other gargoyle gave him a scathing stare, clearly deeply jealous of the comment he made.

'Hi,' I replied.

'Move along, warrior girl… move along, right now!' the female gargoyle said.

'I missed you, Macey and Geoffrey and it feels good to be back home!' Lena said. The gargoyles fell silent and returned to their still state.

Lena knocked on the door and loud, quick footsteps could be heard coming towards the door. Mrs Oak remained behind us all and kept her eyes focused on our surroundings to make sure we hadn't been followed.

The door opened and Lena was almost dragged inside by a blonde woman who put her arms around her and wouldn't let go.

'Lena, my child… you're safe! Your father and I have been terribly worried,' Lena's mother said, towering over us, and her plump rosy cheeks were covered in tears as she embraced her daughter. Once, she let Lena go, she turned her attention to Mrs Oak and said, 'Agatha, welcome back. It has been so long my friend. How are you?'

'Bethelda, I'm fine and I can't say it's good to be back under such dire circumstances,' Mrs Oak replied.

'Mother, where's Father?' Lena asked.

'He's at the Elder Town Hall with Parmona. They've been trying to find out information about your whereabouts. Please come in everyone,' Bethelda said leading us into the house. I noticed Lena's mum was dressed in long black robes. She held a wand in one hand, and she wore a black beaded necklace, which complimented her pale skin.

The hallway was spacious and the light from the crystal chandeliers brightened up the inside of the house, which was a stark contrast to the daunting exterior. I could hear people talking as we were led towards the sitting room, but as soon as we entered the room, the talking ceased.

'Lena's home!' shouted four ugly hag-like statues, situated in each corner of the room. The stone statues twisted and turned towards the door and began to clap as they grinned at Lena.

'Thanks, I'm glad to be back!' Lena replied and like Macey and Geoffrey, the statues returned to their still state.

'Please sit down and rest. Kal you look well and this must be Heera. My child, I'm so sorry for the evil that has befallen you. We will do all we can to help you and your precious family,' Bethelda said kindly as she came over to hug me. I didn't know how to respond to her.

'Mrs Bane, can I be excused? I need to go home and see my parents now that Heera is safe with you,' Kal said.

Lena's surname was Bane. With so much happening, I hadn't even bothered to ask Kal or Lena their full names.

'Yes... of course you can go. Are you sure I can't get you anything though, Kal?' Mrs Bane asked. 'How about a hot drink?'

'No, thank you. My parents will be waiting for me,' Kal said as he stood up.

Lena led him out of the sitting room and out of the front door. Kal didn't even say goodbye to me, even though I was about to stand up and thank him. I felt dejected after the way he simply left without even a backward glance at me.

'Heera, what would you like to eat and drink?' Mrs Bane asked.

'Nothing at the moment, thank you,' I replied.

'Would you like to rest? You must be going through so much! Lena, take Heera upstairs and let her rest for a while,' Mrs Bane added, without letting me reply. I wondered if it was a ploy to get me out of the room so she could talk to Mrs Oak freely.

Lena led me out of the room and up the grand staircase. The house was immaculate, not a speck of dust could be seen.

'Well this is my bedroom,' Lena said, opening the door and allowing me to enter the room first.

I was gobsmacked.

Lena's room was not your normal teenage bedroom. By all means, she had a bed, a desk, cupboards, and a dresser, yet the other half of the room appeared to be a science lab. There were shelves full of jars, some with labels and others without, containing an assortment of what appeared to be ingredients.

I picked up a jar filled with fluorescent yellow liquid and read the label... *Wolf's Blood*... I returned the jar to the shelf.

Another read *Leprechaun Eyelashes* and I could see minuscule green eyelashes floating around the jar.

'Lena dear, is that you?' a wicked voice said behind me. I jumped and turned to see who was standing behind me only to find a table with a huge charcoal grey cauldron placed upon it.

'Iris, yes it's me!' Lena said, placing her hand on my shoulder. 'Heera, it's OK... let me show you something.'

I followed her around the table and placed directly in front of the cauldron was a brown dusty book with black markings on the cover. Still, I couldn't see what Lena was trying to show me.

'Well, hello there! What pretty blue eyes you have, dear, and hair as dark as the night sky!' a voice said and I immediately leapt back. The black markings on the cover of the book had transfigured to form the face of an old lady. Her eyebrows were raised, and she had deep lines around her eyes and cheeks.

'Er... Hi,' I managed to say.

'This is Iris. She's my Spell Keeper!' Lena said.

I managed to smile back at Iris before Lena continued.

'Witches and wizards have Spell Keepers. They are used to protect your spell book and can give you advice on what's wrong and right. They can even help you to become the witch or wizard you aspire, ultimately, to be.'

'How did Iris get in the book, Lena? Is it some sort of spell?' I asked.

'Kind of. Spell Keepers can be good, bad, or both. It used to be common practice that when a wizard or witch wanted to hurt someone, they used to turn their victim into a Spell Keeper and confine them to the pages of a spell book, or even turn them into statues for all eternity. Iris was an innocent witch and was confined to this spell book by a wizard. This spell book was passed down through my family and now it's mine. Iris isn't vengeful and she teaches me right from wrong.

'The four statues in the living room downstairs are Spell Keepers too. They help my parents with spells and potions, and sometimes, depending on their mood, they try to influence us into doing dark magic. We, of course, ignore them when they act this way.'

I was truly fascinated with what Lena had to say, and I wanted to know everything about her life as a witch.

'Lena, who's your friend?' Iris asked.

'This is Heera... the one we had to rescue!' Lena said.

'Welcome, my dear!' Iris said.

'Thank you,' I said, trying to block out the fact I was talking to a book. This day was getting weirder by the minute.

'Lena, bring Heera down! She has visitors who're keen to meet her!' Mrs Bane shouted from downstairs. Visitors had come to see me? It had to be my parents. Who else could it possibly be? I ran out the room and rushed down the stairs and barged into the living room, closely followed by Lena.

I didn't recognise the new faces staring at me. I was disheartened, and it must have shown on my face because Mrs Oak held out her hand to me and pulled me towards an armchair beside her.

'This is Parmona Vestoni and Akaal Cromen, the Elders who govern Kendolen. Landon Tomkins, the third Elder is on his way and will join us shortly,' Mrs Bane said. 'The Elders helped Hayden's family to escape to the human world and placed barriers in Gentley Woods to stop Bulzaar's supporters from entering the town. All residents must abide by their rules to keep us safe.'

The two Elders stared at me. I didn't know why but I felt rather uneasy in their presence, and I couldn't look directly at them.

'Thank you, Bethelda. We'll take it from here,' Parmona said. Mrs Bane sat down beside Lena, clutching her wand to her chest.

Parmona held her head high and gave the impression she was looking down at everyone in the room, especially me. I noticed three warts on her hooked nose and a round mole above her lip, and her white wispy hair gave her the appearance of an old, unkind, hag.

I gulped waiting for her to speak. I felt very intimidated because Parmona was not at all welcoming and didn't smile, and Akaal Cromen was just as serious and straight faced as Parmona. Akaal didn't say a word and sat back in his chair, examining the bowler hat in his lap. Once or twice, I saw his grey moustache twitch and his thin lips pout.

'Heera, you're to start your sword fighting training in secret, and today rather than tomorrow,' Parmona said defiantly. 'You must be prepared to fight before the spy finds out you're already in Kendulen. I also understand you're in the possession of a crystal. I feel it's wise you hand it over to us for safe keeping.'

I was taken aback at the way she spoke to me; she was rather sharp and straight to the point.

I couldn't believe what I was hearing. Sword fighting was out of the question. I wasn't the athletic type and P.E was my least favourite subject. 'I'm afraid I won't be able to sword fight, Mrs Oak,' I said. 'I mean, I've never held a sword. I'm not Hayden and never will be. I can't do this. There must be another way for us to stop Bulzaar and get my family back without having to rely only on me. I can't do this by myself.'

'There is no other option. You must train hard and stop Bulzaar, only... YOU... can stop him!' Parmona said, rather abruptly. 'I thought Agatha would have explained all this to you, but it seems I've been mistaken.'

'Parmona, please I've given Heera my word that I'll do whatever it takes to help her defeat Bulzaar,' Mrs Oak said. 'Heera, please give Parmona the crystal and let's get on with your training.'

I wasn't comfortable giving the crystal to Parmona because there was something not quite right about her. Lena brought over my rucksack and I opened the bag and retrieved the pouch containing the crystal.

A sharp tug around my neck should have stopped me from reluctantly handing over the crystal to Parmona, but I chose to ignore the warning because I trusted Mrs Oak completely, and I didn't want to disobey her instructions.

Parmona handed the crystal over to Akaal and he pocketed it. The living room door opened and an elderly, chubby man with a walking stick, hobbled in with the assistance of an elderly woman.

The man had a kind round face and he was smiling from ear to ear. 'Sorry I'm late. Have I missed anything?' the man said whilst flicking his grey hair away from his face.

'We have the crystal, Landon, and Heera is to start her training today,' Parmona said.

'Hold on there, Parmona. Have you even given the poor girl a chance to breathe, or have you simply jumped down her neck?' Landon asked.

'We have no time for niceties, Landon. The better she trains and sets out to stop Bulzaar and bring the crystals to safety, the better chance she'll have of surviving and helping the Kingdom,' Parmona snapped back.

'That maybe but she is still only a child. Heera, don't mind Parmona… she has your best interest at heart even if she has a funny way of showing it,' Landon smiled. 'Welcome back Aggie! This is Magmus Nessell… she's our Secretary at the

Elder Town Hall and also helps me at home. As you can see my health has severely deteriorated since we last saw each other.'

Magmus greeted Mrs Oak and smiled at me sweetly. Her face was filled with little wrinkles, and her tiny brown eyes twinkled in the light of the room. The lilac hat on her head was far too enormous for her and appeared out of place, and her bright yellow wellies were in sharp contrast to her deep purple floral dress.

'Nice to meet you, Heera. I'm certain you'll be able to defeat Bulzaar,' Magmus said sweetly.

'Thanks,' I replied. I didn't see how I possibly could, though.

'Lena, take Heera with you to meet Kindred,' Parmona demanded. 'We still need to get Landon up to speed with the help of Agatha, and she'll meet you both shortly to see how your training is going.'

'What if they're seen?' Mrs Bane asked. 'Everyone's up and about Parmona.'

'Bethelda, only *we* in this room and the Lancasters know who went over to the human world, and we will, under no circumstances, betray one another,' Parmona replied. 'The spy wants Heera but he hasn't seen her and won't know who she is or where she is. Don't try to draw attention to yourself, Heera. I'm sure you'll blend in fine.'

'Who are the Lancasters?' I asked. I felt as though I was just expected to know everything Parmona mentioned, and how could I possibly blend in when I didn't know how to?

'That's Kal's family,' Mrs Bane replied.

'Heera, go, and I'll see you later,' Mrs Oak said.

'Be careful,' Mrs Bane said.

Lena led me out of the room and we both stood in the hallway in complete silence. Everything had happened quickly. Parmona was very demanding and I couldn't understand how everyone agreed with what she said, even Mrs Oak.

The realisation of having to learn how to sword fight sunk in and I began to panic. Lena placed her hand on my arm and I broke down. I couldn't help but feel everything and everyone was against me.

'How on earth am I going to learn to sword fight, Lena?' I asked, flooding my cheeks with hot tears.

'We'll think of something… don't worry,' Lena said reassuringly.

It was sweet of her to sound optimistic, and yet I couldn't think of anything except complete and utter failure going forward. Amunah had surely picked the wrong person to fight his battles.

CHAPTER 6

Sword Fighting for Beginners

'Going out again? Don't be too late coming home!' Macey said, as Lena closed the gates behind her.

'Mother has them well trained to keep an eye on me,' Lena said casually.

'Lena… Kal really didn't like me, did he?'

'Heera, don't take it personally. He has a lot going on at home, with his mother being really ill, and he's trying to follow in his father's footsteps by becoming a Seer.'

'A Seer, what's that?'

'A Seer is a person who can tell the past, present and future by either reading your palm, touching a specific object or even sensing your aura. Kal's trying to learn these skills from his father… he's found it hard because he spends most of his time taking care of his mother. Mrs Lancaster is a vampire.'

'A vampire! You mean to say Kal is a half vampire?'

'Calm down, Heera,' Lena laughed. 'Trust me… you have nothing to worry about with Kal or his mother.'

'How many Vampires are there in Kendolen? They're supposed to be really dangerous, aren't they?' I asked, peering around me as we continued walking.

'Mrs Lancaster is the only vampire in Kendolen and yes they are dangerous but Mrs Lancaster is different,' Lena said.

I couldn't believe it. Vampires were real, and all this time I'd been in the presence of a vampire's son without even a clue.

'Where exactly are we going?' I asked, trying to focus on the task that lay ahead.

'We're going to the playing field behind my school. It's currently vacant with everyone on school holidays, and your trainer, Kindred, will be waiting for us there. Kindred trains anyone who wants to learn how to fight. It's mostly elves, dwarves, and goblins who attend his lessons. He's an elf himself. I've never attended his lessons but I've heard he's a brilliant sword fighter. Mother would never let me attend even if I wanted to because it's all about spells and potion making with me.'

'I'm going to be absolutely rubbish. Lena, he won't shout at me, will he? I mean he does know I'm only a human right?'

'Why do you say *only* a human? Obviously, Amunah senses something about you to allow you the chance of being his warrior. I wished he could have chosen me… it would've been such a great honour, to tread the same path Hayden had.'

I felt taken aback at how Lena thought it was an honour to be chosen by Amunah, to me it was a burden which was bound to result in failure.

It was a chilly day and the snow was deep. Luckily, we only saw a handful of residents in the distance. I couldn't make out their faces, meaning they too wouldn't see me or Lena clearly, and soon enough, we reached the playing field.

The school itself was rather different to St Claire's. Firstly, it was significantly smaller, and secondly, the building appeared to be a square, stone house rather than a school.

'It's not St Claire's but don't let the outside fool you. The building's enchanted, with hundreds of classrooms and two assembly halls,' Lena said. I could see a figure in the distance, and he approached us once Lena waved at him.

'Is that him, Lena?'

'Yes, that's Kindred,' Lena whispered.

Kindred was slim and tall. The muscles in his arms were well defined under his clothes, and his shoulder length, black hair was a stark contrast to his pale skin. He had a sharp nose, huge violet eyes, and protruding pointed ears. There was something utterly striking about him.

Kindred's clothes were all black, including his high boots, and I could feel myself blushing as he smiled at me, flashing his brilliantly white, straight teeth.

'Good morning, Lena and this must be Heera Watson. I'm Kindred and I'll be training you today,' he beamed as he held out his hand to shake mine. I couldn't look up at him. I knew I was shy, although this was a different kind of shy, and I was pretty confident that as soon as I opened my mouth, I'd start stuttering and make a fool of myself in front of him.

'Errr... hello,' I said, cursing myself, inwardly. Calm down, Heera, I kept telling myself.

'Kindred, Heera's nervous,' Lena said.

'That's understandable but there's nothing to worry about,' Kindred said. 'Let's go around the back of the school out of view of anyone who might be strolling by. Nice earrings by the way... owls... I like owls too.'

'Thanks,' I said.

I staggered up the field, due to the untouched snow over the school grounds, slipping slightly. I hoped Kindred wouldn't glance back and see me struggling.

'Are you, OK?' Lena asked.

'Yeah, I think so... just nervous!' I said, low enough so Kindred couldn't hear.

'Hhmmm, sure it's not something else as well. Do you fancy him?' Lena sniggered.

'Of course not, Lena!' I said, utterly mortified knowing Lena had caught on.

There was a wooden shed at the back of the school into which Kindred disappeared and returned holding two swords and a shield. He laid them down on the ground.

'Before we start, I wanted to give you something. I hope you like it,' Kindred said as he handed me a chainmail suit. I'd seen chainmail in fantasy films as well as in history text books used in school, and I knew it was used as protective clothing.

I gratefully accepted the chainmail from him and tried it on so as not to seem inconsiderate. It covered my arms and upper torso. If I wore it under my clothes, no-one would realise it was there. It was strong, very light and the attention to detail was magnificent. The tiniest chain rings had been constructed into indestructible armour.

'Thank you so much, Kindred. It's beautiful,' I said, flushing crimson.

Lena giggled.

'I'm glad it's to your liking, Heera. Now, shall we begin?' Kindred asked.

I nodded as he handed me a sword with a steel blade that had a jagged edge. The sword was cold to the touch. My pendant began to throb against my chest, and whether it was Amunah or even the mysterious woman, who whispered words of encouragement trying to communicate with me, I felt protected.

The handle of the sword was gold plated and I could see the letters, *H P* inscribed across it.

'Was this Hayden's?' I asked.

'The very same one. May it bring you luck and this… was her shield,' Kindred said, passing me the heavy scratched shield. I noticed he didn't have a shield, which knocked my confidence further because he probably knew how useless I was going to be.

Lena backed away and Kindred and I both stood facing each other. Kindred bowed slightly before raising his sword in front of him, whereas I stood with the sword pointing at him half-heartedly.

Kindred's smiling face now disappeared into a look of full concentration. He was clearly in his element now and I was nothing more than an opponent to defeat.

Kindred made the first strike as he lunged forward at me with his sword. I lifted my shield in front of my face, dropped my sword and screamed. I was a stupid idiot. How was I going to get the hang of this, if I couldn't help but scream?

'I'm sorry but I can't do this,' I said.

'Don't worry, Heera. It takes time to perfect the craft of sword fighting,' Kindred said.

'Keep trying!' Lena shouted from the side.

Again, Kindred stepped forward with his sword directed at me and instead of holding up my sword, I found myself walking backwards trying to get as far away from him as possible. Several more attempts at trying to get me to use my sword weren't fruitful and Kindred called for a short break.

I glumly strolled over to Lena. I thought she would burst out laughing at me but she didn't. 'I'll be right back!' Lena said and rushed off to the shed into which Kindred had disappeared.

Hopelessness engulfed me. My family had no chance if I couldn't fight back. Lena and Kindred reappeared, and I put on a brave face, otherwise I could've easily burst into tears.

'We've come up with an idea to help you, Heera… and I'm warning you it's not going to be very pleasant,' Lena said.

'I'll try anything,' I said.

'No matter what you see, Heera, remember it's only me. I'll be using magic to change my appearance,' Kindred said.

We resumed our position and stood facing each other once more. I lifted my shield up and pointed my sword towards Kindred, who was facing the other way. When he turned around, I no longer saw Kindred. Instead, I found the same dreaded face who I now knew was Bulzaar, sneering at me just as he'd done in my nightmare. He towered over me, and his evil blood-red eyes focused on me with sheer hate on his pallid face.

Bulzaar began to taunt me whilst marching straight towards me, with his sword now held over his head, ready to deliver the fatal blow and finish me.

Bulzaar shouted, 'Heera Watson, you're no match for the Dark King! Lay down your life and I will give your family a swift and painless death!'

'NO!' I screamed at him.

Bulzaar laughed, though in fact it was more like a cackle than a laugh and said, 'What are you going to do about it, Heera? Cry and run to Agatha... she couldn't even help Hayden to defeat me. What chance have you got?'

Fury was raging through my veins, and I held onto my sword and shield with sheer determination. How dare he underestimate me?

Bulzaar approached and I focused my attention on why I was here. It was for my family. Furthermore, I'd been chosen by a God who saw something in me to save his crystals from a monster, and I had magical beings depending on me to save their kingdom from evil. I couldn't wimp out and not even try to help them. I had always lacked confidence, but there was no way I was going down without a fight.

I saw Bulzaar's sword bear down on me; I was too quick for him as I spun to the side and behind him. Bulzaar swiftly turned around to face me. Again, he raised his sword, and I quickly reacted and spun to shield the attack.

We moved around each other, lunging, striking, dodging, and spinning, trying to defeat the other. Every attack I dodged and every contact I made with Bulzaar's sword boosted my confidence.

Now that I'd started fighting, it felt like second nature to me, although I didn't know where I was getting my stamina and strength from. I loved the way my sword sliced through the air. The snow on the ground made the movements tricky. It was challenging and I slipped at times, nevertheless, I speedily steadied myself to shield any blows.

I was so focused on the sword movements and with ducking and diving that I didn't even notice, until much later, that Kindred had returned to his normal self and all signs of Bulzaar had gone. I didn't let this distract me though.

Kindred was swift and the way he held his sword was effortless. His movements were fluid and clean, whereas my strikes were heavy handed and intended to harm. I dodged another clean swipe from Kindred, by using my shield to take the hit, whilst I bent my knees and whirled around behind him to attack with the full force of my sword.

Kindred fell to the ground. He was not quick enough to shield my blow. I was shocked staring down at him and he laughed out loud. 'Well done, Heera! I knew you had it in you! Lena, your plan worked!' Kindred said, getting up.

'You were brilliant, Heera!' Lena said.

'Excellent!' a familiar voice said and I spun around and found Mrs Oak beaming with pride. I was equally stunned to find Mrs Oak wearing a pair of jeans, a black jumper and knee length boots; I'd only ever seen her wear ghastly suits at school and when she came over to the house.

Mrs Oak's hair was no longer tied up in a bun and nor was it grey. It was now brown and loose around her shoulders; the outfit combined with the new hairstyle had taken years off her. She didn't look like a headmistress anymore, and yet, she still had an air of authority about her.

'Did you think I enjoyed being disguised as a headmistress, Heera? I had to put on an appearance so no-one would doubt my intentions,' Mrs Oak laughed, noticing my shocked reaction to seeing her in this new form.

'How long were you here for?' I asked Mrs Oak.

'Long enough, Heera… long enough,' Mrs Oak replied.

We continued duelling for several hours. Mrs Oak was close by, giving me tips on how to improve my techniques, and Lena cheered on.

The sword was an extension of my arm. I simply focused on where I wanted to make the impact and the blade reacted immediately. I wondered if Lena felt the same way when she used her wand. It was an incredible feeling to hear the blade cut through the air. I felt free and in control.

'Let's call it a day!' Mrs Oak said.

'I agree, Agatha. The warrior needs to rest and perhaps we can get some more practice done tomorrow?' Kindred asked.

'Yes, of course. I think we need to give Heera training on how to tackle attacks when the enemy chooses to strike from behind. Bulzaar is an accomplished fighter and won't always fight fair. He's sneaky,' Mrs Oak said.

Even in my nightmare, Bulzaar was behind me on that mountain, and Mrs Oak was right in that he wouldn't play by the rules. I had to learn as much as possible in the little time I had.

'Thank you for everything, Kindred,' I said, without becoming shy. I could've easily continued practising for several more hours, and I was surprised at how much I'd enjoyed sword fighting after a shaky start. For now, we said our goodbyes to Kindred and the three of us made our way back to Lena's home.

My confidence was sky high. I, Heera Watson had duelled with a highly experienced, handsome Elf and I'd won. It began to snow heavily, taking us longer to get home. We encountered several residents in the distance; however, they had their heads down and were completely focused on getting back to the safety of their homes due to the snowfall.

'What took you so long? Don't you know you have guests waiting for you?' Macey and Geoffrey asked in unison.

'Who's here?' Lena asked.

'The Lancasters are here!' Geoffrey shouted.

As the door shut behind me, I instantly recalled Kal's mother was a vampire. After putting my sword and shield by the front door, I stood rooted to the spot.

Lena noticed my hesitation. 'Mrs Lancaster is unwell and will be most likely upstairs resting… don't worry… she's lovely,' she said, before pulling me into the living room.

'Father! You're back!' Lena said rushing into her dad's arms.

'Pleased to meet you, Heera. I'm Thomas, Kal's father,' a meek voice said to the side of me. I turned to find a greying man staring at me with eager enthusiasm. He tried to get up out of his armchair with great difficulty. I rushed forward to help him but he held his arm out to stop me.

'No dear, it's quite all right. I'm getting old,' he said. Mr Lancaster was rather small, frail, and nothing like I'd expected. He inhaled sharply and began to cough uncontrollably. Mrs Oak rushed over to see if he was OK. The living room door opened and Kal brought over a glass of water for his dad.

'Thank you… thank you, Son,' Mr Lancaster said, after taking a gulp of water trying to get his breath back. 'Is your mother settled?'

'Yes,' Kal said. I was standing right next to him and not once did Kal acknowledge my presence.

'WELCOME, HEERA!' Mr Bane shouted. Lena was standing by him and she dragged him over to me. Mr Bane stood overlooking everyone in the room with his hazel eyes, and his larger than life personality filled the room. He too had blonde hair and wore long black robes, and he held his wand in his right hand visible for all to see.

'Thank you, Mr Bane and thanks for letting me stay with your family,' I said.

'Please, call me David. Mr Bane was my father,' he said, laughing.

'Father!' Lena said, rolling her eyes.

'I'm only joking! If you three wish, you can retreat to your room and do what youngsters do nowadays. Leave us to catch up with Agatha,' Mr Bane said whilst moving his arms about as a way of expressing himself. 'I do believe Kal's mother, Eliza, wishes to speak with you, Heera. I'm sure she'll call you when she's ready.'

Mr Bane pointed his wand directly at each of our faces, and I was the only one who moved out of the way when he pointed it at me. The others didn't even flinch when he had directed his wand at each of them.

'Come on, let's go up!' Lena said. Kal followed her out of the room.

Before I left, I turned to Mrs Oak, who appeared to be deep in thought. 'Mrs Oak, please can you come with me when Mrs Lancaster wants to talk to me? I'd rather you be there with me,' I asked discreetly, without Mr Bane and Mr Lancaster hearing.

'Yes, of course. Now go up and get some rest,' she said.

I left the room, picked up my sword and shield and headed upstairs. I hoped Mrs Lancaster was not hard work like her son, who seemed to despise me. I was going to ask Kal straight out what his problem with me was. How was I supposed to know what I'd done if he wouldn't even talk to me?

I lifted up my sword, and I could see my own reflection staring at me in the blade. Was this the same girl who had undervalued her own self-worth and let people walk over her? No, I wasn't the same anymore. I had changed.

If only Laura Foster could see me now, guess I wasn't so pathetic after all.

CHAPTER 7

The Young King's Demise

Kal noticed my sword and shield upon entering the room and smirked to my annoyance, before returning to write in a thick brown diary. Lena was completely engrossed in her spell book.

I placed my shield and sword up against the wall, and I took off my coat and chainmail and placed them on the back of a chair.

'Vincent! Vincent! Come here, please,' the shrill voice of a woman shouted.

Kal flushed red, exiting the bedroom with his brown diary in his hand.

'It's Mrs Lancaster,' Lena said.

'Why is she calling him Vincent?' I asked. Lena didn't have time to reply because Kal returned and he'd heard me ask her the question.

'I hate that name. Vincent is my first name... I was named after my grandfather. Kal is my middle name. Mother is the only one who still calls me Vincent, even after my grandfather tried to kill her for falling in love with my father. I think she still misses him.'

'Is she comfortable?' Lena asked.

'Yes, she wanted me to help her settle,' Kal said. I was taken aback at the fact a vampire was so close to me, and Kal saw a glimmer of panic in my face. 'Mother's not your typical example of a vampire, actually quite the opposite.'

'What do you mean she's not a typical vampire?' I asked, innocently.

Kal didn't look too pleased. 'Just because you are born a certain way, doesn't automatically make you a monster!' he said.

'Mother has never hurt anyone. She refuses to even eat meat and because of her lifestyle, she's had to suffer. She's constantly in pain as she's sacrificed her true traits for the sake of her own beliefs and family.'

'I'm sorry I didn't mean anything by it. I just asked a question,' I said.

Kal diverted his eyes before speaking, 'I'm sorry. I know you didn't mean anything by it... I just get defensive over my mother. She's sacrificed a lot for both father and me, and everyone assumes that just because she's a vampire, she's going to turn on them.'

'Why don't you like me, Kal? I haven't done anything to you, and you constantly snap at me or completely ignore me,' I asked, unable to believe how I'd confronted him so openly.

Lena closed her spell book and cautiously walked over to us. The three of us fell silent. I could see Kal flushing red, once again, in embarrassment.

'There's something that bothers me about you and even scares me,' Kal said, rather bluntly.

'What? Why?' I asked, clearly shocked at the answer he'd given me.

'I'm learning how to open my mind to give readings and sense energies surrounding humans and creatures,' Kal explained. 'And back at St Claire's whilst I was helping you to get to Agatha's office, I tried to see if I could sense anything from you.

'All I could see was a shining bright light and a strong male voice warned me to let go of you. When I ignored it, the light sent a shock through my body. I felt like I was on fire, and all the power I had, drained from me within seconds. You're obviously protected by Amunah and there's also a female presence in the background, and before you ask, no, I don't know who she is. I'm scared at how touching you can drain me of my power rapidly. I've never come across a reading like yours in any of my father's books or heard him mention a scenario such as this. It's not normal.'

'Thanks for telling me, Kal. I hope you realise I've no control over the fact I'm protected by a God and whoever this other person is. I didn't ask for this, and all these things which have happened in the past twenty four hours have scared the life out of me. I don't even know if I'm ever going to see my family again or survive facing Bulzaar. I'm just grateful to you and Lena for helping me so far.'

'I know you didn't ask for this and I apologise for acting this way. It won't happen again,' Kal said.

'Good… now that's all settled, Heera, tell him about your sword fighting lesson with Kindred today. Heera was brilliant!' Lena said, giving us the next few hours to bond without any kind of awkwardness.

Although Kal was being friendly and taking a keen interest in what I had to say, I still found him to be reserved. Now and again, he'd go back to writing in his diary, leaving Lena and me to chat. I wanted to ask him what he was writing about, but I held back for now, feeling it wouldn't be an appropriate question to ask as diaries contained personal information.

There was a knock on the bedroom door and Mrs Oak entered the room. 'Heera, I've spoken with Eliza and she wishes to see you now,' Mrs Oak said.

'OK, do you two want to come with me?' I asked Lena and Kal. They immediately stood up.

'I think it's best if they didn't. We don't know what Eliza wishes to discuss with you, and she may only want to tell you,' Mrs Oak advised. I felt Mrs Oak knew Mrs Lancaster had something important to say to me.

'It's completely fine, Mrs Oak. I trust Lena and Kal, and if it wasn't for them, who knows what Mrs Mead and Mr Powers would've done to me.'

'Very well,' Mrs Oak said.

Kal led us to the very last room on Lena's landing and knocked on the door. 'Mother, can we come in?'

'Yes,' Mrs Lancaster said, gently.

My heart was racing, and I instinctively gripped the cold pendant around my neck. I was being silly reacting this way, but the thought of actually meeting a vampire gave me goose bumps.

Upon entering the dark bedroom, I saw a skeletal figure lying on a king-size, four-poster bed in the middle of the room. The two windows had been covered with black curtains to ensure no light entered the room, and only the dim glow from a lantern, on the far side of the room, gave barely enough light to see where we were treading.

As I came closer to Mrs Lancaster, I was able to see her translucent hollow face, and her white hair was flowing all over the pillow and blanket. Mrs Lancaster's grey eyes were almost lifeless like her body, and you could see the bones in her veiny arms and neck. The way she winced now and again, indicated she was in great pain.

I'd never expected a vampire to look like Mrs Lancaster. Vampires were normally depicted as attractive, dangerous, and immortal beings in movies, whereas Mrs Lancaster was the complete opposite. Having chosen another lifestyle and suppressing her true traits had clearly led Mrs Lancaster down the path of being almost bedridden.

Mrs Oak and Kal sat themselves down on either side of her on the bed. Lena and I stood at the foot of the bed waiting for her to speak.

'Lena, glad to see you back safe and sound. I've been worried sick about you and Vincent,' Mrs Lancaster said.

'Thank you, Mrs Lancaster,' Lena said.

'Heera, come closer... I want to see you properly,' Mrs Lancaster said.

I came closer to Mrs Lancaster and set myself down on the bed next to Mrs Oak. 'Hello, Mrs Lancaster,' I said.

'Hello, sweet child... yes, that's much better... I can see you now. And please, Heera, call me Eliza.' I could see she was trying hard to smile at me through gritted teeth and it seemed she was in excruciating pain.

'Mother,' Kal said, concerned at the look of pain on his mother's face.

'I'm fine. I need to speak with Heera alone. Why don't you and Lena go downstairs and see if Bethelda needs any help with dinner,' Eliza said.

'I asked them to come along, Eliza. I don't mind them staying at all,' I said.

'As you wish, Heera,' Eliza said. 'Agatha, I've heard much about you but never had the chance of meeting you... I understand you know, Thomas, my husband.'

'Yes, Eliza, it's nice to meet you too. Thomas helped me to escape to the human world all those years ago and I have much respect for him,' Mrs Oak replied.

'I've called you both here as I fear something is going to happen very soon, and it may not bode too well for you both,' Eliza explained. 'This journey you are going to take together won't be easy, and I've information that may help you to defeat the Dark King. Agatha, you already know Bulzaar's story, and it's time Heera knew exactly what led him down this dark path because she needs to know what she's dealing with. I'm afraid I'll have to start at the beginning... and Vincent and Lena, it's time you also knew the truth about Bulzaar's beginnings.'

'Go ahead, Eliza,' Mrs Oak said.

'Bulzaar was the eldest son of King Arayan, who held the throne of Fallowmere many years ago. Although King Arayan was an impressive king, his treatment of his first wife, Nerrah and Bulzaar had left the inhabitants questioning his morals,' Eliza explained. 'Bulzaar was only seven years old, when his father banished him along with Nerrah from Cranwell Castle. Nerrah always cared for her son and tried to give Bulzaar the best upbringing she could.

'King Arayan remarried his second wife Zenofur... she bore him another son, Sebastian and a daughter, Zara. Zenofur passed away a few years later, and King Arayan couldn't deny that Bulzaar would be next in line to the throne after his own demise. The King left all his wealth to Sebastian and Zara to ensure they would find another dwelling before Bulzaar entered the castle as the future King of Fallowmere. Up until this day, nobody knows the whereabouts of Bulzaar's step brother and step sister.'

I wondered what'd happened to Zara and Sebastian; it must've been difficult for them to leave the castle they'd grown up in.

'Nevertheless,' Eliza continued, 'King Arayan had served his kingdom well and all hoped his son would also keep the peace. Bulzaar was twenty-five years old, a quiet, reserved, and a handsome prince, who hesitantly took the throne and moved into his father's home at Cranwell Castle with his wife, Saniah, his daughter, Arya, and his mother, Nerrah.'

Eliza stopped talking and tried to get up to rest her back on the head board. Mrs Oak and Kal helped her up. I was surprised to find out Bulzaar had a family. Where were they? Why hadn't they stopped him from following such a dark path?

'Bulzaar could never imagine banishing his own daughter, and he couldn't comprehend how his own father had done such a thing to him,' Eliza continued wearily. 'Bulzaar's family meant the world to him, and he would do anything to keep them happy.

'Saniah, Bulzaar's wife, was a pleasant, quiet woman who cherished her family, until the new found status and wealth of her husband at Cranwell Castle changed her immensely. Bulzaar took to the throne successfully and the kingdom of Fallowmere rejoiced knowing their new King was merciful and treated every creature and human equally. Saniah, on the other hand, became obsessed with the power her husband had. When she heard a small rebellion had begun in Fallowmere, she was frightened, and she didn't want her husband to lose his throne.'

Eliza paused for a few moments and took deep breaths before continuing.

'Saniah, under the cover of darkness, decided to leave the castle and visit a witch, who was well known for her powers, in a nearby village, to ask if there was anything she could do to make Bulzaar undefeatable. The old witch was powerful and cunning. The witch informed Saniah that she could help her husband but only on one condition… the witch wanted protection from Bulzaar, who wanted to banish her from the Kingdom for practising dark magic.

'Saniah would've given anything to make Bulzaar stronger, and naturally, she accepted the witch's offer. The witch gave Saniah five crystals, each wrapped in black material varying in size and colour, and explained the crystals contained power from Amunah himself.'

Lena and Kal, like me, were holding onto every word Eliza was saying. I didn't understand how they didn't know this already as they lived in Fallowmere.

'The witch informed Saniah that the crystals knew the beholder's true desires and would wield their power to help the desires become a reality,' Eliza explained. 'The witch advised that the crystals would have to remain in the black cloth because Saniah would be using them to do evil, and the witch also explained that if the crystals were touched, they would burn the beholder. All Saniah had to do was to take out the crystals each day and let the crystals know her true desires; her true desire was for Bulzaar to have ultimate power so no-one would dare to stand up to him.

'Each day Bulzaar grew darker. He'd set out and go into battle without reason, and he started to enjoy the violence he inflicted on his enemies, which led him to bring out his brutality on his friends and the entire kingdom. Bulzaar found out about the crystals and their power and he forcefully took them from Saniah.'

'Mother, how do you know all this?' Kal asked.

'I knew Bulzaar and his family way before he became a King. I frequented the castle and poor Nerrah was trying so hard to keep the family together, and not long after, Bulzaar started to neglect his own family.

'Agatha, I understand you're aware Bulzaar imprisoned his whole family, but what you don't know is that he held them prisoner in the Caves of Arya, which he named after his daughter. I still believe his family are in those caves and all I can request is that you rescue them if you can. They've been locked away for decades, and that poor girl, Arya, has probably never seen daylight since the day she was imprisoned. I owe that to Nerrah and Saniah. I should've helped them when I had the chance... those were dark times though and I regret it to this day.'

'I knew he'd imprisoned his family, but I didn't realise it was in those caves. I thought they'd be somewhere in the castle. Eliza, we'll do what we can to get his family to safety,' Mrs Oak said.

'Thank you, Agatha. Bulzaar's family may help you defeat him. If you're able to rescue them, make them confront Bulzaar. He imprisoned them because they were his weakness, and they could stop him from committing further acts of evil,' Eliza said.

'We need all the help we can get in defeating Bulzaar, and if it means saving his family to do this, we will do our best,' Mrs Oak said.

'Eliza, do you think he's kept my family there too?' I asked.

'Those caves act as a prison for Bulzaar and yes I believe he may well be holding them there,' she replied.

'Thank you,' I said.

'It's going to be a gruelling task to find an entrance into those caves,' Mrs Oak added.

There was a knock on the door. 'Dinner's ready!' Mrs Bane said as she opened the door. 'Eliza, I'll bring you a tray up. I think that's enough information for one day, now come and eat everyone.'

Mrs Oak followed Lena and Kal out of the room, and Eliza held onto my arm as I stood up.

'Heera, there will be times when you'll feel there's no hope in the world, but always remember what you're fighting for, only then will you be able to finish whatever it is you've set out to accomplish,' Eliza said, tears brimming in her eyes. 'I hope what I'm dreading won't hinder you too much. If only I had the power to know and tell you exactly what is going to happen. Be careful out there.'

'I will, Eliza and thank you for all your help. I'll do my best to defeat Bulzaar and I know it won't be easy,' I said. Eliza smiled and gently pressed my hand.

'Go and have your dinner, Heera. They're probably all waiting for you.'

I closed the door behind me and made my way downstairs. My first encounter with a vampire wasn't as bad as I'd thought it'd be. I had valuable information from Eliza, and most importantly, I was still alive to tell the tale.

CHAPTER 8
Crossing The Barrier

Dinner in the Bane household was like no other. There was music, bad jokes, and laughter, most of it coming from Mr Bane, who kept the guests in high spirits. Lena kept apologising to Kal and me for her father's embarrassing behaviour, but I had thoroughly enjoyed myself, and for an hour or so I'd forgotten about the impending doom of facing a monster and rescuing my family.

Mrs Bane had made fish and chips for our main meal and blueberry pie for dessert. I'd thought food in Fallowmere would've been different because it was a magical world.

'Heera, did you enjoy the food?' Mrs Bane asked. 'It's been such a long time since I've made a human meal for someone… we normally serve squirrel broth or frogspawn soup with toadstool bread for supper.'

'Mrs Bane, it was delicious,' I said. Thankfully, I didn't have to try the broth, soup, and bread Mrs Bane had described.

'Heera, try this… you'll love it,' Lena said, bringing out a plate full of hard dried corn.

'Popcorn!' Kal said.

'Heera, go on, try it. It's not quite like the popcorn back home,' Mrs Oak laughed.

Kal picked up several pieces of corn and put them in his mouth. A few moments later, I could hear the corn pop inside his mouth, and he couldn't keep a straight face as his mouth grew fuller. It was strange hearing the popping sounds. They sounded painful but Kal was trying hard not to laugh.

'Go on, try it,' Lena said.

'OK,' I said, apprehensively. I picked up a few pieces of corn and placed them in my mouth. I could feel the corn resting on my tongue, and in a split second, the corn began to heat up and vibrate.

It was an odd sensation. I closed my eyes because I could feel the corn getting ready to pop, and I could hear it sizzling away in my mouth. A loud, POP, rang out in my ears, and my mouth began to fill with the tasty snack.

I could taste all types of flavours: butter, salt, and even caramel. It was delicious. I wanted to laugh but knew all the popcorn would fall out. I had another few handfuls and could barely contain my laughter. If only popcorn was served like this in the human world, it would make movie night much more fun.

'OK, now, before you go to bed, have some of my famous witch's brew,' Mrs Bane beamed. 'I call it, Dead Fly Sludge. Lena loves this,' Mrs Bane placed three mugs full of green liquid before us proudly.

'It's OK, Mrs Bane. I don't really want any... I'm way too full,' I said. I didn't want to try something called Dead Fly Sludge.

'No, no, you must try it, Heera! You'll love it and it'll make you sleep well,' Mrs Bane replied.

Kal and Lena began to sip the liquid from their mugs, but I couldn't bring myself to try it. I felt sick looking at the slimy green liquid, bubbling away in the mug, and I could see dead flies floating to the top.

'Go on, try it! Don't forget, Heera, it's made by magic and not everything is as it seems,' Lena urged.

'Mrs Bane, this is delicious. Do you mind if I have another mug full?' Kal asked.

'Of course not,' Mrs Bane said, delighted at Kal's request and hurried into the kitchen to refill his mug.

If Kal had asked for more, surely it couldn't be that bad. I lifted the mug to my lips, and before taking a sip, I sniffed the liquid and found it to be odourless. I took a sip and the hot liquid tasted like sweet marshmallows. It was delicious and soothing, and I could feel my insides loosen and relax. It was a lot like hot chocolate, although slightly sweeter with a distinctive taste, and the flies tasted like sour candy.

I could easily have had another mug; however, I was full and my stomach began to hurt with the sheer amount of food I'd eaten. 'Thanks, Mrs Bane,' I said.

'Not a problem, Heera,' she replied.

When dinner was over, Mrs Oak and Mrs Bane ordered the three of us to get some much needed rest and sent us upstairs. Kal was given a room, next door to Lena's, and he said goodnight and disappeared at nine o'clock.

I was going to share Lena's room and was glad of the much needed company. I washed up, put on my pyjamas and entered Lena's room. I immediately noticed a strange mark on the top of her left arm. When she saw me, she quickly put her nightgown over her nightshirt.

I'd only seen a glimpse of the mark. I couldn't make out what it was, but it was dark against her skin, and the way Lena had reacted to me seeing it, made me realise it was something I shouldn't mention.

Iris bellowed from the other side of the room making me jump, 'Goodnight girls!'

'Goodnight,' we both replied. I still couldn't fathom out how a spell book was speaking to me, and yet, I'd replied to it as if Iris was a real person.

'Heera,' Lena said, rather seriously as we climbed into the warm inviting bed.

'Yeah.'

'So tell me the truth. Are you looking more forward to sword fighting tomorrow or meeting Kindred?'

'Sword fighting of course... I have no idea what you're on about with Kindred,' I replied as innocently as I could.

Lena wasn't buying the answer, and she burst into a fit of giggles and began to impersonate how I'd reacted towards him. I couldn't help but chuckle away.

We talked for hours about each of our worlds, and I even took out my mobile phone to show Lena what it was used for and how it worked. Lena was convinced I was joking with her since she didn't understand how another person could hear our voice on the other end. I confused her further by explaining the phone was useless as there was no reception to make a call in Fallowmere.

'So why are you still carrying it around?' Lena asked.

'I have no idea. I guess I'm just used to carrying it everywhere with me in my bag. Trust me, Lena, you'd be amazed at all the things you can do on such a small device in the human world.'

I went on to describe TV and the Internet, and she was fascinated at how humans had used technology to make their lives easier in place of using magic. I told her all about my family, Emma, and the subjects I enjoyed at school.

Lena explained how dull her life had been growing up in Kendolen and how everything was kept secret about Bulzaar's past. She'd never been out of the town until she'd come to my world, and she revelled in telling me all about her training in potions and spells.

We lay in bed, staring up at the ceiling and yawning our way through conversations. My first day in Fallowmere had been hectic with so much information take in, and I realised how tired I was as my body relaxed. Not long after, I fell into a blissful deep sleep.

I was sword fighting with Kindred. He marched up to me with his sword pointing directly at my heart, and as he came closer to me, he fell to the ground before me on one knee. I was almost hypnotised by his violet eyes, and I noticed a diamond ring on the end of the blade of his sword. 'Heera?' Kindred said.

'Yes,' I replied.

'Heera?'

'Yes, what were you about to ask me?' I asked.

'Heera, I haven't asked you anything... you must wake up now,' Mrs Oak's voice whispered.

I opened my eyes to find the bedroom in darkness. I could only just see Mrs Oak's outline.

'What's wrong?' I whispered back.

'Shhh... come quick and get changed,' Mrs Oak said. 'Bring your things and come down straightaway. Don't wake Lena... it's best not to involve her and Kal in all this.'

I carefully climbed out of the bed, tiptoed around the room and retrieved all my belongings, including the sword and shield. Lena stirred in the bed but didn't wake up. I changed in the bathroom, not forgetting to wear the chainmail under my clothes. Before I made my way downstairs, I left a note of thanks for both Lena and Kal on the dresser.

Mrs Oak was waiting for me at the bottom of the stairs; she was dressed already. I saw a rucksack, along with a glistening sword by the front door.

'Leave your things there. Eliza was right... we are in serious trouble,' Mrs Oak said, opening the door to the living room and pulling me inside.

I found Mr and Mrs Bane, Mr Lancaster and the three Elders waiting for me with anxious expressions. Landon Tomkins was clutching at his chest with one hand and had the other firmly on his walking stick. Mrs Bane couldn't contain her distress and bustled out of the room in a flood of tears.

'What's wrong?' I asked, panicking.

'We're extremely sorry for intruding on you like this but the crystal you gave to us has been stolen,' Parmona said. 'Kendolen is no longer protected. You must leave tonight and face Bulzaar sooner than expected. We can no longer guarantee your safety, and once the Dark King uses the power of the five crystals, he'll be able to cross the barrier into Kendolen and have his revenge. We have at least a little time to prepare for this event as it will take a while for the power of the crystals to work to his advantage.'

'Who stole the crystal?' I asked. 'Maybe we can stop them before they leave the town. It will buy me more time. I'm not ready to go into battle... I haven't had enough training!'

'It's my fault. I should never have hidden it in front of her. How was I supposed to know she'd betray me?' Landon said to himself. 'Magmus Nessell took the crystal and fled. I tried to stop her... ' Landon broke down.

'How could she do that?' Mrs Oak demanded.

'Magmus had her own secrets. We've found out she's a Vallaar, an ancient line of creatures, which until now, we'd thought no longer existed in Kendolen,' Parmona explained. 'These creatures are loyal to Bulzaar and are able to change their appearance as they wish. The only way of finding out if you're in company of a Vallaar is by using a shattered mirror, and if the creature looks into the mirror, they'll be seen for what they truly are. She must've been the spy you saw in Gentley Woods.'

'I can't believe it. Magmus fooled me all these years and I never read her for what she was,' Mr Lancaster said, welling up slightly.

'I'll go and see if I can find her,' Mr Bane said.

'NO, David, we must get the town ready to fight. We've no time to search for Magmus… she'll be on her way to the Dark King,' Parmona said. 'Fortunately, it will take days for her to get the crystal to him. Cranwell Castle's a long way away and our only hope is Heera. She must defeat Bulzaar and protect the kingdom. Heera, find the five crystals and bring them to us, and we'll help you use their power to stop Bulzaar and to banish evil once and for all. This is the only way of saving your family, the Kingdom and fulfilling Amunah's wish of bringing the crystals to safety. David and Thomas send word for every resident of the town to meet at the Elder Town Hall.'

'I'll accompany you,' Akaal said directly to David and Thomas. This was the first time I'd heard him speak, and when he stood up, he was shaking and his eyes were darting around the room. I found the way he was acting rather odd but no-one else seemed to notice.

'I'm going to rally up the wizards and send them to the barrier to put up spells to make our defences stronger,' Landon said.

'Come, Heera, we must leave for Cranwell Castle right away!' Mrs Oak said, ushering me out of the room and closing the door.

Mrs Bane was sobbing in the hallway, and when she saw me, she tried to compose herself. 'Oh Heera, please be careful,' she said.

'I'll be fine, Mrs Bane. Please say goodbye to Kal and Lena for me, and thank you all for letting me stay here,' I said. I wanted to say bye to them myself, but maybe it was better this way as it would only make it harder to leave.

Mrs Oak picked up her rucksack, and with a wave of her wand, two sword sheaths complete with leather straps emerged out of thin air on the floor. One was covered in silver embroidered material and the other in gold. Mrs Oak handed me the silver sword sheath, and I copied the way she put the strap of the sword sheath, diagonally over her body.

'Thanks, Mrs Oak,' I said, she smiled at me reassuringly as she put her sword away in the gold sheath.

'Bethelda, thank you for keeping my sword safe for all these years... I knew it'd come in use again one day,' Mrs Oak said.

'Agatha, good luck and keep safe,' Mrs Bane said. Without another word, we left the house and made our way to Gentley Woods in the cold crisp air with only the light from Mrs Oak's wand helping us to see in the darkness.

We trudged through the snow as quickly as we could in complete silence. Once or twice, I slipped on the snow and Mrs Oak helped me up. My ruck sack felt far too heavy, accompanied with the extra weight of the shield and sword and my shoulder was beginning to ache.

'Heera, what's wrong?' Mrs Oak asked.

'Sorry, my rucksack's way too heavy and I'm struggling to keep up with you,' I said.

'How could I forget? Here this should help!' Mrs Oak said. With her wand, she tapped my rucksack and the pain in my shoulder vanished. I lifted my rucksack and it was weightless. I opened it and still found all my things as they were. 'Do you want me to enlarge the rucksack so you can hide your shield in there, Heera?'

'Yes, please,' I said. Mrs Oak again tapped the rucksack, and I could feel it expanding in length and width. I managed to get Hayden's shield to fit inside and I no longer felt hindered.

'Thanks!' I said.

As we sped off again, I heard murmuring from behind us. I turned round to find no-one there. I convinced myself I'd imagined it. Soon, we were at the entrance to Gentley Woods, and the rusty iron gates loomed high above us.

It was pitch black and eerily silent. Mrs Oak opened her rucksack and took out two fire torches and lit them both with her wand.

'Now Heera, please stay close!' Mrs Oak said as she handed me a fire torch. The flames were bright and rather comforting, and we lifted the torches in front of us before we headed into the daunting woods.

We continued deeper into the woodland until we came across something shining in the near distance. 'That's the magical barrier, Heera,' Mrs Oak whispered. 'We have to cross it now before the wizards show up to increase Kendolen's defences.'

My pendant jolted forwards with the chain digging deep into the back of my neck. There was a loud crack and we both spun around towards the sound. A dark figure glided swiftly between the trees coming directly towards us. I reached for my sword, but Mrs Oak pushed me forwards and away from the approaching danger.

'RUN NOW! Go! I'll hold it off. Cross the barrier and I'll catch up with you!' Mrs Oak screamed.

I ran as fast as I could towards the barrier. I could hear Mrs Oak shouting and screaming from behind me. I turned to see the black figure, we'd seen with the Fire Blades in the woods, striking her to the ground with one swift wave of his hand.

I completely freaked out. I had to do something to help Mrs Oak. She was now on her feet duelling with the mysterious figure, and she pointed her wand at him, whereas he simply waved his arm to attack. They were both ducking and diving to avoid each other's spells. Sparks of red and blue flew across the sky and illuminated the duellers.

'Heera!' a familiar voice said. I turned to find Lena followed by Kal appear from the darkness to my right; they too were holding fire torches and carrying rucksacks with them. Lena grabbed me by the arm and pulled me towards the barrier.

'What are you doing here? Let me go… I have to help Mrs Oak,' I yelled.

'You can't help her! She can handle herself and she told you to cross the barrier. Now let's go!' Lena said.

'No, I can't leave her like this!' I retaliated. Again, I went for my sword, and this time the scream emanating from Mrs Oak made my heart fall straight to my stomach. I'd never heard anyone scream like that before and I knew she needed help.

The figure had struck Mrs Oak and he was staring down at her. She was motionless. The figure now turned to gaze directly at me and began to move towards us. We ran as fast as we could towards the glittering barrier. I could hear the figure swiftly approaching us; I could feel a rush of air around my body as he came closer.

There was another loud bang and the figure fell to the ground in pain behind us. We turned and saw Mrs Oak on her knees with her wand pointing towards the dark figure. She'd managed to cast a spell to stop him from attacking us. My heart leapt, seeing her alive.

'GO NOW!' Mrs Oak shouted. The figure was slowly getting to his feet.

We continued running, and before we went through the barrier, we heard the figure shout, 'NOOOO, COME HERE YOU BRAT!'

I felt I'd been hit in the face with ice cold water. When I came out the other side of the barrier, I was dizzy and had to steady myself.

When I glanced back at the barrier hoping to see Mrs Oak, all I found was a solid silver wall, shimmering in the dark. I tried to push myself back through to the other side of the wall to no avail. Lena and Kal stood by my side, and we could hear Mrs Oak's screams grow louder until complete silence fell over Gentley Woods.

'Let's get out of here. That thing may come out of nowhere again,' Lena said, hoisting her rucksack over her shoulder and pointing her wand forward into the trees in the distance.

'We can't just leave Mrs Oak like this,' I said.

'Don't you see, Heera, my mother was right. She said something bad was going to happen and it has. I don't think Agatha is going to come through that barrier,' Kal said.

I clutched my pendant, and I hoped Amunah was watching and would help Mrs Oak be safe. Lena pulled me onwards, and I reluctantly continued walking on.

'Are we going the right way?' Lena asked Kal.

I glimpsed to my left and found Kal holding a map and a compass in one hand. 'We're definitely going the right way, and according to the map, we still have another two miles to walk until we will finally leave these woods well behind us,' Kal said.

My thoughts were still with Mrs Oak. That figure was after me and she'd sacrificed herself to help me get away. Silent tears fell down my cheek. Lena and Kal didn't notice I was crying. How was I going to do this without her?

It seemed like we'd been walking onwards for hours and we were gradually trekking upwards. The trees spread out in front of a steep hill before us, and with the help of the moonlight, we could see where we were going and we lowered the fire torches.

'Is it just me or is there no snow on the ground,' Lena said as she put her fire torch close to the ground.

'Yeah you're right… it's much easier to walk now,' Kal replied.

I could hear them nattering away but I didn't want to join in. I couldn't understand why Kal and Lena were here, knowing they wouldn't be able to cross back into Kendolen.

We came to an abrupt halt at the top of the hill and found a waist-height brick wall in front of us; we couldn't see how steep the downhill path was because of the darkness looming over the other side of the wall. The moonlight, which had been useful for the previous half hour, had disappeared behind black clouds. It was difficult to see anything in front of us without having to lift the fire torches high above our heads.

Kal consulted his map and said, 'Look, we've made it! There's the boundary on the map and the wall signals the exit of Gentley Woods.'

'Let's rest here for a few hours,' I said. 'It's way too dark to even see where we are currently, and it will give Mrs Oak a chance to catch up with us. We'll get up early and carry on.'

The truth was I didn't want to carry on without Mrs Oak. I was optimistic she'd be back and I wanted to stall as much as possible.

'Sounds good to me. I'll get the tent ready,' Lena said. When she saw the surprised look on my face, she grinned, 'You didn't think we'd come and help you without coming prepared do you?'

'But how and why are you both here? How did your parents let you come knowing how dangerous it would be?' I asked.

'We'll talk when we get inside the tent. Set the tent up over there, Lena. The roots of those trees are huge and we'll be well hidden by them,' Kal said pointing towards a secluded area, where the roots of several large trees were growing out of the ground and the tent could easily be hidden from prying eyes.

'Yes, your highness,' Lena mumbled, rolling her eyes at him. Luckily, Kal hadn't heard her.

We found a spot between the giant trees and Lena began to set up the tent. Kal took his brown diary out of his bag and began to write something down with the help of the fire torch in his one hand. Within minutes, Lena had the tent upright by using a spell from her spell book and lit up the tip of her wand to give us enough light to see inside the tent.

We extinguished our fire torches before we entered the tent and climbed into our sleeping bags, which Lena had brought with her.

'Are we going to take it in turns to keep watch?' Kal asked.

'There's no need for anybody to keep watch because Iris will wake us up for six o'clock so we can get a quick start,' Lena replied, taking out her spell book once again.

'Iris, what time is it?' Lena asked.

'Four o'clock in the morning,' Iris replied.

'OK, wake us up at six o'clock, Iris, and if someone approaches our tent, ring some sort of alarm to get our attention,' Lena said.

'Yes, Lena, I will... Lena, my dear, you shouldn't have run away from home. Your poor parents will be worried sick,' Iris said.

'What's done is done, Iris.'

'Yes, my dear,' Iris said.

'Lena, why didn't you get one of these when we went to Heera's world instead of having to rely on your spell book to tell the time?' Kal asked, showing her a watch on his wrist. 'Agatha gave it to me, and it's much better than using a sundial.'

'Because it looks ridiculous! I've always used Iris to tell me the time... that's what witches do,' Lena said in disgust.

'Lena, this is...' Kal started but I interrupted him.

'You two ran away?' I asked.

'Yes, I was awake when Agatha came to get you. I just knew something was wrong when I found my mother sobbing at the foot of the stairs,' Lena explained. 'I woke Kal up as soon as I'd read the note you left us, and Mother came upstairs and told Mrs Lancaster what'd happened. We hid and listened to everything. We even heard the Elders are going to send witches and wizards to guard the boundaries around Kendolen, while other residents will help build an army and train every creature to fight Bulzaar. Not a single soul will be allowed to leave Kendolen.

'We left through the back door of the house. Otherwise, the gargoyles would've made such a racket that we would've been caught. I know my parents are going to be furious, but I have to help you save Kendolen from Bulzaar's wrath. It's our home.'

'We'd have to fight in the end,' Kal said, 'but it would have to be on the Elders terms. When we left, we heard the Elders talking about making each and every one, regardless of their age, to train in the morning. I need to do this for my family too, Heera. We both do. If Bulzaar even thinks about touching my parents, he has another thing coming to him. If Hayden stood up to Bulzaar being a woman, no offense girls, then I can, and plus it's best there is a man accompanying you for your safety.'

'You haven't seen Heera sword fight have you, Kal? Trust me she'll be the one protecting us,' Lena said. This time Kal smiled sarcastically and rolled his eyes

'What about your mother, Kal? I don't think you should've left her,' I said.

'I know my mother would be proud of me making this move, and it would be nice to actually see what's out there in Fallowmere. We've never left Kendolen, well apart from the time we came to your world. I'd rather face Bulzaar sooner than later, and if we can stop him, then he won't even be able to touch anyone in Kendolen.'

'Heera, we're here now and we're going to help you. There's no turning back. Will you let us come with you?' Lena asked.

'Yes, of course... I'm just shocked at what's happened with Mrs Oak and then seeing both of you turn up... it's just been a lot to take in and everything happened so quickly. I only came to Fallowmere yesterday, and I have to find and bring the crystals to safety, defeat Bulzaar, rescue my family and help rid the kingdom from evil. On top of that, Kal's mum wants us to rescue Bulzaar's family from the Caves of Arya, and the Elders want me to bring the crystals to them. The list just seems to be getting longer and I have no idea where to begin. I can't do this.'

'You can, we're here to help you do this, Heera,' Lena assured me.

'Thanks for being here with me you two,' I said.

'OK, now enough of the sentimental stuff... let's get some sleep,' Kal said, tucking himself in. He turned the other way and fell silent.

Lena was nodding her head in dismay, and I tried not to laugh at her reaction. Lena and Kal drifted into sleep almost straightaway. I, on the other hand couldn't nod off. Who was that dark figure in Gentley Woods? If it was Magmus Nessell, then what was she still doing in the woods? Surely, she would've made her way out of Kendolen and Gentley Woods by now? Something just didn't seem right. Could it be possible there was more than one traitor in Kendolen conspiring together? I knew I couldn't possibly know the answers to these questions straightaway, but they kept playing on my mind.

I kept tossing and turning. I tried to think of happier times to focus my mind; however, all the happy memories started and finished with my family, and they were in the hands of a monster. With the last crystal on its way to him, he could do what he wanted to them.

Mrs Oak was convinced I'd be able to defeat him with her help but now she wasn't here. At least, I wasn't alone. I had Lena and Kal with me now, and maybe Mrs Oak would show up soon. With that hope in my mind, I finally managed to drift off to sleep.

I was on my own, looking up at Cranwell Castle, wondering if Bulzaar was hiding there. I gripped the handle of my sword more firmly. It made me feel powerful and in control.

This time, I truly believed I could kill him. The breeze swept through my long black hair and I heard the female voice again. The words were so clear and comforting, 'Heera, be brave... you're only scratching the surface. You have so much to learn... be careful.'

The voice was soothing. I could feel something beating against my chest violently. Maybe it was my heart almost bursting through my skin and I put my hand over a cold, object beating against my chest. I could hear someone calling my name from a distance, and it seemed to be getting louder and frantic.

'Who are you?' I asked hoping I'd get an answer. When I had no reply, I asked again, this time a little louder.

'It's me Lena... get up! We can hear shouting and screaming outside,' Lena whispered. Kal was peering through the opening of the tent.

Even I could hear the scuffle outside and the screaming was becoming louder. There were many voices shouting over each other. 'Kal can you see anything?' Lena whispered.

'No, whoever they are, they must be on the other side of that wall,' Kal whispered.

'Come on, let's pack up silently and get out of here. How come Iris didn't wake us up?' I asked.

'It's only five thirty, Heera, and whoever is shouting must not be close enough for Iris to warn us about any danger,' Lena whispered.

We dressed, packed away our rucksacks, and exited the tent as quietly as we could. Lena quickly pointed her wand at the tent; it fell to the ground and started to fold itself into a compact package. With one final tap of her wand on the folded tent, the package shrunk to fit into the palm of her hand; Lena put the folded tent back into her rucksack and slung it over her shoulder.

I had my sword at the ready. Lena had her wand pointing forwards and Kal had his diary in one hand and the map and the compass in the other. We crept towards the brick wall. I hoped it wasn't the Fire Blades. I hadn't expected to encounter them so soon, and there was still no sign of Mrs Oak anywhere. It suddenly occurred to us that we were truly alone facing danger without anyone to protect us, and the horror of our situation was clearly etched on each of our faces.

CHAPTER 9
Hold Onto Your Head

We stood a few metres away from the brick wall and crouched down onto our hands and knees. We crawled to the far right of the wall and peered out from the side discreetly.

I saw the reason for the scuffle, and fortunately, we were at the peak of the steep hill and the creatures arguing at the foot of the hill were unable to see us hiding behind the wall.

Five ugly, short creatures with beady black eyes and hooked runny noses were shouting at a large rock on the ground. They were circling it, lunging at it, and one was poking it with a branch. They kept flaring their noses as they cackled away. Their faces were covered in fine wrinkles and their ears drooped down the sides of their faces. I couldn't understand why they were acting this way. What was so special about this enormous rock?

The tiny brutes wore identical clothes, consisting of a mustard coloured tunic with an open mouth of a dragon emblazoned on the front in red and black. I'd seen this same dragon on the weapons of the Fire Blades that we'd encountered in Gentley Woods, and it was only too obvious they owed allegiance to Bulzaar.

'They're goblins, Heera,' Lena muttered. 'They're vicious creatures and only out for themselves. They'll take the side of anyone as long as they're going to get something out of it.'

I could hear someone crying. I realised quickly the sobs were coming from the so-called large rock. It was grey in colour and I could see it moving. Whatever this thing was, I couldn't see its face and nor did it appear to be wearing any clothing.

'What is it?' Lena whispered.

'I don't have a clue... we just need to get out of here,' Kal whispered back.

'No, we can't... not yet. We're going to get caught. There's only way out of here and it's straight through them,' I muttered. We carefully peered out again to see what was happening.

'Have you made your mind up yet? Or are you going to keep blubbering on the floor like a little girl?' snarled one goblin.

'Join us, Tallon!' said another directly to the rock. 'The Dark King will be proud if you join his army. Your entire family and clan have joined us without hesitation. You're a Headhunter and you will be of use to him. Bulzaar will want to know who his enemies are, and he'll come for you just as he will for the cowards living in Kendolen. Come with us to the training grounds.'

I'd heard of vampires, witches, wizards and goblins in my world, but I'd never heard of a Headhunter before and neither had Kal or Lena by the looks of it. Whatever Headhunters were, they didn't sound very pleasant. However, this rock like creature named Tallon didn't seem threatening as he lay weeping on the floor with the goblins circling and poking him.

Tallon stopped crying and sat up straight. The goblins stopped in their tracks and were eagerly awaiting a response from him. As Tallon's face turned to face the wall, the three of us gasped together.

The Headhunter was hideous. He had round bloodshot eyes, a crooked nose, and his circular mouth was enormous. Tallon's teeth appeared to be razor-sharp and he seemed to have way too many of them. His mouth and teeth were like those of a large bloodsucking leech I'd once seen on a nature programme on TV, and I couldn't help but shudder looking at him. He had stick thin legs, gangly arms and he had long, slim fingers with dirty sharp nails.

'No way! I'll never join your King. All the others have lost their minds and do you think I'm stupid?' Tallon sobbed. 'I remember how it was when your so-called Dark King had complete power. What did he do? He only caused my kind misery and pain. You're the cowards... not me or those creatures back in Kendolen... you can't make me join.'

The goblins were confused. They thought they'd broken his will by their antics but the Headhunter was not at all afraid.

'You're going to regret this... you should be ashamed of yourself. You are the Chief Headhunter's only son and you should be following his example,' a goblin spat.

'The Chief? He has no right to call himself the Chief. He's leading the entire clan to ruin. Why haven't you left yet? Go back to the castle and tell your beloved Dark King that I'm waiting for him. Go now or do you want me to wear your head?' Tallon said, directing his question at the goblin that'd lunged at him with a stick earlier.

'There is only one of you and five of us, and we aren't leaving here without teaching you a lesson about respect,' the goblin said.

The goblins without warning pounced on the Headhunter and did something I didn't expect to see nor did I have time to look away. One of the goblins had ripped the Headhunter's head off and flung it several feet away. They laughed and picked it up and started to pass the head to one another.

To my horror the body of the Headhunter was still moving around, and its gangly arms were flailing on the ground, trying to stabilise himself. His head was still shouting as it was thrown between the goblins.

'Put my head down right now! I'm warning you! Give me back my head!' the Headhunter said.

'No, we'll be back though to see if you change your mind, and we might even bring a few Fire Blades with us to convince you the hard way,' a goblin said. 'Morty, throw his head far away. It will take him ages to find it… might do him some good as he has a lot to think about.'

Morty did as he was told and flung the head several feet away from the Headhunter's body. 'I'll get you next time,' Tallon's head said. The goblins ignored his remark and ran towards a forked path, with one path heading to the left, and the other to the right.

The goblins veered off to the left.

'Now's our chance… let's get out of here,' Kal said.

Lena agreed with him and they began to run down the hill, veering away from the Headhunter.

'Wait… we can't leave him here like this. We have to help him,' I said as I ran after them. Lena and Kal stopped once they were at the bottom of the hill, and we could see Tallon's head still screaming for help while his body was still running around trying to find his head.

'Heera, are you crazy? It is called a Headhunter for a reason. It will take yours off if you're not careful! Now let's go,' Kal said, scared. 'Whatever happened between them is none of our business.'

'Yeah, he's right! Let's go,' Lena said.

'No, I can't believe you're not going to help him, and in case you haven't noticed, he can't be that bad if he threatened the goblins,' I replied and headed straight for the Headhunter's head.

'Oh!!! What am I going to do? I can't see where my body is. Help! Help!' the head was shouting. The head went quiet as it heard me approaching; it was facing away from me. 'Hello, is anybody there? Please help me,' the head pleaded.

'Erm hello… I will try to help but I don't know how too,' I honestly replied.

'OK, don't panic! Pick my head up nice and gently and return it to my hands. I will take care of the rest and thank you so much in advance for helping,' Tallon's head said.

I didn't mind helping, although I felt disgusted at the thought of handling a head without a body. I took a deep breath and picked up the head, which was still facing away from me. The back of Tallon's head felt dry and rough and I couldn't bear to hold it any longer. I ran over to Tallon's body and placed the head in his hands.

Soon enough, the head was firmly attached to his neck, and he moved it side to side to make sure it didn't fall off. He had his eyes closed as he was rubbing his head and he said, 'Thank you so much. I don't know how I could ever repay you... it would have taken me forever trying to find my head. I'm Tallon.'

He opened his eyes and saw me standing in front of him, and he stared at me in shock. 'Hayden... is that you?' he asked. 'No it can't be... but you look so similar to her. Oh Hayden, It must be you, otherwise who'd have helped a Headhunter... I thought Bulzaar had killed you. Where have you been my dear friend? You've had an ageing spell put on you, haven't you? You look very young and the colour of your eyes has changed. Are you disguising yourself as someone else? Still carrying your sword, I see!'

I didn't know what to say because Tallon was babbling away too quickly and asking too many questions all at once. I managed to speak when Tallon took a deep breath to say something else, 'I'm sorry, but I'm not Hayden. I found this sword back in Kendolen and I didn't realise it was hers. My name is Heera.'

I didn't want to tell him who I was to be on the safe side.

'You look like her... I'm sorry. I just thought maybe all our problems would be solved if she was back,' Tallon said, looking into the distance as if deep in thought. He spotted Lena and Kal, 'Who are they?' he asked.

'They're my friends,' I replied. 'How did you know Hayden?' I asked. Lena and Kal strolled over apprehensively and stood a short distance away.

'It was a very long time ago, and believe it or not, we went to school together,' Tallon continued. 'She was always kind to me and saw me for my good deeds. Not once did she judge me for being a Headhunter. Our kind are known to be savages but I've never taken anybody's head for my own. This is my original head.' Tallon seemed to be proud of still having his own head with the way he was beaming at me.

'That's great! Well, we really should be getting on now. It was lovely to meet you,' I said, rather uncomfortably, after hearing Tallon talk about his head. I turned around and gestured to the others to walk the other way.

'No wait! Where are you going? Have you come from Kendolen?' Tallon asked.

'Yeah we have. We are going to… ' I didn't get to finish my sentence.

'Heera, can you come over here please,' Kal said abruptly. Tallon didn't seem to care that Kal had interrupted the conversation. He just stood staring at me with a goofy grin on his face.

'Erm… excuse me, Tallon. I'll be right back,' I said smiling back as I walked over to Kal.

'Very well, I'm not going anywhere,' Tallon replied.

I couldn't believe how Kal was reacting. 'What's wrong with you, Kal?' I asked. 'That was so rude of you. Why did you do that?'

'I didn't know how else to stop you from putting our lives in danger. You can't tell him everything, Heera,' Kal replied. 'How do we know he's even a good creature? Okay, I know you're going to say he didn't join Bulzaar's goblins, but what if he has other ideas. I mean what if he's after our heads.'

'You really amaze me Kal... of course he's telling the truth. Do you think if he was lying about hunting heads that he would choose the one he has on now?' I asked. 'I'm not saying we should trust him, but maybe we can at least ask him for some advice about which way we should go. Can you not tell whether he's good or bad?'

I turned around to find Tallon still gaping at us. I felt guilty we were whispering about him while he stood watching us in awe. Usually, at school, I was the one who'd always be whispered about, and I knew how that felt.

'I can't concentrate right now,' Kal heated up. 'And in case you haven't realised, my powers in this world aren't as sharp as they were in your world because there was hardly any magic there, and it was easy to pick up a magical presence but here my powers are limited.'

'I didn't mean anything by it...' I said.

The last thing I wanted was to offend Kal, and he always took things out of context; however, he was here with me out of choice and I let him have his rant.

'Heera, just ask him quickly so we can make a move. I think he might want to tag along,' Lena said.

'Fine, I'll be as quick as I can.' I went back over to Tallon. 'Tallon, we were wondering if you can help us... you see we've left Kendolen and we're trying to get to Cranwell Castle. Do you know which way would be the best way to go from here?'

'Why do you want to go there? Do you know about the crystals, Heera?' Tallon asked grimly. 'Bulzaar has found them, and he'll soon be powerful enough to destroy the kingdom once again. You should go back to your family. It's not safe for you out here.'

'Thanks for your advice, Tallon, but please can you tell us the best and safest way to get to Cranwell Castle? You see, my family have been taken by Bulzaar and I need to find them,' I asked again, politely.

'If your family is with Bulzaar, they probably won't be the same anymore… they probably won't even know who you are. You see he does things to creatures nobody would ever dream about. My family hate me because Bulzaar has turned them against me, and they keep sending those goblins to demand I join them or else they'll disown me. Are you really sure about finding them?'

'Yes, I'm sure,' I replied.

'OK then… well you can either go to the left of that path ahead and it will take you to Morden Village, or if you take the right at the path, you'll end up at the Purple Lotus Marsh. Each path has positive and negative points. Morden Village is full of Bulzaar's supporters… the good point is they won't expect Bulzaar's enemies to roam around freely.' Tallon took a deep breath before continuing.

'The Purple Lotus Marsh on your right is a good option because it will be quiet as everyone is scared of the beast that lives in the water… even though it hasn't been seen for many years. Oh yes and the high temperatures might cause a problem with having to walk a long distance… you certainly won't be needing those boots and warm coat.'

'What kind of beast? Have you seen it, Tallon?'

'No I haven't seen it. It hasn't been spotted for years and some say it died.'

'Thank you for all your help, Tallon. We best get going now and please don't tell anyone you saw us here,' I said backing away.

'No, thank you for getting my head back for me, Heera, and I won't say a word to anyone. Good luck,' he smiled.

I turned around expecting to be called back by Tallon. I walked over to the other two, and when I turned around, I saw Tallon disappearing down the pathway towards Morden Village.

'What do you think? Morden Village or the Purple Lotus Marsh?' I asked.

'Purple Lotus Marsh,' Kal and Lena said in unison.

'I was thinking the same. Those goblins went towards the village and I wouldn't want to run into them.'

'It will be less crowded and who knows if this evil beast Tallon was talking about even exists. If it hasn't been seen in years, it could've died,' Lena said. 'Bulzaar's supporters will have the village on lockdown. If we do see this so-called beast, we can turn back and think of another plan.'

'At least we don't have to see him again. He was so weird,' Kal declared.

'He wasn't that bad. He was just lonely, that's all,' I said.

Tallon was strange and yet he was standing against Bulzaar. If you saw Tallon, you'd think he was an evil creature who'd sympathise with Bulzaar; however, he'd proved me wrong, and he'd even gone as far as leaving his family for what he believed in.

My journey had only just begun and I'd learnt my very first lesson: not to judge a creature based on their appearance. With that in mind, I continued onwards towards the Purple Lotus Marsh with Lena and Kal by my side.

CHAPTER 10
The Beautiful Beast

The Purple Lotus Marsh, according to Kal's map, was nine miles away, and he led the way with the map, compass, and brown leather diary open in his hands.

The path was narrow and winding. We steadily found ourselves surrounded by trees with giant green leaves swooping down to the ground from the vine like branches, and the moss covered bark glistened in the ever increasing temperature.

Sweat began to pour down our faces with it becoming increasingly humid, and at one point, we stopped to take off our coats and put them away in our rucksacks.

We each had a drink of water from flasks Lena handed over to us, and we ate a few pieces of bread she'd taken from her kitchen. Unusual flowers in a variety of colours encircled us, and minuscule green and blue birds hovered around the luminous plants nearby.

'It's only quarter past seven. I think our parents will know we're missing,' said Kal. 'I bet they're panicking.'

'I feel bad about how we left them without saying something, but I'm glad we've come along on this journey,' Lena said.

'I wonder how Mrs Oak is,' I said.

'She'll be OK, Heera. Mrs Oak can take care of herself,' Lena smiled. 'I bet she's rallying everyone to stand up and face Bulzaar back in Kendolen.'

'Let's hope so,' I said.

We decided to move on in the sweltering heat. Three hours later of trailing through the luscious greenery, the path led to an area of open water covered in green algae.

Floating on the surface of the wetland were gigantic lily pads, blossoming with purple lotus flowers, which sparkled like jewels under the blinding sun. I saw steps leading up to a broken stone bridge, which was partially submerged in the water; the bridge re-emerged half way across the marsh before it disappeared again. There was no way of making it to the other side.

'What a waste of time! How are we going to get across, now?' Lena said, slightly crestfallen. 'I don't want to have to walk all the way back in this heat.'

'I'm not getting a good feeling... there's something in the water. I can feel its energy and it's not good,' Kal said putting away his diary in his bag. He retrieved a sword from his rucksack and gripped it tightly.

'Where did you get that from Kal?' Lena asked, obviously flabbergasted. 'And, most importantly, why're you only just taking that out now?'

'I had to bring something to defend myself with, and I found this in Agatha's room,' Kal replied. 'I think your mother had kept quite a few of her swords, ready for her to return, and I picked one up before we left last night. It's not as good as yours, Heera, by the looks of it, but it'll do for emergencies, and in case you haven't noticed Lena, this *is* an emergency.'

'Can you tell what it is? I mean is it alive?' I asked Kal before Lena had a chance to reply to him. I didn't want them to argue, especially not now. I took out my sword from its sheath and pointed it towards the open water. Lena had her wand at the ready.

'I really can't tell if it's alive. I only know it's dangerous,' Kal said panicking and backing away from the water. 'I think we should try going through Morden Village. We can't take a risk.'

'We can't go back now. For all we know, it's dead,' Lena said. 'Tallon did say nobody had seen it for years, and you could be feeling its residual energy from the time it was living?'

'Oh, I don't know Lena! How are we going to get across anyway? The bridge is broken,' Kal pointed out, getting further aggravated with Lena.

We heard a loud croak and saw an enormous toad jump onto a lily pad. We were surprised to find the lily pad remained completely still; we'd expected it to sink slightly. Lena's eyes lit up.

'Hang on, let me try something,' Lena said. She picked up a rock from the side of the bridge and used her wand to increase it in size. She levitated the rock towards the closest lily pad to us and slowly lowered it onto the lily pad. To our amazement, the lily pad didn't sink.

'We can use the lily pads to cross over,' I said as Kal shook his head in disbelief at what I was suggesting. 'I know it's not what you want to do, Kal, but we don't know for sure if this beast is alive or dead, and turning back is going to cost us time.'

'I think we should go for it and it's not too far a distance to the other side,' Lena said. 'If we're quick, it won't take us thirty seconds. Heera and I can go first if you want, Kal?'

'No, I'll go. I can't let you girls go first, and I'd rather get it over and done with,' Kal said while going red in the face. Clearly, he didn't want to sound like a wimp in front of us both.

The murky water seemed perfectly calm, and Kal was determined to cross over to the other side. I felt he wanted to prove to us both that he wasn't afraid to cross the marsh, and we left him to it.

He stepped onto the bridge, focused on the deep purple lotus flower resting on a lily pad to his left, took a deep breath, and jumped as far as he could, landing heavily on the plant. Miraculously, the plant did not move.

Kal became terribly confident. He jumped to the next lily pad to his right, and he kept on jumping until he landed on the broken bridge that emerged from the water. He was now halfway across the marsh.

He swiftly and calmly leapt across the remaining eight lily pads, making it across to the other side. Kal was thrilled and started to signal to us to jump across; he was overcome with excitement at being the first to cross over without harm.

'Heera, do you want to go next?' Lena asked.

'How about we do it together? I mean we won't be able to land on the lily pads together because there's not enough room for both of us to stand on them, but we can wait for each other as we jump across each plant. Let's show Kal how fast we can cross over compared to him. It will make him so angry.'

We both saw Kal watching us and he kept telling us to hurry up. He was becoming more and more impatient. He was either too scared to be on his own on the other side or he was feeling rather too pleased with himself for having to wait for us.

'Yes, let's do this,' Lena said.

We stepped onto the edge of the bridge, and I leapt onto the lily pad nearest to me. I kept my eyes focused on the purple lotus flowers and leapt onto the next one with Lena following closely behind. We crossed six lily pads and found ourselves standing on the partly immersed bridge.

Just as I was about to jump onto the lily pad in front of me, something shot out of the water with great force. I was knocked back onto the broken bridge and bumped into Lena. We both screamed in shock. It was so sudden that we nearly lost our balance.

Lena had her wand at the ready and pointed it at the creature staring down at us with a sneering smile on her face. It had a tall-elongated scaly body, resembling a snake, and each yellow segment on the inner side of its belly was marked alternatively with a red and black pulsating spot.

The body was moving to the left and to the right gently. The upper torso and face was of a woman, a beautiful woman at that. She had golden brown hair and yellow eyes. She was playing with her hair, curling it behind her slim, long fingers, whilst grinning at us.

There was a crown on her head and the white diamonds sparkled in the sun. The creature bent down a little closer to us. There wasn't a single speck of water on her, even though she'd only just appeared from the depths of the marsh, mere seconds ago.

This had to be the beast Tallon had warned us about. I couldn't stop staring at her. The beast might've had half the body of a snake but I'd never seen such a stunning face before. I held my sword behind my back. I didn't want to give the creature an excuse to disarm me before I could properly defend myself, and the snake like creature had not as yet seen my sword.

The beast briefly twisted around to glance at Kal before turning back to face us. Lena was petrified and stood rooted to the spot with her wand still pointing at the creature. I tried to remain as calm as I could. I wanted us to come away from this encounter in one piece, and my mind was racing trying to find a way to escape.

Finally, the creature spoke in a sweet voice and bowed a little, 'How strange? I was expecting to see one girl up here, but there are two of you. How very strange? Anyhow, I am pleased to make your acquaintance. What are your names?'

'My name is Lena and this… is Heera,' gulped Lena.

'Lena, it's rude to point. I'm not going to hurt you,' she said, ever so gently.

Lena slowly lowered her wand to her side, and I could see from the corner of my eye that she'd tightened her grip on it.

The creature set her eyes on me and hissed. This time when she spoke, her slippery tongue was revealed and it was forked and white in colour, 'Heera... what a wonderful name. Sss... sss... say Heera, I believe we have met before, have we not? I hope you have forgiven me after our last meeting, many years ago. I didn't mean to have caused you any harm. You look different and yet so much like her. I wonder what sorcery this is.'

'I'm afraid you're mistaken. I've never met you before and this is the first time we've come here. You've confused me with some else. Who are you?' I asked politely, knowing she was referring to Hayden. I didn't trust this creature, not one bit.

She laughed. 'I'm Naaga. I am the serpent queen of the Purple Lotus Marsh. This...' she said, pointing at the water around her, 'is my home and has been for over five hundred years. Forget about me... tell me about you, Heera. Who exactly are you? Where are you going? Is that boy with you?'

Kal was looking straight at us, paralysed with terror.

'Sorry we don't have the time. We're already so late but maybe some other time,' Lena said glimpsing up at Naaga, who remained focused on me.

'Lena's right. We really have to get going. Could you please let us pass?' I asked smiling back at the creature. I thought being nice would help and she might let us go.

'Why? I want to know why two pretty girls like you are running around in Fallowmere when there is so much danger around. You do know there are rumours Bulzaar is regaining strength and will wage war on everyone who has betrayed him? Aren't you sss... sss... scared?' Naaga hissed, directing her question at me.

I had to lie to Naaga because she wasn't going to let us go anywhere very soon. 'Well you see, we have been sent by Bulzaar to find more fighters to join the Fire Blades' army,' I said convincingly and even Lena started to nod her head vigorously. 'We're his cousins and this is why we're free to roam around Fallowmere without any danger. We're on our way to see him.'

'Now I'm disappointed. If you're going to lie at least do it well, Heera. I'm a little hurt. I've been nice to you and you are lying to me. Yesss… you have truly disappointed me,' Naaga hissed as she thrashed her body slightly, and I saw her long tail emerge out of the water momentarily.

'I'm not lying to you, Naaga. I promise I'm telling you the truth,' I said.

'Bulzaar has no cousins. The only family he had, he imprisoned. Why did he let you two go?' Naaga said with an angry huff and placed her hands on her hips. Her lower snake-like body pulsated and started oscillating to the left and then to the right again.

'We ARE his cousins! We'll go get him and he'll tell you,' I said confidently.

Naaga laughed aloud. Lena pointed her wand directly at the beast's body and muttered something. Two green sparks flew out of the wand and hit the scaly body, except they rebounded and nearly hit me straight in the face.

'Stupid little girl, magic can't kill me. I'm older than magic itself,' she said threateningly.

'When Bulzaar finds out how you treated us, he'll kill you once he regains his power,' I said, trying to think of ways to scare Naaga into letting us pass.

'Do you think I'm scared?' Naaga grinned. 'Even Bulzaar would think twice about coming into my territory. Your war means nothing to me. I do not intend to take sides and as for you two, you're coming with me.'

Naaga moved towards us.

'No we're not! Let us go, please. What do you want from us?' Lena cried.

I could tell Lena was petrified, especially now that her magic was useless against the beast. I could feel her trembling body beside me, and I thought she was going to faint.

'Isn't it obvious? I'm five hundred and seventeen years old; however, I have retained my beauty and youth. When I felt a female presence in the water, I knew I had to come and have a sneak peek,' Naaga announced excitedly and her tongue lashed in and out of her mouth. 'Pretty girls are what I want and you are beautiful, Lena. And Heera when I saw you, I simply had to have you. I will devour both of you. I will devour you first, Lena, and use your magic to strengthen me because there is something that lurks beneath your skin that is oh so powerful.

'Then Heera, you'll be next. You possess something much more irresistible, an indescribable power which I've never seen before in any creature, except Hayden.'

Naaga cackled, and when she opened her mouth, in place of the white forked tongue, a vicious black scaly snake with red eyes appeared hissing away. Instantly, Naaga's human face and torso shedded away, and all that was left was a monstrous serpent hissing threateningly at us.

'Now come here beautiful,' Naaga said as she tried to bite Lena, who ducked just in time. Although, Naaga now resembled a snake, I was surprised to find her voice remained unchanged. 'Now, now don't be like that Lena… come nicely,' she laughed as she lunged towards Lena now baring her red forked tongue. 'I'll make it a quick bite. I'm so hungry, I'll devour you whole. There is no use fighting me, Lena! Your wand and magic can't hurt me.'

'Oh yeah but I bet THIS can,' I shouted as I used my hidden sword to slice the forked tongue. Naaga's attention now turned to me.

Naaga opened her mouth wide, and I could see another tongue growing, the same as the last. I found the opportunity to save Lena, 'Lena, go now! Get across the water while you can.' Lena took the opportunity to run across the lily pads into the arms of Kal.

'That's a pretty little toy you have there, Heera. Do you even know how to use it or is it just for show?' Naaga grinned. 'You can't harm me. Never mind about Lena, I only wanted you. Lena was more of a starter rather than a main meal like you.'

I was getting angry with her. I knew Naaga was only trying to find my weak spot, and I couldn't let her get the better of me. I tried to focus on the snake and lunged at it with my sword. The snake was too fast as it swerved to the left and missed the blow.

'If you think I'm scared of you, I'm not. I'll fight you and I will kill you!' I screamed. It could've been due to the impending danger or the sheer desperation to save my family that pure adrenaline rushed through my body, and I tightened my grip on the sword and stared back at the creature.

'Good girl. Now you're talking my kind of language. Give me your best shot, pretty girl!' Naaga mocked. 'Let's see if your big blue eyes can keep up with me.'

I decided to run back to the starting point to confuse the snake, and I moved backwards onto the lily pad behind me. I was followed closely by Naaga. She submerged into the water and with a huge splash resurfaced in front of me. I tried to stab her with my sword and yet again I missed.

Naaga was fast. The lily pads I was jumping back and forth on began to shake. Naaga was desperately trying to get me into the water, and I had to keep moving back and forth speedily to steady myself.

I took another two steps back and again the snake disappeared. I moved forward onto the broken bridge and tried to run for it across the last remaining lily pads. It was of no use. Naaga found me again and tried to take a bite out of my arm.

I kept moving and trying to strike the snake. If only I could distract her long enough to join Kal and Lena, who were now trying to search for something to throw at her.

I was standing on the submerged bridge once again. I began to panic slightly because Naaga had disappeared back into the water, and this time she didn't resurface. I knew I hadn't hurt her because the blade of my sword was clean.

I thought of running for it. But I knew that would be far too easy and I was absolutely certain Naaga would catch up in no time. I searched around to see if I could see any ripples in the water. The marsh was still, and I stood rooted to the spot, while Kal and Lena were frantically gesturing to me to run to them.

I cleared my mind and remembered what Mrs Oak had said to me after my training session with Kindred. She'd mentioned I'd need training on how to fight enemies who could attack me from behind. Naaga was cunning like Bulzaar, and she too would play dirty and possibly attack me whilst I was unaware she was even behind me. I wasn't going to let go so easily of someone as evil and dangerous as her.

I raised my sword. As I did so, I could see my own determined face in the gleaming blade, my eyes searching for a sign of the beast. I turned the sword slightly to the left and saw Naaga's human face behind me, and her arms were stretching out to grab me.

Naaga was beginning to open her mouth up wide. With a backward turn and with the sheer force of the way I wielded the sword, I spun around and the sword sliced through the thick body of the serpent queen.

Naaga smiled her sweet smile as if nothing had happened until her eyes fell on her own blood on my sword; it dawned on her that she'd been hurt, and she opened her mouth and eyes wide in shock. The top half of her human body fell away into the water, while the body of the snake thrashed about in the water.

The lily pads began to sink and I sprinted across those which remained and landed on the ground in front of Lena. I glanced back and saw the remnants of the broken bridge, the lily pads, and the purple lotus flowers disappearing into the water, and the marsh began to bubble up.

The water turned to a deep red and white and silver balls of hazy vapour emerged from the murky depths. Within these ghostly spheres, I could make out faces of girls, shooting towards the sky.

Some spheres were coming towards me, yelling, 'THANK YOU FOR FREEING US!' Other girls were distraught and said, 'She killed us and wouldn't let us go!'

My eyes welled up at hearing the many voices and seeing the pretty faces of the young girls Naaga had so mercilessly killed and consumed in order to remain strong and beautiful.

Lena and Kal stood beside me. Lena put her arms around me and we watched until every last soul was freed from the watery grave and ascended to the bright blue sky above.

'Heera, you were fantastic!' Kal said, after a short while.

'Thank you, Kal,' I smiled through my tears.

My heart sunk slightly at the thought of Mrs Oak not being here to witness what I'd accomplished. I knew she'd have been proud of how I'd handled the beast. My pendant throbbed against my chest frantically. I thought it was odd that the pendant didn't warn me of the upcoming danger before crossing the marsh.

The pendant had secrets of its own, and for now, I took its reaction as a reminder that I still had a long way to go, and it wasn't the time for me to celebrate a win. I wondered how many Naaga's I'd have to meet on the way to Cranwell Castle.

CHAPTER 11

The Close Encounter

We left the Purple Lotus Marsh behind us and continued onwards. We were still in shock at how we'd managed to escape from Naaga's clutches. We came across a meadow with a spring flowing through it, and we rested for some time, taking shade under a pear tree, to take a break from the blazing sun.

Lena collected all three flasks and went to the spring to refill them. Kal retrieved his diary from his bag and began to write in it. I had a feeling he was making an account of our journey.

I retrieved my sword from its sheath and found it covered in Naaga's blood. I didn't think to clean it before I'd placed it away at the marsh. Immediately, a sharp jolt went straight to my heart. I had actually killed someone or a something, and although it felt right at the time because it was either me or her, guilt took over my heart and mind.

I took the opportunity to clean my sword in the spring water and tried to convince myself I'd done the right thing in killing Naaga. I admired the sharp jagged edge of the sword, and my fingers felt Hayden's engraved initials on the glistening gold handle. I contemplated how many creatures Hayden had slain before she came face to face with Bulzaar and whether I'd even survive the journey to get to him.

'Kal, I'm sorry we didn't take you seriously about what you'd sensed on the bridge,' I heard Lena say as she sat down beside him.

'I'm sorry too, Kal,' I said.

'It's fine. Maybe next time though, we shouldn't rush and make a hasty decision,' Kal suggested.

'I know Naaga was a vicious monster,' Lena said, 'but she'll never hurt anyone ever again, and those innocent girls were set free. We did that. We made a difference and I'm glad we chose the path we did.'

Lena was absolutely right and what she said made me feel a tiny bit better about myself.

'Yes, well when you say it like that, I guess you're right,' Kal said, rather reluctantly.

'Kal, please check the map before we leave to make sure we're on the right track,' I said.

'I've already checked and we're definitely going the right way. The path we're following will lead us to the Forest of Eedon, and we'll have to pass through there to get to Cranwell Castle. It will take us at least three days to get to the forest.'

'Let's go then because the sooner we leave here, the sooner we'll get there,' I said, placing my clean sword back into its sheath. I filled my rucksack with pears I plucked from the tree, and we packed up our things and made our way towards the Forest of Eedon.

The scenery started to change around us as we walked further north over the coming hours. Instead of picturesque meadows and streams, we were passing fields of tall-uncut grass, and it was gradually becoming dark.

Most of the time, we whispered to each other in case we were heard by anyone; however, as the day dragged on, we all fell quiet and I noticed Lena did not look too well.

'Lena, you OK?' I asked.

'Yeah, I'm fine… just tired and I don't think I'll be able to walk too far now.'

'I'm getting tired as well, and it's getting colder. The weather is changing again,' Kal said.

'Don't worry, let's find a place to rest for tonight and we can make a…' I didn't get a chance to finish my sentence because loud screams came from across the field we were walking by. A flash of orange lit up the sky and the shrill screams were getting louder.

'Quick, let's hide. I don't get a good feeling about this,' Kal whispered as he grabbed and pulled us into the uncut grass, which was several inches taller than us.

We could hear the uproar from the other side of the field, and the screams were becoming intolerable to hear. The pendant around my neck tugged with great force, pulling me forwards towards danger, and all this time, I'd been thinking the pendant was there to protect me. The pendant had a secret agenda of its own it seemed.

I had to see what was happening and I crept through the towering dry grass towards the uproar. Kal grabbed my hand and pulled me back. 'Are you insane? Get back here and wait till whoever it is has gone, or do you want to get us killed?' Kal glared. 'Whatever is out there, it's evil.'

'Whoever or whatever it is, can't see us and I want to know what's happening. Stay here with, Lena. I won't be long,' I said. Facing Naaga had somehow given me the courage to face danger, and Kal was surprised at how I pulled away from him.

'No, we're going to stick together and that's final. Heera, promise you won't get involved. I don't think I can cope with another fight,' Lena whispered.

I nodded in agreement and carried on moving forward. The smell of smoke was in the air, and we cupped our hands in front of our mouths and noses, so as not to inhale the thick black fumes.

We came to a stop where we could see what was happening. A beautiful white cottage was on fire. The upper two windows were filled with orange flames and thick black smoke was escaping from the roof.

Before I could even make sense of the situation, Kal tapped me on my shoulder, and I found him pointing towards the door of the house. The symbol of a dragon's vicious face, which was carved into the Fire Blades' weapons and visible on the tunics of the goblins, was also scorched into the wooden door. It simmered in red and orange against the brown door. I knew now that we were in the presence of Bulzaar's supporters.

I was shocked to find Morog, one of the Fire Blades we'd seen the other day in Gentley Woods, pointing his axe at the cottage. The axe itself was searing red hot against the darkening sky. The dragon, which was engraved on the blade, had its mouth open wide with its sharp teeth on show, and it was then that I knew Morog had set the cottage on fire with his axe.

I could see four people as I moved a little closer. A middle-aged, skinny man held a little girl in his arms. She was crying her heart out. A young boy, around the age of ten, was standing close by, weeping and looking on in fear. A plump, kind-faced woman was on her knees begging Morog to leave her family alone.

Three more Fire Blades came into view and stood behind Morog, waiting for his command and eyeing the helpless family with loathing and disgust. I could see their deformed noses snorting away in laughter at the damage they were causing the family.

'GET UP! Stop embarrassing yourself, Martha. We need both you and Percy to obey our orders or should I say the Dark King's orders,' Morog laughed, baring his black tongue. 'Now get up or else your family will have to pay and we don't want that now, do we? You've already lost half of your house.'

The woman named Martha didn't dare argue with Morog; she immediately sprang to her feet and ran back towards her family. They stood holding each other closely while weeping silently.

'Good move, Martha,' Morog grinned. 'If only you could've listened before we set your house on fire. Well, never mind, you can build another house. Percy, are you ready to come with us or are you going to put your innocent children in danger?'

'Please Morog, I can't leave my family now… they have nowhere to go,' the man named Percy, who'd stood silently beside his children now pleaded. 'Where will they live now? I promise, once we find a suitable place to stay, I'll personally come to you.'

Morog threw up his arms and let out a high pitched cackle before speaking, 'Lagak, get the boy and bring him to me. They just don't get the message. If the father won't come with us, we'll take the son instead.'

The Fire Blade named Lagak came forwards, and Percy quickly gave his daughter to his wife and moved towards the Fire Blades. 'I'll come but please leave my family alone,' Percy said, freeing himself from his wife's grasp as she tried to hold him back.

Percy glanced back at his family, pleading with his wife through his eyes not to protest against his decision. Martha held her children tightly and tears flowed freely down her face.

'Finally the message has sunk in with you all,' Morog said, rolling his eyes. 'I'm sure you'll make a fine soldier, Percy. Now return to Cranwell Castle with Lagak and Jorg. Durk, you remain behind with me because our business has not yet finished. We must go and see Naaga.'

Percy stared longingly at his family as the two Fire Blades marched him away, and he disappeared from view. Martha in shock and grief sat down on the floor cuddling her children. Morog and Durk didn't even bat an eyelid. Instead, they stood conversing with each other as if the remaining family members didn't exist and nor did they care about the devastation they'd caused.

'Well, Durk,' Morog said, 'it has been a good day for numbers. That's nineteen new recruits for the army including Percy. Not long now before the fun really starts. We'll be ready to cross into Kendolen soon and the town won't know what's hit it!'

'Morog, we have done well but will Naaga be tempted so easily?' Durk asked.

'It's not going to be easy. Bulzaar warned us it would be hard to convince her to join our cause, but this time we're going to tempt her with her favourite feast, which reminds me... Durk, bring the little girl,' Morog commanded.

Durk marched up to the weeping family and prised the small, screaming girl out of her mother's arms. Martha did all she could to stop him from taking her, but she knew there was no way she could save her child. 'Let go Martha! You never know Naaga might not be hungry, and if she's not, we'll bring your daughter back,' Durk laughed.

I was so angry with the Fire Blades. I knew I couldn't take them on, but also, I couldn't let them take the girl. I moved closer and was getting ready to get out my sword when Kal whispered, 'Heera, don't do anything to draw attention to us. The snake's dead anyway and they'll have to bring her back to her mother.' Lena didn't take any notice to us talking; she was transfixed by Morog and Durk.

'How do you know they won't just kill her anyway?' I asked Kal.

'The little girl has a long life ahead of her. I can feel it. She'll be OK,' Kal said confidently. 'You didn't believe me last time, and I knew there was something in the water. My powers aren't very strong, I know, but I can still sense things.'

'I know and I'm sorry. I just feel so bad for her family,' I said looking at Martha and her son still crying in front of the burning cottage. The Fire Blades had now taken the girl away, and her screams couldn't be heard anymore as they made their way towards the Purple Lotus Marsh.

'Let's go,' Kal said.

'Wait a second, we may be able to help,' Lena whispered.

Lena laid her spell book on the ground and I could see Iris's face frowning at us. She knelt down and opened the book to a specific page and read from it. Lena stood up, murmuring the spell under her breath, and pointed her wand directly above the burning cottage.

As Lena kept repeating the spell, in a language I couldn't understand, tiny droplets of water appeared in the sky out of nowhere and merged together to form dense heavy clouds. Each cloud began to move in a circular motion creating whirlwinds, encircling the entire cottage.

The whirlwinds were growing rapidly. Martha grabbed her son and backed away watching the whirlwinds as they gushed through the chimney, the front door, and the windows, flooding the whole cottage with water.

The water extinguished the fire as it flowed through the rooms until there was not a single flame in sight. Even the dragon's face burnt into the front door had been drenched and was fizzling out. Martha and her son watched on in disbelief.

Once the house was free from the flames, the damage the fire had caused began to disappear, and the symbol of the dragon vanished from the front door. I could hear the broken windows and objects being repaired, and shortly, Martha's cottage was as good as new.

Martha ran into her house with her son and ran back out alone. It seemed she'd heard something from the field opposite her, and she stood listening silently as tears rolled down her face.

Her son called for her but she didn't reply. Instead, she began shouting and peering around for a glimpse of whoever had saved her house from burning to the ground. Martha didn't receive a reply because we'd left the field behind us, and we were treading the main path once again, focused on hiding and resting somewhere safe for the night.

CHAPTER 12

Footsteps

We camped down in a different field covered in tall uncut grass, a mile away from Martha's cottage, and our tent was safely concealed from prying eyes.

Lena commanded Iris to wake us up for a seven o'clock start the following morning. After making sure everything was in order, we could take a deep breath and try to unwind.

We sat up in our sleeping bags and reflected on the day's events from meeting Tallon and Naaga to our close encounter with the Fire Blades.

'I still can't get over the fact, it's only my second day in Fallowmere and we've had to face so much,' I said.

'I know,' Lena smiled, 'and we're absolutely fine!'

'Heera, when I pulled your hand back in the field, I could touch you without being hurt,' Kal said. 'I think Amunah knows I mean you no harm, but I still can't read you.'

'That means he must know you two are with me. Do you think he can see us right now?' I asked.

'Well he is a God, he can probably see everything,' Lena said.

'I don't think he can see everything,' Kal said.

Kal's comment was all that was needed for Lena and him to bicker between themselves. I didn't have the energy to keep them from arguing, and even if I did, they wouldn't have listened anyway. I started to feel the muscles in my legs relax and my body ease and I drifted off into a deep sleep.

'Get up, Heera!' I heard Lena say.

'What now?' I mumbled, hastily sitting up. I was surprised to find Lena fast asleep. I didn't have time to comprehend where the voice had come from because I was distracted by a noise coming from outside the tent.

I could hear muffled footsteps making their way around the tent. I panicked a little, thinking about the Fire Blades we'd seen earlier, but the footsteps seemed to belong to someone much smaller, almost childlike.

'You two get up, someone's outside,' I whispered while trying to get out of my sleeping bag.

Lena and Kal sat up and listened to the footsteps still tottering around the tent before getting out of their sleeping bags.

I lifted my sword, ready to go outside and confront whoever was roaming around our tent.

'You don't need your sword, Heera. It's not a bad thing,' Kal whispered.

Abruptly, the footsteps slowed down and muffled laughter could be heard. Lena had her wand pointed towards the opening of the tent and again Kal whispered, 'It's not going to hurt us. Let me open the tent.'

'OK, do it slowly,' Lena said. Kal carefully unzipped the opening of the tent. The footsteps and the muffled laughter came to a stop, and whoever it was made a quick run through the tall grass and disappeared from view.

'It's six o'clock now and there's no way we're going to get back to sleep. I think we should make a move,' Kal said.

We gathered our things and Lena packed up the tent. Kal examined his map and compass, and we began our journey onwards. I shared out some pears between us, which I'd collected from the meadow, and we ate them as we walked on. Lena was not her normal self this morning; she seemed deep in thought. I wanted to ask her what was wrong; however, everyone needed time and space to think about things, and for now, I let her have some thinking time.

I could hear the same footsteps I'd heard earlier, and I turned around to see if anyone was behind us. There was no-one there. Kal and Lena had also heard the footsteps and were peering around trying to find the culprit.

Whoever it was had followed us from the field and I decided to confront them. I knew they wouldn't do any harm because they would've attacked us by now.

'Who is it?' I asked, firmly placing my hand over the handle of the sword in case somebody decided to attack. No-one came forward. I called out a few more times and was about to give up when I heard rustling coming from a field to the left of where we were standing.

A creature, around three feet tall, peered out from behind the tall grass. He had bright green eyes and a round face with red chubby cheeks. He stood there with his chubby fingers in front of his face, laughing shyly, and when I addressed him, he hid behind the grass and burst into a fit of giggles.

His clothes were unusual. He was wearing lime green trousers, a yellow t-shirt, and his black shoes were shiny and had large gold buckles on the side. To complete his look, he wore a black top hat with a single red feather perched on the top.

He looked like a cross between an ornamental gnome my neighbours had in their back garden and a leprechaun I'd seen in a book when I was a kid. He was the cutest thing I'd ever seen.

I walked over to him and bent down to talk to him, 'Hi, I'm Heera, what's your name?'

Kal, also intrigued, knelt down beside me.

Very slowly the creature lowered his hands from his face, showing his big red chubby cheeks and a bright white smile. He spoke with a high-pitched squeak, 'I'm Fergal.'

'Very nice to meet you, Fergal. This is Kal and that over there is Lena,' I gestured towards Lena, who didn't seem the least bit interested in this cute unique creature. Lena simply waved back unenthusiastically and retrieved her spell book and began to whisper to Iris.

Fergal didn't notice or seem to care the way Lena had reacted towards him. He was so overjoyed we'd spoken to him that he began to giggle again.

I tried to calm him down. Not only did I want to find out more about him, but I was also concerned Fergal was going to faint because he was finding it hard to breathe due to laughing so hard. I tried to talk to him again, 'Fergal, can you please stop laughing while we talk to you? We want to know more about you. Who are you? Where do you live?'

Fergal calmed down and began hopping from one foot to the other in sheer excitement. 'I'm a forest dwarf!' he screeched. Kal was writing away in his diary and now and again he'd glance at the forest dwarf.

'Why were you pacing around our tent and following us?' Lena asked Fergal.

'I saw her,' he said pointing at me, 'last night before she went into the triangle house with the sword, and I waited till daylight to see her again. I was so excited and began to run around because I was hoping she'd help me get my house back from the Fire Blades.'

'Why did you run away, Fergal?' I asked.

'I was scared and thought you'd want to hurt me like everyone else in Fallowmere. There'd be no reason for you to help a forest dwarf. Everyone ignores us, and when somebody wants our land, they take it from us because we cannot fight. We don't know how to and that's why they took my house.'

'Why did they take your house, Fergal?' Kal asked.

'I live in the Forest of Eedon. Our kind live in forests, woods and the undergrowth. We've built clay houses on the ground and networks of tunnels, but the Fire Blades wanted to use our land to make a training camp. They picked up my belongings and me and threw me out of the forest. Some of my friends ran away, while the others still live in these fields.'

'Do you have any family?' Kal asked still writing down what Fergal had told us.

'No, I'm on my own. Forest dwarves fend for themselves after they're born and make their own way in life. Many don't survive because for countless creatures, we're their food,' he said solemnly.

'Well why did you follow us then, if you didn't think we would help you?' Lena snapped.

'I wanted to spy on you to see if you were good or bad and whether you were going to the Forest of Eedon,' Fergal said. 'If you were kind enough, I was going to ask you to help me get back my house.'

'Of course we'll help you, Fergal. In fact, we are heading towards the Forest of Eedon,' I said.

'We can't possibly get his house back. We're no match for the Fire Blades! Fergal, we're sorry but we can't help you,' Lena said sternly.

'Lena, we're going to the forest anyway, and we can at least try to help him. What's wrong with you? Why are you acting like this?' I asked. Fergal didn't say a word; he glanced at each of our faces as we argued back and forth.

'Nothing is wrong with me. I just don't think we should get involved with Fergal,' Lena, calmly explained. 'How do we know he's not going to lead us straight to the Fire Blades? He might be a spy. I simply think we shouldn't trust everyone we meet and even Iris has her suspicions.'

'Kal, what do you think?' Lena asked.

'I don't think he'll betray us. I mean look at him,' Kal said. 'I think we should try to help him, and Fergal, there may be a possibility we might not be able to get your home back,

137

especially if the Fire Blades have destroyed it. You do understand that, don't you?' Fergal nodded his head and smiled. 'I think it may be a good idea if he does come along as he must know a fair bit about the forest since he lives there.'

Lena was furious. Fergal saw the look on Lena's face and hid behind Kal's long legs and began to shiver.

'Lena, you're scaring him,' Kal said, whilst trying to console Fergal, who seemed to be on the verge of bursting into tears.

'She doesn't like forest dwarves,' Fergal said rather quietly.

'No it's nothing like that Fergal, is it Lena?' I asked.

Lena didn't reply and looked the other way; she knew she had no option but to allow Fergal to come along with us. Fergal told Kal everything about his background; Kal was thrilled to have all this detailed information and wrote down every word Fergal said.

A few hours later, Lena sighed heavily and strolled towards a field and sat down on the ground. We followed her lead. Lena was massaging her legs and I sat beside her and took a drink from my flask. Kal and Fergal sat further away from us, and Kal began to show his new friend his diary.

'Are your legs still aching from yesterday?' I asked.

'Yeah, I don't know why though. They keep throbbing, even after having a good rest. I just hope we get there soon,' Lena replied, quietly.

'We will. Kal has us travelling on the right path... we will be there in...' I didn't get to complete my sentence because Lena burst into tears. Kal and Fergal glanced over and saw Lena crying, but Kal purposely began to engage in a conversation with his new friend, and he pretended he hadn't noticed she was upset.

Lena put her head on my shoulder and let out deep shuddering sobs. Her pretty button nose was drowning with the tears flowing down her face.

'Lena, tell me what's on your mind. Take your time. Maybe if we talk about it, you'll feel so much better. Let me help you,' I said softly.

Lena laughed through her sobs and took a deep breath before speaking, 'It's so stupid. You know when you woke me this morning, I was dreaming about my parents. It was like they were right there beside me, and when I woke up, all I could think about was them. I'm always thinking about them, but today, I'm really missing them. Sometimes I get so scared I'm never going to see them again.'

'Lena, I can't guarantee what will happen, but I promise you I'll do everything to make sure you're protected,' I said.

'I know it was my choice to come with you and I stick by the decision. I don't know why, but for some reason, it's all really got to me today.'

'That's completely understandable and you will definitely see you parents again, Lena,' I said. Lena dried her tears, took a deep breath and managed to smile.

Kal came over to us with a huge grin on his face, rather conveniently, once Lena had stopped crying. 'You two need to come over here, we have something to show you,' he said. Fergal was bouncing on his heels with excitement.

I was glad we'd met Fergal. He'd lightened the mood and Kal had found a friend in him. They were inseparable. I only hoped we'd be able to help Fergal and not let him down, and as for trusting him, I went with my gut instinct. There was no reason for him to be disloyal. Fergal hadn't asked us who we were or where we'd come from, and he was innocent as far I could see.

Lena and Iris had their doubts, but Kal had been right about Naaga, and he was adamant Fergal was harmless. I was too trusting at the best of times, and now that Fergal was accompanying us, I vowed to keep a close eye on him, and if he was lying then he'd have the three of us to answer to.

CHAPTER 13

Boot Camp

Kal pointed towards the map he'd laid out on the ground and excitedly exclaimed, 'Fergal knows a short cut into the Forest of Eedon, and we'll get there tomorrow evening at the latest!'

'What's the shortcut?' I asked intrigued. 'Most importantly, is it safe?'

'Yes, it's completely safe,' Fergal said. 'If you go by your old map, it will take you longer to reach the Forest of Eedon. If we go off track, you'll reach one of the closest entrances to the forest and reach Cranwell Castle sooner.'

'Nice one, Kal! You've told a complete stranger we're going to Cranwell Castle,' Lena glared.

'Sorry,' Kal blushed.

'There's nothing we can do about that now, but Fergal, please don't tell anyone about where we're going. Promise me, you'll keep it a secret?' I asked.

'I promise I won't tell anyone,' Fergal said meekly.

'I don't know about going off track,' Lena said.

'I think we should listen to him, and I trust him completely,' Kal said, confidently.

'Lena, I do trust Fergal, and I think we should give him a chance. If we do encounter danger, we'll turn back, I promise,' I said.

'OK,' Lena replied half-heartedly.

Fergal led the way and we followed. Both Kal and Fergal were chatting nonstop about various things such as life in the Forest of Eedon, and Kal told his new friend all about his life back in Kendolen. Lena and I simply listened, taking in our surroundings and making sure we weren't followed.

We'd been walking for most of the day, and we were becoming irritable by the minute. Not only were we were tired and hungry but Fergal stayed true to his word and took us down a beaten track. We'd left the fields way behind us.

It was truly awful. We had to cut through bushes with stinging nettles and sharp thorns, and sometimes the thorns dug into our clothing, scratching our skin.

Once or twice, I slipped when we travelled down a path at a steep gradient and grazed my legs and hands.

I couldn't help but swear, much to the dismay of Fergal. Each time, I apologised profusely, whereas Lena didn't and remained in a foul mood for most of the journey down this route.

When we trudged up almost vertical slopes of a hill, the three of us had to take our time, and we found at one point or another, we were kneeling on the ground, taking deep long breaths and clutching our chests. It truly was hard work, and the lack of stamina did not help any of us on this trail.

The only positive I could find was the path was completely isolated and we didn't encounter a single soul.

It was nearing midnight when we decided we could no longer carry on, and we set up camp for the night in the midst of bushes. The mood in the tent was rather sombre, and we felt extremely shattered. We ate stale pieces of bread quietly before we drifted off to sleep in our comfortable sleeping bags.

I managed to sleep all the way through without any visions of Bulzaar.

The following morning, we were awoken by Iris shouting at the top of her voice, 'WAKE UP! WAKE UP! TIME TO WAKE UP!' Anyone in close proximity could have easily heard her, and Lena ended up shouting back at Iris for not being discreet.

Everyone seemed to have slightly cheered up with the thought of reaching the Forest of Eedon fairly soon. The journey still took most of the day, and we arrived at the Forest of Eedon at quarter past seven in the evening, tired and hungry.

It had started to rain and flashes of lighting could be seen in the distance followed by the sound of a heavy blow of thunder. We decided we would find a safe place in the forest to settle down for the evening and make another fresh start in the morning.

'Fergal, tell us which way we should go? We don't want to get lost, and please let's hurry, we're getting drenched!' I now spoke directly to Kal and Lena, 'Let's see what we can do for him first thing tomorrow.'

Fergal seemed unhappy to be back in the forest. This was understandable because we'd seen what the Fire Blades were like, and they'd make anyone tremble with fear.

Lena used her wand as a light instead of fire torches in case we came across any unwanted attention, and it provided enough light for us to see where we were treading. I grasped my sword tightly in my hand. It made me feel safe, and I could feel the pendant grow hot against my flesh.

I didn't have a good feeling about what lay ahead in the forest and wondered if the pendant was giving me a sign to turn back. I ignored my thoughts and stepped into the Forest of Eedon as there was no other way to Cranwell Castle than through the dark forest.

There were two paths to choose from once we'd entered the forest. One led to the left and the other to the right. Gigantic oak trees enclosed us, and it was difficult to see where we were treading, but we kept close together and let Fergal lead the way.

Fergal pointed us towards the right path and squeaked, 'Let's go down Blodmer Path. My house is down the left path, but if we're going to spend the night here, let's make sure we're far away as possible from the Fire Blades. I'll show you my house tomorrow because it's not safe to do it now. There are many dark creatures that live here, and if they see us, they'll take us to the Fire Blades.'

Just as Fergal led us deeper into the forest, the rain and thunder stopped. We could smell burning, and a dull orange glow in the distance was rising before us. We could hear singing and shouting from ahead, and Lena gestured to go back and take the other pathway. I agreed with her until I saw Fergal crying and Kal was trying to console him. 'I want to take a closer look and see if I can see any of my friends,' Fergal sobbed. 'Some of them may still be alive.'

I nodded in agreement, much to the dismay of Lena and Kal. We crept up slowly and hid behind two conjoined trees. Fergal was shaking like a leaf. Kal even allowed his friend to perch on his shoulder while we investigated the scene before us.

Lena put out the light on her wand and pointed it forwards. I gripped my sword tightly and saw Kal retrieve the sword he'd taken from Mrs Oak's room from his rucksack.

We peered out from the sides of the trees, armed and ready.

A roaring fire burned in the middle of what appeared to be a camp. Several white tepees were set up around the fire, and wicker chairs and hammocks with several Fire Blades occupying them were spread out across the clearing. It seemed the Fire Blades had set up more than one camp because Fergal had said his home was down the path to the left as we entered the forest, and it was there that the Fire Blades had initially set up a training camp.

The Fire Blades were still in their heavy armour. It was as if their armour had become their natural skin, and every time I'd encountered them so far, they were never without their armour or weapons. They cackled between themselves and their yellow, "cat's", eyes sparkled with the light from the roaring fire and sweat dripped from their matted hair.

I noticed another group of creatures who were laughing and jeering with the Fire Blades. Fergal noticed the look of confusion on each of our faces and he whispered softly, 'They are the Critanites. They're nothing more than vicious mutated dogs that support Bulzaar, and the Fire Blades have been training them.'

The Critanites were strange creatures. They stood on their dog-like hind legs and had pointed ears like wolves. Some had vivid green eyes, others had grey and they had long runny noses. Their arms and hands resembled those of humans, however, in place of fingernails, they had huge dirty claws.

I saw their unusually long tails slamming against the ground like whips, at the sheer excitement of being in the company of the Fire Blades. Each one of these creatures held silver daggers and some were even play fighting with each other.

When they spoke, they bared their sharp teeth and drool was falling from the sides of their mouths. 'Their spit is like acid, and if it touches your skin, your skin will melt away,' Fergal whispered. 'They were one of Bulzaar's secret weapons, and he used them to scare other creatures who dared stand up to him. It seems he's planning to use them again.'

I didn't get a chance to ask questions because complete silence had fallen in the camp, and dense thuds could be heard approaching the site. The Fire Blades and the Critanites stood up to greet the figure approaching them.

A voice I'd heard not so long ago spoke and it made me shudder. It was Morog. 'Now, don't let me spoil your fun!' Morog laughed. 'Each and every one of you has worked hard and you have earned a break. Bulzaar will be very proud.'

'Please Morog, we have a seat for you here,' a Fire Blade said.

'Always trying to please, Fray. Very well, I will sit at your given seat,' Morog sniggered.

The others laughed and remained standing until Morog had sat down directly opposite us. Morog wouldn't be able to see us from where he was sitting because of the darkness beyond the trees and the sheer amount of smoke from the fire clouding us from view. Morog was alone, and I wondered if he'd returned the little girl to her mother.

'Morog, what took you so long? We were expecting to see you the day before yesterday,' a Critanite spoke.

'Noman that was the expected plan, however, Durk and I, were side tracked. I am glad to see you have, once again, joined forces with the Fire Blades. The Dark King always told me, he could count on the Critanites to help our cause.'

'Morog, there is one pressing issue I have,' Noman said, 'and as the leader of the Critanites, I must advise you there are two Critanites still living in this forest who refuse to join us. Word has it that Bulzaar will deal with them directly.'

'Ahh yes, Bulzaar did mention there would be two who wouldn't join in the battle… he has asked us to leave them be for now. If he is going to deal with them himself, they must have done something disastrous, oh well, not our problem. How has the training been going?'

'It has been most excellent, Morog, but we require more weapons and armour. And do you know when our great King will regain enough power to go into battle?' a tall Fire Blade spoke, he seemed to be in charge of the boot camp. 'I want to put everyone through as many training sessions as I can for us to be ready in time for his return.'

'I will make sure we have more weapons and armour, Stolmir, and as for Bulzaar, I have not spoken to him recently, and therefore, I cannot comment on his health. As you already know, Durk and I were side tracked by a certain issue and I haven't been back to Cranwell Castle yet. It will take time for Bulzaar to become powerful as he once was and even the greatest warrior needs to train. It could be as early as next week before we claim Kendolen as our own. Have you scoured the forest and surrounding areas for more recruits?'

'We found another six and sent them to the castle grounds with Lagak this morning,' Stolmir said proudly, 'and we're going to search in another nearby village tomorrow. Morog did you manage to get Naaga on our side?'

'No, in fact she is the issue we came across. Naaga has been killed.' Everyone in the camp gasped.

'How could this happen? Who could've killed her, Morog?' Noman asked in shock.

'No idea,' Morog said. 'Whoever it was had some power to kill a beast like her. We even took her an offering of a girl, to persuade her to join Bulzaar, but the Purple Lotus Marsh was dissolving her remains. We had no use for the girl anymore, and we headed back to her mother to take her son with me to Cranwell Castle. What was equally strange was that the house we'd set on fire was as good as new. When we asked the mother how she'd dowsed the roaring fire, she explained it was a miracle from Amunah himself. I burned her cottage to the ground for lying to me and sent all three of them to Bulzaar's training grounds in the castle. Something doesn't seem right. I know it can't possibly be Amunah, but who could've done it?' Morog asked the last question to himself rather than the others staring at him.

'Do you think it's someone from Kendolen?' Noman asked.

'I really can't say. It has deeply troubled me though and Bulzaar needs to be made aware of this,' Morog said darkly. 'In the meantime I used a spy to snoop around to see if they could find out anything for me, and as soon as I hear from him, I'll report back to Bulzaar. If it is someone from Kendolen, we've underestimated them because it takes a lot more than luck to kill something like Naaga, and not only that, they could be among us right now and we wouldn't even know.'

'So who is the spy, Morog?' Noman asked.

'Nobody important, Noman. He'll be here shortly if he knows what's best for him.'

The four of us listened intently. Fergal whispered in Kal's ear and Kal helped him down to the ground from his shoulder. Fergal crouched down and tugged on our clothes to follow his lead, and now that we were on our knees, we were unable to see the camp.

'I'm sorry for lying to you, but they have Ruby. Please forgive me,' Fergal whispered through his tears. 'When I say the words 'clay hut' go back the way we came and take the left path to 'Adenway', follow the path until you come to an area where there are tree houses above you. Mine is the one with a sunflower in the window. Wait for me there and please don't judge me. If you can't see the tree houses, wait for me at the entrance of the forest.'

Fergal ran from us before we could respond.

Lena and I were dumbstruck and Kal had his mouth wide open in shock. After all, it was Kal who Fergal had spoken to the most and all this time he'd been spying on us. I didn't know whether I could believe him after his disloyalty. What if he was still lying and was going to turn us over to the Fire Blades?

Before we could make our next move, I could hear a Fire Blade approaching Morog and he was holding Fergal by his clothes in mid-air. 'Morog, is this the spy you were waiting for?' the Fire Blade said, as he dropped Fergal on the floor with a thud in front of Morog. Fergal got on his knees as Morog stood up.

'Yes it is indeed. I hope you've brought me good news, Fergal. Ruby is desperately hoping for you to rescue her,' Morog laughed.

'You sent a forest dwarf to gather information?' Noman questioned.

'I know they're good for nothing, Noman, but I captured his wife and threatened him to spy for me,' Morog explained. 'He's small and can hide easily, and even if someone came across him, they'd think he was too insignificant to worry about. They don't have any powers, and they cannot be put under any spells either, and what he'll tell me... WILL be the truth, or otherwise, I will eat him and his wife as a snack. Now what did you find out for me?'

'M... M... Morog, I found out a few things, but can I see Ruby first to make sure she is alright?' Fergal said with his eyes closed, simply too scared to look at Morog.

Morog screeched loudly and shook his head from side to side before speaking, 'I'm surprised you have the nerve to demand this of me, however, to hurry things along, Stolmir, go get her.'

Kal whispered, 'What if he shows them where we're hidden? Let's get out of here.'

'I don't think he will. Why would he tell us the truth, beforehand?' Lena said.

'What if they see us?' I said. 'We can't risk leaving yet because we're directly opposite Morog, and he's standing up. We have no choice but to wait for the right moment.'

'LET GO OF ME YOU BRUTE!' a squeaky voice shouted.

I saw Stolmir bring out a female version of Fergal, and Fergal glanced up in delight to see she was alive and well. Stolmir brought her over to Morog, put his hand over her mouth to stop her from shouting, dangled her over the campfire, and glared at Fergal to make him answer Morog's question.

'See, she is fine. Now SPEAK, Fergal. You don't want Stolmir to accidently drop her now, do you?' Morog threatened.

The three of us took a deep breath together and waited for Fergal to give us away. I almost began to tremble with fear and gripped my sword tightly with both hands.

'The day before yesterday, when you sent me to spy for you, I saw nothing in the fields, so I decided to go to the Purple Lotus Marsh, and I waited to see if anybody could be seen, but I still had no luck,' Fergal paused as if contemplating what to say next.

He became very nervous and at one point glanced at the trees where we were hiding, and my heart almost stopped. Surely, Fergal would be caught lying and he'd tell Morog about us. How would we ever get out of this mess?

'AND! Come on, I haven't got all day!' barked Morog. Fergal shuddered with terror and continued.

'Sorry! Sorry! Where was I? Ummm… I didn't see anything until I went past the Purple Lotus Marsh and waited to see if I could see anyone entering or leaving Gentley Woods. I waited and that's when I saw him. At first I thought it was a girl because the person had shoulder length, brown hair, but when he turned around, it was a man.

'He was holding a sword and a wand, and he ventured towards Morden Village. I followed him as best as I could, but he kept looking around, and eventually, he disappeared out of sight completely. I think he may have used a spell because one second he was there and the next he was gone. Even yesterday and today, I spent time searching and hiding to see if I could find him, but he's completely vanished.'

The whole story told by Fergal was a lie; nevertheless, he had said it convincingly and left Morog deep in thought. 'Are you sure he had a wand *and* a sword?' Morog asked and Fergal nodded. 'How strange? Why would you carry both?

Sure enough if he is a wizard, why would he need the sword?' Fergal gulped and was petrified and even Morog noticed the expression on his face. 'Is there *anything else* you haven't told me? You best not be lying to me, Fergal. This is very important, or I'll take you to Bulzaar.'

'No, I promise I'm not lying to you about what I saw but there is something else,' Fergal said slowly and the Critanites and the Fire Blades were holding onto his every word. 'The man kept mumbling he was going to finish Bulzaar off, and he couldn't wait to find the Fire Blades so he could destroy them like he did Naaga.'

'Did he, now?' Morog asked calmly this time. 'Well we'll see about that. We need to change our plans, Stolmir! I'm going to leave right now and go to Bulzaar. I'll be able to reach him quicker by using Dragmatus tonight... Vlork get him ready for me. Stolmir and Kroman, I want you both to head out to Morden Village first thing tomorrow and see if you can track this man down quickly and bring him to Bulzaar. He has to have ties with Kendolen... where else could he have come from to threaten our King?' Stolmir and Kroman bowed slightly at Morog to show him they would obey his instructions.

'Morog, please let Ruby go! You promised you'd let her go if I spied for you. You've already destroyed our home, and we'll have to rebuild our clay hut,' Fergal pleaded, who was now standing behind Morog. Everyone turned around to face Fergal, and they each had their back to the conjoined trees. Fergal had used the safety words, and we silently managed to flee the spot and swiftly headed back the same way we'd come.

We kept quiet and succeeded in getting back to where we started and followed the path to the left. I did have doubts as to whether I should trust Fergal, but he could've turned the three of us over to Morog and yet he didn't.

Honestly, deep down, I did trust him, and bearing in mind our situation, we had no other option but to trust Fergal. I wanted answers from him about his involvement with the Fire Blades, that was, of course, if we'd ever see him again. Morog might've easily gone back on his word and taken Fergal and Ruby to Bulzaar, or even worse, he could've eaten them. All we could do was wait and see if we ever saw our small companion again.

CHAPTER 14

The Tree House

Our journey to Adenway didn't go smoothly. It was pitch black. The dark sky, combined with the dense trees, caused us to keep bumping into each other. Lena lit her wand to help us see.

We seemed to be trekking downhill and sounds of insects could be heard chirping away making my skin crawl. I found myself having to slap bugs away with my hand as they flew across my face. The ground was covered with damp grass, which helped to cushion our footsteps.

We followed the steep path downwards for a quarter of a mile, and even the light from the wand was not strong enough for us to see anything around us. It was even becoming more humid as we delved further into the forest.

Something hit me in the face, and I put my hand over my mouth to stop myself from screaming. I could hear Lena and Kal struggling with whatever was flying around in the dark, and each time I batted the creature away, it kept rebounding and obstructing my face.

'Wait, let's get out those fire torches... you can't see anything. This seems like another trap to me,' Lena said.

We huddled close to each other, and Lena lit up the torches and handed them out to us. We lifted the flame torches high into the air and moved around to get a bearing of our surroundings.

We finally saw what was causing so much alarm, and it wasn't an animal or a particular creature, but it was the several hundred twisting vines drooping down from the trees around us. The trees were thin and tall, and you had to really strain your neck to peer up at them.

'Look!' Kal said pointing up into the trees and perched on the monstrous, thick branches were tree houses. The glowing lights in their windows sparkled like yellow diamonds in the dark.

'These vines must be used as ladders. Look at this one over here,' Lena said.

The vine ladder was sturdy and solid, making it easy to climb.

'We're definitely in the right place!' I said. 'Search for a tree house with a sunflower in the window. It has to be here somewhere.'

We spread out and tried to find Fergal's tree house. Several minutes later, Lena called us over and pointed at a tree house. It was difficult to see the door and windows due to number of branches obstructing our view, but if we squinted, we were able to make out something yellow resembling a flower in the window. We decided to slowly make our way up the ladder to the house.

The vine, although strong, made it very difficult for all three of us to climb together. I climbed up first and waited outside the door to the tree house for Lena and Kal to join me.

I pushed the wooden door and the whole tree house vibrated. For a moment, I thought we'd fall to the ground, however, we grabbed each other and swung ourselves into the house and closed the door behind us. The reason for the shaking became apparent; the tree house seemed to be growing larger.

The minuscule sofa, six chairs, and a dining table suitable for Fergal and Ruby were being pushed to the right, leaving a trail of human sized replicas on the left.

It didn't make sense. It was impossible for such a tremendously huge tree house to be built on the branches of a tree. It was obvious that magic played an integral part in how the house was built, and it was fascinating to see how it was making room for us, complete with furnishings, to make us feel comfortable. The three of us stood watching in awe.

There was a kitchen, small enough for Fergal and Ruby, on the far right of the room, complete with forest dwarf sized cutlery and crockery on the shelves.

The tree house had two floors and a carved wooden ladder twisted itself up to the second floor. Two square windows were on either side of the main door, and the room itself was surprisingly warm and extremely cosy. We made ourselves comfortable on the replica sofa, which had been made for us, and waited for Fergal to come home.

'I can't believe he lied to us and all those things I wrote in my diary are probably all wrong,' Kal said, flicking through the pages he'd written about Fergal. 'I'm going to kill him.'

'At least he didn't hand us over to the Fire Blades,' Lena said.

Kal was distraught. He simply sat staring into space and left his diary open in his lap refusing to look at it.

We heard muffled voices a short distance away; one was a female and the other a male. The male voice was husky, nothing like Fergal's, and even the female voice sounded normal and not at all squeaky.

We immediately stood up, ready to attack whoever was going to come up the vine ladder because it certainly wasn't Fergal and Ruby. We heard footsteps, and the door opened, and to our relief, Fergal and Ruby stood before us. Fergal was stunned, being faced with a wand and two swords, and Ruby acted as if nothing unusual was happening. I was taken aback because the voices we'd heard had belonged to the dwarves, and they were no longer the high pitched squeaks we'd become accustomed to.

'Thank goodness you found the tree house! It's great to see the house has even made room to accommodate you. We were afraid you mightn't have been able to see it,' Ruby said to the three of us. She then turned to Fergal and huffed, 'Look at them, Fergal. Look at what you've done to them. You should be ashamed of yourself and you must explain everything to them.'

Fergal stood rooted to the spot, almost cowering as Ruby scolded him.

'He told me everything on the way back here,' Ruby said to the three of us, 'and don't you worry about anything. Nobody knows of this place because we're invisible to the outside world. Now would you like a cup of dandelion tea?'

Ruby had a friendly jovial face and big vivid brown eyes with long eyelashes. She wore a blue dress and yellow sandals and was even shorter than Fergal.

'Erm, yes please,' I said politely whilst putting my sword to one side. Ruby smiled back, and the three of us turned to Fergal demanding answers. He appeared to be a little scared as he entered the house and shut the door behind him.

Ruby put on her pinafore and stood in front of the tiny stove to prepare tea for us all. Fergal sat on one of the chairs at the tiny dining table and glimpsed at us glumly, and he spoke in his natural deep voice, 'I'm so sorry, Kal, Heera, and Lena. I had no choice but to lie to you. Morog had threatened me with hurting Ruby if I didn't spy for him. After meeting you three, I couldn't hand you over to the Fire Blades. I wouldn't have forgiven myself.'

'It's not that we don't understand why you did it, but you could've at least told us, and we could've helped you, Fergal,' Kal said solemnly. 'All the things you told us about yourself were a lie, and to be honest, I'm a little hurt.'

Fergal was devastated. 'Kal, my friend, I'm truly sorry,' Fergal said. 'I lost my mind and I had to do it for Ruby. I hope you can forgive me. This *is* the real me. Everything from the squeaky voice and childish behaviour to the Fire Blades taking my home were a lie. I wanted you to somehow trust me. I'm sorry for betraying you.' Kal remained quiet and Fergal shook his head and stared down at the floor.

'How did you find us so quickly after being thrown out of the forest? It doesn't make sense,' I asked.

'Morog doesn't sleep, Heera, or rest for that matter. He is quick when getting things done. What takes you a full day to do, he does in mere hours. By the time you awoke that morning and heard me outside your tent, he'd already sent me to spy on you after finding Naaga dead and Martha's cottage as good as new. Morog was also keeping an eye out for anyone coming from Kendolen and I checked every single field before I managed to find you. I knew it had to be you three who killed Naaga... why else would three teenagers be roaming around Fallowmere completely alone with a wand and two swords?'

'Fergal, if this place is hidden, how did Morog find you?' Lena asked.

'We weren't here the day Morog found us,' Fergal explained. 'Several of us had ventured out foraging for wild mushrooms in the early hours of the morning near the undergrowth, and normally, we can't be seen if we don't want to be. It was a nice fresh morning and nobody seemed to be around, so we let our guard down and started foraging, thinking nothing of it.

'We wandered over to the little clay huts, which forest dwarves used to live in, to see if they were still standing after so many years. Some of our friends saw Morog coming and either hid or disappeared into thin air, but Ruby and I were too slow. We had our backs turned away from him, and we didn't even hear him coming. He threatened me and took Ruby prisoner.'

'If you're magical creatures then why doesn't magic work on you? And how is it that these tree houses can't be seen by the enemy?' I asked.

'Fergal, pour the tea and give everybody some cake, and how about introducing me to your friends?' Ruby interrupted us and ushered us to the human sized dining table.

Fergal introduced each of us to Ruby. 'Have your tea,' Ruby said sweetly to us. 'It's been a long day for all of us and there will be plenty of time for questions a little later.'

There was a loud knock on the door and each one of us jumped up startled. 'Don't worry, you three! You're safe here,' Ruby reassured us. She turned to Fergal directly and said, 'I think Hosemee knows we have visitors who shouldn't be here.'

Ruby opened the door and there stood an old dwarf with a walking stick. He was trembling from head to toe. He was furious and stared straight ahead at the three of us at the dining table. I smiled at him but he didn't return the smile.

Ruby let him in. 'Please, come in Hosemee. We will explain everything,' she said.

Hosemee greeted Fergal, nodded his head at us and took a seat on the petite sofa. Hosemee was wearing a red dressing gown with striped pyjamas underneath, and he was wearing a thick pair of blue glasses and a blue nightcap.

Ruby took his walking stick from him and placed it at the side of the sofa and once he'd sat down comfortably, Hosemee turned to Fergal and said, 'I'm glad to see you and Ruby safe and sound, but Fergal you shouldn't have risked bringing them here. News has spread that there's a powerful warrior from Kendolen scouring the kingdom, and the Fire Blades and Critanites are starting to search for him tonight, rather than tomorrow. We can't leave the tree houses until things calm down. What if these three children expose our world? What will we do? I have betrayed him, and when I meet him again, what will I say to him?' Hosemee broke down.

'Hosemee, please don't say that,' Ruby said softly. 'They will *not* expose us and you haven't betrayed him... they could see the vines and the tree houses. He has given them the sight to see our world, and surely that means something.'

I wanted to know who Hosemee was referring to as 'him', and I wanted to desperately reassure the forest dwarf we meant him no harm, and we'd never reveal this place to anyone.

'I can't help the way I feel,' Hosemee croaked as tears rolled down his face. He turned to the three of us and said, 'I don't want to make you feel unwelcome, but there are things you simply don't understand.'

'We won't tell anybody about this place,' I said sincerely. 'We promise you, Hosemee.' Lena and Kal agreed by nodding their heads vigorously.

Hosemee tried to smile unsuccessfully. He turned his attention to Fergal, who told him everything from the moment Morog had threatened him, to meeting us and to the last encounter in the forest, while we listened and sipped our tea.

Hosemee was quiet throughout the explanation. He was deep in thought, and he turned to look at me, directing his gaze at the pendant around my neck.

'Where are you three from? And, why are you wandering around in Fallowmere all alone?' Hosemee asked.

I didn't want to lie to Hosemee. There was something about him which made me want to be honest with him. I went onto explain who I was and what had brought me here, and even Lena and Kal didn't stop me from revealing the truth.

'You are young and yet confident in your mission. Are you not afraid you may not succeed?' Hosemee asked us.

'We each made the decision to fight and we stick by it. All we can do is try,' Kal replied while Hosemee still had his eyes set firmly on me.

'I have my family to rescue and it's because of me they're with that monster in the first place. I can't sit back and do nothing,' I said.

'I understand,' Hosemee replied.

'Hosemee, they wanted to know about our kind and how other creatures are unable to use magic on us or against us, and why our houses are invisible to the outside world?' Fergal said. 'As you're here, I leave it to you to make the decision of whether we should tell them about our history. I know how important it is for it to remain a secret.'

Hosemee was watching us closely, as if sizing us up and wondering if we could be trusted.

All we could do was wait for his reply.

Hosemee spoke at last, 'I will answer your questions, although I must point out, this information cannot be divulged to anyone. I believe you're trustworthy, hence why you are sitting here in this house which nobody but forest dwarves can see, and that alone is a sign that you mean us no harm. There are some things I need to discuss with you later, Heera.' Hosemee glared at me and again he stared at the pendant around my neck.

'Can I have your word when it comes to not sharing this information with anybody or even writing it down?' he asked kindly, glancing at Kal, who was opening his diary and starting to write about Fergal's secret world.

Kal's face fell. He was taken aback at this request. He was so used to writing everything down, and he had no option but to put down his pen and close his diary.

Hosemee began, 'Ruby, please light a candle and place it in the middle of the table. I think it's best I show them how it all began. Our kind used to live in the undergrowth in this very forest centuries ago and made little clays huts to live in with our families.

'We dislike conflict, and there's never been a forest dwarf who's been rude, spiteful, or aggressive to anyone. We are known to be docile, kind, and keep ourselves to ourselves, and because of our qualities, other creatures in Fallowmere have always thought little of us and have always treated us like vermin. Our lives changed because of him.'

Fergal brought Hosemee over to our table, and Ruby stood with a candle in her hand. Kal lifted the three dwarves onto the larger chairs. Ruby reached over placing the candle in the middle of the table, and with a click of her fingers, a yellow flame engulfed the wick. Hosemee sat beside me and I felt awkward with the way he studied me; however, I put that to one side because I wanted to find out who'd changed the lives of the forest dwarves forever.

I wanted to ask him who this mystical being was, but I knew the answer would come in Hosemee's own time, so I let him continue. For now, we waited for Hosemee's story to unfold.

CHAPTER 15

The Unlikeliest of Friends

Hosemee concentrated on the candle and attempted to blow out the flame. I was surprised to find the colour of the flame become brighter; the flame changed from a light yellow, to orange, and finally to blue.

Suddenly, the flame disappeared.

I could see a colourless vapour rising from the candle, forming ripples and hovering before our eyes. Hosemee took out a green velvet bag from the inner pocket of his nightgown, which he opened, and poured grains of golden sand onto the palm of his tiny hand.

Carefully, he began to blow the minuscule particles into the vapour and the sand simply floated in mid-air.

'We had no powers to begin with,' Hosemee explained. 'A chance meeting in this very forest between a stranger and a forest dwarf, hundreds of years ago, changed the lives of our kind forever. The magic I'm using was given to us by the stranger and the images you'll see are mere memories of the forest dwarf.'

The ripples in the dense vapour began to vibrate, as did the particles of sand, and slowly, images began to move around us. It was as though, we were in the images themselves. We saw minuscule clay huts surrounded by moss and deep dense trees.

It was an odd sensation. I could feel the humidity of the Undergrowth on my skin, and when I glanced down, I found myself still sitting at Fergal's table. When I glanced up once more, I was transported into another part of the forest. Lena and Kal looked on in wonder.

I didn't glance down again. I let myself become accustomed to what Hosemee was trying to show me. The forest was quiet. There was a scuffling noise, and the wooden door of a clay hut was thrown open, and a young forest dwarf ventured out. He was scruffy, wearing an odd assortment of clothes; he wore a dirty white vest, blue shorts and pink coloured socks without any shoes.

A voice from within the hut shouted, 'Make sure you find some dry wood! We can light a fire in the evening when it gets cold, and be careful my son.'

'I will, Mother. I always am careful,' he replied as he made his way out of the Undergrowth.

The memory changed and showed the forest dwarf holding armfuls of dry firewood, making his way back home until he found two goblins blocking his way. The young dwarf was scared and tried to move to the left and to the right to get past the goblins, but they purposely mimicked the dwarf's every move stopping him from getting away. I wanted to help him, and I could see the fear in the dwarf's eyes.

The dwarf dropped his firewood and tried to run away. The goblins tripped him up and started to make fun of him and laughed at his dirty clothes. 'You dirty little rat! Who said you can be out here. Go back to the Undergrowth, where you belong, and never show your ugly face again,' a goblin laughed while the other picked up a long piece of firewood the dwarf had dropped and started to prod him in his ribs.

Unbeknownst to the goblins and the dwarf, a young boy, around the age of ten, was watching them from behind a tree and stepped forward to confront the goblins. 'Hello! Are you playing a game? Can I play?' the boy asked politely.

The young boy was well groomed. He had dark brown hair, light brown eyes, and was handsome. The boy looked out of place standing in the forest wearing expensive, clean clothes.

The stranger stood observing the scene before him with a grin on his face.

'Yes, come join us,' a goblin said, excitedly. 'We're playing a game and the aim is to prod the dirty little dwarf until he cries, but make sure you don't touch him because you don't want to make your nice and clean clothes dirty.'

The dwarf remained sitting on the ground and wouldn't look up at them. He seemed to be ashamed at being a dwarf and began to whimper. The goblins encouraged the young boy to mock the dwarf; nevertheless, the boy stood rooted to the spot and stared at the goblins. The young dwarf managed to glance up at the boy, and he was surprised to see that even though no words were spoken between the boy and the two bullies, the goblins trembled with terror and fled from the scene.

The young boy helped the dwarf to his feet and asked kindly, 'Are you OK?' The dwarf didn't reply. He was red in the face and clearly ashamed of what'd happened to him. 'Do you want help with those sticks? I'll help you carry them to your house.'

'Why are you helping me? You know I'm a forest dwarf, don't you? It's fine… I'll manage,' the dwarf said.

'So? What's that got to do with anything?' the boy smiled. 'My name is Amunah. What's yours?'

I smiled at Kal and Lena and we couldn't believe we were looking at the great God, Amunah, as a child.

'Hosemee,' the young dwarf replied. This time, the three of us turned to the present Hosemee, and he smiled through his tears. We returned to gaze in disbelief at Amunah and Hosemee as their younger selves, and I was eager to find out what'd happened next.

Hosemee put up his hand and the image before us turned into a golden mist of moving particles.

Hosemee turned to us and spoke in a low voice, 'You've now seen how Amunah and I met for the very first time, and this was the beginning of a friendship which I still hold dear to me.'

'Did he show you any of his powers?' Lena asked Hosemee. 'Because, he must have done something to those goblins to make them run away like that.'

'I never saw him use his powers early on. If he had any, he never showed them to me until much later on when he granted us protection and gave us a status of equality alongside other creatures. Heera, I want you to pay close attention to what Amunah gives me in the next memory. It's important.'

Hosemee pointed to the mist again, clapped his hands and the golden sand now formed another image.

Both Hosemee and Amunah were strolling through the forest side by side. Amunah had grown and was tall; his face was soft and even more handsome, while Hosemee had remained exactly the same. They were talking and laughing and Hosemee spoke first, glancing up at his friend, 'It's been so long, Amunah. I thought I'd never see you again.'

'I'm sorry, Hosemee,' Amunah said. 'Ever since my parents passed away, all the responsibility of the Kingdom has fallen upon me, and I have to take care of Raven too. I never get time to do the things I want to. I've missed you too and I can never forget our friendship.'

Hosemee took a deep breath, clearly relieved his friend hadn't forgotten him.

'Hosemee, there's something I must tell you though. I don't know when I'll be able to see you next, but I promise I'll do my best to see you when I can.'

'It's because I'm a forest dwarf, isn't it? You can't be my friend because you're the King of Fallowmere and everyone will think poorly of you if they see you with me,' Hosemee croaked and his eyes brimmed with tears.

Amunah was taken aback.

'Hosemee, I would've thought you knew me better than that. I *am* proud to say that *you're* my best friend, and why do you think so poorly of yourself? You are equal to me, and I'll prove to you how much our friendship means, but please take these doubts out of your mind.'

Amunah closed his eyes and moved his hand from the ground upwards towards the sky; tall, healthy trees grew out of the earth and shot high into the sky. With one hand movement, they stopped growing and were now over a hundred feet above the ground. Hosemee was amazed and excited and couldn't believe how Amunah had done this magic.

Amunah closed his eyes once again, and slowly the branches of the trees began to move like arms, and they were building tree houses using their own bark, branches and leaves. Just as the natural bark was used up, the trees were replenishing themselves magically.

The branches sprouted long vines down to the ground, twisting and forming ladders to make a way up to the tree houses. Other vines were growing across to the other trees, allowing the dwarves access to each other's homes. Hosemee didn't know what to say. One second, he was staring at the trees, then at the tree houses, at the vines, then back at the trees.

Hosemee could hear Amunah muttering under his breath at the ground below them, and a dirt wall sprung out of the ground with great force and encircled them and the tree houses. The wall was building higher and higher until it was above the trees, and when Amunah opened his eyes, the dirt wall vanished into thin air.

'My dear Hosemee, *this* is your new home. Bring your family, your friends and all the forest dwarves. You wanted protection from other creatures and I'm giving it to you and to your kind. You're not below any creature in this forest! You'll live like a

King also, in a house higher than the creatures who torment you, my friend.

'Nobody can see these trees. All they'll find is a clearing and you'll be able to keep watch from above. From this day forward, nobody will be able to cast a spell on you or your kind. Instead, you'll have enough magic to keep yourselves hidden and safe. If you don't want to be seen, think it and you'll be invisible.'

'Who are you? I mean… what are you, Amunah?' Hosemee stuttered.

'Why, your friend of course,' Amunah laughed and Hosemee gave him a hug. 'I have one more gift for you, Hosemee. It's something to remember our friendship by and I have one just like it. It's very special.' Amunah took out two pendants from his pocket just like I was wearing and handed one to Hosemee and put the other one back in his pocket.

'Thank you so very much! I'll keep it with me always. You've changed my life, Amunah. How can I ever repay you?' Hosemee said meekly while admiring the gold pendant his best friend had given him. 'I do feel there's something troubling you, Amunah. Is there anything I can do to help you?'

'Hosemee, you don't have to repay me. I take it you already know about my powers,' Amunah chuckled. 'I want to help the Kingdom in a way that has never been done before. My followers are beginning to suspect I have powers and are treating me like I'm their God, and not even I understand how I was given these powers. I don't want to be their God. I want to be normal.

'I have so many people and creatures around me, but still I feel so alone. Nobody understands me except you. I'm planning to leave the throne and leave my brother in charge for a while until I find a way to help the Kingdom. I think I know how to help Fallowmere… I just have to put my plans into action.'

'You can stay here with me,' Hosemee said excitedly.

'Thank you Hosemee but I can't stay here. It will be a great inconvenience to you and to the other forest dwarves. Several of my followers are building a temple for me and it's high above Mount Orias. I'll live there for a while and experiment with the ideas I have. Very few will know its exact location, but once it's built, I'll let you know where it is and you can visit whenever you want.'

The image faded and Hosemee blew out the candle and the mist cleared. We were all silent, thinking about and remembering what we'd seen. I was anxious to find out what the elderly dwarf was going to tell me about the pendant around my neck.

'Look at the time! It's ten o' clock and I haven't even started dinner yet,' Ruby said, getting out pots and pans and placing them on the stove. 'Fergal, help me make dinner.'

'Yes, yes, OK,' Fergal sulked. He clearly wanted to stay with us and hear what Hosemee was going to tell us. 'You three, please make yourselves comfortable on the sofa. I'm sure Hosemee wants to talk to you.'

Kal stood up and helped Hosemee back to the sofa; Lena and I followed them.

We manoeuvred the larger sofa so it was opposite the dwarf sized one and the three of us sat down with Hosemee sitting directly opposite us.

'Now, where shall we start?' Hosemee asked smiling at us.

'Was that the last time you saw, Amunah?' Kal asked.

'No, we met a few times after that meeting in the forest. I even went to see him in the temple that was made for him. His followers called the temple, the 'Sorin', and it was built high up in the mountain behind Cranwell Castle. The entrance to the Sorin faced the sun; the kingdom felt the location was fitting for him as the sun gives us life and light and Amunah was seen as a bright hope for the future.'

Hosemee paused and stared into space, perhaps thinking about Amunah. He took a deep sigh before continuing.

'The last time we met, he was devastated and said he had to go and would never return to Fallowmere because he'd failed to protect his Kingdom from evil. He blamed himself for what his younger brother had done and felt ashamed that his own brother could turn out so evil.

'Amunah gave me a jar full of gold particles, which you saw back at the table, and they are fragments of the memories he left me with. He also gave our kind a prolonged life. Amunah was the greatest King that Fallowmere ever had and will ever see and he was my friend and my God.' Hosemee welled up.

'I just don't understand why Amunah couldn't stop his brother? He had so much power himself,' Lena said.

'Lena, if you had to fight Heera to the death, would you?' he asked frankly and Lena was taken aback. 'See it's not easy to fight your own friend, let alone your own flesh and blood. Raven was still dear to him and I believe Amunah couldn't face having to hurt his brother.'

'Did he say where he was going?' Lena asked.

'I don't think he was sure either,' Hosemee explained. 'He said he'd meet me one day, though not in Fallowmere. I asked if I could come with him, but he refused, explaining it was not my time to leave Fallowmere. He explained there would be a time, when true warriors would try to bring the crystals together again to use them for good, and if I was to meet any of them, I should help them on the right course.

'You see it's not a matter of simply getting the crystals from Bulzaar… they need to be taken to the Sorin and returned to their rightful place. The temple is hidden to all, except the one who is chosen by him.

'Hayden, of course didn't know this. Even if she'd found all five crystals, she still would've failed to protect Fallowmere, because if the crystals are still in the kingdom, there will always be someone who wants them and will keep searching for them. Amunah has managed to bring you here somehow, Heera, and you will complete this journey.'

The Elders had instructed me to bring the crystals to them, so they would help me to use their power to defeat Bulzaar, but I knew now I couldn't trust anyone with them. I would make sure if I did rescue my family and find the crystals, I'd return them to the temple. There was no way I was going to use the crystals to defeat Bulzaar; it was more important to take the source of Bulzaar's power away, and once the crystals were no longer in the kingdom, others wouldn't try to use their power to do evil. I'd have to find another way to defeat Bulzaar.

'I want to know more about this pendant. It's exactly the same as yours and Amunah's,' I said.

'I have mine right here,' he took out the pendant and showed it to me, 'Yours is Amunah's,' he smiled.

'What? How can that be?' Lena asked.

'There were only two identical pendants, and Amunah lost his pendant when he fought with his brother,' Hosemee continued. 'In time, the pendant was picked up by different creatures. They didn't know it was Amunah's nor did they know how the pendant worked. If you're full of hate and want to do harm to others, the pendant will burn you and you'll never be able to touch it. I assume a clean soul would be able to wear it, but only the chosen warrior would be able to communicate with Amunah through the pendant like Hayden, and now you of course.'

No wonder the pendant had a life of its own. I grabbed the pendant and felt it vibrate against my hand.

'Hosemee, did you ever go to Cranwell Castle with Amunah? I need to know of a simple way to get in there without being seen,' I asked.

'No, I never went to the castle. Amunah always came to see me... he tried to get away from the castle as much as he could. There is another entrance though... through the Caves of Arya.'

'Dinner's ready! You can finish your conversations tomorrow. It's already late,' Ruby called over. Although I was hungry, I wanted to know the answers to all the questions I had floating around in my head. I kept quiet for now because I knew Ruby wouldn't let us continue speaking tonight.

We sat down for a hearty meal of mushroom soup and tomato and onion bread. Once we'd had our fill, we were ready to drop on the dinner table with tiredness. We laid our sleeping beds on the floor, and Ruby made arrangements for Hosemee to sleep in their bed upstairs while Fergal laid blankets on the sofa for Ruby and him.

'I'll help you make a plan of how to get to the Caves of Arya tomorrow. Now sleep well and goodnight,' Hosemee called over before heading upstairs.

'Goodnight,' we said in unison.

'Fergal, I forgive you and thanks for saving us,' Kal said, out of the blue.

'Thank you, my friend,' Fergal beamed.

Lena and I shook our heads at how long it had taken Kal to forgive poor Fergal. We both smirked at each other and turned in for the night.

CHAPTER 16

The Chief's Guidance

The following morning, I was the first to awake out of the three of us, and unlike other early mornings in Fallowmere, I felt completely safe and at ease in Fergal's tree house. I lay in the warm sleeping bag, and I could hear Hosemee whispering nearby. I simply lay thinking without opening my eyes.

I'd been in this new world for five days now and the time had flown by. I wondered if any of our relatives had noticed our absence in the human world and were now desperately searching for us. Emma, surely would've tried to get a hold of me and left messages.

If anyone did raise the alarm, they'd find our house in a state and the police would be involved. How would we explain our absence to them? We couldn't tell them the truth because they'd think the whole Watson family had lost their marbles.

Ruby could be heard opening and shutting the kitchen cupboards, and not before long, the tempting smell of toast being made and eggs being fried, forced me to get up.

I sat up and Ruby, Fergal, and Hosemee immediately looked my way. 'Good morning, everyone,' I said as they each returned the greeting while smiling at me. Ruby was cooking at the stove, and Hosemee and Fergal were sitting on the sofa chattering away.

Lena and Kal also stirred in their sleep and were up and out of their sleeping bags in no time. We washed up and came to the table to eat breakfast.

'After you eat, we'll talk about how to get you to Cranwell Castle,' Hosemee said from the sofa. 'Kal, you'll be happy to know, you can note everything down in your diary.' Hosemee chuckled.

'Thank you,' Kal replied while getting up through the middle of his breakfast to get out his diary from his rucksack. 'What?' he asked of Lena when he found her looking at him in disbelief.

'Nothing at all, Kal,' she sighed.

Once we'd eaten our fill, Ruby ordered the three of us to the sofa after we tried to help her clear up. 'You have a lot on your plates already, and you need as much rest as possible,' she said.

We made ourselves comfortable on the sofa. 'Now that you're all fed and watered, Fergal and I need to find a way to get you three to the Caves of Arya safely,' Hosemee said, 'and without detection. I'll also tell you more about the location of the Sorin. Fergal has given me a copy of the map you're using.' Hosemee placed it on the table before him. 'You are here,' he said pointing at the centre of the Forest of Eedon on the map.

'The Caves of Arya are further north. It will take you at least five days to reach them, and you'll not find any more creatures that'll help you to get rid of Bulzaar in this forest,' Hosemee continued. 'Bulzaar has a stronghold on them, and they can be extremely brutal when they want to be and will hand you over to the Fire Blades without thought.

'Fergal, will of course accompany you since he knows the way to the Caves of Arya. But he will remain invisible to everyone except the three of you for his safety.'

Kal was over the moon, and although I was grateful, I felt guilty about him having to leave Ruby behind.

'Are you sure, Fergal? Ruby will be all alone and it might be dangerous,' I said.

'No, he *will* accompany you three. This is the least we can do to help with defeating Bulzaar,' Ruby replied.

'There are many paths to the castle,' Hosemee added, 'and the strongest Fire Blades are stationed at each entrance to ensure nobody passes through.'

'How will we find the temple?' I asked.

'You'll know where the temple and crystals are Heera because that will guide you,' Hosemee said pointing at my pendant. 'Kal and Lena, you're very good and dear friends, but you must understand that Heera will be at her weakest, and she may not know what's happening around her. You must protect her when she's at her most vulnerable. The closer she gets to the crystals and the temple, the more powerful her pendant will become because it senses Amunah's power too.'

'Will it help if we take it off and wear it for her if it gets too much?' Lena asked.

'The pendant will not work in the same way for you,' Hosemee explained. 'Amunah's chosen Heera to communicate with and he may not do so with someone else. As for the crystals, they'll need to be placed in the temple in the cradle, the location of which was only known to Amunah. Once they're placed there, Fallowmere will be safe once more, unless someone finds another way to bring evil to the kingdom.'

'Hosemee, how will we get into the caves?' Fergal asked. 'I've been there and the Fire Blades never leave the area and are always on the lookout for enemies.'

'You'll have to sit and wait, Fergal. Surely they must rest, or have change overs, giving you the opportunity to enter the caves.'

'Fergal, don't worry... just take us to the border of the caves and we'll think of something. If need be we can always create a diversion,' I said.

'Yes, we can do some magic to distract them. I'll go over my spell book and mark the pages which may be of use and ask Iris to help me,' Lena said, immediately getting up and fetching her book of spells.

'Kal, have you noted everything down?' Hosemee asked with humour in his voice.

'Yes, and thank you for letting me.'

'Fergal tells me your father is a Seer and your mother is a vampire?' Hosemee asked.

'Yes, that's correct,' Kal replied.

'How unusual, and your powers?' Hosemee asked intrigued. 'How are you coping with them?'

'Well to be honest, they come and go but Father says it takes time. He didn't get his full powers till he was twenty five,' Kal explained.

'If you don't mind, can I suggest something?'

'Yes, of course,' Kal said.

Hosemee took out an old bronze coin and blew over it before continuing, 'Take this and keep it with you. It will help you to channel your powers, so you won't have to rely on books too much. Once you start to think and feel for yourself, your powers will begin to grow stronger.' Kal took the coin and thanked him. 'Do you have any traits from being the son of a vampire, yet?'

'No. Not at all. My mother doesn't practise the customs.'

'Yes but it doesn't mean you don't have any of her powers. Do you think being the son of a vampire is somewhat shameful?'

Fergal, Lena and I peeked awkwardly at each other. I was surprised Hosemee was talking so openly with Kal, and it was even more surprising that Kal was answering all his questions.

'Of course not, I love my mother and I'm proud she's my mother.'

'You are proud of her, yes, but are you proud because she has managed to control her natural instincts? Let me ask you something else then. What if your mother was a cold blooded killer? Would you still love her? Would you be proud of her?'

I felt sorry for Kal. He appeared to be truly dumbfounded at being asked these questions, and Hosemee was still continuing to glare at him, clearly waiting for a response.

'Of course, I'd love her and be proud of her. She's my mother,' Kal hesitated in his answer.

'Sorry to be so blunt but being a vampire is not a crime, Kal. Amunah knew a few vampires who practised their customs, harmed no-one and were peaceful beings. If you have such powers in you, don't be afraid to use them as long as you don't hurt anyone, of course.'

'Thank you for your advice, Hosemee, and I am certain, I have no powers from my mother.'

'We will see, but keep your mind open,' Hosemee said smiling. Kal nodded but didn't look too happy with Hosemee's advice. 'Now you three, it's already one o'clock in the afternoon, and I suggest you rest as much as you can because you won't have an easy journey. Also Lena, can I have a word with you alone?'

'Sure,' Lena said and Hosemee led her outside the tree house. Kal and I didn't think anything of it as we both knew Hosemee was trying to help us in his own way, and we left them to it.

Once Lena returned, she was rather sullen, and I saw her hold onto her left arm a couple of times. I wondered if Hosemee had said something to her about the strange mark I'd seen on her arm on my first night in Kendolen.

'Lena, is everything OK?' I asked.

'Yeah, everything's fine. You know what Hosemee's like… he likes to interrogate everyone,' she said. I didn't ask her anything else. I couldn't. It wasn't any of my business, and a few moments later, she was back to her normal self.

The rest of the afternoon was spent resting on the sofa. Lena humoured us with possible ways to distract the Fire Blades who were stationed at the entrance to the Caves of Arya, and each distraction involved turning Kal into a gruesome beast. I couldn't help but laugh, and even Hosemee, Fergal and Ruby joined in, much to the annoyance of Kal. He was furious with all of us.

Dinner was very subdued and hardly anybody spoke. We were all lost in our own thoughts while we ate the delicious food Ruby had made. We had vegetable soup and homemade bread, followed by apple pie and custard. It was soon time for us to depart, and it was difficult having to leave Ruby and Hosemee behind. They'd been so kind and hospitable and had shared so much with us. It was very hard to say goodbye.

Ruby was brave and fighting back her tears, and Hosemee who'd remained so strong and had given us so much advice was in a flood of tears. He kept on giving us words of encouragement and said we'd all make Amunah proud.

We each hugged Ruby and Hosemee and thanked them for everything they had done for us. We left Fergal alone to say his goodbyes, and we climbed down the vine ladder to the ground and waited for him.

'Okay, let's go,' Fergal said when he joined us. He pointed into the distance and we crept out into the not so quiet night.

We could see roaring camp fires burning here and there. We trod slowly and silently so as not to cause attention to ourselves. I could hear snippets of conversations, and the content of the chatter confirmed the speakers' owed allegiance to Bulzaar.

'Guess what?' a hooded figure said to a group of goblins. 'Bulzaar's sent word, through the Fire Blades, that whoever finds Heera Watson and brings her to him will be rewarded most generously. I'm setting out tomorrow to find her... even if it means trying to find a way into Kendolen. She must be still there. A fifteen year old human girl won't last a day in Fallowmere.'

'Morog has been in touch!' exclaimed a strange-looking creature. His face resembled a buffalo and the rest of his torso was human. 'He's brought Dragmatus back with him, and the beast will help the Fire Blades guard the caves in case the warrior from Kendolen shows up.'

'They caught that good for nothing Headhunter, Tallon! They have taken him straight to the training camp back at Cranwell Castle against his will,' a Critanite laughed around another fire. I was shocked at hearing about Tallon because although he was strange, he'd still fought so hard not to get involved in Bulzaar's plan and still he'd been taken away.

Fergal led us deeper into the forest where there were fewer camp fires. I wondered who or what Dragmatus was. I'd heard that name before when Morog had mentioned it back at the camp. If the beast was now helping to guard the caves, I knew this would be another barrier we'd have to overcome.

We walked on, for almost six hours straight, in silence. It was still the early hours of the morning, and even though we'd spent most of the previous day resting at Fergal's tree house, sheer darkness and the drop in temperature was slowing us down.

Fergal pointed to a path verging off to the right in front of us and whispered, 'We can camp out here tonight. The Fire Blades have already searched this part of the forest and hopefully we won't be disturbed. There's no point in continuing if we can't see where we're going.'

Lena set up the tent and once we were inside it and in our sleeping bags, we began to talk with each other without worrying we'd be heard.

'Fergal, who or what is Dragmatus?' I asked.

'It's a creature Bulzaar created, by using the power of the crystals, to protect himself from the enemy. He uses it when travelling great distances. The night Morog was at the camp, he used it to fly back to the castle to inform Bulzaar about the mysterious warrior. I haven't seen it myself and from what I've heard it's not a pleasant creature. Why do you ask?'

'I heard a creature talking about it around a fire, shortly after we set off. He was saying it's now guarding the Caves of Arya with the Fire Blades.'

Fergal looked scared.

'Don't worry, Fergal. Like we all agreed yesterday, we'll sit it out and see exactly how the caves are guarded,' Lena assured him. 'We'll think of something.' Fergal tried to relax as best as he could.

'Bulzaar's told all the creatures they'll be rewarded generously, if they can find me and take me to him,' I said. 'Poor Tallon's been taken to Cranwell Castle as well.'

'Heera, we're going to have to be so careful,' Lena said, worriedly.

'I know,' I said.

We settled in, knowing we had a long day ahead of us, and each of us lay in our sleeping bags in silence before sleep claimed us.

I was peering down at Fallowmere from such a great height. The sun was blazing, and it was impossible to look straight ahead. I felt a hand on my shoulder and turned around and immediately regretted my decision. Bulzaar snatched at my pendant, and I heard a new voice. It was powerful, controlling and belonged to a female. She screamed out, 'TAKE IT FROM HER BULZAAR! SNATCH IT FROM HER! DON'T LET HER TAKE IT TO THE TEMPLE! ALL WILL BE LOST!'

Bulzaar began pushing me to the edge of the mountain, and in another few steps, I'd fall. He had his hand around my pendant. He was about to snatch it away from me, but his hand glowed bright orange, and he let go quickly. Once more the harsh voice of the woman shouted loudly, 'GRAB IT!'

I awoke with sweat pouring down my face and with the pendant beating against my chest.

CHAPTER 17

The City of Dalmain

'Heera, what's wrong?' Fergal asked getting up, prompting Lena and Kal to stir and awake.

'Nothing, I just had a bad dream, that's all,' I whispered.

'What was it?' Fergal asked.

I told them all about my nightmares of Bulzaar, and they were taken aback with the new voice I'd heard, this time encouraging the Dark King to take away my pendant.

'Isn't it obvious? It's Saniah trying to get her husband back into power,' Kal said, sleepily.

'Why didn't you tell Hosemee about your nightmares?' Fergal asked.

'I didn't want everybody to think I was afraid of some nightmares.'

'They might not be nightmares though, Heera,' Lena said.

'I feel you made a mistake in not telling Hosemee about them,' Fergal said.

'There's nothing I can do about it now. I'll use what I see in the nightmares or whatever they may be to help me face Bulzaar,' I said.

Each one of them stared at me like I was insane. Either way, ignoring the nightmares, or whatever they were, or even taking them seriously, didn't take away from the fact I still had to face Bulzaar. I chose not to dwell on what I saw.

We ate from the individual food parcels Ruby had packed for us and ventured out of the tent. Lena used magic, once again, to fold the tent away and Fergal led the way onwards.

This part of Eedon Forest was tranquil. There were no camp fires or groups of different creatures wondering around, however, night time was the complete opposite.

We were whispering away and I abruptly stopped in my tracks and held out my arm to stall Lena and Kal. I saw a Fire Blade making his way towards us in the distance. He had his head down and was humming away.

'What's wrong?' Lena asked.

'Look,' I whispered. 'Fergal run somewhere safe.'

Fergal ran behind a nearby tree. He was invisible anyway, but I still wanted him out of harm's way. I began to tremble. All this time, we hadn't met with one face to face and currently one was heading straight towards us. There was nowhere to hide. If we made any sudden movements, he'd see us right away. Lena and Kal, like me, stood rooted to the spot.

The Fire Blade glanced up and saw us. His yellow eyes widened, and instead of running towards us, he made a run for it in the opposite direction. I was confused because the Fire Blades we'd encountered on our journey so far weren't cowards. They struck fear into their victims and showed no mercy. Maybe, this Fire Blade was going to raise the alarm to the others and tell them they'd found me.

I ran after him; Lena and Kal followed lagging behind. I couldn't let him run back and tell the other Fire Blades about us, and at least with one against three, we had a chance of stopping him. The Fire Blade was fast, but I managed to catch up with him.

I reached out my arm and grabbed his metallic clothing, and he fell to the ground on his front. I knelt down with my knee on his back, waiting for Kal and Lena to catch up. The Fire Blade was desperately trying to get away, and once or twice, I had to dig my knee deeper into his back.

'Heera, turn him… around,' Lena panted. Kal stood beside her trying to catch his breath.

I turned him around and the figure before us was no Fire Blade. He'd been wearing a mask resembling one that was half way up his face. I stood up and placed the blade of my sword at his chest.

'Who are you?' I asked.

'What's your problem?' the figure said, removing the mask completely off his face. He was a boy, around sixteen years old I would have said, with black, shoulder length, wavy hair, and his skin was very pale, as if he'd never been outside. His eyes were turning from vivid yellow to deep brown and were now fixated on me with the deepest of loathing. The way his eyes changed colour made me wonder if he'd used magic to change his appearance to blend in with the Fire Blades.

'No, *we* ask the questions around here,' Kal said arrogantly. Lena and I glanced at each other; neither of us knew where to look when Kal reacted this way. It was embarrassing.

'Good to see you've got your breath back,' the boy laughed at Kal and then he turned to stare directly at me, 'and YOU, thinking you're real powerful holding a sword.'

'Who are you?' I asked again. I saw that Fergal had come to stand a few metres away from us, but I ignored him as I didn't want to draw attention to him.

'Answer her!' Lena said.

'My name's Jack and that's all you need to know,' the boy said and immediately, he grabbed the blade of my sword and pulled me forward, and I fell on top of him. He swiftly turned over and pulled me up. He had my sword in his hand; the blade was placed carefully against my neck and his other arm was holding me close.

'What? How… did he do that?' Kal said panicking, and he dropped his bag accidently while retrieving his sword.

'NO, GET AWAY FROM HER!' Lena shouted and pointed her wand towards him. Jack was strong, and every time I tried to move, I couldn't budge.

'Don't point your wand at me! You don't want to hurt your friend accidentally, do you?' he said.

'Let go of her,' Kal threatened with his sword and moved closer.

Jack laughed and said, 'You three are coming with me. You've seen me and that's not good for you. Oi, butter fingers, bring that witch forward, or else your friend here gets it.'

'OK, fine! Just don't hurt her!' Kal said.

'MOVE!' Jack bellowed. Kal and Lena moved forwards. Jack, still holding me tight, followed them closely. I could feel the blade of the sword touch my skin gently, and with each touch, I inhaled trying to steady myself. There was no way I could get out of this without seriously hurting myself.

Lena looked back towards us and asked, 'Where are you taking us?'

'You'll see... NOW KEEP MOVING!' Jack shouted.

Lena and Kal kept moving onwards between the trees and Jack followed with me in his grasp. We came to a stand in front of a hill made of black stone, and Kal and Lena glanced back at Jack. 'What do you expect us to do? We can't walk through this,' Kal said.

'Now you two get behind... I said GET BEHIND!' Lena and Kal moved back, and Jack and I moved towards the face of the hill, still keeping Lena and Kal in sight. 'Now you, listen carefully. If you try anything, you've had it,' Jack whispered in my ear. He released me from his grip, although he still had the sword firmly in place under my neck.

'OUCH!!! What bit me?' Jack yelled, and yet, he still managed to hold the sword firmly in place against my throat. Fergal had managed to bite him on his leg, and because Jack couldn't see the dwarf, he kicked out and hit Fergal straight in his face. Poor Fergal fell to the ground holding his nose as it began to bleed. It was foolish for us to try to help him right away; we had to get away from Jack before we could acknowledge Fergal's presence, and for now, it was best he remained concealed for his own safety.

Jack stood still peering around in the distance, and once he was certain we hadn't been followed, with his free hand, he pushed a particular section of the hill, and the stone wall moved back to reveal a hidden entrance. It was dark behind the secret opening and a flight of stairs could just be seen going downwards into the ground.

'Now you three, get down there!' Jack said, shoving me towards the stairs, followed by Lena and Kal. I couldn't see anything and there was nothing to hold onto to steady myself. I trod carefully, taking my time to climb down the steps.

There was a glimmer of light in the distance. I kept moving down the stairs and I could hear talking and laughter. It had to be the Fire Blades. My heart was thumping against my chest whilst my pendant remained still. My feet stalled with sheer terror at one point, leading Lena and Kal to bump into me.

'MOVE!' Jack shouted from behind and pushed Kal roughly. Lena toppled into me, and I lost my balance and came hurtling down the stairs. I landed hard on concrete floor.

'WHOA!' I heard Kal say.

I stood up and my eyes opened wide in wonder. A golden arch towered in the distance and people bustled here and there. To my right, I saw a mountainous pile of costumes resembling different creatures, and to my left, I found several market stalls completely covered in vegetables and fruit.

Children were playing in a fenced area, complete with swings and slides, and teenagers were perched on a brick wall gossiping heartily.

Nobody seemed to have noticed our presence.

'What is this place?' Lena asked.

'It's some sort of underground city,' Kal said.

'MOVE!' Jack shouted again, pointing my sword onwards. We were forced into the midst of a crowd of people who began to notice us as we walked by. The crowd stepped back allowing us through, and silence began to fall as more and more faces eyed us curiously.

'Where are you taking them, Son?' a man said, bowing at Jack as he marched on behind us.

'To my father, he'll know what to do with them,' Jack said.

As we came closer to the golden arch, I found hundreds of tea lights placed in tiny crevices all over the arch, making the golden colour more prominent and flooding the entire area with light.

Beyond the arch, I could see houses on either side of a cobbled street, which carried on into the distance. It was unbelievable to see the sheer number of houses in this underground realm. Who were these people? And where had they come from?

'In here, NOW!' Jack shouted and pushed us into a building to our left. When I opened the door, we found ourselves in a waiting room with empty chairs placed against the grey walls. There was a closed office door directly opposite us at the back of the room.

The door behind us shut. Jack ushered us into the middle of the room and shouted out, 'FATHER, WE HAVE A PROBLEM!' The closed office door opened, and a tall, bald man with a black beard and moustache walked through, eyeing us suspiciously. He was wearing a black cloak. Following him, were seven other boys, wearing different coloured robes and who were around the same age as Jack. They flooded the room and circled us.

'What's the matter, Jack? Who are they?' the man asked his son.

'I found them in the forest and they attacked me,' Jack said.

'Who are you?' the man asked of us.

'Let us go, please,' I said.

'We can't let you go… I assume they saw you in disguise my son?' Jack's father asked with deep concern.

'Yes, she caught up with me and pushed me to the ground and my mask came off,' Jack said.

The other boys smirked and giggled at Jack being pushed down by me.

'ENOUGH!' Jack shouted at the laughing boys, 'Wait till you're ready to go out there… let's see how you all fare.'

The boys fell silent, trying hard to keep straight faces.

'Jack, enough. Go change out of your clothes and let's sort this mess out,' his father said. Jack made his way into the office, still wearing his Fire Blade costume, with my sword by his side, and he slammed the door shut. 'Boys, leave us now and send for Felicity Shyre, immediately.'

'Please, we have to go,' I pleaded.

'That's out of the question, I'm afraid. Please sit down and tell me who you are. I'm Nathaniel Webber,' he said.

We reluctantly sat down on the available chairs. 'I'm Heera and this is Lena and Kal. Mr Webber, we have to leave. We won't tell anyone about Jack, or you, or this place,' I said.

'It's not as simple as that, Heera. What are you three youngsters doing in the forest when you know there is danger out there?' Mr Webber said.

'Are you going to kill us?' Kal asked outright.

Mr Webber laughed and said, 'Kill? I would never dream of killing anyone.'

'If we tell you everything, will you let us go then?' I asked.

'No, Heera. Once you've entered the city of Dalmain, there's no going back,' Mr Webber said. 'You've seen too much, and if the Dark King comes to know of this hidden city, he'll kill each and every one of us.'

'We won't tell anyone! In fact we've come to save the Kingdom of Fallowmere from Bulzaar,' I said, hoping this would persuade him to let us go.

'You three? That's impossible,' Mr Webber said.

'Heera's been chosen by Amunah himself to come to our world and save our kingdom,' Lena said.

'Wait a moment... are you, 'The Chosen One', the Fire Blades and Bulzaar are searching for?' Mr Webber asked.

'Mr Webber, I will tell you everything, but please don't hurt us. We have to go and I have to save my family,' I pleaded. I could feel myself almost welling up at the thought of him keeping us prisoner.

'I won't hurt you. Now speak,' Mr Webber said gently.

I turned to Lena and Kal and they nodded for me to continue. Unexpectedly, the office door shot open and Jack stood at the door. He glared straight at me, and I could feel myself flushing red.

His appearance was completely different. He was no longer wearing a costume but was dressed in black jeans and a red T-shirt. I could see the defined muscles in his upper arms; no wonder he was able to hold me with one arm. His black hair against his pale face and bright T-shirt made him stand out, and his brown eyes narrowed as he scowled at me. He gripped my sword tightly and entered the room.

Jack didn't say a word and took a seat opposite me with his dad. The door to the building opened and a woman walked in. The woman was black and was wearing dark glasses. She was rather tall and my eyes were drawn to her long yellow braided hair. One of the boys, who'd left earlier, guided the woman into the room. She was wearing a long black cloak, and a blue medallion necklace rested against her chest.

'Oh dear me, Jack... what have you found?' the woman said. 'I knew someone powerful had entered Dalmain. It's a girl, isn't it? Not an ordinary girl mind.'

'Felicity, come here please,' Mr Webber said and the boy helped her take a seat next to Jack. 'Thank you, Anderson,' Mr Webber said to the young boy, who smiled and made his way out the front door.

'You're right, Felicity. It is a girl, but she's not as powerful as you think, and that's why she's sitting right here with her friends, against her wishes,' Jack smirked.

'Jack, that's no way to talk to someone,' Mr Webber said.

'Whatever,' Jack replied, taking out a wand from the pocket of his jeans and resting it on his leg.

Felicity didn't say a word. 'Heera, continue, please,' Mr Webber said.

They listened carefully as I told them about my journey from the human world to Fallowmere. I explained I was here to rescue my family and to stop Bulzaar from opening a portal for Raven to come through by taking the crystals from him, and to bring those very crystals to safety. Jack sat with his arms folded and stared directly at me and rolled his eyes and huffed at what I said.

'It's true then... Amunah has chosen someone. We'd heard the rumours but we weren't convinced a young girl could stop the King,' Felicity said in a low voice. 'How do you control the vast power you've been given?' It seemed as if she was in a trance like state. I couldn't see her eyes behind her dark glasses and she made me feel nervous.

'Felicity, trust me, she's not powerful,' Jack smirked whilst lifting up my sword.

'STUPID BOY, DON'T YOU DARE SPEAK TO THE CHOSEN ONE IN THAT MANNER!' Felicity bellowed. 'YOU DON'T UNDERSTAND THE POWER SHE HAS BECAUSE YOU ARE BLINDED BY YOUR OWN ARROGANCE!'

Mr Webber nearly fell off his chair, whereas Jack went bright red, and Kal sniggered.

'Oh come on Felicity, you must be joking! She's not powerful!' Jack said.

'QUIET!!!' Felicity shouted.

'Jack, if you can't keep quiet, then leave,' Mr Webber said.

'This is what I get for risking my life to serve this city?' Jack asked.

'Jack, this is not about you,' Felicity said and Jack simmered down.

'Felicity, what do we do with them?' Mr Webber asked.

'I can erase their memory of this place,' Felicity said, 'but I do not think it is wise to do so. The girl is well protected by Amunah and the spell may backfire.'

'Please let us go! We won't tell a single soul about this place,' Lena pleaded.

'YOU! What is your background?' Felicity asked Lena, holding onto her blue stone medallion.

'Me... I'm a witch and my parents live in Kendolen. I'm Lena Bane,' Lena said.

'No... it can't be...' Felicity said, shaking her head and letting go of the blue stone.

'What's wrong?' Kal asked. Lena lost all colour from her face and stared down at her feet. I was confused as to why Felicity had reacted this way to Lena, and I waited for her to answer Kal's question.

'No... it's... nothing. Sorry to startle you, Lena. I'm overcome with the amount of power in this room from Heera

189

and it's impacting my senses,' Felicity said. I noticed Lena and Kal glance at one another before Lena took a long, deep breath.

I wasn't convinced Felicity was telling the truth because she'd definitely sensed something. Lena fell silent and appeared to be rather upset. What was Lena hiding and why couldn't she confide in Kal and me? Once this journey was over and I had somehow miraculously survived, I'd ask Lena outright and help her as she had helped me.

'Nathaniel, let them go. I do not want to go against Amunah's will,' Felicity said. I breathed a sigh of relief; Kal and Lena also loosened up a little knowing we were going to be let go.

Jack stood up, furious and spoke directly to Felicity, 'What if they're lying! You ever think of that Felicity?'

'Boy don't take me for a fool,' Felicity said. 'You're only seventeen years old and you think you know the ways of the world. I may not have eyes, but I can sense the power the girl brings with her. A power so divine that it can come from no-one other than Amunah! I remember feeling the power Hayden had, and it's the *exact* same power Heera now has. I know they're not lying.'

With a final look of contempt at the three of us, Jack marched outside and slammed the door shut. Once again, he took my sword with him.

'Jack!' Mr Webber said.

'Leave him be, Nathaniel. He can't be angry with me for too long,' Felicity smiled.

'Did you know, Hayden?' I asked.

'Oh yes, I knew her very well. There are few who didn't know her,' Felicity said.

'But how? Did Hayden know this place existed?' Kal asked.

'No, how could she? This place only came into existence after Hayden was defeated,' Felicity replied.

'It was a dark time for all of us,' Mr Webber said. 'Once witches and wizards had helped the remaining humans to escape to the human world, we had nowhere to hide, and even Kendolen had closed their border. Bulzaar was after us, wanting to take his revenge by killing all the members of our coven, and it was then that Felicity used her magic to create and conceal this wonderful city for us.'

'Don't you ever go out?' I asked.

'No, we have everything here,' Mr Webber replied. 'Jack and some of the other boys venture out, disguised as other creatures, to gather information about Bulzaar's plans from our trusted informants in the forest.'

'There are so many of you here,' Kal said, 'why can't you stand up to Bulzaar? If you're all witches and wizards, you could stop him?'

'The same can be said about those in Kendolen,' Mr Webber replied. 'They have plenty of magic and like them it's fear that's stopping us. Why risk our lives when we know we don't stand a chance against him?'

'Those crystals contain Amunah's pure power and that very power runs through Bulzaar's veins. Not even my magic will work against that power,' Felicity said. 'I'm what they call an 'Absolute', meaning I'm the head of the coven, and my power is stronger than the rest in Dalmain, but in front of Bulzaar, my power is worthless.'

'What if Bulzaar is defeated, will you still keep to yourselves?' I asked.

'No-one likes to be caged no matter how wonderful that cage maybe,' Felicity said. 'I long for a breath of fresh air, and when that time comes, Heera, when you've stopped him, we will re-join the kingdom and live with our fellow witches and wizards in Kendolen. Our true home is there.'

'Did you know my parents?' Lena asked.

'Yes, Bethelda and David Bane... they too were in our coven and great power they had too,' Felicity said.

'Can we go now?' Kal asked.

'Yes and can we count on you three for keeping our city safe?' Felicity asked.

'Yes,' we replied in unison.

'I know you won't tell anyone. Arthur, here, sees and tells me everything. There were four of you, where's the dwarf?' Felicity asked holding onto the medallion around her neck.

'He's injured outside... Jack kicked him,' I said, stunned.

'Lena, tell your parents, when you see them, that Felicity Shyre is alive and well and would like to meet them. We have much to discuss,' Felicity said.

'I will,' Lena said.

'Now go, finish the monster once and for all,' Felicity said.

'I'll get Jack to take you back to the forest,' Mr Webber said standing up and making his way out the front door.

'What happened to your eyes?' Kal asked.

'*Kal?*' I said in frustration. I found it rather rude how he'd asked outright.

Felicity laughed before continuing, 'A vampire and a Seer, what a mix! I like you a lot, Kal. I can feel the pain inside of you boy, but don't you worry... you're powerful... you just don't know it yet!'

'How did you know about my parents?' Kal asked, completely taken aback.

'I told you, Arthur sees everything... he's my eyes,' Felicity said, as she removed her glasses. We gasped. In place of her eyes, we could see light, the same blue colour of her medallion, shining straight at us. 'How were my eyes taken? Now that's a long story, maybe I'll tell you about it another time.' Felicity put her black glasses back on.

The door opened and Jack appeared. 'Come, I'll take you three back,' Jack said reluctantly.

'Give her sword back,' Felicity said.

'I will, when we get to the top,' Jack replied.

'What am I going to do with you, Jack?' Felicity asked, smiling.

'No, don't smile at me, Felicity. I'm mad at you right now,' Jack said.

'Now go,' Felicity said.

'Thank you for letting us go,' I said before leaving. I saw her smile and turn away before the door shut.

We were surrounded by witches, wizards, and their young. They stood watching us three with keen curiosity and began to whisper to each other as we followed Jack through the underground city. It was awkward being gawped at. I had my eyes on the ground until we came to the flight of stairs leading up to the forest.

'Not going to get into a costume, Jack?' Kal smirked.

'SHUT UP, BUTTER FINGERS, BEFORE I PUNCH YOU IN YOUR FACE!' Jack flared up.

'Stop, Kal, let's just get out of here,' Lena said.

Fuming, Jack, out of pride, walked by the mountain of costumes and led us up the flight of stairs in silence. He opened the stone door, ever so slightly, and waited before opening it fully once he was happy all was clear.

'Get out, butter fingers,' he spat when Kal went out first, followed by Lena. Just as I was about to go out, he pulled me back and closed the door slightly. I could hear Lena and Kal talking to Fergal; they didn't notice I had been pulled back by Jack.

Jack pushed me against the stone wall and whispered in my ear, 'Here's your sword, beautiful.' I could feel his arms pinning me to the wall. I should've pushed him away but I didn't. I sort of didn't want to.

I grabbed my sword and I could hear Jack sniggering away. 'Thanks,' I replied.

I moved forward to leave, and he grabbed my hand, pulled me back and kissed me on my lips. It was so quick that I didn't have time to register what was happening, and when I did, I pushed him away now feeling myself blush red. The moment I had pushed him away, I secretly wanted him to be kissing me again.

'When this is all over, come find me, Heera. I'll be waiting for you,' Jack said.

'Heera!' I heard Lena say.

'I have to go,' I said and with a final glance at Jack, I returned to the forest. I heard the stone fit back into place and there was no sign of Jack.

'What happened? Did he say something to you?' Kal asked, concerned.

'No, nothing at all,' I said abruptly.

Kal accepted the answer; however, Lena raised an eyebrow and smiled. I couldn't look at her.

'Lena healed me, Heera!' Fergal said excitedly.

'Fergal!' I exclaimed, hugging him, then picking him up off the ground and swinging him around.

'Heera, can you let me down now? I'm feeling dizzy,' Fergal said.

'I'm sorry, lead the way onwards, please,' I said, letting Fergal down on the ground.

'Are you feeling OK, Heera?' Kal asked.

'Yeah, I'm fine, just glad we were allowed to leave,' I said, which was true, whereas the other part of me was glad I'd met Jack. He was rude when I'd met him at first, not to mention arrogant, but what I'd encountered moments earlier was not the same boy.

I hoped I did meet him again, but this was not the time to fall head over heels over a boy. I had a mission to complete and Jack and my feelings for him would have to be set aside. If only Kal knew what'd happened, I grinned to myself.

Fergal carried onwards and we continued our journey for the rest of the day.

CHAPTER 18

The Fiery Fiend

By the time it was beginning to get dark again, we were shattered from having travelled such a great distance. Fergal led us to a section of flat land covered with huge stone boulders varying in shape and size.

Kal found six giant stones resting on each other in an almost perfect circle, and we decided to set down our tent amidst them to remain hidden from prying eyes.

We sat down on the cold ground to catch our breath before setting up the tent while Lena went to explore the vast stone land. It was hard to believe we were still in the Forest of Eedon as the trees had disappeared, and it seemed as if we'd entered some sort of stone minefield.

We appeared to be in a stone valley with steep stone slate hills around us in the near distance. Kal and Fergal walked in the opposite direction to Lena and began to explore the landscape around them. Kal and Fergal returned shortly. 'What did you find Kal?' I asked as Kal began writing in his diary.

'Nothing much... I'm just noting down as much as I can of our journey. It will be a good recollection to have if something goes wrong and someone finds our things. This diary will tell them how far we journeyed, and what we encountered. I know you and Lena think it's stupid because I've seen you both laughing about my diary.'

Fergal, all of a sudden, took great interest in the stone boulder behind him.

'I don't think it's stupid at all Kal, and even Lena will agree. Lena, come over here,' I said. There was an awkward silence.

I knew we'd both wondered what Kal was writing in his diary and noticed how possessive he was over it, but I certainly didn't want him to think we were mocking him.

'Lena?' I called again and still there was no sign of her. I stood up at once and began to search around the stones. I couldn't see her anywhere. 'Kal, Fergal, where has she gone?'

I panicked and started to run around searching for her. I looked behind several boulders and Kal and Fergal went the opposite way to search for her. I couldn't understand where she could've gone, and I started to run up the steep slate hills and call out aloud. I didn't care who heard as long as I had Lena back beside me.

'HEERA, SHE'S HERE! COME OVER HERE, QUICK!' Kal shouted with urgency. I ran as fast as I could. I saw Kal and Fergal on their knees beside Lena's still body.

'NO! GET UP, LENA. WHAT'S HAPPENED TO YOU?' I screamed.

I tried to shake her awake. Kal and Fergal were lost for words and all colour drained from their faces. My heart began to race, and out of nowhere, I was picked up by something and thrown high into the air before being slammed against a boulder a few feet away.

I was so shocked that I didn't register what'd happened. My whole body was in pain with being struck so hard against the boulder, and I fell forwards and lay on the ground with blood running down the side of my face. My head was pounding, and when I placed my hand on my head, I could feel a large bump oozing fresh blood, which was making its way down my face. I could hear Kal shouting at someone to leave us alone.

I felt dazed. Nevertheless, I put all my energy into getting back to Lena and Kal. I tried to sit up and retrieve my sword from its sheath. I could vaguely make out a dragon like beast trying to attack Kal, who was now hiding behind a boulder with Fergal.

They were terrified as they shot peeks at the beast several feet away. I knew Fergal would be protected as he was invisible to the beast. I had to get Kal to safety but I didn't know how to, and worst of all, the beast was trampling the ground near to where Lena was lying, and I didn't want her to be crushed.

As I focused my mind and tried to get back to my feet, I saw the mutated dragon clearly for the first time. The beast had thick, matted, dark green fur all over his body. His face was black and scaly, and his enormous, yellow and green pupil glared down at the boulder Kal and Fergal were hiding behind.

Suddenly, his jaw and sharp metal teeth were on display. He breathed out intensely hot fire and the boulder in front glowed orange. This scared Kal, and he leapt to the side and started to run in the opposite direction, trying to find another boulder to hide behind to bide some time.

The beast was having none of this. He opened up his wide and leathery wings, flew a few feet and managed to catch up with Kal.

Fergal made a run for Lena and was desperately trying to wake her up.

I noticed a saddle on the back of the beast's body, and as he flapped his wings, his tail thrashed from side to side. The yellow spikes covering the tail made a rattling noise.

Could the creature before me be Dragmatus, I wondered? If it was, then the Fire Blades could show up any minute. I had to do something fast.

Kal managed to squeeze into a tiny gap between boulders and the beast couldn't see him.

The bump on my head had disoriented me; I stood up with all the force I could muster and tried to get my footing right. I clutched the sword close to me and ran as quickly as I could to Lena. I pulled her to the side so she was out of harm's way. 'Fergal, try and get her to open her eyes,' I called out to him.

'I'm trying, Heera,' he cried.

The beast was still trying to find Kal; I crept up on the creature from behind, and although he was a few feet from the ground in mid-air, I knew if I could climb up the boulders, I might be able to attack him with my sword.

It was of no use. He quickly turned around, and his luminous eye was solely focused on me, following my every move. He opened his mouth and lunged forward, and I dodged the scorching flame he sent my way.

'Kal, go to Lena and help her! I've got this,' I shouted.

Kal ran and the beast almost seemed to grin at his attempt to flee; he thrashed his tail violently on the ground, causing a boulder to fall and knock down Kal, who went out like a light.

'NOOO!' I screamed as I lunged at the beast. He kept moving, and I tried to think of a way to outsmart him.

I ran in different directions as fast as I could to confuse the flying beast. Luckily, Fergal threw a rock, and the beast was distracted, turning his head away to find who else he could go after, but he couldn't see Fergal.

With his attention on something else, I managed to escape his gaze and found a suitable hiding spot where I couldn't be seen, yet I could keep an eye on the beast. He was looking everywhere for me. He flew over the area a few times and he still couldn't find me; he landed rather abruptly and began stamping on the ground, determined to find me.

I crept up close to a boulder where the creature was about to pass by; I could hear his heavy raspy breath close to me, and the thuds were getting louder. The sword in my hand was becoming restless, and I plunged it into the beast. It punctured his underbelly, and he let out a monstrous shriek.

This was it. The Fire Blades were bound to hear its screams and come running. I had to keep attacking. I stabbed him once more and green gloopy blood covered the ground where he lay. His huge eye focused on me, and he bared his teeth.

Knowing the beast wouldn't be able to stand, I ran to where Kal had fallen, but he'd disappeared. He must have woken up and gone to help Lena, I thought. I ran, with blood still running down the side of my face, to where I'd left Lena and Fergal, only to find that they too had vanished. I was too late to help them; the Fire Blades had them and they were going to kill them.

I was in such desperation that I didn't know what to do. I didn't even notice that the beast I'd wounded moments earlier had followed me slowly and silently. When I turned around, the last thing I saw was his great eye staring at me and his tail coming towards me. I was knocked to the ground.

Was I dead or alive? That I didn't know. I could feel my sore body being dragged over the hard ground. I had lost Kal, Lena and Fergal, and they were going to die just like me. I would never see them or my family ever again, and I had to tell them I was sorry. It was too late. Before I lost all consciousness again, all my hopes dissolved and I was in a state of despair.

It felt like an eternity had passed before I was able to feel my body again. It felt broken and bruised and I couldn't move my arms and legs. I felt like a motionless mannequin, however, I could hear voices close by. The voices were becoming increasing louder. They belonged to a man and a woman squabbling with each other; if only I could open my eyes to see who they were.

The female voice was directly above me, and a warm soft hand was tapping my face to try to wake me, but when I opened my eyes ever so slightly, I found a Critanite grinning down at me.

I lost consciousness again.

CHAPTER 19

The Cursed

I had no idea how long I'd drifted in and out of consciousness. I gradually began to move my arms and legs and felt my body lying on something soft.

'How long before she wakes up?' a sharp cold voice said. I was in danger. A voice so harsh could only belong to Bulzaar; I was probably in his castle and he was waiting for me to wake up. 'She's been like this for almost two days now. I told you before you should've left them all, but no… you always want to be a hero, don't you?'

I couldn't believe we'd lost so much time. It was simply flying by and I'd never been away from my family for this long. I tried to move with more force but it was too painful.

'I couldn't just leave them there. They were…' the gentle voice of a female was cut off mid-sentence.

'YES, YOU COULD HAVE! They mean nothing to us and because of you… we'll be punished again! Bulzaar is definitely going to kill us now… well done, Nova!'

'I'm sorry, Mykha. I didn't think about that,' she said calmly.

'You just don't think, that's your problem, and that little swine they brought in with them, bit me,' he argued. 'I swear he wasn't there when we carried them in here. He just appeared out of nowhere attacking me like a vicious puppy.'

'He seems strange, I agree, but he means well. He's not left their side since they arrived here.'

'The other girl is a full-blown witch, and the boy, well, he's simply strange, and then her, did you see what she did to poor Dragmatus?' he coldly said. 'Amunah only knows what those three are up too, and when Bulzaar comes, which will be any day now, you can explain why they're here. Obviously they're leading some sort of rebellion against him.'

'There will be no need to explain anything because they'll leave before he comes,' the subdued female replied.

I tried to speak; however, I only managed to make mumbling noises. The two voices stopped bickering, and I heard footsteps coming towards me. 'Wake up, Heera… wake up,' she gently whispered in my ear.

I opened my eyes and my vision was blurred. I found myself in a well-lit room, and when I lifted my head slightly off the soft pillow, I saw a Critanite sitting on a wooden stool, observing me. The Critanite smiled, baring its sharp teeth. Its nose was long and runny, and yet its eyes examined me with deep concern.

'Be careful and don't strain yourself too much. Here, I'll help you sit up,' the female Critanite said, as she put her hands under my arms and helped to lift me up. I winced slightly as her sharp claws dug into my clothes and skin.

I found myself lying in a bed with a heavy, white quilt over me. As my eyes skimmed the cosy room, I found another Critanite standing near the only window in the room, sneering over at me. I tried to find words to communicate but only managed to let out a slight whimper. The gentle Critanite reassured me that Lena, Kal and Fergal were perfectly fine.

She stood up to open the only door to the room, and I noticed her canine like hind legs and long tail; she called the other three into the room, while the other Critanite kept peering out of the window. Both Critanites had vivid green eyes, and each time the Critanite, who stood at the window, looked over at me, his eyes narrowed threateningly, and his long tail whipped the floor as he flared his long runny nose. I remembered Fergal had said their saliva was like acid, and they owed allegiance to Bulzaar, during the night we first saw Critanites in the forest.

Fergal was the first one to run into the room. He used the stool to leap onto the bed to console me. The male Critanite snorted and folded his arms and muttered under his breath in a loud enough voice so everyone could here, 'Preposterous.'

Fergal glared at him with deep loathing and the glare was returned. Lena and Kal arrived in the room, appearing well enough to smile. They both were limping. Lena was covered in purple bruises, and Kal had a black eye and deep scratches on the side of his face.

I was so happy to see them safe and sound. I couldn't speak yet and I felt extremely weak. Lena gave me a comforting hug whilst Kal simply watched awkwardly. He didn't know how to greet me, but he soon bent down and gave me a hug.

'Don't make her speak,' the female Critanite said. 'She's still not well and needs time to recover.' All eyes on the room were on me, and the male Critanite was now glaring at me, almost in disgust.

'Nova, you said you'd answer our questions once Heera was awake. Well she is now, so please tell us who you are?' Kal asked. 'Why did you help us if you're Critanites?' Nova was lost for words. She kept glancing at the other Critanite, who was staring out of the window again as if he was expecting someone to come.

'Oh, erm we are...' she didn't know what to say and she glanced over at the other Critanite for answers. He simply shrugged his shoulders at her and refused to talk. 'That's my elder brother, Mykha, and as you know, I'm Nova. We live here in the forest. I found you hurt and we brought you back to our cottage.'

'Why did you save us? Don't you owe allegiance to Bulzaar?' Kal asked. Nova remained silent and started to move around the room trying to busy herself as Mykha snorted in disgust.

'How did you find us?' Lena asked Nova, trying to make her talk. Mykha snorted again and this time it was directed towards Nova. It seemed he wanted to hear what his sister was going to tell us.

'Errr... umm... I was walking through the forest and stumbled upon you and Kal lying unresponsive on the ground. I ran back to fetch Mykha to help me to carry you both back to the cottage. Then I saw Heera attacking Dragmatus, and when he threw her to the ground, we rescued her before he trampled her.'

'What happened with Dragmatus? Didn't he attack you?' Kal asked.

'No, he flew away,' Nova said.

'He couldn't have... I injured him with my sword. He could barely walk,' I managed to say without wincing.

'ENOUGH!' Mykha shouted from across the room. 'First, Nova and I save the three of you from death, and now you have the audacity to question us like we're some sort of villains? Who do you think you are? You're under our roof, and we're the ones who should be asking you, who you are?'

Nova looked pleadingly at her brother to stop being so loud and intimidating, but he ignored her silent pleas. 'No, Nova, how dare they? We want answers from you! Who are you?' he demanded of us. 'What are you doing alone in this forest when you know how much danger is out there? Bulzaar will be restored to good health shortly, and he's going to come for us all.'

'Mykha, please, not now,' Nova pleaded.

'Let's get out of here,' Lena said. 'We can manage and thanks for everything, Nova. We don't owe you any explanation because you chose to help us, we didn't ask you to.'

'Heera has not healed properly yet. She can't go!' Nova pleaded. Kal stood up from the edge of the bed and tried to help me stand up. Nova stopped him as Mykha watched on closely. Fergal and Lena were furious with Mykha and both stood with their hands on their hips, glowering at him.

'See I told you, they're no good, Nova,' Mykha said. 'Ungrateful little… they're not even telling us who they are, or why they were wondering around the forest alone? The way they've just reacted proves they're up to no good, and Bulzaar will surely kill us once he finds out we've helped his enemies. Did you see what they did to Dragmatus, Nova?'

'Why do you talk about Dragmatus as if *he* was the victim?' Kal confronted Mykha. 'Why are you so concerned about Bulzaar punishing you if he finds out we're here?'

'Please everybody, calm down… Mykha… please stop now. Once Heera is well enough, they will leave, and he will never have to know they were here.'

'Nova, how can you do this to us? Haven't we been through enough? And now you're risking our life, for them?'

'I can't just leave them out there to die and I don't care if Bulzaar comes here. Do you think our parents would've left them to die?' Nova asked of her brother. At the mention of his parents, Mykha calmed down. 'Is this how they raised us?'

'Thank you for everything, Nova, but we don't want to cause any further arguments between you two,' Lena said calmly. 'And if Mykha supports Bulzaar's views then he is entitled to them, but it's not right for us to stay here. We will look after Heera and anyway we have things to do.'

'Support, Bulzaar! You couldn't be much further from the truth. Nova is right, you must get better first,' Mykha said reluctantly.

I didn't really believe these Critanites were Bulzaar's supporters; otherwise the Fire Blades would've been knocking down the door to the house by now.

'Now rest, Heera, and lay back down,' Nova said gently.

'No, I'm fine thank you,' I replied.

'How can we be so sure, you won't hand us over to the Fire Blades?' Kal asked. I wished he'd give it a rest and not aggravate the situation further; Mykha had just calmed down but now snapped his head around to face Kal.

'If we wanted to hand you over to Bulzaar and his army, you wouldn't be here right now. It's not us who are the monsters, IT'S YOU!' Mykha shouted.

'What do you mean by WE'RE the monsters?' Lena retaliated. 'What've we done, and if you are referring to trying to kill that beast, then of course we had too, otherwise he would've killed us first!'

'Did it not ever occur to you that the creatures Bulzaar corrupted were once innocent and deep down they're not evil?' Mykha asked. 'It's the magic that runs through their veins that makes them evil. The same can be said for the Fire Blades too because they were once innocent humans.'

'Mykha, leave it,' Nova said again.

'Well if they attack us, obviously we have to fight back,' Kal fumed. Mykha laughed at him, which enraged Kal even more. 'What would you do then? I'd like to see how you would react if YOU were confronted by Dragmatus.'

'I think YOU'RE forgetting something, Kal! How do you think we snatched Heera away from him?' Mykha retaliated. 'Do you see any wounds on either, Nova or me?'

Nova became increasingly panicked and kept on begging Mykha to stop answering back; she was clearly frightened at what he may do or say.

'How do we know you actually fought Dragmatus?' Lena flared up. 'You could be lying to us. He could have flown off and you want us to believe you came away unhurt.' Mykha just laughed.

'Stupid girl, you can't face the Fire Blades,' Mykha spat, 'or any of the beasts Bulzaar has created by evil magic. You're young, inexperienced little children who seem to think you'll make a difference to the Kingdom. HOW PITIFUL!'

'Mykha stop shouting at them. Lena and Kal, please calm yourself,' Nova pleaded.

I was getting really irritated with the constant questioning and shouting, and even poor Fergal was fed up and had his head in his hands.

'If you claim to be Bulzaar's enemy, how come you know so much about him and his magic?' Kal asked. 'Sounds to me like you're right in with him and we're the ones who're trying to stop him! We aren't like you… simply hiding away and not doing anything to stop him *even though* you claim to be his enemy.'

Mykha, seething, stepped right up to Kal and Lena. Nova started to cry but nobody paid attention to her. 'You… stop Bulzaar? Yeah right! Nova, can you believe they're going to stop Bulzaar?' Mykha cackled. Nova was sobbing while pleading with each of them to stop arguing.

'At least we ARE trying!' Lena spat.

'Keep trying then, but you will fail.'

'How do you know that?' Kal said. 'You have no idea what we're capable of. You don't even know us, and yet you claim to know Bulzaar, oh so very well. At least we aren't cowards like you, Mykha! We'll do whatever it takes to defeat him.'

'Don't you dare call me a COWARD!' Mykha shouted.

'No don't, Mykha.'

'Don't worry, Nova, he likes to pick fights with children, and yet he's afraid of Bulzaar,' Lena mocked. 'Mykha, why don't you pick a fight with your good old buddy, Bulzaar?'

'BECAUSE HE IS OUR…'

'Mykha, NO!' Nova shouted.

'BROTHER!' Mykha shouted.

CHAPTER 20

The Black Panther

'No!' Lena shouted, backing away from Mykha.

I wondered if I'd misheard Mykha proclaiming that Bulzaar was his brother. I had nothing to say at this time. My mind was racing with all sorts of thoughts and questions.

'How do you expect us to believe you? They were called Zara and Sebastian and they weren't... you know... Critanites,' Kal said.

'We don't have to explain anything. I shouldn't have said what I said, forget it ever happened,' Mykha said and then turned towards his sister. 'Sorry Nova, I really didn't mean to say anything... it just came out.' He stepped towards his sister and wiped her tears away. 'Nova's right, you must stay here until you all heal, and then you're free to go wherever you choose and do whatever you wish,' he said before he left the room and shut the door behind him.

Silence filled the room. We were trying to digest what we'd heard, and how was it possible these Critanites were Bulzaar's siblings? Why on earth did they look the way they did? Something bad had happened to them after they'd left Cranwell Castle, all those years ago.

Nova left the room to check after her brother and closed the door behind her, giving the four of us a chance to talk.

'What do you think, Heera?' Lena asked as Kal sat down on the stool and Lena and Fergal perched on the side of the bed. I suddenly remembered something I'd heard the night Fergal had brought us to the forest.

'Do you remember the night when the Fire Blades and Critanites were talking around the camp fire?' I asked. They each nodded. 'Well the leader of the Critanites informed Morog that there were two Critanites who wouldn't join Bulzaar's cause and lived in this forest. Morog had said Bulzaar knew about the two and would deal with them himself. Don't you think that's strange? Why would Bulzaar bother to come down to this part of the forest to confront these two Critanites, all by himself? It doesn't make sense.'

'Do you think he *is* their brother?' Kal asked.

'I really don't know but we have to find out the truth. We need to remain calm and polite. If they were bad, they would've killed us by now or handed us to the Fire Blades.' I stopped talking as the door to the room opened, and both Nova and Mykha entered with bowls of meat broth and a pot of tea for us all. Mykha went back out and dragged in a table and five chairs.

'We thought it'd be nice to sit down and have food together now that Heera is feeling better,' Nova said, setting out the crockery and cutlery around the table. 'Heera, would you like to eat at the table or shall I bring you a tray to the bed?'

'I want to try to get up and eat with you all,' I replied. Kal and Lena helped me up and sat me opposite Mykha, who watched me with great interest, presumably because I was the only one who hadn't argued with him.

Lena and Kal sat on either side of me. Fergal decided to stay on the bed as the table was far too high for him, and he wouldn't be able to see anything if he sat on the chair. Nova served his food on a tray.

'Thank you for helping us,' I said. 'I understand you want to know more about us and I'll explain everything to you. In turn, we'd be grateful, if you could tell us what happened to you both because it may be of use for when I meet Bulzaar. If you can't tell us what happened to you, then that is OK with us also. I'll face Bulzaar regardless to save my family and protect all those back in Kendolen.'

Mykha and Nova listened while deep in thought.

The three of us took it in turns to describe our entire journey. We left out the time we'd spent with the forest dwarves and with Jack and Felicity Shyre as there was no way, we were going to betray them and break our promises.

'Bulzaar, has taken your family?' Mykha asked somewhat intrigued.

'Yes, I need to find them, and I have a feeling they're being kept prisoner in the Caves of Arya, along with Bulzaar's family,' I explained.

'There's been talk about a mysterious warrior who is leading a rebellion against Bulzaar in the forest. Do you know anything about him?' Mykha asked.

'That's a story I made up to protect Kal, Lena and Heera when Morog had sent me to find and spy on them,' Fergal replied.

'You have them completely baffled,' Mykha grinned.

'Mykha, we should help them,' Nova said to her brother.

'Hmmm, I don't know,' Mykha said.

'Please, Heera's family and the kingdom is in danger,' Nova said.

Mykha fell silent, deep in contemplation. After a few moments, he looked over at Nova, sighed and said, 'Fine.'

Kal immediately left the room and returned with his diary and a pen ready to write down everything about Nova and Mykha.

'You don't mind if he writes down what you tell us, do you?' Lena asked. Kal ignored this question and opened up his diary anyway.

'I don't mind at all. It's not going to be easy to tell you though. Nova, you tell them,' Mykha said and focused his gaze towards the window again.

'I'm sure you've heard many stories about our family. Especially, the one where my father threw out his first wife and first son, Nerrah and Bulzaar, from Cranwell Castle,' Nova said. 'Well, the stories were all lies… he never threw them out.

'Father's marriage to Nerrah had been arranged a long time ago by their parents', and as Father had grown up, he fell in love with our mother, Zenofur, who worked in the castle as a maid. When father married Nerrah, our mother was left heartbroken and so was our father. Still, in order to protect his parents' reputation, our father tried to make his marriage with Nerrah work. Bulzaar was born soon after, and there was gossip amongst the staff that the King and Queen didn't love each other.'

'So if your father didn't throw them out, why did Nerrah leave with Bulzaar then?' Kal asked rather impatiently, glancing up from his diary with his pen poised.

'One day, Father caught a glimpse of Mother in the kitchens and ran after her to speak to her,' Nova continued. 'He took her to one side of the castle and told her that he still had feelings for her and that he didn't love the Queen. Nerrah, however, caught them. Nerrah had heard their conversation and the truth was she never loved our father either. They decided amongst themselves they'd go their separate ways, but Nerrah wanted to take Bulzaar with her because he was all she had. Father opposed this. Nerrah argued that Father and Mother could start another family together, and it was only fair she take her only son. Eventually, Father had no other option but to let Bulzaar go.'

'Where did they go, Nova?' I asked.

'Nerrah went to live with her parents. My father and my mother married and she had Sebastian and me. He deeply missed Bulzaar and even Nerrah to some extent. Father knew he'd done them an injustice by falling for our mother again. He never really forgave himself.'

'Did he try to see Bulzaar?' I asked.

'He always tried to,' Nova replied. 'Nerrah's parents were furious at Father and wouldn't let their grandson have any contact with him. Even Nerrah had to listen to them since she was living in their house and didn't want to disobey them.'

'Why have you changed your names?' Lena asked.

'Our parents gave us these nicknames. We use the names because it reminds us of them, and we were told never to tell anyone who we really are,' Nova explained.

'What happened to you? Who said you couldn't tell anyone who you really are?' I asked. Nova fell quiet. Mykha stood up and went out of the room and returned with a gigantic gold frame. It was heavy, and he was struggling trying to carry it over to us.

'This is the reason for what happened to us... our parents' portrait,' Mykha said.

He turned the portrait around. It was an oil painting of a striking King wearing a royal blue robe and a gold crown. The King had short auburn hair, large brown eyes and a thin smile.

He was standing behind a pretty woman who was wearing similar robes to her husband. She had long blonde hair to her waist, with curls around her soft pleasant face, dark blue eyes and high defined cheek bones. She was sitting on a red cushion placed on a dark mahogany chair.

'What do you mean? How can a painting do that to you?' Kal asked confused.

'After Mother passed away from an unexpected fever, Father was not the same,' Nova continued. 'He too started to fall ill with constant longing for Mother. Father told us it would be better for us to leave before Bulzaar and his family moved to Cranwell Castle after his death because he felt it may cause friction between us.

'We packed our things and moved out of Cranwell Castle, the day after he passed away, taking our beloved pet dog which Father had brought Nova for her ninth birthday,' Mykha explained. 'We took what belonged to us and decided to settle down in a nice house in a village not too far from Kendolen. We were somewhat content at first, and even the villagers treated us like we were royalty, giving us much respect.

'Ten months passed since Bulzaar moved into the castle and Nova was only eleven. The move from the castle really distressed her, as well as losing our parents within months of each other. I was eighteen and spent most of my days caring for her. She was in such shock that she was bedridden for months, and I decided enough was enough. I made her promise me she'd get out of bed the following morning, or I'd leave her all alone. I only said this to make her respond but...'

Nova interrupted and finished the sentence for him, 'I said... I'd only get up if he would get our parents' portrait from their bedroom back in the castle. It would be almost like they were there in the house with us. I missed them terribly. Mykha agreed to go and ask for the portrait.'

I imagined how Nova must have felt. She was still so young, and now I saw Mykha in a different light because regardless of how he had treated the four of us at the start, it was obvious he'd do anything for his younger sister.

'How did they treat you?' I asked.

'Well as you can see we did get our painting back,' Mykha said.

'We both went together and met with Nerrah at first. She was really welcoming,' Nova said. 'We were frightened of telling her who we were because we just didn't know how she'd react towards us. She sat down with us and asked us how she could help. We told her who we were and why we'd come to the castle. Nerrah was shocked to begin with and then later complimented us on our manners. She called the maid to get us some tea and spoke to us about our parents and Bulzaar. She was really nice to us.'

'Did you meet Bulzaar?' Lena asked intrigued.

'Yes, he came after a good half an hour and Nerrah introduced us to him,' Nova continued. 'He was slightly taken aback but was really happy to meet us. Sometimes it felt like he was in a world of his own, like he wasn't all there. He asked questions about Father, and we told him as much as we could about him. We even told Bulzaar how Father had always missed him. Bulzaar requested one of his servants to bring down the family portrait. He handed the portrait over to Mykha and we were getting on really well until...' A tear ran down Nova's cheek and she didn't finish the sentence.

'Until what, Nova?' I asked. Mykha put his arm around his sister and she began to cry.

'Everything was fine until Bulzaar's wife, Saniah, entered the room,' Mykha said. 'Saniah lost all colour from her face and asked us directly what we were doing in the castle. She glared at Bulzaar questioningly, as if implying he was wrong to be sitting having tea with us. She even gave Nerrah a filthy look and the smiles were wiped off their faces. Saniah kept telling everyone that nobody had the right to take anything from the castle.'

'How did you manage to leave with it?' Kal asked, momentarily glancing up. Kal gazed at the portrait of Zenofur and Arayan and started to scribble further details down in his beloved diary.

'Bulzaar apologised and took Saniah out of the room,' Nova said. 'Nerrah was kind enough to hush us out of the castle with the picture and apologised at how Saniah had acted towards us. She was unhappy to see us go upset but wished us all the best and told us to look after the portrait of our parents.'

'When we returned to our house after several days of travelling back from the castle,' Mykha explained, 'we hung up our portrait, and that very night we heard a crashing sound in the living room while we were asleep. We ran out of our bedrooms to see where the noise was coming from, and this is going to sound really strange, but we saw a black panther facing the mantelpiece, staring at the portrait of our parents.

'The panther turned towards us and his green eyes watched us closely. Without notice, in a whirlwind of black and grey dust, spiralling in mid-air in front of us, a woman wearing a long, black hooded cloak stood where the panther had been a split second earlier. She said she'd come to punish us for stealing Bulzaar's things, and she knew one day we'd try to overthrow him and take the throne.'

'Saniah… she must be using dark magic to change into an animal,' I said more to myself than the others.

Lena's face drained of all colour. I hoped hearing this about Saniah hadn't scared her; I didn't want her to feel like all hope was lost. Furthermore, Saniah was locked away in the caves and was now powerless, and there was no way she could hurt us.

'Saniah was so cold towards us, and we really thought she was going to kill us when she retrieved the crystals from her black robe,' Nova said. 'The crystals glowed bright as they rested on black material in the palm of her hands, and we thought we were going to be blinded with the intensity of the light. We could see black particles flying out of the crystals towards us and we couldn't escape. It was as if an unseen, powerful force had us rooted to the spot. We could feel our energy being drawn from us as it was being pulled into the crystals. We saw and felt our bodies change. We could see claws protruding from our fingernails and felt our tails thrashing the ground behind us, and then our legs changed. She just laughed at us and …' Nova broke down.

'Saniah said she didn't want to see us again, and we were cursed to look like this for the rest of our lives,' Mykha continued. 'She even said we'd never be accepted as royalty again because nobody would believe our story. She even took our dog with her, saying she had use for him, and we stood there and did nothing. We were helpless.'

'That creature you fought back in the forest… he was our dog, Dragmatus. Look at what she did to him,' Nova wept.

I could hardly believe the creature we'd faced used to be an innocent dog.

'We ran out to the villagers for help,' Nova explained, 'but they wouldn't believe our story. They thought we'd gone mad and were scared of us. Others thought we'd eaten the real prince and princess and wanted to hurt us. They started to threaten us and told us to leave the house before dawn, or they'd kill us. We fled into the forest and found this empty cottage to live in.'

'Thank you so much for sharing…' I was interrupted mid-sentence.

'No, we aren't finished yet, Heera,' Mykha said. 'If you want to get to him, we have a way. We'll help you to get into the castle, but just promise you'll do everything you can to stop him.'

'I'll give everything I have, Mykha. I need to find my family and get them back safe,' I said.

'As we were growing up, our father had planned many routes into the castle. He knew it was always best to have a secret entrance to the castle, in case of an enemy attack,' Mykha reminisced. 'There is a secret tunnel his trusted workers built, and we used it several times with our father when he wanted to escape from the castle without anyone knowing.'

'Are you sure the tunnel hasn't been found by anybody? We don't want to fall straight into the hands of the Fire Blades,' I asked.

'No, the tunnel is still secret and leads to the castle laundry room through the Caves of Arya. It's well hidden. We know it's still a secret because the Fire Blades never guard the entrance to the tunnel,' Mykha said gravely.

'Where's the tunnel?' I asked.

'Well, you'll have to wait until you're better, and we'll show you,' Mykha grinned.

We couldn't believe our luck. I turned to face Fergal and he smiled at me. I guess facing Dragmatus hadn't been such a bad thing, and I couldn't help but smile back.

CHAPTER 21

Down the Tunnel

Mykha, Fergal and Kal left the room, leaving Nova and Lena to take out the used cutlery and crockery. I tried to help them but Nova wouldn't let me; instead, she directed me to the other room.

'Noman was definitely referring to two Critanites living in the woods,' Kal said to Mykha as I entered the living room, 'and Morog said that Bulzaar would deal with them himself since they weren't joining his cause. I think he may be referring to you and Nova.'

'Please sit down, Heera, you must rest,' Mykha said politely, pushing a tall elegant chair towards me. 'Yes, Noman was talking about us. He did come to persuade us to join him in helping Bulzaar, but we refused. We know we'll have to face Bulzaar soon, and we aren't hiding from him. He knows where we live, and we wouldn't want our parents to be ashamed of us by hiding away.'

Nova and Lena pulled up chairs beside me and sat down and listened to Kal and Mykha. Fergal was sitting on a comfortable armchair and appeared to be dozing off. Nova gave him a blanket, which he gratefully accepted before he fell fast asleep.

I took in the room around me. It was very dark with mahogany furniture. The walls were made of long wooden oak panels and dimmed lights were fixed on the walls giving a dull glow to the spacious room. It was homely and snug.

I glanced behind me and saw a spectacular white marble fireplace littered with taper lit candles and a fire blazing in the grate. Directly above the fireplace, I saw the portrait of King

Arayan and Queen Zenofur peering over us. To my right, I saw three more closed doors leading off into other rooms.

'Heera,' Lena said, grabbing her spell book, 'I'm going to try to heal your wounds tonight. I've tried it on myself and it worked.'

'Brilliant, I hope it works on me too,' I replied.

We sat and talked for hours. Nova and Mykha asked me loads of questions about the human world, and I had a really hard time explaining what life was like in our world. They too, like Lena, had trouble understanding how a mobile or a TV worked.

'Mykha and Nova, can you take us to the tunnel tomorrow?' I asked.

'You're leaving already? You're not fully healed yet, Heera,' Nova said.

'I'm fine, Nova. We really need to make a move. If you don't mind, can we set out tomorrow?' I asked.

'If you're sure you're feeling better, we'll take you tomorrow,' Mykha said and the rest of the evening was spent talking about defeating Naaga to life in Kendolen without Bulzaar.

Nova, Lena and I decided to sleep in one room together, and Nova told us about her life in Cranwell Castle. So much laughter filled the room that even Mykha and Kal came in twice and told us to keep the noise down, which we took no notice of.

It was nice to see Nova laughing over the funny stories Lena was telling us about mishaps she'd had with practising spells. The night ended with Lena trying to heal my bruises and the spell really did work; I could move without wincing and I could feel my muscles relax.

When the lights went out in the room and the conversations between the three of us dwindled away, sleep came over me in tidal waves.

Fergal was the first to awake and woke us all at six o'clock. We each rushed to get dressed. The healing spells Lena had used on me worked wonders, and I could move without any pain in my body.

I found my sword lying under the bed covered in the sticky green blood of Dragmatus. Mykha found me cleaning the sword and admired the beauty of the blade, even asking me to show him a few moves. I shied away and he laughed as I flushed red.

Nova was hurrying around, trying to make porridge for us all and filling bags with fruit and pastries to give to us. It was decided that Fergal would accompany us to the tunnel and then return to Ruby in the tree house. Kal was rather glum after Fergal announced he'd be leaving.

By seven o'clock, we were ready to leave. 'Stay behind us,' Mykha instructed.

'How far is it?' I asked.

'Not too far. It's near where you met with Dragmatus,' Mykha replied.

Nova moved to the front to walk alongside her brother, shielding the four of us as we headed towards the location of the secret tunnel. It'd turned out to be a bitterly cold and frosty morning, and the rugged ground glittered with ice particles forming on the rocks.

Shortly, we arrived at the spot where we'd come face to face with Dragmatus. I recognised the huge boulders in front of us, as well as the steep stone slate hills beyond, and there was green blood spattered around.

Mykah led us up the steep hill, which was a challenge in itself. I could feel myself sliding back down as the slates shifted below me. Kal had to carry Fergal up the hill because he was struggling with his short stature, and Lena and I grabbed hold of each other as we attempted to reach the top. Mykha and

Nova waited for us at the top and held out their hands to pull us up.

Once over the hill, we came across an area covered with thousands of black slates and rocks, and a white cliff stood in the distance. Numerous, shadowy caves had formed in the cliff face. Mykah and Nova marched straight ahead, getting closer to the other side and veered off to the left of the cliff towards one of the caves.

There was enough room for us all to step into the dark cave. Once inside, we couldn't see anything, and I trod on Lena's foot. She howled out in pain and I apologised, 'Lena, I'm sorry. I can't see anything.'

'It's OK,' Lena replied hopping on one leg.

We could hear Mykha and Nova patting the back of the cave trying to find something. Lena dropped her rucksack to the floor and started to rummage around. She hurriedly lit a fire torch with her wand and bright orange flames lit up the cave. Lena passed the torch to Nova.

'Thank you, Lena. I'm glad one of us has come prepared. I just need to find the lever now,' Nova said.

Different shaped holes, some to fit your hand through and others you could put your head through, could be seen on the back wall of the cave. I wondered about the sheer amount of bugs they must be harbouring and shuddered at the thought of being covered in creepy crawlies.

'It's OK, I've found it,' Mykha said excitedly. 'Now everyone, please move back.'

We moved back slightly and I could see Mykha had his hand in one of the many holes. He was grabbing onto something and he moved his hand upwards; the bottom of the cave floor dropped down, revealing a platform leading into another part of the cave.

Kal steadied himself by placing his hands on the wall beside him, and Fergal, who was perched on Kal's shoulders, had his arms around his neck. Lena and I were not so lucky; we both came tumbling forwards and slid down the platform. Nova and Mykha already knew what was going to happen and steadied themselves.

Lena and I found ourselves in a dim open space where the ground was extremely wet and cold. Mykha and Nova, followed by Kal and Fergal, walked down the platform towards us carrying the fire torch, flooding the space with light. Our eyes opened wide; shimmering walls encircled us and directly in front of us stood a glittering tunnel. It seemed we'd entered a cave full of crystals and gems.

Mykha saw the looks on each of our faces and laughed. 'Our father wasn't going to make any old dirty tunnel now, was he?' he said.

'It's brilliant! What's the tunnel made of?' Lena asked.

'Crystallite rock. It forms the foundation of the Forest of Eedon and the surrounding areas. Look at this, you won't even need a light,' Nova said placing the burning torch at the entrance of the tunnel. The specks of silver within the bluish rock started to glow, and a blue light spread like wild fire through the tunnel.

Nova and Mykha stood silently, possibly reminiscing about the time they'd spent here with their beloved dad. They stepped into the tunnel and felt its glittering walls.

'How long till we get to the Caves of Arya?' Kal asked rather abruptly, scribbling away in his diary.

'It's at least a day's walk,' Mykha said. 'It's the easiest and quickest way to get into the castle. Once the tunnel starts to get darker and narrower, you'll need to keep quiet and listen for any movement from the other side of it. Don't forget other routes are known to the Fire Blades and may run parallel to this one, and they or the prisoners may hear you. The prisoners will report you for a shorter sentence, so please be careful. Good luck you three.'

Nova stepped forward to give us a tight hug.

'Thank you Nova and Mykha for saving our lives. We'll do our very best to stop him,' I said.

'We know you will,' Mykha said, with a reassuring smile, and both siblings moved towards the platform.

Nova told Fergal she'd be waiting for him inside the cave until he'd said his goodbyes, and with one last glance at us all, she left with Mykha. Lena and I gave Fergal a hug, thanked him and promised him profusely that we'd visit him as soon as we could.

'Heera, Lena, be careful out there. Remember what Hosemee told you and get those crystals to their rightful place,' Fergal said.

'We will, Fergal and thanks for everything,' I replied.

Fergal wiped away his tears and he turned his attention to Kal.

We both stood at the foot of the tunnel waiting for Kal; I knew Kal and Fergal would be better left alone to say goodbye as they were close. Within a few moments, we heard a noise like a door shutting and Kal re-joined us. I noticed he'd been crying. His eyes were red and watery, and he wouldn't look directly at us. I felt it was best to not draw attention to him being upset.

I decided to change the subject, 'What was that noise?'

'The platform was raised back. Mykha and Nova must've done it to close the entrance to this chamber,' he replied.

I felt my pendant begin to pulsate against my skin. I knew we were on the right track, and we started to make our way through the tunnel. The tunnel itself was warm. It wound its way upwards quite steeply to begin with, and sometimes it felt as though the tunnel was dropping further deeper into the ground. For the first few hours, it had been almost fun to walk through until the novelty of being in a secret tunnel was beginning to wear off as we walked for miles on end.

We stopped now and again to drink some water and to eat when we were hungry. We decided to call it a day when our legs began to ache, and we laid our sleeping bags in the middle of the tunnel.

'Heera, just think if your family are in the caves, you may get to see them,' Lena said as she laid her head down on a soft pillow, which she'd just plumped up before getting into her sleeping bag.

'I hope so, Lena,' I replied. Lena smiled and turned to look over at Kal, who was lying on his front, writing away in his diary. She narrowed her eyes.

'Kal, what ARE you doing?' Lena asked. 'You've ignored what Hosemee told you to do. It's because of *you* that we ended up hurt when we were attacked by Dragmatus. If you'd listened to him, you could've sensed danger... but as per usual... you had your head buried in that stupid diary of yours all day long. Even when we were taken by Jack, it was Heera who'd seen him first. You should've sensed his presence. What's your problem?'

I was taken aback at what Lena had said, and I certainly didn't blame Kal for what happened with Jack and Dragmatus.

I thought Kal would shout back, but he just looked at Lena and said in a low voice, 'Why don't you mind your own business, Lena? If you think I'm to blame for what happened with that IDIOT, Jack Webber and with Dragmatus, then you need to grow up. Who told you to go off wondering on your own when we encountered Dragmatus?'

Lena was livid.

'Please don't fight you two, not now, especially when we're so close...'

'Just ignore him, Heera. Let's leave him to write and read his stupid diary,' Lena snapped, 'because at the end of the day, we're going to be the ones who save him just like we've been doing since leaving Kendolen.'

Kal said nothing and returned to reading his diary again. Lena and I lay down and stared up at the tunnel ceiling in silence. I could hear Lena telling Iris to wake us up early the following morning. We all drifted off into a deep sleep in the tunnel as the fire torch we'd placed at the entrance slowly went out, plunging the tunnel into complete darkness.

I stirred awake and heard light whispering in the distance. It was Lena's voice.

'I can't do it Iris. I can't tell them. What will they think?' Lena asked.

'You can't lie to them dear, especially not Heera. She deserves to know what Hosemee told you,' Iris whispered.

'It may not be true and they'll only worry. I don't understand why my mother and father didn't tell me. And you, why didn't you say anything, Iris?'

'My dear, it wasn't my place to do so… you need to tell them.'

'No, Iris… I'll tell them when it's the right time. Now, I need to sleep. Be quiet or you'll wake them,' Lena whispered.

'But…'

'Goodnight, Iris,' Lena said.

'Goodnight, dear but you're making a mistake.'

I heard Lena tiptoe towards us. She made herself comfortable in her sleeping bag and was soon fast asleep.

I desperately wanted to know what Lena was hiding from us. It was obviously something very personal to her, and it would only be right for me to wait till she told me herself and in her own time. Hosemee must have given her some sort of advice about channelling her powers, like he had with Kal, and to be truthful, there was no need for me to suspect her of doing something wrong. I trusted both Kal and Lena.

Without their help, I wouldn't have made it this far. I tried to fall back to sleep. In the end I did, but not easily.

CHAPTER 22

The Caves of Arya

'Wake up everyone!' Iris said, loud enough to startle us.

'Huh... hmmmm... thanks... Iris... that'll be... alllll,' Lena yawned.

I opened my eyes, and I could feel the pendant beating gently against my chest. I automatically put my hand over it and prayed to Amunah to keep my family safe.

Lena lit a fire torch and placed it against the wall of the tunnel. Instantly, the tunnel returned to the ice blue colour we were accustomed to, allowing us to see what we were doing and where we were going.

Kal was out of his sleeping bag and avoided eye contact with us both. Lena kept giving him dirty looks.

'Heera... Lena, I'm sorry for the way I've been acting lately. I shouldn't have ignored what Hosemee had said to me, but I can't help it,' Kal explained looking slightly crestfallen. 'I find comfort in writing my thoughts down. It's almost like talking to a friend without being judged and ridiculed.'

'It's OK, Kal,' I replied and Lena stopped glaring at him.

'You need to try to do what Hosemee advised. You never know he might be right about channelling your powers,' Lena assured him.

'It's not that. It's just... you won't understand,' he said solemnly.

'You're frightened because you think you won't be able to control your powers like your mother has, aren't you?' I said.

Kal nodded silently.

'You should be confident, Kal. If your mother can do it, so can you,' Lena said. 'Even Felicity Shyre said you're powerful, but you just don't know it yet.'

'It's not only that though. I'm afraid I won't be good enough,' Kal explained. 'Don't you think I feel bad that you two save me every time? It makes me feel really inferior. Lena, you're brilliant with your spell work, and you're not even fully trained yet. And Heera, you may not have magical powers but Amunah chose you! Plus, your sword fighting is out of this world. As for me, I hide in my diary and books, and the little power I have, simply isn't good enough. I can't confide in anyone because I don't have any friends, and I find it hard to talk to you both.'

'Kal you're not inferior to anybody,' Lena said. 'We'll help you to realise your true powers and we can help you to control them too. We'll always be friends. We have a bond no-one can break, and we'll always help each other right, Heera?'

'Definitely,' I said.

Kal smiled, and for the first time, he happily put his diary away, took out the bronze coin Hosemee had given him and gripped it in his hands tightly in an attempt to channel his powers. We started to move forwards together as one and looked forward to what the day would bring.

The tunnel became more demanding with severe drops, sharp corners and steep uphill climbs as the day went on. It was tiring us out slowly, but we soldiered on for several hours.

I was about to mention to the others about having a little break and something to eat when Kal stopped in his tracks and whispered, 'Wait, there's someone up ahead.'

'Wow Kal, told you it would work,' Lena whispered back pointing at the coin in Kal's hand.

'No, I haven't had a reading. I can hear someone mumbling… shhhhh just listen,' he muttered.

We listened very carefully, and a feint mumbling voice could be heard up ahead. We moved towards the sound. With each step, the tunnel was getting narrower, darker and colder. We had to be somewhere in the Caves of Arya, and if Mykha and Nova were right, the mumbling sound could either belong to a prisoner or a Fire Blade.

The mumbling was getting louder, and we could make out words coming from a male disorientated voice. He sounded like he was sobbing, but in the next moment, he was screeching at the top of his lungs, 'LET ME OUT! LET ME OUT!'

I could sense the despair in the voice and it was difficult to concentrate. As we moved onwards, we came to a set of concrete stairs with almost fifty small steps leading upwards and towards the voice. I retrieved my sword from its sheath. Lena gripped her wand, and Kal tightened his hold on the coin Hosemee had given him. I led the way up the stairs, followed closely by Kal and Lena. We left the tunnel behind us.

There was a narrow gulley straight up ahead. The walls on either side of us were made of cold hard crumbling brick, and the smell of damp filled our lungs. We began to tiptoe through the gulley, and I noticed there were gaps between several of the bricks to my right, some large enough to see through.

I stopped to take a peek through the gaps, and Lena and Kal waited patiently behind me. I could make out thick iron bars directly on the other side of the wall and further in the distance, and I realised then the voice I'd heard was of a prisoner.

'LET ME OUT PLEASE!' the prisoner screamed again. I found a gap further down the brick wall where I could see the back of someone's head. He had his head in his hands and was taking deep long breaths. 'You filthy cowards, let me out! Show YOUR faces!' he shouted as he stood up peering out to someone outside of my vision. Nobody came forth, and the prisoner now turned around to face the brick wall. He had his eyes closed and continued to sob. I recognised him immediately.

'It's Tallon,' I whispered to Lena and Kal, who were equally startled.

I felt I was in a terrible internal dilemma; I didn't know whether to speak to him or not. What if the Fire Blades heard us talking? And what if Tallon somehow gave us away? Kal dropped the coin Hosemee had given him, and Tallon glanced up towards the brick wall, which concealed us from him.

He narrowed his eyes and whispered threateningly, 'Who's there? Are you spying on me? Don't have the guts to come face me... you really are cowards.' Tallon came right up to the wall and tried to peer through the small gaps, attempting to get a glimpse of someone who he thought was spying on him. Now was the perfect time to get his attention, with him being close to the wall, as I wouldn't have to shout.

'Tallon, it's me, Heera,' I whispered. Tallon was completely still and had his ears glued to the brick wall.

'Is that really you, Heera? What *are* you doing behind the wall?' he whispered back.

'I don't have time to explain. Lena and Kal are also here.'

'Tallon, where are the guards? We don't want to get caught talking to you, or our plan is going to go to waste,' Lena butted in.

'The guards aren't here, but please don't leave me here. Please, Heera take me with you. I'll try to get some of these loose bricks out from this shadowy corner, but you'll have to crouch down to talk to me.'

I didn't have the heart to refuse him. He began pulling out enough bricks for him to see us and for us to see into the prison cell. It was dirty and depressing. No wonder, Tallon was shouting for someone to let him out. When I thought of my family, I welled up, knowing they too were probably in a gloomy cell such as this. How would they ever recover from such an event?

'Tallon, have you seen Bulzaar?' Kal asked. I tried to focus and not get too emotional. I had to finish what I'd started.

'No, but the guards talk about him, claiming he's put plans into place to go to war with Kendolen. One of them said his most trusted spy has been working with him, somebody from Kendolen itself. What are you three doing here in the caves, anyway?'

'Well, we're here to stop Bulzaar and find Heera's family, but Tallon you can't tell anyone OK,' Lena whispered. 'We can't take you with us right now as we don't have much time. We promise you'll be set free soon.'

'Do you promise me, Heera?' Tallon cried. Lena was taken aback at how Tallon specifically asked me to promise him, but I didn't think anything of it.

'Yes, we all do,' I replied. 'Tallon, have you seen my family, at all?'

'No, Heera. I haven't even heard the Fire Blades mention them. I don't think they're in these caves,' Tallon said. I felt another pang go straight to my heart. They had to be somewhere in the castle, or he had turned them into Fire Blades. 'Heera, I know someone who can help you three, and she'll be…'

Tallon stopped whispering. We heard a heavy door opening and then closing and heavy thuds came towards us. I felt my pendant jolt, warning me of the approaching danger.

'Quick, hide in case they see you. They're back with Arya, who visits me every day,' Tallon whispered. 'She's kind, and the guards let her spend time in my cell because they want me to be quiet. She'll be able to help you.'

I wanted to throttle Tallon. He'd left out the fact that Bulzaar's daughter was being brought into his cell. The three of us froze. What if Tallon told Arya about us and then she told the guards? We were stuck now and couldn't do anything. I hadn't expected to see Arya at all; I assumed she'd be locked in a cell with guards watching her every move. I certainly didn't think she'd be able to meet with the other prisoners.

We heard Tallon get up and run to the bars on the other side of the cell. 'Arya, I had to see you,' he said. 'I was going mad with loneliness, and these beasts wouldn't listen to me.'

'Shut up you disgusting animal and get away from the bars! Princess Arya, you're free to go in the cell,' one grumpy voice said. We heard the sound of keys, followed by the sound of the door to the cell being flung open.

'Please, leave us alone,' a sweet voice said. The guards left, and a heavy thud again was heard as they closed the door behind them. 'Oh Tallon, my kind friend, look at you. Don't be so sad, I'm here now.'

'Arya, I can't take it anymore. I can't be locked away like this… It drives me mad,' Tallon's voice gave way to more tears. 'Those cowards say I'm a disgrace to my father, and they shout abuse and laugh at me all day. My father despises me because I'm different.'

Arya laughed and said, 'Well my father has had me imprisoned since I was a baby, and not even my own mother has bothered to come down and see me. Father allowed my mother and my grandmother to stay in the castle, and he left me here to rot on my own. Anyway, let's not talk about things we cannot change… we've only a couple of hours together.'

Lena and Kal seemed to relax a little. Arya didn't seem like a threat, but we couldn't be so sure yet.

'Arya, guess what?' Tallon said excitedly. 'Hang on, first you have to promise me you won't tell anyone, and you have to promise to help me.'

'Oh Tallon, I promise I'll help you. Who am I going to tell anyway? I only talk to you except for when Father and Grandmother come to see me. What's the matter?'

'I want you to meet some of my friends,' Tallon said rather proudly, walking over to the wall we were hiding behind, whilst Arya appeared rather confused. 'Heera, are you still there? Arya will help you, won't you Arya?'

'Yes... yes of course,' Arya replied, uncertainly. I think she thought Tallon had truly lost his mind.

We had no option but to step to the side and crouch down to look into the cell.

I found a petite, pretty woman sitting on a chair in the middle of the cell. She was puzzled and rather lost for words. Arya had black hair with large curls that fell around her pale face. She had hazel eyes, plump lips and wore a beautiful white dress, and although she'd spent nearly all her life as a prisoner, she was well groomed.

'Hi Arya, I'm Heera and this is Lena and Kal.'

'Hello. Tallon, what are they doing here?' she asked Tallon politely, who stood beaming at us all. 'It's not safe for them here, especially now my father is ready to go to war.'

'They're here to stop your father from going to war. You must help them, Arya,' Tallon suggested.

'Stop my father? But nobody can stop him, even Hayden lost against him,' Arya said.

'I'm here to find my family and I *have* to try and stop Bulzaar. Arya, do you know anything about my family? And would you know where in the castle they would be kept?' I asked.

'No sorry, I haven't seen them, and I don't know what the inside of the castle looks like to tell you where your family will be imprisoned. I've been down here nearly all my life.'

'Sorry, Arya,' I said. How could I be so stupid? Arya had been kept in these caves for most of her life, and I was so consumed with finding my family that I was asking her questions which, most probably, caused her a lot of pain.

'What about your mother and grandmother, where are they?' Lena asked.

'Initially, my father imprisoned Mother, Grandmother and me in these caves. He thought we were his weakness and would stop him from becoming powerful,' Arya said. 'Mother persuaded Father to let her back into the castle, and she's the one who's using the crystals to bring him to strength.

'My grandmother isn't a prisoner either. Mother wanted to humiliate her because she tried to stop her only son from following the path to destruction, and Mother has kept her as a slave. Grandmother tries to come and see me whenever she can and makes sure the guards treat me right. She even sent down four maids to take care of me since I was a child. She's like a mother to me, and to be honest, I can't even remember what my real mother looks like anymore.'

I felt sorry for Arya. I couldn't imagine how her parents could be so cruel, but at least she had her grandmother to speak to.

'Please don't kill him, Heera. It's those crystals that are changing him,' Arya said sadly.

'We'll do anything we can to stop him without hurting him, Arya,' I said. 'All I want is to return home with my family, and hopefully, you can have yours back.'

'Arya, how can they get inside the castle and not be found out?' Tallon asked. Arya fell silent in deep thought and then jolted up right in her chair and grinned.

'I have an idea! I think it may be your only option to get into the castle and blend right in and not get caught,' Arya said. 'You have to pretend to be servants. All three of you can go anywhere in the castle, and you only have to speak when spoken to.

'You aren't allowed to speak to each other, and when you're in the presence of my family, you have to look at the ground. Your faces must be covered with a thin veil at all times. These were all rules Mother ordered when she took control over the castle. I can get you uniforms, but you,' she pointed at Kal, 'will also have to wear what is given to you because I have no male servants taking care of me.'

Kal flushed red as he understood he'd have to wear female servants clothes; Lena turned away from him before she began to grin at his plight.

'I could always tell Grandmother, maybe she can help you.'

'No that's OK, Arya,' I said, 'please don't tell anyone anything. We don't want anybody in the castle to know about us because your mother may hurt them, thinking they were in on the whole plan.'

'Okay, you need to hide again,' Arya said. 'I'm going to call for the guards and request them to take me to my cell. I'll take three uniforms from my personal maids and bring them to you. Tallon, I'll say I'm bringing clothing for you because you're cold and that's why you always call for the guards. They won't suspect anything. They'll just be grateful I'm doing them a favour by keeping you quiet.'

'Actually, if you have a few blankets I could use them because it does get cold in here. Arya, you can even hide the uniforms inside the blankets,' Tallon suggested. The three of us hid again. We heard Arya call to the guards, and after a brief wait, they came and took her away.

'Where is she?' Lena whispered, after a good ten minutes.

'I have no idea. Arya didn't seem the type to tell on us,' Kal whispered back.

I heard heavy footsteps approaching and Tallon ran up to the bars. I heard the sound of the keys opening the cell door and Arya telling the guards to leave her again. We waited until the guards had disappeared before we crouched down. I saw Arya had an oversized royal blue blanket folded in her lap.

'Sorry I took so long. I had to wait for the guards to leave and had to send my maids to do errands for me while I rummaged through their drawers to get the uniforms,' she opened up the blanket and folded in the middle were three white uniforms for maids, complete with hats. She passed them to us, and she put the blue blanket around Tallon, who was sitting on the floor beside her chair.

'Thank you both but we must go now. We don't have much time. We have to follow this path and get into the castle,' I said. Tallon hung his head in sadness at the thought of us leaving, but Arya jumped up and came over to us.

'Good luck and please remember it's not my father who's bad… it's the power of the crystals that has changed him,' Arya said, tearfully. 'He's still my father despite what he's done. Please try not to hurt him. I really hope you find your family, Heera.' I realised Arya still loved Bulzaar even after the way he'd treated her.

'We'll do our best, Arya, and please take care of Tallon,' I said.

'We'll come and get you,' Kal said. 'My mother knew your family and she asked us to rescue you all from these dreadful caves.' Eliza had asked us to free Bulzaar's family and to make them confront him, but this was not possible at this moment in time. The only way was to defeat him first and then we'd rescue everyone.

'Thank you,' Arya said.

Tallon was bawling his eyes out and even Arya had tears running down her cheeks. With a last look at both their faces, we carried onwards. I was consumed with guilt having to leave them behind, as I'm sure Lena and Kal were.

CHAPTER 23

Dinner with the King

We hurried up more flights of stairs. We could hear terrible high-pitched screams and shouting from other prisoners on the other side of the wall as we passed their cells. I tried as hard as possible to block out the noise. It was deafening. Each shrill scream was filled with pain and desperation, and it was difficult to ignore the calls for help, but I had to focus on the task at hand.

The stairs led us to a narrow corridor. There was a tiny wooden door beyond, and I tried to gather as much courage as possible to walk through to the other side and step foot in Bulzaar's territory. Simply thinking about entering the castle made me shudder.

We changed our clothes before continuing. Our uniforms consisted of a billowing white dress, which came down to our feet, and an accompanying cloth hat with ribbons to tie below our chin. A veil had to be placed over our faces and tucked under the hat to hold it in place.

Kal didn't seem too pleased with the uniform. Lena assured him his face was well covered, and nobody would ever know he'd worn these clothes. Kal flushed red and went awfully quiet.

Lena used her spell book to shrink our bags, so they'd be hidden underneath our clothes. Lena explained, if we ever needed to use any of the items from within the bags and rucksacks, they'd appear in their original size once we'd pulled the item from the bag.

'Okay let's go. Remember to act as the others do and try not to talk. Let's stick together and rescue my family first,' I said.

'No, Heera, let's find the crystals first,' Lena suggested, 'and get them to the temple. If your family are here, it's better to keep them out the way for their own safety. Once we've stopped Bulzaar, we can come back and rescue them and everyone in the Caves of Arya.'

'Lena's right,' Kal agreed.

'But, that's my family…'

'We know, but the best place for your family is right here,' Lena said, 'while we get Bulzaar's ammunition away from him. And when you do fight him, he'll hopefully be much weaker as he won't have the power of the crystals helping him.'

It pained me to agree with them.

'OK, let's go,' I said and we made our way down the corridor. I reached the door first and took a deep breath. OK, this was it. Bulzaar's castle was on the other side, and I knew I had to go through the door, but I was terrified. There was so much depending on me and thoughts of failure plagued my mind. My pendant vibrated under my clothing, reminding me I had to finish what I'd started, and this was enough to make me push open the door slightly and ever so quietly.

We were staring down on a spacious, empty room with wicker baskets sprawled across the floor, full of laundry. There were a number of washbasins in the corner with a water pump nearby. I jumped down first, closely followed by Kal and finally Lena, who used her wand to close the tiny door behind us.

From where we were standing, you wouldn't have been able to tell there was an opening in the wall. It had been a clever disguise by King Arayan to secure the perfect route out of the castle; no-one would bother to come into this part of the castle, thinking it was only occupied by the maids and servants.

There was an open door on the other side of the room. I took the lead and headed up the stone steps that were dimly lit by lanterns fixed to the walls. The following room we entered erupted with noise and was clouded with steam. There were maids, bustling here, there and everywhere, carrying pots and pans over to the stove, while others were cutting up vegetables and meat.

'WHAT ARE YOU DOING?' a harsh voice shouted from the other end of the room. The three of us spun around quickly. It was over and we'd been caught. A tall, plump, big-shouldered woman was marching towards us with a meat cleaver in her hand. She was red in the face and was wearing a black uniform.

We cowered on the spot. As she came closer, we stared at the floor, but she went past us and headed straight for a young girl who was trying to cut up a chicken using scissors. 'WHAT is your name?' demanded the woman.

'It's Jenny… Doreen… Ma'am,' the little girl said in a meek voice. She too was staring at her feet and shivering from head to toe with terror.

'How dare you call me by my name? Only call me Ma'am,' Doreen sneered. 'Now listen you lot, I'm warning you. I only have to make one complaint and you'll be out of here in no time, and your families will be severely punished. You're lucky you're all still alive, or you would have met a fate much worse than this!'

Jenny was now crying her eyes out, and the scissors she was holding dropped out of her hands. 'Pick those up, right now, you useless girl and take a hold of this,' she said handing the meat cleaver to her. 'What nonsense, cutting up chicken with a pair of scissors, stupid brat. NOW, HURRY UP!'

Everybody went back to completing their individual tasks. All around us, pots were bubbling with food, and the head maid was watching everyone. I moved towards a table where the maids were making balls of pastry. Kal and Lena followed me closely. We didn't want to appear to be standing around being idle.

I picked up a rolling pin and started to roll out a ball of pastry. A voice right next to my ear screamed out, 'NOW WHAT DO YOU THINK YOU'RE DOING, MISSY?' It was Doreen.

'Rolling out pastry, Ma'am,' I replied confidently.

'Yes, I can see that... I'm not blind... but WHY?' Doreen barked. 'You know the pastry is for dessert, not for dinner. We're preparing dinner first! You stupid girl! I've just about had enough. You three step forward right now, oh yes don't think me stupid girls... I've seen you standing there doing absolutely NOTHING! Now you'll be made to work all evening, and you'll be the ones waiting on the King and his special guests while we finish the work and retire early for the night.

'BELINDA, get the serving trolley loaded! These good for nothing brats are taking food to the King. Once they meet him, they'll think twice about standing around doing nothing. NOW GO, you good for nothing lumps. I expect to see you working harder tomorrow, and yes... once you come back down, don't forget to wash up and collect the serving trolley from outside the Queen's room in the tower. Don't you even think of going in her room because she does not like to be seen.'

I was dreading meeting Bulzaar. What if he found out I was the one who Amunah had chosen to get the crystals to safety? I tried not to tremble at the mere thought of being in his presence. I knew I'd have to face him eventually, yet this seemed way too soon; we'd only just entered the castle moments earlier.

We walked over to Belinda, who was equally as rude as Doreen. Belinda was busy loading up a trolley full of delicious smelling food; there was roast lamb, roast potatoes, a gravy boat with thick brown gravy, all sorts of vegetables, and a big pitcher of ale.

'You'll have to set the table in the dining room,' Belinda said, 'which you'll find down the corridor to the left, at the top of the grand staircase. You must wait for the King and his guests to arrive, and you may only leave once they've asked you to. Make sure you bring down the cutlery and dishes from outside the Queen's chamber.'

Belinda nearly pushed the trolley into the three of us; Kal stopped it before the food and crockery toppled over.

'Where is the Queen's chamber?' I asked with my head down.

'At the top of the highest tower in the castle,' Belinda smirked. 'Go through the door opposite the grand staircase and it'll be an upward climb from thereon girls. You're in for a tough evening. It's a good lesson for being lazy… don't forget you'll have to clean up all our dishes too, and before you even ask, you will NOT be allowed supper tonight.'

Kal took hold of the trolley and pushed it. Lena and I directed it from the front and we headed towards the exit. We came to a standstill before a set of high, spiralling stairs, and directly to the left of us, we noticed a dumbwaiter lift, which would help us to take the food trolley from one floor to the next. The lift had a wheel lever attached on the outside to operate it.

Kal pushed the trolley into the modest space, shut the door and spun the wheel to the right, and we could hear the trolley being lifted from the ground.

'That should do it,' he whispered after the wheel wouldn't turn anymore.

We went up the spiral staircase and retrieved the trolley and pushed it over a thick red carpet covering the floor of the hallway. Candelabras, colourful vases and ornaments were placed upon the wooden, antique furniture resting against the dark maroon coloured walls.

At the other end of the hallway, we came to a grand staircase, lined with the same red carpet. Kal found another dumbwaiter lift close by and pushed the food trolley inside and began to spin the wheel. The stairs led up to a further set of smaller staircases; one set veering to the left corridor and the other to the right.

I noticed the door which led to the tower, but Lena and I, continued up the staircase and admired the crystal chandelier hanging down from the high ceiling. Kal hurried past us and busied himself with collecting the food trolley at the top of the second set of stairs leading to the corridor on the left.

So far, the castle reminded me of being inside one of the many stately homes I'd visited with my family over the years. Every object, whether it was flowers, a chair, or a painting, was in its rightful place. Everything appeared to be immaculate; it did not appear to be the home of a monster.

Kal whispered, 'Heera, Lena, let's go. We still have to set the table… the dining room should be down here according to Belinda… come on.' Kal led us down the corridor to the left whilst pushing the trolley. It was strange seeing Kal take the lead in Bulzaar's castle; I expected it to be Lena or me and yet we tiptoed behind him.

We found the enormous dining room. A huge table was occupying the middle of the room, and there were lit candelabras hanging down from the ceiling, making the gold cutlery gleam on the table. Kal began unloading the trolley and setting the food on the table.

A door from the farthest corner of the room opened; I took a deep breath and stared down at the ground. I was consumed with fear. How could I forget Bulzaar was a monster, inhuman, and he didn't care about anyone? I could feel myself shake and my heart thumped. The pendant was hot against my flesh.

Soft footsteps came to a standstill before us and a kind voice spoke, 'Thank you girls… Bulzaar's on his way with his guests. You don't have to wait around. There's a screen you can stand behind over there, and you only have to come out when they call for you.'

The kind woman led us to the opposite side of the room; we had to be careful not to look at her. We could see her dragging three chairs behind a black screen from the corner of our eyes. The three of us took a seat behind the screen and were out of sight until we'd be called upon.

The door opened once again and my pendant went crazy. Not only was it thrashing against my skin under my clothes but I could feel the chain twisting around my neck. A cold chill filled the room. Heavy steel footsteps crashed on the flooring and a hoarse male voice spoke, 'Mother, are you in here?'

Lena and Kal were paralysed with fear, knowing they were in the presence of evil. We could've retrieved our weapons, but we knew we couldn't stand up to him right now. All we could do was sit and wait and hope we didn't get caught.

'I'm over here,' Nerrah answered softly. We realised now it was Nerrah who'd met us in the dining room. I felt sorry for her because even Bulzaar had imprisoned her at one time, but she still greeted him as if he was a normal man. I could hear Bulzaar's breathing; it was heavy and raspy and made my skin crawl.

'Mother, join us for dinner,' Bulzaar said.

'You know I can't, Bulzaar. Saniah will never let me. She doesn't want me to spend time with you, and I don't like you like this. You should never have become this… this monster. When was the last time you saw, Arya?' Nerrah sounded really disappointed in her son.

'Arya?' Bulzaar asked, if trying to remember who Nerrah was referring to.

'You've forgotten your own daughter, how shameful, Bulzaar?' Nerrah said. 'You really need to wake up and stop Saniah from ruining you further. There's still time left.' Nerrah was interrupted by the door opening and more footsteps could be heard entering the dining room. The footsteps came to a halt, rather abruptly.

'Will you ask Saniah to see me, Mother? I haven't seen her in years. Will she bring those crystals to me? I don't know how she can simply take my crystals from me, and she even took the ones that were only recently brought to me,' Bulzaar croaked.

'How many times do I have to tell you, Bulzaar? She doesn't want to see you, even I'm afraid to bring up the subject. She would never listen to me anyway. I am nothing more than both your slaves,' Nerrah said as her voice broke down. 'I only live for Arya and in the hope you'll change your evil ways. As for those crystals, she'll not let you have them again after you imprisoned her... she certainly won't make the same mistake twice, Bulzaar. She's cunning... she recently took the three crystals from your room when you began your training a few days ago. Saniah wants full control over your destiny, and I hope someone destroys those crystals before you cause more harm to the kingdom.'

'NOOO! Don't you DARE say that mother! I will k... k... kill... NO... NO, I didn't mean that Mother,' Bulzaar seethed as we heard him taking further steps towards her. Nerrah shrieked and we heard her hurrying out of the room.

'NO MOTHER, DON'T GO! Why don't you understand?' Bulzaar shouted. Bulzaar kicked something in anger at his mother leaving and he began to laugh. 'No-one will destroy those crystals, Mother, not even you,' he said sinisterly.

'Is everything OK?' a familiar voice said. We'd all heard this voice before and we were trying to recall whose it was.

'Yes, both of you sit, eat, and tell me what news you bring,' Bulzaar commanded. I gathered there were two guests who had entered the room, but the second guest had not as yet spoken.

'Everything is in order back in Kendolen, and they have no idea I'm going to lead them straight to you,' the man laughed.

'Landon, my friend, sorry I haven't been able to spend time with you. I'm still trying to regain my strength… the power is too much to bear,' Bulzaar said. 'Thankfully, Agatha Oak didn't see you for what you truly are on the day you met with Morog and Bastian in Gentley Woods, or our plan would've failed. If only you'd realised Agatha and the girl were watching you the whole time during the secret meeting, the Fire Blades could've killed Agatha and brought the girl to me straightaway.'

I couldn't understand the betrayal. Why would Landon be so cruel and betray Kendolen? For how long had he been working for Bulzaar? Kal and Lena appeared to be even more shocked. After all, they thought they knew him and trusted him with his position as an Elder. I found it hard to believe an Elder who was in charge of protecting the town had simply left those very residents to be brutally harmed or even killed by Bulzaar.

'I didn't enter those woods as me. I transformed into a fox, and no-one would suspect a fox entering the woods now, would they?' Landon laughed, clearly trying to impress Bulzaar. 'No-one knows I'm a Vallaar. Can you actually believe they let a creature like me become an Elder? They only see what I want them to see.'

'Well done, Landon, I always knew you could be trusted, and thank you to your friend, Magmus Nessell. Oh dear she still doesn't know where she is, does she?' Bulzaar laughed coldly. Magmus Nessell was the third person present in the room and still she hadn't spoken a word.

'No, she won't recover anytime soon. The power of the crystals was too much for her, and the thought of losing her family has also driven her insane, isn't that so Maggie?' Landon mocked, however, Magmus didn't reply.

'They still don't suspect anything?' Bulzaar asked of Landon.

'No, they still believe Maggie is behind the whole thing. I'd hoodwinked her, and she crossed the barrier with the crystals and gave them to your waiting Fire Blades. They brought her and the crystal here straightaway using Dragmatus, while I played the innocent victim of betrayal.

'They think Maggie waited in Gentley Woods and went after Agatha and Heera, the night they left Kendolen, when it was in fact me. Heera was too quick but at least I managed to stop Agatha going with her. By the time Agatha had gained consciousness, I was nowhere near her, and as for coming out of Kendolen, I offered to go out and search for Heera Watson and the other two teenagers who left with her.'

I knew then I had been right in thinking there was a possibility that more than one person was involved in betraying Kendolen when Mrs Oak had been attacked. It all made sense now, and poor Magmus had no idea she had been used to betray a town, which was now in complete danger.

'I convinced the residents to allow Oliver Brooke, an accomplished tracker and warlock to come with me,' Landon gloated. 'Parmona and Akaal were keen to let me go, thinking I'd hold up their pathetic training of the residents. I told them we'd come back once we had any information, but I haven't been back. It's been four days now.'

'Oliver Brooke? Where is he?' Bulzaar asked.

'Four-letter word, my friend… starts with the letter D and ends with D,' Landon laughed. 'I told him I'd meet him in Gentley Woods, but Agatha Oak, the meddling hound, sent him to my house to help me gather my belongings, and the boy saw me strolling around, fit as a fiddle, without my walking stick from the window. He stuck around and saw my true reflection in the mirror in my bedroom. Luckily, I saw him too and the poor boy didn't make it out of Kendolen.'

Bulzaar laughed heartily before speaking, 'I need that girl, Landon. I must finish her once and for all… only then will I have ultimate power of the crystals to open a portal for Raven.

I have the Fire Blades searching the kingdom for her and her supposed friends, but still there's no sign of her. If she was dead, I know I'd feel it.'

'Heera Watson is an ancestor of Hayden and she shouldn't be underestimated, Bulzaar,' Landon said.

'She will be no match for me. Her biggest weakness will be her family and she will come to me herself. Once, the plan is enforced, Raven will enter this Kingdom and I'll rule alongside him.'

The following hour was filled with petty talk between the two about how they'd make Fallowmere obey Bulzaar. They were taking their time eating and drinking, and not a single word had been said by Magmus Nessell.

Bulzaar was cold, hostile and over confident. I wanted nothing more than to burst his bubble. The way he spoke about the kingdom made my blood boil. At one point he even suggested using innocent young creatures to fight for him in battle.

Landon was agreeing and egging him on, and I listened with hatred in my heart for them both. At least Bulzaar wasn't pretending to be evil. Landon, I believe was even worse than the King, a two faced, slimy brute, who I hoped would get his comeuppance.

'Oi, we've finished! Clear the table,' Bulzaar barked. We slowly came out from behind the screen and were careful not to look up at the table.

Kal swiftly brought over the trolley to the table, and we hurriedly started to empty the contents of the table onto the trolley to take back down with us. I was standing in between Bulzaar and Landon, and I felt I couldn't breathe. The pendant was throbbing violently against my chest, and my heart was racing.

I felt Bulzaar's eyes on me. I wondered whether he'd noticed or sensed the pendant beating under my clothing. Fortunately, he continued to talk to Landon.

'So this girl then, we know she's Hayden's ancestor, but who are the other two?' Bulzaar asked casually, as the three of us collected dirty plates and cutlery off the table. I could see Magmus from the corner of my eye; she sat on the other side of Landon, completely rigid. I wondered if she even knew where she was.

'Lena is the daughter of powerful warlocks, and the other is Kal, the son of a vampire and a gifted Seer,' Landon said.

'Not even Morog has seen these two accomplices. They must not have made it passed Naaga or the spies in Morden Village, or they could've met with the unknown warrior,' Bulzaar said.

'Warrior?' Landon asked, intrigued.

'He's been spotted near Morden Village. He's responsible for killing Naaga, and recently Dragmatus was attacked near the caves, and I think he may be behind it,' Bulzaar said coldly. 'The Fire Blades are searching for this mysterious warrior. I need to know who he is and I have word he's from Kendolen.' The trolley was now loaded and we were about to push it out.

'WHERE ARE YOU THREE GOING?' Bulzaar shouted and we jumped with terror. 'We're not finished yet! Get back behind the screen and serve our new visitors when they arrive. Landon, I would like you to meet the guests… Morog has gone to collect them and will be here any minute now.'

Before we could return behind the screen, the door opened and shouting could be heard. 'GET IN HERE!' Morog said and it sounded like he'd pushed the new guests into the room because they landed on the floor with a thud.

'Come, Morog. Maids, don't just stand there, get drinks for all of us!' Bulzaar laughed. We rushed forwards and filled golden goblets with ale. My heart sank when I saw Nova and

Mykha on the floor before us. 'Don't worry maids, they won't hurt you. Come forward with the drinks. Landon, these two ugly monsters are my step brother and sister.' We had to step over them to place the drinks on the table.

'Oh, but they are… Critanites,' Landon said.

'Yes, they've been cursed by Saniah,' Bulzaar laughed hysterically.

We walked back towards Nova and Mykha. As I passed Nova, I had my back towards the main table and I lifted my veil slightly to indicate to her that we were pretending to be maids. Nova and Mykha peered up just in time, and I winked at them and put my finger over my mouth to stop them from acknowledging me.

I could see Morog from the corner of my eye. I didn't have the courage to look directly at him; I remembered how Arya had told us the maids at Cranwell Castle had to keep their heads down, and I couldn't risk glancing up. The three of us went back behind the screen.

'Where did you find them?' Bulzaar addressed Morog.

'I went to their cottage yesterday and gave them your message,' Morog explained, 'and when they didn't cooperate, well I brought them to you as you instructed me to.'

'And who's that behind you, Morog?' Bulzaar asked.

'Oh him… he's going to join our cause. I found him at the cottage with Mykha and Nova and I brought him in to train for battle… goes by the name of Jack Webber, and that's all I could get out of the weasel.'

My heart began to race. What was Jack doing here? Why was he caught in Mykha and Nova's cottage? I tried to think of a possible connection between them, but my mind was so clouded that I couldn't think straight. Kal and Lena, who weren't so keen on Jack, appeared to be worried. I waited with bated breath for more information about him.

'Morog, you've blindfolded him and gagged him! No wonder I couldn't hear him,' Bulzaar laughed.

'Best thing for him, Bulzaar! He has a big mouth, and since he had the nerve to be dressed like a Fire Blade, he must now learn to fight like one,' Morog said.

'Ungag him, Morog. Let's see what he has to say for himself,' Bulzaar demanded.

I could hear some shuffling and some footsteps draw nearer.

'LET ME GO!' Jack shouted.

Bulzaar cackled and said, 'Where are you from? And what were you doing dressed as a Fire Blade in my filthy step siblings' cottage?'

'I don't have to tell you anything and nor will I,' Jack replied defiantly.

'How dare you speak to the Dark King in this manner!' Morog threatened.

'Morog, have you forgotten what you once were?' Jack asked. 'You used to be human and THAT so-called Dark King of yours has ruined you. How can you be so blind?'

'HOLD YOUR TONGUE, BOY!' Bulzaar flared up and complete silence fell in the room. His voice shook me to the core; Kal almost fell off his chair and Lena clutched at her heart. 'Morog, tell him how we treat disobedient guests at Cranwell Castle.'

'No, please don't,' I heard Nova plead.

We heard a loud sharp sound, followed by a deafening thud, and Nova burst into sobs.

I stood up. Jack had been hurt and I had to do something. Lena and Kal grabbed my hand and pulled me back down into my chair and shook their heads.

'Now's not the time,' Lena whispered.

I could do nothing to help him, and it was killing me having to act like nothing had happened.

'Once we've finished here, take him to the battle ground, Morog,' Bulzaar demanded. 'Leave him in chains throughout the night, and tomorrow, I'll transform him into the cold hearted beast, he was pretending to be. It's not only filthy humans I can transform into Fire Blades... I can turn any creature or magical being. And from this moment forward, anyone who disobeys me, WILL become a Fire Blade.'

Bulzaar cackled to his heart's content.

'No, please, Bulzaar, don't turn him into a Fire Blade,' Nova said.

'SILENCE!' Bulzaar bellowed. 'Well then, my dearest brother and sister, tell me, are you going to join me in taking down Kendolen? If not, then you'll go down with them.'

'No way will we join you, Bulzaar, and soon you *will* meet your match,' Mykha threatened.

'Oh really, little brother, where is this match? I'm waiting for whoever wants to stop me,' Bulzaar laughed.

'Bulzaar, there's still no sign of Heera Watson and her friends,' Morog said. 'We need to increase security in and outside the castle. We shouldn't take Heera and the other two lightly. I mean for all we know, the three of them could be in this very room and we may not even know about it.'

Bulzaar laughed before continuing, 'So you mean to say, Morog, those maids could be the three missing brats from Kendolen? Let's see, shall we. You three come back out and show us your faces.'

We stared at each other in horror; we knew we were no match for Bulzaar and Morog. We'd have to come clean and just hope Landon wouldn't recognise us. We had to do as he said or Bulzaar would get suspicious. We emerged from behind the screen, trembling from head to foot.

I could see the look of horror on Nova's face, but Mykha was seething with anger. I saw Jack lying face down on the floor a few feet away and there was a pool of blood under his head. I wanted to run to him. What kind of person was I to leave someone who was hurt and not do anything to help them? Lena was right in that this was not the right time to act, and even if I did something now, Bulzaar would kill me.

Mykha began to laugh like a mad person and said, 'You really are stupid. If you only knew what you really are up against, you wouldn't waste your time on those missing teenagers because they're all dead. Amunah's new chosen warrior killed them along with Naaga, and he can't wait to meet you Bulzaar.'

'You're lying Mykha because the only way Amunah chooses a new warrior is if they touch the crystals and those crystals are in my possession. Nice try!' Bulzaar said.

'Oh so you honestly think that the rules Amunah put in place to choose a warrior can't be changed?' Mykha said. 'It turns out, Amunah was wrong about Hecra. She was selfish and wanted to use the crystals to rule Fallowmere, so Amunah stopped guiding her. We saw a man kill her, and when he took her pendant, the light from it almost blinded us. The pendant has power too and it seems that's how Amunah's chosen his new warrior. Of course, this way, you won't have heard his name being called out because he didn't touch the crystals. You should be preparing to lose, Bulzaar because the warrior will defeat you.'

Mykha cackled, and Nova rolled her eyes towards the exit of the dining room. We took the hint and left with the trolley now that the attention of the room was diverted.

'Where is he now? Why should we believe you?' Morog asked. 'We've searched everywhere for him and we can't find him anywhere.'

'You're not looking hard enough,' Mykha said confidently. 'He's a powerful warlock sent by Amunah to destroy all of you, and he can hide anywhere he likes and disappear whenever he wants. You don't have to believe us, but who killed Naaga, and why haven't those teenagers been found?'

I knew Mykha was lying to Bulzaar about this mysterious warrior. Initially, it was a lie which Fergal had told Morog back at the camp, and if Bulzaar actually believed Mykha, then it would take his attention off the three of us for the time being. I waited to find out what Bulzaar's reaction would be to Mykha's lies.

'THAT'S ENOUGH!' Bulzaar barked. 'Heera Watson can't be dead! Morog take Mykha and Nova with you and scour the land to find this warrior and Heera Watson. I'll kill everyone if I have to, but I need to have full control over those crystals,' Bulzaar continued. He had obviously believed Mykha's story for now and was sending Morog to find the warrior and me. 'Dragmatus is still healing from his wounds, so you'll have to take another beast with you if you want to fly. Landon, we need to get ready and prepare for battle.'

This was the last thing I heard Bulzaar say, and when we were outside the door with the trolley, I couldn't resist glimpsing back at him through my veil. I saw him for the first time in flesh and blood, and he looked exactly as he had done in my nightmares. Lena and Kal took turns to have a glimpse of him and shuddered at what they saw.

He had dark features. Black hair obscured his blood-red eyes and his face was gaunt and full of hate. He frightened me beyond belief. He was wearing thick metallic armour like the Fire Blades, and he picked up his goblet and took a swig of ale, which ran down the sides of his mouth. He simply wiped away the fluid with his weighty bruised hand. He loomed over his guests, and when he exhaled, I could see his cold breath on the air.

As for Landon, he was full of youth and didn't resemble the Elder we'd seen in Kendolen. He was ecstatic. He had a slimy grin on his face and was bouncing on his heels, and his unkempt blonde quiff was obstructing his eyes. I saw him roughly pulling Magmus off her chair with great force, and I thought she'd lose her footing and tumble with the way he was treating her.

Morog pulled Mykha and Nova off the ground and pushed them towards the door at the far end of the room. He picked Jack up and flung him over his shoulder. I could see blood trickling down his pale face, and I hoped I'd be able to do something to help him. Each of them left through the door and the dining hall became empty once more.

We were running out of time. We had to find the crystals and Saniah quickly.

CHAPTER 24

The Panther's Cage

We dared not speak to each other. We went back down to the kitchen with the trolley; all the kitchen staff had retired for the evening. We emptied the trolley and Lena washed the dishes including the kitchen staffs' by using a cleaning spell, and in no time, we were ready to go up to the tower.

We climbed the staircase leading away from the kitchen and followed the hallway to the door, which Belinda had mentioned to us. The black door that led to the tower was opposite the grand staircase. The door seemed menacing, almost as if it was daring us to open it. I turned the gold doorknob, and with a backward glance at the spectacular staircase, we entered a dimly lit corridor. I shut the door behind us.

We followed the daunting corridor and came to a spiral staircase, leading both upwards and downwards. I led the way upstairs, followed by Kal and Lena.

Soon enough, we stepped off the staircase and found ourselves in another dark corridor. Six closed doors were on either side of us. There was a double window at the end of the corridor, and although it was dark outside, we saw the shadowy outline of a mountain to the left of the window.

'Mount Orias,' I whispered. It was so high that we couldn't even see the peak.

'How will we climb that?' Kal gulped.

'Let's find the crystals first and we can worry about that later,' I replied.

I looked down and could make out hundreds of cabins with no windows. This had to be where Bulzaar's army was billeted. Exactly how many soldiers did this monster have?

It was so quiet that you could've have heard a pin drop in the silence. The corridor was completely bare; there were no portraits or furniture in this part of the castle. We turned a corner and saw the trolley we had to collect at the bottom of a staircase, meaning the staircase led to the tower and the crystals.

We grabbed the trolley and wheeled it back down the corridor where we'd seen the closed doors. There was no way we were going to go back down to the kitchens. I stood at the first door, next to the window and listened to make sure I couldn't hear any movement in there, and when I didn't hear any sound, I quietly opened the door to find a pitch black room.

With the help of Lena and her wand, casting light into the room, we saw hidden objects concealed in sheets and littered with dust. The room appeared to be used for storage. Kal pushed the trolley into the room and we closed the door behind us, proceeding swiftly to the staircase leading to the tower.

At the top of the tower, in front of a stained glass window at the far end of the landing, there was one glowing candle placed on a ledge. A single door was visible and the silver doorknob was shaped like a panther's open mouth.

I remembered Mykha and Nova had seen a black panther in their house, the night Saniah had cursed them to look like Critanites. The three of us stood still, facing the door with apprehension.

Kal was nervous. He took out the coin Hosemee had given him and clutched it to his chest, and Lena's hand was in her pocket, holding onto her wand for dear life. I could feel my sword in its sheath underneath my clothes; it would remain hidden until I had to use it.

After staring at the handle, I turned to Kal and Lena and whispered, 'I'm going to open it.'

I gently turned the doorknob and pushed the door open quietly. At the same time, I took a deep breath in case Saniah would hear my breathing. To my surprise, the room was almost dark with barely enough light filtering through from the second, slightly ajar, door on the other side of the room.

We closed the door behind us and tiptoed on the carpet, getting closer towards the second door.

My pendant began to vibrate and I put my hand over it to keep it still. I didn't need the distraction at such a time. We tiptoed past tables and armchairs, and as we came closer to the other end of the room, we could hear a sharp female voice.

We peeked through the gap in the door. We could see the figure of a woman, wearing a black hooded cape facing the other way. She was sitting in front of a dressing table and was wrapping something away in black material. I couldn't believe it. Here was Saniah, a few feet from me, the woman who'd ruined so many lives.

'IT'S NOT FAIR!' Saniah vented her anger by thumping her fist on the table before her. 'If only we can catch and kill Heera Watson, only then will Bulzaar be impossible to defeat, and he'll finally fulfil his destiny.'

'No, you have to stop him,' a second kinder and quieter voice said from the corner of the room. 'Don't you remember how he was the last time he had this much power? Poor Arya, you're keeping the poor girl from her own father.' I knew the voice to be of Nerrah as it was rather subdued. Unfortunately, we couldn't see Nerrah from where we were hiding.

'Raven WILL be brought back! NOW QUIET!' Saniah shouted. 'I need to speak with him.' Saniah pointed her hand in the air towards the direction of Nerrah and she immediately fell silent.

Saniah stood up and placed the items in the black cloth in a cupboard beside her dressing table. I knew those had to be the crystals because she had to wrap them in material, or she would be burned if she touched them. Saniah retrieved a gold goblet from the drawer of her dressing table and placed it on the table. She then retrieved a beaker full of red liquid and filled up the goblet. Immediately, the goblet started to shake and thick, pungent, green smoke was pouring out of it.

Saniah was talking into the goblet and yet nobody could be heard responding back, 'Everything is arranged, Raven. I will not disappoint you, Raven... yes... the crystals are safe with me. Once Bulzaar has full control over the crystals and Fallowmere, he'll open the portal and you will return to where you rightfully belong. It won't be long now... you have my word.'

My pendant began to beat violently against my chest. I couldn't hear Saniah talking anymore. Instead Amunah spoke to me, 'Heera, take the crystals and bring them to me. He cannot return and spread his poison over Fallowmere. Bring them to me or else all will be lost. Don't be afraid, Heera... I will guide you to me. Hurry my child.'

I was no longer standing. Kal and Lena were crouching next to me; thankfully, Saniah hadn't noticed the disruption going on behind her door. Amunah's voice had brought me to my knees, and I couldn't think straight. His voice was still swimming through my body.

I needed to focus on the situation at hand. I took off my pendant and put it in the pocket of my dress, and the vibrations subsided for now.

Kal pulled me up and tried to push me into a dark corner because Saniah was about to come through the door we were crouching behind.

'I'll be back. I need to check everything's in order in the castle and make sure the Fire Blades are well rested,' Saniah said as she whisked through the door into the room where Lena and Kal were trying to silently steady me against a wall. Saniah didn't even turn on the light and hurried out of the main door.

I came to my senses as it dawned on me there was no greater time than the present to take the crystals from the cupboard and to rescue Nerrah from Saniah's clutches.

We entered the Queen's chamber.

I noticed a second standing glass cupboard as I entered the room. The cupboard was crammed with glass jars filled with various ingredients. There were no labels on the jars; they simply had pictures of grotesque images of humans and creatures transforming into hideous monsters on the front.

'This is some powerful magic, Heera. Saniah is a monster,' Lena said to me as she examined the labels on the jars.

'Heera, Lena... I think you need to come over here right now. We have a problem,' Kal said from the other side of the room.

I could see he was crouching down on the floor next to Nerrah, who was unresponsive and lying on a mattress on the ground, despite there being a king size bed in the corner. We rushed over and I couldn't believe what I saw.

We were staring down at a pallid unrecognisable face. The woman was skeletal; her face was sunken and her hair was completely white, yet she didn't seem old enough to be Bulzaar's mother. Her clothes were filthy, and it seemed this woman had not seen the light of day in decades. It became clear to me that this was in fact Saniah.

Although we hadn't seen Nerrah's face in the dining room, the way she ran out of the room when Bulzaar had shouted at her, showed she was strong unlike the woman before us. Saniah was the one who was being held prisoner and Nerrah was the one who'd been using the crystals to control Bulzaar.

'We need to wake her up and find out what's been happening in the castle. I can't believe this,' I said while trying to shake Saniah awake.

'Let me try something,' Lena said as she pointed her wand at Saniah. Lena closed her eyes and muttered under her breath, and instantly water poured from the wand and splashed over Saniah's face.

Saniah began to stir as the water sprinkled over her eyes, and she tried to get up but couldn't. Her arms wouldn't lift up from the mattress, no matter how hard she tried. It was as if something unseen was holding her down and was restricting her movements.

Kal touched Saniah's hand and quickly let go. He opened up his hand and stared down at the coin Hosemee had given him. 'Can you two see the things that are tying her down?' he asked in horror.

'No why? How can you see them?' Lena asked, trying to squint to see if she could see anything. Even I couldn't see anything.

'No I can't see them myself,' Kal said, 'but with the help of Hosemee's coin, I've managed to see through her eyes. The ropes she's tied down with are living breathing things, like black serpents with no faces, and they taunt her. It's horrible and we have to do something.'

Instinctively, I pulled the pendant out of the pocket of my uniform; it jolted in my hand, filling the room with an intense light.

Saniah sat up straight, moving her arms freely, and she gazed into the light and started to cry. 'Thank you! Thank you!' Saniah wept. 'I'm sorry, Amunah, I couldn't do anything to stop her.'

Saniah managed to stand up and was only focused on the intense white light shining above her. She hadn't even noticed the three intruders in the room.

Lena and Kal shut their eyes. I looked on as Saniah was communicating with the light. I didn't have to close my eyes, and I could feel an immense sense of power rushing through my body. The pendant was pulling me upwards, and the light was hovering above me now.

The light vanished just as it had come, and Saniah stood completely alert on her feet, moving her arms without any restraint. Lena and Kal opened their eyes cautiously; Kal stepped forward and touched Saniah's hand. 'They're gone and she's no longer bound,' he said.

'Amunah's freed me after all these years,' Saniah exclaimed. 'I know who you are and why you've come here. Amunah has told me everything. You're the ones who are destined to stop her and you'll have to do it quickly.'

'Why is Nerrah doing this? Why is she so intent on bringing back true evil to Fallowmere? Who and what is she?' I asked all at once. Lena stood guard near the door in case Nerrah came back, and Kal, on cue, retrieved his diary and pen out of his backpack and waited for Saniah to speak.

'I don't know where to start, Heera, but all the stories that have been told about me are all vicious lies. I had no idea the crystals could be used for dark magic. Nerrah misled me.'

'What happened, Saniah?' I asked whilst putting my necklace back on and the pendant rested against my chest once more.

'Nerrah always kept to herself. She was pleasant and loving towards me, even though she never shared anything with me about her life. All she cared about was Bulzaar and her parents. Bulzaar and I married and started our own family, and Nerrah became very attached to Arya and would do anything for her.

'After we moved to Cranwell Castle, Nerrah chose to live separately so as not to intrude on our family and occupied this very room. One morning, when I was passing the kitchen, I heard the cooks whispering that Nerrah was dealing in sorcery. They said she was a powerful witch and this was the reason why she was banished by King Arayan.'

'If her magic is anything to go by, she is way more than a powerful witch. She doesn't even have to use a wand to do her spells,' Lena said.

'If I'd known her true intentions, I wouldn't have gone to visit her that same evening,' Saniah explained. 'When I knocked and entered the chamber, I found her sitting at the dressing table looking into a circular mirror, which she was holding in her hand. She was talking to somebody and I could hear them replying.'

'Was it Raven?' I asked.

'No, it was Nerrah's mother, Mable. She was telling Nerrah all about a witch in the Forest of Eidon, who had five crystals crafted by Amunah. Mable alerted Nerrah to my presence in the room, and when Nerrah glanced at me, I was almost sure I could see her eyes burning bright red for a split second.'

'Was she angry with you?' Lena asked.

'No not all. On the contrary, she smiled and said goodbye to her mother and came running forward to pick up Arya. Nerrah, kindly asked me to sit down, and for the first time ever, she began to tell me a bit about herself, from her upbringing to how she'd struggled to bring Bulzaar up alone and how King Arayan had left her for another woman.

'Nerrah told me Queen Zenofur had instructed Zara and Sebastian to kill Bulzaar. This shocked me, and she asked me if I wanted to help her save him from such a fate to which I agreed. Who wouldn't want the best for their loved ones?'

'Did she make you get the crystals for her?' I asked.

'No, she told me she was going to go collect them herself from the witch, for Bulzaar's own protection, against Zara and Sebastian, who would be ready to attack him at any time.

'I found out later that Nerrah and Mable had killed the witch, who had the crystals. It turned out the old witch was harmless and was shielding the crystals from the outside world, and somehow Mable had found out about the valuable items.

'The day Nerrah brought the crystals into this castle, my life started to spiral out of control. Nerrah convinced me the crystals would be used to protect Bulzaar from harm, and by the time I found out the truth, she'd used their power to make him merciless.

'I began to rebel, but she started to use the magic on me, making me do things which were out of my control. Bulzaar believed in Amunah and was and still is a good person. He is just poisoned by hate and vengeance.'

Saniah broke down.

'When Mykha and Nova came to take back their parents' portrait, were you being influenced then, Saniah?' Kal asked.

'Yes, I hated the sight of them because I thought they were going to hurt Bulzaar after what Nerrah had made me believe. She was the one who went after them and framed me for the whole thing. She had me imprisoned by controlling Bulzaar but changed her mind, and she brought me back up here to make me look like the bad one in front of the whole kingdom.

'Nerrah has never let me see Arya because I dared go against her plans. Arya was too little to remember anything. She still thinks her father imprisoned the three of us, and my poor daughter doesn't even know that her own grandmother hasn't spent a day in those caves. I hope you can stop them both, Heera, I really do. I want to see Arya so desperately. Hayden was so close, but Nerrah killed her too.'

'What? I thought it was Bulzaar,' I said.

'Nerrah was using magic against me as well as Bulzaar at the time Hayden was captured,' continued Saniah. 'I couldn't even think for myself. Bulzaar locked Hayden away in a room in the castle and visited her now and again. Nerrah instructed me to torture her by using dark magic. Without thinking, I went down to the chamber where Hayden was held. I was simply a vessel for Nerrah's dark magic. I couldn't think for myself, and I could only hear Nerrah's voice instructing me to do horrific things.'

I couldn't comprehend how evil Nerrah was as I listened to Saniah.

'I saw Hayden standing with her back to me,' Saniah continued, 'staring out of the window at Mount Orias, and she didn't even flinch when she heard me entering the room. Hayden turned around with a smile, opened her arms and I saw the pendant around her neck. The light from the pendant was so bright I thought it'd blind me at first, and I could feel the light entering my body and cleaning my soul of the darkness Nerrah had put in it. I was free from her binding at last.'

Saniah paused before continuing.

'I left the room unlocked and Hayden escaped,' Saniah explained. 'She managed to steal three crystals and fled the castle. She found Agatha Oak and gave her the pendant and the three crystals. Hayden told Agatha that she was coming back to the castle to get the other crystals, but Nerrah caught her taking the other two and Nerrah killed her on the spot. Nerrah has used the power of the crystals to make Bulzaar think he killed Hayden himself, and he tells everyone she died at his own hands.

'The only way Nerrah has been able to control me is by using serpentine rope to keep me physically tied down. She can't use spells to control my mind because they don't work so well against Amunah's protection.'

Hearing what had happened to Hayden made me furious, and I couldn't believe how she was killed without a thought by Nerrah.

'Do you know where she's kept my family?' I asked.

'Yes, I do. They've been kept in the same room where Hayden had been imprisoned. They've been rendered unconscious though, and they haven't been awoken since they came here. Both Nerrah and Bulzaar thought it was best this way as they already have enough to do without having to worry about humans.

'Heera, there is something else you should know and it's truly dreadful. Bulzaar is also planning to sacrifice your family when he opens the portal for Raven. The power of the crystals will only allow Raven to cross over, but Nerrah has learnt the power of the crystals, if radiated through human vessels, will keep the portal open for every evil soul from the Realm of the Shadows to enter Fallowmere.'

'What?' I asked in disbelief.

'Heera, let's go now,' Lena said, equally shocked at what we'd heard about the fate of my family.

I was trembling with anger. I was going to take Nerrah down too and I'd make sure she'd pay for all the misery she'd caused.

CHAPTER 25
Trapped

'We have to replace the crystals with something else,' I said rushing towards the cupboard.

'Saniah, do you think she'll check the crystals before she goes to sleep?' Lena asked.

'She will check the cupboard but she won't look inside the cloth. Search her drawer for heavy jewellery which you can replace the crystals with. Nerrah has never been able to touch them and has to wear gloves or use a cloth to pick them up to tell them her true desires.'

I opened the cupboard and uncovered the crystals from the black cloth while Lena rummaged through the drawers retrieving jewellery to put in place of the crystals.

The crystals were here and twinkled against the back set of the black cloth. Amongst the green, yellow and blue crystals I'd found back in my dad's office, there was also a ruby red and a purple coloured crystal. I touched the two crystals I'd seen for the first time, and my pendant sent a surge of energy throughout my body.

Lena rushed over with mounds of jewellery in her hands whilst I took the five crystals and placed them carefully in my bag, and she placed the bundle of jewellery concealed in the black cloth back in the cupboard.

'How do we get out of the castle?' Kal asked Saniah.

'The best way is to take the right corridor at the top of the grand staircase. Carry on straight ahead until you come to a flight of stairs going down to the ground floor and into the sitting area. You'll find a side door there to get into the gardens.

As for Mount Orias, I've never known anyone to go up that mountain. When the battle between Raven and Amunah took place, they say his temple was destroyed, and no-one even bothered to try to look for it because only his chosen followers can see it. I'm certain Amunah will be able to guide you there.'

'Ouch!' Lena gasped as she picked up the blue crystal out of my bag to take a look at it. 'I don't understand. I'm not a bad person so why can't I hold it?' Lena was distraught.

'I don't know, Lena. Maybe they've been near Nerrah too long and aren't working properly,' I said.

'Well they didn't hurt you,' Lena said flushing bright red. She rubbed her hand and I could see a red streak where the crystal had burned her.

'We don't have time for this you two, come on let's hurry,' Kal warned. 'And aren't we forgetting something? Nerrah's going to know something's wrong when she comes up to find Saniah is no longer bound by those snake like ropes.'

'No, she won't take any notice of me,' Saniah said. 'She'll check to see the crystals are in the cupboard and go straight to bed. By the time she gets back, I'll be pretending to be asleep, and she already has enough on her mind to worry about me.'

'Saniah, we *will* come back for you and Arya,' I said taking her hand.

'Be careful you three and don't worry about me, but make sure you get Arya out of those caves,' Saniah said. As I was about to leave, she pulled my hand and continued, 'Don't trust anyone and listen to what Amunah tells you.'

We left Saniah behind, and before we stepped onto the landing of the tower, I tucked my pendant back into my top in case we were caught. We were careful and tiptoed around corners, listening for any footsteps, and in no time, we'd reached the top of the grand staircase. We crept past several closed doors on either side of us down the corridor to the right.

Kal stopped and pointed to a room further down the end of the corridor. The door was fully open. Bright light was flooding out of the room and onto the red carpet, and we could hear voices coming from within.

We tiptoed up to the room. I pointed to the flight of stairs going down to the sitting room on the other side of the open door. We had to tread carefully now; one mistake could stop us from saving my family and Fallowmere.

'Mother, tell Saniah I need those crystals tomorrow,' Bulzaar demanded. 'I'm going to accompany Landon and go to Kendolen and wipe them all out. Maybe Heera Watson somehow never left the town and they're hiding her. I need to be prepared. This warrior has me on edge as well, and I can't tell whether Mykha is lying to me or not. I can't fail Raven again. I can't!'

'You won't fail, Bulzaar,' Landon said. 'It's best if you let me fly over first. Once I've crossed the barrier, I'll take the magical guard down. You can follow with the Fire Blades and have your revenge.'

We each had our mouths' open in shock with the plans of Landon and Bulzaar attacking Kendolen tomorrow. There was so much at stake and the only way to stop Bulzaar was to get the crystals to safety. We still had some time left.

'Saniah wishes for you to communicate with Raven tonight,' Nerrah said. 'She's sent this potion and goblet. Landon, you can stay, but you'll not hear Raven because he doesn't trust easily.'

'That's understandable,' Landon said.

I managed to take a sneaky sideward glance and found their backs were turned away from the door. They were focused on the goblet on the table before them, which was overflowing with the same green smoke I'd seen in Nerrah's chamber.

I signalled to Lena and Kal that it was safe to pass. We took a deep breath and silently crossed the door to the other side.

Bulzaar shouted out, 'WAIT!' We froze at the top of the flight of stairs we were about to head down. He'd heard us or seen us and we had failed in our mission. I couldn't breathe.

'Shut the door, Landon. Anyone could be listening,' Bulzaar said.

We heard footsteps and the door to the room slammed shut. We drew breath and ran down the stairs. I listened at the bottom of the stairs for any disturbances before entering the sitting room. Lena lit up her wand, and we huddled together as the light was not bright enough to fill the dark room.

'Look for the side door to get into the gardens. It's here somewhere,' I whispered. We moved around the room trying to find a side door and found it hidden behind a set of curtains. It was locked.

Lena pointed her wand at the lock on the door, and as she concentrated all her energy into the incoherent words she whispered, we heard the door shake. Kal turned the handle, and the door creaked open. Before we left, we took off our uniforms and Lena put them all in her bag. Kal retrieved his sword and kept it close, and he still had Hosemee's coin in one hand.

I too, retrieved my sword from its sheath, and with sheer determination, we stepped outside and fresh air hit us as we made our way into the night.

Lena extinguished her wand. We didn't want to be seen by anyone from within the castle or run into the Fire Blades, who could be anywhere. We only had the moon and hundreds of twinkling stars to give us enough light to see where we were stepping. It was almost impossible to see what was ahead of us.

We followed a winding brick path in and out of bushes and trees, and although Mount Orias couldn't be seen, I knew it was towering high above us in the near distance.

We continued deeper into the castle grounds; there was an overwhelming feeling of dread in the pit of my stomach. It was so strong that at one point, I felt nauseous and stopped in my tracks.

'Are you OK, Heera?' Lena asked as quietly as she could.

'Yeah I feel as though I'm going to be sick, but I know we need to keep going,' I replied.

'It's the pendant and the crystals weighing you down,' Kal said. 'That's way too much power for one person to handle. Hosemee had said you'd feel weak, the closer you came to the crystals and the temple.'

Shortly, the path opened up to an enclosed arena to the right of us. There were fire torches around the circular area, and I believed this was some sort of training ground. From what I could see, many obstacles were spread out over the ground and various weapons and armour lay against the side of the fencing. The area could have easily held an army of a thousand or possibly more. For now though, it was completely deserted except for a lonely figure lying on the ground.

It was Jack. I felt another blow to the pit of my stomach; I knew I had to try to help him.

'Heera, come on,' Kal whispered.

'No it's Jack, I have to help him,' I whispered back.

'We haven't got time,' Lena said.

'I have to…'

'We'll keep watch then, but please hurry, Heera,' Lena said.

'No we can't just stand around waiting,' Kal said to Lena. I ignored him.

Without another word, I left them standing in the dark and ran towards Jack. I knelt down and whispered his name, 'Jack, it's me Heera. Please, wake up.'

There was no movement; he was lying on his side. I began to move him with as much strength as I could gather and managed to lay him down on his back. His face was unrecognisable. His eyes were bruised and deep scratches covered his face and arms. His wavy black hair and the white T-Shirt he was wearing were soaked in blood, and his skin was almost white from the amount of blood he'd lost.

Heavy chains around his ankles had him tied to the ground of the enormous arena. I tried to pull the chains away from him; however, they were on too tight and had dug deep into his battered and bruised skin. I turned to glance back at Kal and Lena for help, but as I was about to speak, Jack grabbed my wrist.

'Heera...' Jack winced.

'Jack, yes it's me. I'm right here,' I whispered as I bent down closer to him.

'I never thought I'd look like this when I saw you again...' he said.

'Jack, don't worry about that now. I'll get Lena to try to get these chains off you with a spell,' I said.

'No... go before you get caught. You've come so far and you have to carry on. If they find me missing, they'll know something's wrong. Please go, Heera... I'll be fine.'

'I can't go and leave you like this,' I said.

'You have too... Bulzaar has to be stopped,' Jack said. 'When Mykah and Nova told me they'd seen you, I knew I was wrong about you. Sorry for the way I treated and underestimated you when we first met.'

'I was the one who chased you and you're not to blame. I didn't know you knew Mykha and Nova,' I said.

'They're our informants. I visit them, now and again, and they give me valuable information and tell me what's going on in the kingdom. I mentioned your name to them during my last visit to their cottage, and they told me they'd seen you. And as you can see, Morog turned up unannounced.'

I remembered Jack's dad telling me they had informants in the forest; he must have been referring to Mykha and Nova.

'Heera,' Lena said softly. I turned to see her standing behind me. 'We need to go.'

'She's coming, Lena. Heera, please go now,' Jack said as Lena left us alone again.

'I'll come back for you, I promise...' I said.

'I know you will. How's butter fingers?' Jack said trying to lighten the mood.

'He's... fine,' I just about managed to say. I felt the pendant send a shock throughout my body. I knew I had to carry on, time was running out. I stood up and I detested the fact that I was about to turn my back on Jack when he was in such a dire state.

'Bye, Heera and good luck, and I promise when I see you again, I'll sweep you off your feet,' Jack laughed.

'I'll hold you to that, Jack,' I replied and with that I turned around and tears flooded my eyes. I clutched my pendant, hoping this wasn't the last time I'd see him.

I didn't look back. I returned to Kal and Lena, who were huddled together in the dark, keeping watch.

'There she is! It's about time, Heera,' Kal huffed.

'Kal,' Lena warned.

'Let's carry on,' I said. I didn't want to argue with Kal and I didn't respond to his comment.

We followed the path forward and found concrete buildings on either side of us. Kal dragged us to the right of one of these cabins, and even I felt something was wrong. I was clutching at my chest and the pendant was growing hot and vibrating. I dropped to the ground.

'I think the Fire Blades are in here,' Kal whispered. 'I can feel danger close by.'

Eventually, I stood up and continued to pass the cabins, row after row. There were hundreds of them. We were nearly approaching the last few of them; long pipes, iron sheets, broken shields, armoury, weapons, and other objects littered the sides of these structures.

Kal, once again, pulled us to the side of one of the cabins. He dragged and pushed us behind a pile of iron sheets and shields with such force that our backs slammed hard against the building. We heard sharp heavy footsteps coming towards us and there was a flash of light. We leaned back to hide ourselves and I gripped my sword tightly. The light was coming towards us; the Fire Blades had lit a fire torch and were in close proximity to us.

'Leave it! It's probably vermin running around,' a deep raspy voice said from a distance.

'I heard footsteps,' said another.

'Come back, nobody's out here. If you want we can stand watch for a few hours, as it is, I can't sleep anyway,' the heavy voice said once again. The Fire Blade with the fire torch went away for the time being.

The three of us sat down on the ground and huddled together. We could hear the Fire Blades murmuring, a short distance away. We had no option but to sit and wait for the danger to pass. It would be too risky to make a move. We were too scared to speak, and we listened to the Fire Blades pacing up and down for what seemed like hours.

The warmth from huddling together made us realise how exhausted we were. The Fire Blades were still pacing and chatting away. I felt Lena drop her head on my shoulders and heard deep breathing against my ear; Lena had fallen asleep, and it did not take too long for me to drift off, against my wishes.

When I awoke, the sky was no longer dark. Streaks of red and yellow were beginning to cut through the greyish sky. I panicked. Bulzaar was supposed to go to war in Kendolen in a few hours and I was still in the castle grounds. I was furious with myself. How could I have been so stupid? My family and the entire kingdom were in danger and here I was sleeping.

I listened to see if the Fire Blades were still pacing up and down but there was no sound. I nudged both Lena and Kal on either side of me. Kal stood up and crept towards the side of the pile of sheets and shields to see if he could see the Fire Blades.

'They've gone,' he confirmed.

'We have to keep moving,' I murmured.

Mount Orias came into view. It was a monstrous block mountain as it loomed above us and the peak was hidden above the clouds. The further up the mountain your eyes went, the colour of the rock changed. It started off with a deep grey, which merged with white and brown towards the middle, and almost at the top, you could just about see a darker shade of greyish black, partly covered in ice. How on earth were we going to climb this mountain?

We continued on as quickly and quietly as we could and passed the last remaining cabins. There was another circular enclosure ahead of us closed off by a metal door. As we approached the building, we heard a huge roar and heavy footsteps came running towards us.

The three of us freaked out. We ran straight towards the sound of the roar through the heavy metal door, and we came face to face with ferocious creatures with severe deformities, all bound to the ground in metal chains.

The creatures were both vicious and gruesome. They seemed to be a hybrid of different animals. They were staring at us with hunger in their eyes, and wherever we moved, hundreds of eyes followed us. We were edging around the metal fencing separating us from the beasts, who were now snapping their teeth hungrily at us. One creature was built like an ostrich and had three beady eyes; when it snapped its beak, I could see hundreds of tiny sharp teeth. It was definitely not a friendly creature.

I noticed the enclosure had no roof. The door opened and closed with a "clank", and with the hybrid creatures now standing up and hiding the three of us from view, we managed to hide behind one that was lying on its side. The beast, which was motionless and appeared to be hurt, had its own separate enclosure.

We couldn't see anybody approaching, but we could hear footsteps. The creatures tied to the ground were going hysterical, and the noise level was deafening. The creature shielding us was unresponsive.

A throaty voice said, 'They need feeding. We have to saddle one up for Landon also, but let's get them fed first before we attempt to move closer to them.' The heavy metal door slammed shut and I stood up trying to think of a way to escape.

I could see the creatures were saddled up and were branded with Bulzaar's mark, depicting an open mouthed dragon, which was burned into their flesh. These creatures were used in many ways such as transport, in wars, and to attack the enemy as Bulzaar and the Fire Blades wished. I focused on the creature lying before us and took a closer look at his face. I realised we'd met him before and both Kal and Lena had recognised him too.

'Dragmatus,' I said softly, looking at the creature, not as a monster anymore but through the eyes of Mykha and Nova. He was their beloved pet at one time, and because of me, he was lying wounded on the ground. I gently stroked the fur on his head. His eyes were closed and he gently moved his head against my hand.

'Nova and Mykha were with us a few days ago… do you remember them?' I whispered in his ears, and he opened his eyes slowly and turned around to look at me. He gritted and bared his teeth at us; he must have also remembered our last fight.

'What are we going to do?' Lena asked in exasperation. 'The Fire Blades will be back any minute now! How are we going to get to the mountain?'

I glanced down at Dragmatus, then up at the lightening sky, and back down at the chains he was tied to. Kal was following my eye movements and sat down in a huff, crossed his arms and shook his head. Lena catching on excitedly said, 'Brilliant!'

'Dragmatus, we can take you to Nova and Mykha if you help us please. We can heal you as well,' I said as I took out my pendant, hoping it would heal him just as it had freed Saniah from Nerrah's binding. The pendant began to glow once again.

As Dragmatus opened his eyes and turned to look at what I was showing him, a flash of white from the pendant blinded him momentarily. The light of the pendant slowly dimmed, and Dragmatus tried to get up as Kal and Lena backed away from his rapid movements.

Dragmatus flapped his wings with such force that the three of us were thrown against the wall of the enclosure. He appeared to be different than before. He was a lot more willing to communicate with me through movement and no longer bared his teeth at us.

He came closer to me, bent down and I climbed onto the saddle on his back. It was uncomfortable and I held onto the handle of the saddle ready to fly into the air. Lena was up next without a problem. We both waited for Kal to jump on, but he stood rooted to the spot with his arms crossed looking livid.

'I'm not going with you! I can't do it… what if he changes back?' he said.

'Kal if you stay here, the Fire Blades will find you and kill you anyway,' I said. 'At least this way we have a chance and he's not going to change back, Kal. Saniah didn't and we are only using him to get to the mountain. After that he can go find Mykha and Nova.'

The metal door creaked open. The Fire Blades had come back to feed the creatures. We had to make a move or our cover would be blown once they came around to feed the many creatures near us.

'Come on now or we'll leave you here, Kal,' Lena threatened.

Footsteps and shouting from the Fire Blades could be heard as they taunted the creatures. I could see pieces of meat being thrown from all angles and the footsteps were coming towards us.

I was terrified of being caught. We were completely trapped; Dragmatus was now healed and would need feeding, and we couldn't hide behind him without being seen, and if we flew away on him, we'd be seen escaping.

I did what was best and used my sword to strike the metal chains, which bound Dragmatus, with force and freed him. Fire Blades approached from either side of us, but they were concentrating on the creatures trying to snap at them.

My heart almost stopped with fear.

This surely was the end.

CHAPTER 26
Mount Orias

Kal jumped behind Lena and grabbed her hard. She appeared to have been winded temporarily. A Fire Blade spotted us and ran for us. 'WAIT!!! WHAT ARE YOU DOING?' he shouted. His yellow eyes scrutinised us and now more Fire Blades came from either side; there were six Fire Blades in total.

'They're only children! Let's take them to Bulzaar, or better still, let's feed them to the other creatures,' a Fire Blade laughed as he came nearer. He wielded his sword in a cutting motion to scare the three of us.

I bent down and whispered into Dragmatus' ear, 'Please save us, Dragmatus and take us to the mountain.' He remained standing still. The Fire Blades were only a few feet away staring at us, and when we refused to get off the saddle, it angered them further.

'Get off Dragmatus or he'll hurt you! He's not a toy… get down now!' one of them mocked as he took a step forward.

I pointed my sword at them threateningly and Lena pointed her wand. 'LOOK AT THAT PENDANT! THAT'S HEERA WATSON, GRAB THEM NOW!' a Fire Blade shouted, running forwards to grab us.

Suddenly, Dragmatus opened his wings and flapped them with great strength. The Fire Blades took a few steps back and he bared his teeth at them as a warning. One Fire Blade opened his mouth and a ball of fire erupted from him; Dragmatus dodged the fireball coming straight for us in time.

All six Fire Blades were now attempting to strike Dragmatus with their weapons, hoping he would drop us as several fireballs hurtled towards us. Dragmatus panicked, flapped his wings and we were off the ground.

I saw two Fire Blades run out of the enclosure; they'd probably gone to call for help, and the other four tried to jump and grab Dragmatus to pull him back down. They couldn't because we were now high up and out of reach, and the balls of fire were now coming towards us from every angle.

I could see several more Fire Blades entering the enclosure staring up at us, and the higher we flew, hundreds could be seen flowing out of the concrete cabins as the alarm had been raised that an intruder had escaped from their grasp.

From a height, the Fire Blades resembled little gleaming ants on the ground with their yellow eyes and with the balls of fire erupting from their mouths and weapons into the sky. Several of them were now scrambling to get on the other creatures to chase us; Dragmatus, however, veered off to the left instead of heading to the mountain to confuse the Fire Blades below.

The wind blew through my hair and allowed me to think clearly. I glanced around us to see if we were being followed, but the speed at which we were flying, it would be impossible for anyone to catch up with us. I had to laugh at what we'd accomplished and I held my sword high up in the air to celebrate our escape. Lena was laughing in my ear, and when I looked back at Kal, he was holding onto her tightly and had his eyes shut.

Instantaneously, a cloud ahead split into two and moved apart to reveal three huge fireballs suspended in the sky; the fireballs merged to form the face of a black and orange dragon. The mouth of the dragon shot open and it sent a dozen fireballs racing towards us.

Dragmatus swerved rapidly to avoid several of them and all I could do was hold on tight. Kal and Lena were screaming. The dragon now transformed into Bulzaar's face; his blood red eyes pierced my soul and I shuddered. I was about to scream until something else caught my eye.

A cloud above Bulzaar's face began to brighten with an illuminating white glow, and I could see straight into the cloud to the other side where the peak of Mount Orias was revealed. *'Don't be frightened, Heera. He can't harm you here. Amunah is with you,'* a female voice said in my ear as my pendant began to pulsate once more.

'Dragmatus fly through that cloud,' I whispered to him but he was focused on Bulzaar's face and was backing away slowly. 'Come on don't be scared.'

The bright cloud shot white lightening sparks towards Bulzaar's face, and he turned his eyes upwards and opened his mouth in slight bewilderment. The cloud seemed to be expanding, growing larger, and was emitting frequent sparks. Bulzaar's eyes widened and he let out a fireball from his mouth; at the same time, the cloud above sent a gleaming white spark towards Bulzaar. The spark and the fireball connected and the fireball exploded in mid-air.

'Come on Dragmatus, please!' I urged and he flew upwards and headed directly for the cloud. Lena and Kal screamed at the sheer force with which Dragmatus was flying towards a cloud that was ablaze with a blinding light.

Dragmatus flew out of the other side of the cloud. I turned back and I could see Bulzaar's face was no longer floating in the sky, and the cloud we'd flown through was still emitting short sharp sparks.

Dragmatus glided through the air and took the longer route to fly to the opposite side of the mountain in case we were being followed. Dragmatus hovered at the side of the mountain, trying to find somewhere suitable to drop us off; he saw an area, halfway up the mountain, where he could sit comfortably to allow the three of us to climb down safely.

I patted Dragmatus on his head. 'Thank you for saving our lives, Dragmatus. I need you to do one more thing for me though… hang on one moment,' I said while dropping my sword on the hard ground. I began to rummage through my bag to find a piece of paper and a pen.

I quickly wrote a note and placed it on the ground in front of Dragmatus and said, 'Will you please take this note to Mykha and Nova? They're with Morog, and you're the only one who can deliver this message to them. If they read this, they can send word to Agatha Oak about Landon's betrayal and about Bulzaar's and Nerrah's plan?'

He nodded his head at me. Lena also stepped forward and stroked Dragmatus; Kal managed to find string in his bag and tied the letter to Dragmatus' front paw with great hesitation.

As Dragmatus flew off the mountain towards the brightening sky, the three of us waved and watched until he was out of view. I hoped he'd be able to find Mykha and Nova and they could send a warning to Mrs Oak.

I picked up my sword from the ground.

'Heera, do you think Bulzaar knows what we're doing?' Lena asked scared. 'He appeared out of nowhere in the sky.'

'I think he was trying to scare us. I doubt he knows the crystals are missing and that we're heading to the Sorin,' I assured her. Kal had lost all colour from his face and listened to us speak.

I waited for my pendant to give me some sort of sign. I even listened for Amunah's voice for help because I had no idea where exactly on the mountain, the Sorin was hidden.

When no sign came, I placed my sword back into the sheath and began to climb the mountain with Lena and Kal following behind. Once or twice, we lost our footing, and when we gazed down, we could see nothing except brown and green patches of land.

Climbing the rocky terrain was extremely difficult and tiring. After half an hour, I decided I couldn't climb any further, and reaching a level edge, I rested with Kal and Lena. I stared down, and to my surprise, we hadn't made much progress in climbing.

Kal rummaged through his diary, flicking through the pages and Lena had taken out her spell book and was whispering to Iris. I saw the sun appear from behind clouds, shining down on the side of the mountain. I closed my eyes, feeling the warmth of the sun on my face.

I opened my eyes and turned back to talk to Kal and Lena, but they'd disappeared. I wasn't alone though; I felt there was another presence near me. I should've retrieved my sword, yet I didn't feel threatened. I felt a warm feeling on my shoulder as though a hand was placed on it; still, I couldn't see anyone.

I gasped.

'Keep moving, Heera. You don't have enough time… these events have already taken place,' Amunah's voice said. I looked straight ahead of me, expecting to see the sky and clouds; instead, a dense fog came towards me, carrying an image. The image vanished and was followed immediately with another.

I saw Fire Blades storming the castle searching for Bulzaar. They found him in the drawing room with Landon Tomkins. He was livid at how they'd barged into the castle; however, they wasted no time in telling him we'd left on Dragmatus.

Nerrah in long black robes and a hood covering her face listened to what the Fire Blades had to say. She ran up to her room, ignored Saniah on the floor, and headed straight to the cupboard and retrieved the black bundle, she thought contained the crystals.

When she found the crystals missing, she screamed loudly as she clutched the jewellery to her chest. She walked over to Saniah, who in turn didn't move or flinch. Nerrah asked her who took the crystals but hysterical laughter from Saniah filled the room.

Nerrah with sheer fury transformed into Saniah and ran back down to inform Bulzaar the crystals were now missing. I still hadn't seen Nerrah's true face with her hood obscuring it from view. Bulzaar was shocked to see his wife when she first entered the room; even he couldn't see her face and nor did he pay her any attention after hearing what'd happened to the crystals. He told them all he'd search for the three of us and would kill each of us slowly.

He followed the Fire Blades outside with Landon Tomkins by his side. Landon informed him that the Elders had told me to deliver the crystals to them and that I'd be on my way back to Kendolen. Several Fire Blades dragged a gigantic, fierce red dragon by a rope, which was around its neck, out of another enclosure. The dragon was covered with sharp, long, black spikes and was enormous compared to Dragmatus. Bulzaar greeted the dragon as an old friend, and with one stroke to the back of the dragon's head, he flew into the air with such force that he showered the Fire Blades with dust from the ground.

'You will find the temple where the first rays of the sun meet the entrance, Heera. It will reveal itself to you for a short time only,' Amunah said.

'But how will I defeat Bulzaar?' I asked.

'Heera, who are you talking to?' Kal asked and when I glanced behind me, I saw both Kal and Lena staring at me.

'It was Amunah, wasn't it? Did he tell you where to find the Sorin?' Lena asked. I told them what Amunah had told me about the temple. 'That doesn't tell us much, Lena continued. 'We'll have to wait until the sun's rays hit every inch of the mountain.'

'He's showed me what happened after we left,' I explained. 'Bulzaar knows we have the crystals and he's looking for us. He's gone towards Kendolen for now, which is of course completely the wrong direction, but it's only a matter of time before he realises where we are.'

'How did he show you?' Kal asked intrigued. I explained how I saw the visions, and I told them what Bulzaar had said about killing us slowly, not to mention the dragon which made the other creatures we'd seen in the enclosure seem like cute puppies. They were both frightened; the fact we'd now been exposed was very real to them. Bulzaar would be coming for us and I hoped we were ready for him.

Without another word and too consumed with our own thoughts, we began to climb more quickly now that Bulzaar was coming for us. I felt more and more weighed down as we continued on. My vision blurred now and again, and when I glanced back at Kal and Lena, they'd simply disappear right in front of my eyes and reappear later.

I could hear them talking to me, asking if I was okay and when I tried to speak I couldn't. I was breathless climbing the steep rock, and I could only think about finding Amunah's temple fast.

I heard Amunah's voice clearly in my ear, 'Heera, you're getting closer. You need to reach the platform above you and search for me there.'

I peered up and saw a rock jutting out of the mountain; I had to reach it somehow. When I looked down, to my horror Kal and Lena were gone, and all that could be seen was the same dense fog, I'd seen earlier all around me.

I knew what I was seeing wasn't real; how could Lena and Kal disappear like that? It was the crystals and my pendant working together to get me to the temple.

'Heera, he knows... be brave,' Amunah's voice reverberated from the fog and more images came forth.

I saw Bulzaar flying on the dragon. He was worriedly searching the ground below for us and he was in deep thought. The same fog around me entered his ear and I could see Bulzaar's memories and hear his thoughts. Bulzaar was talking into the goblet filled with blood and green smoke was erupting from the cup.

Nerrah and Landon were there too; Bulzaar shouted at Landon to close the door. This had to be last night's memory, I thought. A hoarse voice echoed from the goblet and it made me feel nauseous. The voice was deep and malicious and I understood it belonged to Raven. Bulzaar listened and didn't dare speak until he was allowed to, and Raven kept repeating the same thing over and over again.

'LISTEN CLOSELY SERVANT OF THE DARK... GUARD THE SORIN AS THE TRUE SAVIOUR, HEERA WATSON MAY FIND HER WAY THERE... YOU WILL NOT BE FORGIVEN FOR ANY MISTAKES THIS TIME,' Raven shouted.

Bulzaar was arguing with his own thoughts. One thing was certain: Mykha had been lying all along about the new warrior because even Raven had confirmed the warrior was Heera Watson. Now would the saviour take the crystals to Kendolen or to the Sorin? Heera Watson was not of this world; could she be smart enough to take the crystals to their rightful place? Hayden had been blinded by Agatha Oak and the Elders, and that's why she'd failed.

Very few knew the crystals had to be taken to the Sorin; the Elders and Agatha Oak didn't have a clue, but could it be that someone else gave this valuable information to Heera? No, she couldn't possibly know... but she'd slipped straight past me and I didn't have an inkling. Heera Watson was another breed of Amunah's chosen warrior. She had to be stopped and she would know not to make the same mistake Hayden did.

Bulzaar had made up his mind. 'To Mount Orias, Belle!' he said and immediately turned the dragon around with sheer hatred and determination in his face. The fog disappeared and so did Bulzaar, and I became aware of my surroundings.

I pulled myself onto the platform where Amunah had told me to search for the Sorin and peered around. I felt a pat on my back and I jumped. It was Lena and Kal. 'Kal, it's that pendant. She's talking to Amunah, and I don't think she can hear us,' Lena said while still staring at me and waving her hand in front of my eyes.

'He's coming here and he knows what we're doing... I heard Raven's voice saying my name and Bulzaar knew last night Mykha had lied about the new warrior,' I said shaking from head to toe. Kal and Lena gulped and their eyes widened in terror.

'Raven???' Kal said.

'The temple's around here somewhere... Amunah told me so himself. Let's search, we're running out of time,' I said ignoring Kal. I desperately began to search everywhere. The ground was flat, and there were caves and crevices all over the place. Boulders were littered here and there, and still there was no sign of the temple.

We split up and tried to search among the rocks and the many caves, but there was simply no door or entrance which could be the entrance to the Sorin. I walked again to the edge of the mountain and peered down. I saw nothing except clouds below.

Light from the blazing sun pierced my eyes. I quickly closed them. I tried to squint as the sunlight was beginning to travel onto the rock platform in front of me, and the rays of light were slowly making their way over the entire area.

'It has to be here somewhere... let's keep searching,' I said.

We spread out again to search in different areas. There was a lot of area to cover and we needed to do it speedily. I was getting frustrated. Bulzaar would be here any minute.

Lena and Kal were still searching and I leaned against a slanting rock to catch my breath. I retrieved my flask from my bag and drank from it. I noticed the crystals in the bag were getting hotter and the pendant around my neck was getting heavier.

The sun had lit up the entire area of where we were searching, yet I couldn't see any opening. As I lifted the flask to my mouth, something caught my eye and it was shimmering in the sunlight.

In the distance, I saw what appeared to be two rock pillars, and in between these pillars, I could see another rock face shimmering with golden symbols carved into it. If it wasn't for the shimmering rock face, the pillars would've been easily overlooked due to their crumbling state. I ran towards it and Kal and Lena followed.

'You've found it, Heera!' Lena said excitedly, staring up at the entrance. Kal had his mouth slightly ajar, in awe of being at the foot of the Sorin.

I don't know why but I put my hands on the pillars and whispered, 'I'm here, Amunah.'

I could feel the pillars vibrate against my hands and I saw the carvings move inwards into the rock; it was as if a key had been turned and a door was unlocking. The rock moved backwards and an entrance to the temple emerged.

'Heera, he is near, my child,' Amunah's voice said.

'We can enter,' I said and I took a step over the threshold and entered the Sorin with Kal and Lena beside me.

CHAPTER 27

The Sorin

I found myself in a large, dusky room. The entrance remained open with a few rays of sun coming through. Ancient lanterns placed on mantels, unseen by us until now, lit themselves all around the room completely flooding it with light.

'Heera, look at this,' Lena said and I found her staring at the image of Amunah carved into a wall at the back of the room. The pendant around his neck caught my eye immediately. He was wearing a crown on his head, long robes and his face was the same as I'd seen in Hosemee's memory. He was smiling down upon us.

My pendant suddenly lit up with white light and jolted upwards. It too knew it had returned home and was becoming hot and weighing me down. I took it off and placed it on one of the mantels, which shelved the lanterns for the time being. Lena and Kal were still examining the room, and I couldn't see anywhere I was supposed to put the crystals.

'Kal, Lena, where would Amunah have put the crystals?' I asked.

'I have no idea. It must have been secret. There has to be another room somewhere,' Kal said while Lena started to search for any signs of another hidden door or corner.

I started back at the entrance of the temple and walked along the wall, trying to feel for any clues that would suggest there was another room in the temple, but I found nothing. The pendant I'd placed on a mantel was still burning bright and the white light was helping us to search.

I, once again found myself in front of the carving of Amunah. I took a closer look at the carving this time and placed my hand over it to feel the outline, and as I did so, I felt like a magnetic force was pushing me away. I took this sign to mean I was on the right track.

I traced the outline of Amunah to the pendant around his neck, and in the same moment, I turned to look at the pendant resting on the mantel. The pendant rose in the air and with quick speed, like a bullet, darted towards me and stopped immediately in front of my face. Kal and Lena ran up to me and tried to grab the pendant to stop it from hitting me in the face, but as they touched it, they let go because it was scorching hot.

The pendant was vibrating in front of my face with the tip dangerously close to my right eye, and I knew what I had to do as soon as I grabbed it.

'Heera, are you OK?' Lena asked as she saw the pendant burning up in my hand.

'Yeah, I think so,' I said placing the pendant into the spot where Amunah's pendant was carved into the stone wall. It was a perfect fit. The light shone from it, and like a snake, the light travelled all around the carving. The image of Amunah was now brightly lit, and the stone wall moved outwards, revealing another entrance.

We waited until the wall had fully opened, and I retrieved my pendant from the carving before entering the other chamber. I could hear bells in the distance and followed their sound. The second chamber was well lit with huge candles on pillars in the four corners of the room.

There was a desk in the corner, littered with paper, old quills and ink pots. Opposite the desk, stood a glass cabinet holding jars full of various ingredients; on another table, I found measuring scales and bowls. This must have been the room where Amunah was experimenting to protect Fallowmere from evil as Hosemee had said.

'Look over here, come quick,' Kal said. Lena was examining the jars in the cabinet and she rushed over to join us. Kal had found a wall made of what appeared to be ice. It was opaque and I tapped it with my sword; it was made of glass.

'This has to be it, but how do we get through this glass?' I said.

'I can try a spell to see if it will shatter,' Lena said. She pointed her wand and focused, directing her spell at the glass but nothing happened.

'What about those ingredients over there? Can't you use them in your spell, Lena?' Kal asked. 'Amunah must've used them for something?'

'Those aren't any old ingredients,' Lena answered back sharply. 'Amunah was not a mere wizard Kal... he was a God. I can't just pick up any ingredient and use it in a spell.' Lena tried the same spell again for longer, and once again, nothing happened to the glass.

'Well excuse me,' Kal snapped back.

'Heera, only you can pass,' a female voice said. 'Come forward, Amunah's waiting for you. Well done, you've done it.' It was the same kind voice I'd heard many times before, whispering words of encouragement.

'Lena, Kal, I've heard a voice saying only I can go through the glass.'

'Heera, go,' Lena said and Kal nodded.

I moved forward and touched the glass wall with both my hands, and in my mind I said, 'I'm here, Amunah.' The glass disappeared in the blink of an eye and a wooden door appeared in its place.

Before I opened the door, I looked back and said, 'Kal, Lena, please wait for me here.'

'We'll be right here, Heera,' Kal replied as Lena smiled.

I opened the door and faced another wall made of gold particles; the door closed behind me and the gold particles came together to create a dense barrier. I took a step into the mass of gold particles with my eyes closed. I felt a rush of fresh air against my skin, and when I came out the other side, I opened my eyes slowly.

I was no longer on the mountain or in the temple, but I was standing on a hill observing thousands of flowers below. The sky above was cloudless and blue. In the distance, I could see night falling and the stars and galaxies were twinkling against the dusky sky.

There was no-one in sight; where was this place?

I couldn't help but admire the beauty of the place I'd stepped into. Colourful insects and birds were flying above me and making their way towards the night sky in the far distance.

'Heera, you've made it,' a familiar voice said.

I turned around to find Amunah standing behind me, for how long he'd been there, I didn't know. Amunah's light brown eyes were bright and twinkled in the sunlight, and he was very handsome. He appeared to be around the age of forty; I hadn't expected him to look this young considering he was a God.

I had to strain my neck to look up at him as he was rather tall and well built. I was drawn to the jewels gleaming in the crown he wore on his head, and his elegant plain robes were spotless and appeared to glow and radiate white light.

'Come, let's sit,' Amunah said while sitting down on the hill. I took a seat next to him, staring into the distance. I was confused. If Amunah was here, why couldn't he have taken the crystals back and defeated Bulzaar once and for all?

'What is this place?' I asked.

'It's a sanctuary for my believers. They come here after they leave their own world and continue their life in my world. There are other kingdoms and other sanctuaries which exist and I have to spend my time equally between them.'

'Why can't you come back to Fallowmere and stop Bulzaar and Nerrah?' I asked. 'They're planning to bring back your brother, and if he does manage to cross over, Fallowmere will be destroyed.'

'Heera, I do not need to come back because you'll stop them. I can only come back to Fallowmere when I believe all hope is lost. As long as I have one person or creature who believes in me in Fallowmere, I will help them to succeed.'

'I'm not from Fallowmere. I'm from the human world and Bulzaar's taken my whole family… I never knew you and this other world even existed,' I explained.

'Heera, Hayden was from Fallowmere and you have ties to this world through her. Deep down, I knew you would believe in me like Hayden did. I have every faith in you and I know you will bring your family back home.'

'I can't do it by myself, Amunah. I'll fail. I can't stop Bulzaar,' I said.

'Yes you can stop him and you will. You're a fighter, Heera, and when you realise this, you'll be able to defeat anybody. I certainly believe in you and there are some things I need you to do and to tell you. Let's start with getting the crystals safe first of all, and Heera this will not mean Bulzaar will become weak. He has had enough use of their power to last him for days, and you'll have to find his other weaknesses to defeat him.'

I searched around trying to find a place I could put them. I followed Amunah down the hill but I could only see field after field of flowers. I glanced up at Amunah and was about to ask him where I was supposed to place the crystals but found him staring towards the sky.

It was as though, he was expecting to see something. In the next moment, he lifted his arms and gold particles fell from the sky, spinning around in the air in a circular motion. The particles began to solidify into the shape of a gold chest in the air above a field of flowers close by, and the field vanished in front of my very eyes, leaving an area of clear blue water in its place.

The remaining particles began moving around the chest before coming towards us; as they moved closer, they formed golden steps in the water leading towards the chest.

'Heera, you must take the crystals to the chest and place them inside. You've proven yourself to me by not using the power of the crystals for any type of gain. Along with me, the chest will only reveal itself to you. It will recognise your touch and your presence, and it will open and close for you,' Amunah said, moving me forward.

I took the first step on the golden solid particles and walked across to where the chest was floating in the air. I glanced back to find with each step I took, the previous step dissolved into golden particles which glided towards and hovered under the golden chest.

When I stood on the last step, the golden particles floating under the chest came together to form a solid column, and I reached out to touch the golden chest.

The chest raised itself in the air; as it lowered back down onto the column, it opened to reveal five compartments. I retrieved the crystals from my bag and carefully placed each crystal into each compartment.

When I placed the final stone in the chest, it shuddered and lifted into the air circling above my head. Multi-coloured sparks were flying from within the chest; the lid opened and closed several times, and with a final spark of green and yellow, the chest fell gently onto the column.

The crystals were now resting in their rightful place. The column and the golden step I was standing on dissolved into the water, solidifying it. The chest rose into the air and shot up into the sky out of view. I walked back towards Amunah on the blue solid surface.

'Well done, Heera,' Amunah said proudly. 'Heera, I want you to listen to what I have to tell you.'

'Yes,' I replied.

'Even if Bulzaar no longer has the crystals, he will still have a great deal of power in him, and the evil he has spread in Fallowmere will not completely vanish. Choosing between good and evil, regardless of the crystals, leads you down different paths in life, and Bulzaar may still follow the path of evil once the power drains from him.

'However, that does not mean you've lost your battle. It's no fault of yours when someone decides to follow and believe in evil. I also understand Nerrah and Bulzaar want to bring back Raven to Fallowmere. He like Bulzaar became tempted by the crystals, which he couldn't take from me. I banished him to another kingdom and he began to find a way to get revenge. He wanted to steal the power from within the crystals and to destroy me once and for all. He wants to rule every world and kingdom, Heera, but he will never let a shred of good enter any of the worlds he rules. To him, being good is weak. Who knows what he's been up to since I last saw him? I dread to think what my brother has become. '

'Where is his kingdom?' I asked.

'In a vast land, where only despair fills the air and where my brother awaits to get his revenge.'

'Can he still come to Fallowmere?' I gulped.

'I cast a spell on Raven before he was banished and it cannot be broken by my brother. Raven only has power over his own world at the moment due to this spell, and only a powerful entity can break it. This powerful entity is not destined to be Bulzaar. Even if Bulzaar had full command of the crystals, he still would not be powerful enough to break my spell and return from Raven's realm.

'Both Nerrah and Bulzaar know that if they go to Raven's realm, they will not be able to come back. That's why they are using a portal to indirectly open a pathway without entering Raven's realm and breaking my spell.'

I wondered if Mrs Oak and Hosemee knew about the spell Amunah had cast on Raven. If I ever saw them again, I'd have to let them know that there was another way for Raven to return.

'Nerrah's ancestors worshipped my brother and many went to the Realm of the Shadows with him,' Amunah continued. 'They were all part of a powerful coven, but they too didn't know they wouldn't be able to travel between the kingdoms. Nerrah wanted to bring her ancestors and Raven back to Fallowmere, and she'd planned all along to marry King Arayan to bear him a child, who'd one day reign over Fallowmere with Raven.

'Nerrah knew perfectly well that Bulzaar wasn't powerful enough to open up a portal without the crystals, and when she managed to find the crystals, she used their power to make Bulzaar evil and powerful in order to help Raven return. Nerrah hoped Raven, in return for bringing him to Fallowmere, would share power with Bulzaar. She's very much mistaken because my brother would never share power, and if he returns, the Kingdom will never have seen such darkness. Raven has his eyes set on the human world too, and if Raven ever steps out of his world, it won't be long before he makes his mark there too.'

'Who is powerful enough to bring him back?' I asked. I dreaded the thought of Raven coming to the human world, and I hoped he would never be set free from his own realm.

'I'm certain it won't come to that. You've been here a while, Heera, and I think it's time you went back to Lena and Kal,' Amunah said, skipping over the question I'd asked him.

'But... what if?'

'Heera, you've brought me back my crystals and you've stopped a portal from opening to allow Raven's return. You've done so well and I'm proud of you. However, your main priority now is to face Bulzaar, rescue your family and return home, my child. You don't need to think about Raven any longer.'

'Did you want your pendant back?' I asked. I felt guilty wearing something which belonged to Amunah.

'No, of course not, the pendant belongs to you. Take care of it and don't let it fall into the wrong hands. The pendant also has some power and will help you to face Bulzaar.'

'Amunah, who was the woman helping me?' I asked.

'Hayden,' he replied. 'I allowed her to communicate with you through the pendant after you found the crystals. She is proud of all three of you.'

'Can I see her?' I asked.

'I'm afraid not. Once you come to my world, there are rules you have to abide by and Hayden has moved onto another world. She will not communicate with you again as you've fulfilled what was meant to be her destiny, and she is now at peace.'

I felt sad at hearing this. I wished I could've thanked my ancestor and said goodbye to her.

'Hayden says there's no need to thank her and it's not really goodbye. She'll always look down on you with Mamma by her side,' Amunah said. I was amazed at Amunah knowing what I was thinking and hearing him mention my grandmother made me well up.

'How can I speak to you if I need you?' I asked.

'I'm always listening, Heera. You can do this and well done for bringing the crystals back to safety. I must go now for I'm needed elsewhere.' I felt myself being pulled back quickly and Amunah was waving at me.

I had so many questions I needed to ask but I couldn't speak. The fields, the sky, the green hills were all blending into each other, and I was moving away from Amunah and his world. In a blink of an eye and a soft thud to the floor, I was back in the room where Lena and Kal should've been waiting for me.

CHAPTER 28

Facing the Enemy

There was no sign of them. What if they were now in danger? I started to panic. It didn't seem as if I was with Amunah for long. 'Lena... Kal! Where are you?' I said, not very loudly, in case they were in the main room of the temple. I did not get a reply.

I pushed the door fully open and entered the first chamber. They were nowhere to be found. Bright sunlight was now entering the temple through the entrance and it was very calm and quiet.

They had to be outside. I gripped my sword tightly with determination, retrieved my shield from my bag and marched out of the entrance, leaving the bag outside the temple. The sun, which was directly opposite me, was blinding. I lifted my hand over my forehead in an attempt to shield the sun from view as my eyes skimmed the area trying to find my friends.

I couldn't see or hear them; it was deadly silent. I pointed my sword straight out in front of me, expecting someone to attack me at any minute, but all was still.

As I searched around, I felt a cold breeze and heard someone whisper to me. I found my way to the edge of the mountain, still peering around and my heart was thumping against my chest. Where could they have gone? Lena and Kal would've waited for me. I looked down at Fallowmere below me and I remembered seeing this scene in my nightmare on the very night I'd found the crystals.

I closed my eyes expecting to hear the familiar voice of Amunah; however, this time no voice whispered words of encouragement. I knew something wasn't right; I could feel the presence of someone behind me, waiting for me to turn around. I kept myself calm as an overwhelming feeling of dread filled me. I didn't want Bulzaar to know that I knew he was there. I knew it must be him; if it was a friend they would've called out to me. I tightened my grip on the sword and with a deep breath steadied myself.

I moved swiftly. Spinning around, I saw Bulzaar standing leering at me with his red vicious eyes. He was livid and his distorted face enhanced his dark features further. I couldn't bear to look at him. He ducked immediately. I didn't stop to see if he would retaliate; I kept my shield against my chest wielding my sword towards him, yet he kept dodging every time.

'You stupid girl! Give the crystals to me!' Bulzaar said grinning from ear to ear like a mad man.

'Never!' I yelled back at him.

For a fraction of a second, I glanced around us. Several creatures I'd seen in the enclosure in the castle grounds were circling the mountain. Fire Blades were jumping off the fierce beasts and running towards me.

'Don't step forward, I'll manage,' Bulzaar warned the Fire Blades. They obediently waited to be called upon to help their King. 'She's nothing compared to me and it won't be long before she's dead!'

Bulzaar laughed mocking and leering at me.

I took my chance with his attention diverted and began to strike him with my sword. Bulzaar was powerful. The crystals had made him undefeatable, and he simply shielded himself from every blow with his thick metal armour.

He retrieved a sword from within his armour, hidden away, and this time he wielded his sword at me. He completely missed as I dodged his strike. He was furious. He managed to grab my arm and flung me into a pile of rocks. I lost my shield as I flew through the air and skidded across the ground, landing heavily against the sharp rocks. I grazed myself, but I managed to stand up quickly despite the stinging sensation on my hands and legs.

Warm blood trickled down my face and I saw Bulzaar raising his sword to strike me; I managed to duck his blow in time by quickly side stepping away from him. Hundreds of Fire Blades were encircling us and their yellow unblinking eyes were glaring at me.

'LET GO OF ME!' I heard Lena shriek. I turned to find both Lena and Kal being held by two Fire Blades close to the edge of the mountain. They were both struggling to get away from them, but to no avail. I felt relief at seeing them both alive; however, there was no way Bulzaar and the Fire Blades were going to spare the three of us.

I had to do something fast. Bulzaar was too strong and my sword was not helping in the slightest. I had to focus on his weaknesses like Amunah had mentioned, and his family were his ultimate weak point, but they weren't here.

He stomped towards me with his teeth bared, and his terrifying eyes focused on my every move. The heavy armoury he was wearing made a high-pitched clunk with every movement he made. I took a swipe at him, over and over again, ducking and diving, moving around him as best I could, and each time our swords met, sparks flew but still my sword made no impact on him.

He raised his sword and I ducked. This time, he knew exactly what I was going to do and he was ready for me. He grabbed my hair and pushed me to the ground and stamped on my stomach. I'd never felt such pain before and I thought I was going to die. I screamed and images of my family flooded my mind. Bulzaar stomped around me, laughing at my plight.

I tried to roll away from him but he stood over me with his sword pointed at my chest. 'Pathetic,' Bulzaar spat.

He stood waiting for my next move. It took me a few moments to come to my senses and the pain was unbearable. I managed to get on my knees; Bulzaar used his foot to slam me down once more and my face hit the ground.

He began to joke around with the Fire Blades, who loved the attention of their master, giving me the chance to crawl away from the monster. I tried to stand against a rock face but my legs kept giving way.

When I managed to get to my feet, he came to stand in front of me and pointed his sword at my throat. I lowered my sword; this surely was the stupidest thing I'd done so far, but my pendant began to beat against my chest, reassuring me that I was doing the right thing.

Bulzaar grinned, seeing me lay down the sword on the ground. Suddenly, we heard screams of pain. Bulzaar and I turned at the same time to find Lena escaping the clutches of the Fire Blade, who had been holding her hostage. Lena used her wand to wound the Fire Blades who'd captured Kal and her, and both fiends fell to the ground in pain. Kal and Lena stood side by side now as more Fire Blades circled around them.

Kal was holding out his sword, determined to protect Lena.

Bulzaar cackled. 'Your friend has given up and it's no use fighting,' he shouted towards Kal and Lena. He turned to me, 'You will meet the same fate as Hayden, but if you want to save your friends, give me the crystals and I promise your death will be swift. You will not feel a thing.'

I began to laugh at him. Bulzaar appeared to be confused and I said, 'The crystals are gone! If you want them, go into the temple and get them yourself. Oh I forgot, the temple won't reveal itself to you, never mind.'

'In the temple?' Bulzaar said to himself.

'Yes, you heard me right, Bulzaar. And by the way, Amunah says "hello", but he isn't impressed with you at all,' I said. The colour in Bulzaar's face drained and he backed a little away from me.

'You're lying! Amunah isn't here because he deserted his kingdom and the real God will reign along with me soon. The temple is no longer here,' he said, moving closer and raising his fist. Maybe, he thought I'd believe him and hand over the crystals. He didn't seem to realise I'd already delivered the crystals to Amunah and I knew I had to dig deep to get to him.

I laughed again and said, 'If the temple is no longer here, then why are you here? Oh yeah, I know why because Raven told you to guard the temple… even he knows the temple exists. The Sorin revealed itself to me, but it won't for you. You like picking on those weaker than you, don't you? If you could imprison your own daughter, Arya, then you could harm anyone. How is she Bulzaar? Still alive, I presume, or have you killed her like you're going to kill me?'

Bulzaar lowered his fist.

'Arya,' he said softly and turned away from me as if trying to remember who she was. 'Stop this nonsense,' he said while hitting the side of his head. He seemed to be getting more confused. He thumped the rock wall behind me and fragments of rock fell to the floor around us. He whacked me again to the ground; I blocked out the pain and managed to get back to my feet, and not once did I lower my gaze.

'It's not nonsense, Bulzaar. Where is your family?' I asked. 'Do you actually see them or do you only see what you want to see?'

'Heera, watch out!' Lena shouted.

'We're his family,' a familiar voice spoke from behind Bulzaar and he turned to see who was standing behind him. I saw both Arya and a woman dressed in black robes with a long hood covering her face, and she was holding Arya's hand.

Arya didn't seem to know where she was because, although her eyes were fully open, she was staring ahead and not making eye contact with either myself or Bulzaar. It seemed Nerrah had worked dark magic against her.

'Saniah... Arya. See, girl... THIS... is my family,' Bulzaar said and he struck me across the face. I was worried he'd cracked my jaw; my head was spinning and I became dazed. Every inch of my body was in pain and I could partially see the Fire Blades drawing closer. I knew they were bloodthirsty. I began to wonder how long it would take me to die, and then it hit me that I was never going to see my family again.

'Get up, Heera, you are not so weak,' Amunah whispered to me. Bulzaar was laughing at me once again, clearly impressed at the damage he'd caused to the young girl standing broken before him. Even with blood flowing down my face onto the ground, I gathered as much strength as I could to carry on.

His other weakness was his love of power. He wanted everyone to be scared of him; in truth he was nothing more than a bully, who'd intimidate anyone to get his way. I had to show him I wasn't scared of him, so despite my injuries and the pain I was in, I began to laugh at him. I wasn't going to let him win so easily, and I focused my eyes on the monster before me.

I could see Kal and Lena from the corner of my eye; they were standing with their backs to each other as two Fire Blades, threateningly, wielded their weapons at them.

'Where are the crystals?' the woman said as she came forward now. She lifted her hood and Saniah came face to face with me, but I knew it wasn't really her. Nerrah used dark magic to change herself into anything or anyone she wanted, and she was disguised as Saniah, a younger and more elegant version of Saniah at that. Arya was standing by her grandmother's side still staring into space.

I laughed.

'The crystals, where are they?' Nerrah barked and as she did so, she waved her hand; I lifted off the ground and fell back into hard stone behind me. I screamed in pain as my knees gave way and I collapsed to the ground. I never expected Nerrah to do this to me. Nerrah pushed Bulzaar to the side and moved closer to me and screamed, 'I said... GIVE ME THE CRYSTALS!'

Nerrah bent down and put her hands on my arms and legs. I felt I was being electrocuted, and every inch of my body was writhing in pain. I couldn't think at all. I thought I was surely going to faint. Nerrah stood back up and grinned at me and bellowed once again, 'I said GIVE ME THE CRYSTALS!'

I heard a scuffle from behind Nerrah. I could see that Lena and Kal had started to attack the Fire Blades around them. I could see flames flying through the air and the Fire Blades running towards the edge of the mountain. I heard someone approach Bulzaar.

'Bulzaar, they're here! We need to fight!' a raspy voice said. It sounded like a Fire Blade.

'Who are they?' Bulzaar said calmly.

'Those traitors from Kendolen! We've been tricked and they've stormed the castle! It seems they left Kendolen a few days ago, and Zara and Sebastian have brought several of them straight to the castle on Dragmatus. They're using the other beasts to come up to the mountain!'

'Let them come, they have no chance anyway,' Bulzaar said, while looking directly at me. 'I'm still strong and I can defeat them, but first I need my crystals. Go and help the others but remember don't leave any of them alive.'

Shouting and screaming filled the air, and I could see more beasts approaching the mountain. The thought of having friends helping me to fight Bulzaar gave me the strength to get up on my feet once more. Kendolen had risen to help me, along with Mykha and Nova, and not forgetting Lena and Kal. I had to do this. I grabbed my sword from the ground.

'The crystals, where are they?' Nerrah asked again. 'Those crystals belong to me! GIVE THEM TO ME NOW!'

I raised my sword and Nerrah and Bulzaar began to laugh; they did not believe I was a threat. The screams were growing stronger and more and more flames were now flying across the mountain.

I lashed out at Nerrah with my sword and a surge of energy flew through my body, all the way to my arm, and down the sword I was holding. Nerrah and Bulzaar were shocked to see the sword glow bright silver for a moment, and the force of the blow threw them back, even though the sword had not touched them.

They started to back away from me. 'I already told you once, if you want those crystals, you go and get them from Amunah yourself,' I said calmly.

Nerrah panicked, 'Amunah... is he here?'

I smirked. They were both backing into the middle of the battle; I was fully aware of the fighting going on around me. I knew if I could deal with them and make them back down, the Fire Blades would do the same.

Nerrah grabbed Arya and moved backwards. 'I'm warning you girl, give me the crystals,' Nerrah shrieked, while moving her arm in the air towards me. She was unable to hurt me and I kept walking towards them.

'I see... you're using the power of the crystals to defeat me,' Nerrah said. 'You see pathetic girl, I don't believe such a young girl would've found that temple all by herself in such a short time.'

'Wrong again... I use no magic and I need no magic, and I will defeat you both,' I said smiling. 'The crystals are gone and you'll have to tell Raven you've lost again. He won't be too happy about that. I don't care if you don't believe me... I don't have to prove anything to you.'

Nerrah's face dropped.

'NOOOOOO! She lies... move aside, Saniah, I will take care of this,' Bulzaar said pushing both Nerrah and Arya to the side. He moved forward with his sword raised; he was ready to slash me, and I was going to move as soon as he wielded his sword, but someone caught his eye behind me and he lowered his sword. 'Saniah?' he said.

I turned and found the real Saniah glaring at Nerrah disguised as her; Nerrah had been caught red handed in front of Bulzaar. It seemed Saniah had managed to escape the castle and used one of the beasts to fly up to the mountain. The fighting around us slowly stopped, and every eye was now on the two Saniah's standing face to face amidst all the mayhem.

The real Saniah was skeletal and pale and her long white hair came to her shoulders, whereas Nerrah resembled a younger version of Saniah, with a glowing, pretty face, and long brown, wavy hair. It was difficult to witness how the real Saniah had changed, when compared to the young woman she once was.

'Get away from my daughter,' Saniah said to Nerrah, who still did not let go of Arya.

'What's happening?' Bulzaar asked Nerrah.

'She's an imposter, Bulzaar. This girl is playing a nasty trick on us,' Nerrah said pointing towards me. 'She's using the crystals to cast evil magic. Bulzaar, how could such a young girl find Amunah's temple and put the crystals back? Hayden couldn't, what makes you think she's telling the truth?'

'If I was using the power of the crystals, you wouldn't have been able to lay a finger on me, and yet here I am battered and bruised,' I laughed. 'I stand before you and I have no crystals as you can see. Now back to you, Bulzaar, you claim to love your wife very much, so tell me which one is Saniah?'

'How can this be?' he asked staring at both women standing before him.

'Heera!' Kal and Lena said, running towards me. They came to stand on either side of me; Lena directed her wand at Nerrah and Kal directed his sword at Bulzaar.

'Tell me, Bulzaar, which one?' I asked again.

'QUIET, Heera Watson,' Nerrah shouted. 'Just because you're the chosen warrior, albeit by a false God, doesn't mean you can say what you wish and tell lies. Don't listen to her anymore Bulzaar! We'll find another way for Raven to enter our world.'

Bulzaar stared at his real wife and he started to bang his hand against his head. I was finally getting through to him.

'After all these years, you claim you love your family, but you still don't know which out of the two is your real wife. How sad?' I said.

'Don't listen to her, Bulzaar! Let's go. There are other ways to bring back your power,' Nerrah said while letting go of Arya and holding out her hand to Bulzaar. Lena took the opportunity to grab hold of Arya and pushed her towards her real mother. 'NOOO!' Nerrah screamed.

Arya was still under the spell and she didn't react to anything going on around her. The real Saniah held Arya, who she'd not seen since she was a small child, and comforted her. Bulzaar kept banging the side of his head, trying to figure out what was going on.

'Bulzaar! Watch out!' a Fire Blade shrieked. I saw Dragmatus flying towards us with Nova and Mykha on his back; to my delight, Mrs Oak, Parmona and Akaal were also sitting behind them.

Nerrah's eyes opened wide in fear as the new guests dismounted Dragmatus and came running towards us. Nerrah moved her hand towards Nova and Mykha and was about to cast a spell to knock them over, when Lena rushed forward and used her wand to stop her with a shielding spell.

Lena was knocked to the floor. The spell Nerrah had cast was too powerful and Lena had taken the full force of the blow; this allowed Nova and Mykha to knock Nerrah over and she fell to the ground. Mrs Oak, Parmona and Akaal were following close behind, but a group of Fire Blades intercepted them and were now holding each of them prisoner.

Bulzaar hit Mykha across the face and Nova screamed. The Fire Blades rushed forward to help their King. I knew if Bulzaar wasn't stopped, he'd kill each and every one of us. I focused myself and wielded my sword high above my head and I struck Bulzaar with it, knocking him over.

Nova was now holding Nerrah down and Saniah moved Arya out of the way. Luckily, Mykha and Nova hadn't recognised the real Saniah; her appearance had changed so drastically since they'd last met. Nerrah had chosen to appear as the Saniah, Mykha and Nova would've remembered, and that's why Nova was holding Nerrah down.

Kal was trying his best to intimidate the Fire Blades with his sword, and with Bulzaar now struggling to stand, the Fire Blades were too scared to approach me, given the impact that my sword had made on their leader. I used my sword to keep Bulzaar pinned down. He was becoming angrier and weaker as he no longer fed off the energy of the crystals, and he was using his remaining power to fight me. I don't believe he'd anticipated the fight to go on for so long.

He became breathless and kept closing his eyes, which were still glowing red, and I found him staring into space every few minutes. I grew in confidence, seeing him this way. I had hope in my heart that I could end this and my fear of him vanished. Bulzaar had to know the truth about the dangerous game his mother had played against him.

Bulzaar grabbed my leg as I turned away from him to keep an eye on Nerrah, but with one final strike to Bulzaar's chest, he lay flat on the ground, breathing fast. The armour he was wearing was solid and the sword did not cause him any permanent damage.

I didn't want to hurt him; I wanted Bulzaar to wake up to what had happened to him. He glared up at me and I saw his eyes flick from red to orange and finally to a deep brown. I hadn't expected the power of the crystals to drain from him so fast and it seemed he hadn't expected this either.

'Bulzaar, you need to know the truth. You've been cheated by someone close to you. You have to listen to me, do you understand?' I said staring deep into his eyes. 'Tell the Fire Blades to back off. They are under your instruction and they will only obey you, or else you'll lose everything. I *will* kill you, make no mistake about that.'

I heard a whisper from Amunah in my ear, 'Good, it's working. Keep going, Heera.'

I moved the sword off his chest to allow him to get up. 'Bulzaar kill her and end this madness!' Nerrah shouted as Nova was holding her down and Lena pointed her wand directly in the evil woman's face.

Bulzaar stood up panting and addressed the Fire Blades, 'Lay… down… your weapons. The girl has something to tell me.' He threw down his sword, put his head in his hands and rocked back and forth. 'What's happening to me?' Bulzaar whimpered. I saw his face begin to change before my eyes, and the distorted gaunt dark features were beginning to subside.

'What have you done?' Nerrah said, in disbelief.

CHAPTER 29

The Beginning of the End

The Fire Blades dropped their weapons without delay and stood staring at their King; the soldiers were waiting for their next command. Agatha Oak, Parmona and Akaal were let go and they came running towards me, but I put my hand up to stop them coming closer in order to protect them.

Even though the crystals were safe and the power from them was slowly draining from Bulzaar, he could still decide to follow the path of evil as Amunah had warned me. Nova didn't let go of Nerrah and Mykha had managed to stagger over to her side.

'Saniah, she has something to tell me. Someone has cheated me and I want to know who it is,' he addressed Nerrah.

'No-one has cheated you, Bulzaar! SHE IS LYING!' Nerrah shouted but Bulzaar focused on me.

'She's the one who's been lying to you,' I said, pointing my sword at Nerrah. Bulzaar moved towards me to grab my sword, but I was too swift for him. I pointed the blade at Bulzaar and I shouted, 'STOP THERE! I told you don't push me because I'll hurt you! She's not your wife!' I turned to Nerrah and shouted, 'TELL HIM THE TRUTH!'

Nova glanced at me and said, 'Heera, it *was* Saniah who attacked Mykha and me and cursed us to look like this.'

'Yes, Nova,' I said, 'I know it was Saniah who attacked you and Mykha, but Saniah isn't who you think she is. Isn't that right?' I asked Nerrah again.

Nerrah stared at me and began to cackle. 'How did you know, clever girl?' Nerrah replied. 'Nothing you say or do will change anything. I will follow my plan through.'

'Bulzaar,' I said, 'she's your mother, Nerrah! She has lied to you all these years. Saniah and Arya were taken away from you on purpose.'

Nerrah laughed, while Bulzaar, judging from the look of complete bewilderment on his contorted face, couldn't understand what he was hearing.

Nerrah laughed and suddenly pushed Nova and Mykha away. She moved closer to me and shook her head from side to side; her robes, her face, her hair, all shed away and vanished into thin air as she changed back to herself to everyone's horror. Nerrah was now a petite woman and her long, plaited, black hair fell down to her waist, and her soulless, black eyes were transfixed on her son. Her shoes, jewellery and her robes were all black and you couldn't see any other colour on her.

To look at her, you wouldn't think she'd be so cunning; she appeared to be approachable and kind, but underneath that false persona, she was an evil and manipulative woman.

'Bulzaar, my son, I did everything for you. You will be the most powerful King that Fallowmere has ever seen,' she said strolling up to him and touching his face. I thought Bulzaar was going to embrace his mother; however, he pushed her away and yelled. His face was gradually gaining colour and his eyes were completely brown in colour.

Nerrah didn't say anything and glowered at me. I addressed Bulzaar, 'Amunah told me himself that Raven doesn't share power. He'll only bring eternal darkness with him. You can still change your ways, Bulzaar. Your father believed in Amunah and you did as well at some point... just think who introduced you to the darkness of Raven?' Bulzaar stood silently, deep in thought at what I'd said.

'She lies! She doesn't speak with Amunah. He left centuries ago and hasn't come to help any of his followers,' Nerrah said. 'The true God will come here soon and I will bring him back with your help, Bulzaar.' Bulzaar couldn't look at her and moved away from her.

'You're wrong again, Nerrah! Amunah is alive and knows and sees everything,' I said.

'Why did you do it, Mother? What else have you lied about?' Bulzaar asked.

'I did everything for you Bulzaar, and I will explain everything to you later. NOW KILL HER!' Nerrah said pointing towards me. Bulzaar completely blanked out his mother.

'Saniah, I didn't know, please forgive me,' he spoke to his wife and approached her. He was standing in front of everyone as a defeated man. I was seeing the man beneath the darkness, which the crystals had conjured inside of him. Saniah backed away him from him; she was scared of what he'd become and he was taken aback at her reaction. He embraced Arya but she did not respond to him. He glared angrily at his mother and shouted across to her. Nerrah was not expecting her son to react to her this way.

'What have you done to, Arya?' Bulzaar asked. 'Lift the curse you have placed upon her mother, and on Zara and Sebastian. You're going to put everyone and everything back as it should've been. I can't believe my own mother would tear my life apart.'

'Bulzaar, my son... what are you saying? You are not in your right mind. Think of what you can achieve,' Nerrah said, sounding very hopeful she could bring her son around to her way of thinking. 'You will have the whole kingdom bowing down to you... think about it, Bulzaar. All the power and glory you could ever want will be yours. I will fix Arya, Zara, and Sebastian too if you want, but promise me you will help get the rightful God back to his kingdom.'

Bulzaar shot a glance at me while responding, 'Fine, Mother... you need to fix them first, and then I will do as you say.'

'Bulzaar, what are you doing? Please no,' Saniah said as tears rolled down her face. I was ready to hurt Bulzaar; he was still evil underneath. I stepped forward and Bulzaar glanced at me, silently pleading with me to wait. My pendant throbbed again and I stood waiting to attack him.

Nerrah came over to Arya, whispered in her ear and put her hand on her head, and Arya awoke instantly. Saniah and Bulzaar hugged her and she was trying to fathom out where she was and what was happening.

Nerrah strolled over to Zara and Sebastian staring at them with disgust. She retrieved a handful of black dust from a red pouch that appeared out of the pocket of her robes. She placed the dust on her hand and blew it towards both the siblings; the dust spiralled around their body and lifted them a few inches off the ground.

When they landed back on the ground, the black dust flew back into Nerrah's hand and Zara and Sebastian returned to normality. They both resembled their mother, Zenofur; they had wavy blonde hair, blue eyes and perfect smiles. They were happy to see each other as their true selves again and hugged each other while sobbing away. They'd even returned to the ages they were before they'd been transformed into Critanites.

'Come, now Bulzaar, I've done as you've said. No-one has come to harm,' Nerrah said glaring at me. 'This girl has ruined everything. I don't think Raven will allow you to rule with him after losing the crystals... maybe... if we can bring him back another way, he may give you another established position. I had so much planned for you and now because of HER, it's all lost!'

Nerrah walked towards the edge of the mountain but Bulzaar stood next to his wife and daughter.

Nerrah turned around to find Bulzaar standing still. 'Come I said and bring the Fire Blades with you,' she said.

314

'No, I'm not going anywhere,' Bulzaar replied, staring at his mother.

'What? What do you mean? I did what you said,' Nerrah said. 'You're choosing all of them, over me? What about the sacrifices I've made to help you become the King you are today?'

'Mother you made me a failure. You kept my family from me and I even hated my father because of you. And my own daughter, Arya, doesn't know who I really am... all because of you!'

'You don't understand, Bulzaar, they were all distractions. Arya is a part of me as well. I have loved and cared for her, haven't I? Come to me, Arya,' Nerrah said smiling but Arya turned her face the other way.

'Mother, please don't do this. Let's ask for forgiveness from Amunah. We can do it together if you wish but what you're doing is wrong,' Bulzaar pleaded.

The Fire Blades, who'd been forgotten amidst this family feud, were standing quite still, with their yellow eyes focused on their master.

'What will I tell Raven?' Nerrah said. 'I spent all these years depending on my own flesh and blood to do the right thing by using the crystals to bring the true God, Raven, back to Fallowmere. You would have been rewarded with everlasting power, Bulzaar... you've thrown everything away. Raven *will* take the crystals from Amunah himself.'

'Mother please, just listen.'

'No you're a big disappointment, Bulzaar. You will all pay and I will bring him back somehow. Heera, you will meet me again and I will destroy you,' Nerrah seethed.

Nerrah was dangerously close to the mountain edge; Bulzaar was moving towards his mother, pleading with her to stay, and she was ignoring both him and his pleas.

We all moved a little closer now trying to make Nerrah understand. She wouldn't listen and she waved her hand in the air, and the black dust, with which she had healed Mykha and Nova, was coming out of her mouth towards us at high speed.

We couldn't see anything. There was a lot of confusion with shouting and screaming coming from everywhere. Nerrah could be heard laughing and cursing everyone in sight. Once the dust settled, we found her standing at the edge of the mountain. Lena sent a spell her way and Nerrah, with a wave of her hand, made the spell rebound back towards her.

Lena fell backwards. The spell hit her on her left arm and the entire sleeve of her top was torn off. Nerrah moved closer to Lena and fixed her eyes on the black mark at the top of her arm. I saw it clearly for the first time and it was in the shape of a black panther. Mrs Oak's eyes widened.

'Lena, step away from Nerrah now!' Mrs Oak said.

Lena tried to cover her arm and stood up, ready to come towards us, but within seconds, Nerrah glided towards her with her feet off the ground, and she had her arm around Lena's neck.

I screamed.

'Heera, this is a little reminder of what it means to ruin my plans and to take my son away from me,' Nerrah said coldly. 'Say goodbye to Lena for now! I'm going to make each and every one of you pay for what you've done to me!' With those cold words, and terror in Lena's eyes, Nerrah jumped back over the edge of the mountain.

I rushed forward screaming for Lena with Kal by my side. Mykha and Nova followed us to the edge of the mountain and I saw a fierce black dragon, baring his sharp teeth at us. Mrs Oak sent spells to hurt the dragon but he sent fireballs her way and we ducked.

'To the Realm of the Shadows,' we heard Nerrah shout and in the blink of an eye, the dragon had vanished with Nerrah and Lena.

I screamed and dropped to the cold rock floor. I was disorientated. Lena had gone and it was entirely my fault. Mrs Oak comforted me but I wanted to see Kal; after all, it was the three of us who'd taken this journey together, and now that Lena had gone, he was the only one who'd understand what I was going through.

I crawled to see where he was and found him sitting on the ground with tears in his eyes, shaking like a leaf. He saw me and ran over to console me. What happened next, I didn't know. *Amunah, please help me,* I said to myself, *bring her back to me, please.*

CHAPTER 30

A Kingdom Restored

Two long days had passed since I'd collapsed on the mountain. I was still seeing moving shadows in my mind that were slowly becoming clear, and I could make out familiar voices. I lay still with my eyes closed.

Mount Orias came into view and I could hear Lena calling out to me. I rushed to the edge and saw her on the black dragon, screaming for help. The dragon was moving closer to me, and Lena held out her hand for me to grab her, but it was unsafe.

Lena tried to stand on the dragon's back so that she could reach my hand. She raised one arm and the dragon moved; she fell hurtling to the ground, screaming out my name, and I sat bolt upright calling out her name.

'Heera, you're safe… calm down,' Mrs Oak said.

I didn't want to speak to anybody. Memories of how Lena was taken by Nerrah came speeding back to me, and I felt that raw pain again. I couldn't breathe. Instead of looking at Mrs Oak and the rush of familiar faces coming into the room, I tried to get out of the bed.

Mrs Oak was stopping me. Didn't she realise Lena was waiting to be rescued? I was in a comfortable high bed, with purple velvet drapes around the sides. The room itself was elegant, littered with expensive cabinets and trinkets. There were several candle holders and lit candles placed on every available surface making the room warm and cosy.

'Mrs Oak, my family, where are they?' I asked. How could I forget them? I couldn't bear to hear any more bad news.

'Heera, they've been rescued and are back home safely. They were put under a deep sleeping spell, and I personally took them back through the portal. They won't remember a thing.'

I breathed a sigh of total relief and broke down. My family were safe and I was glad they didn't know what had happened to them.

'We need to get Heera home,' Kal said. I hadn't noticed him standing at the door and he appeared not to have slept a wink.

'Yes, Agatha, take her home. She's done enough for this Kingdom,' Hosemee said. I hadn't seen him either; he was standing behind Mykha and Nova, who were grinning at me.

'You've done so well,' Nova said.

'You did it! And good thinking sending Dragmatus to find us,' Mykha said. 'We gave Morog the slip and found Agatha and the others and brought them to the mountain. Sorry I ever doubted you, Heera.'

'Heera, you're awake,' another voice spoke as he entered the room with Saniah and Arya by his side. It was Bulzaar. I started to look for my sword. I had to be prepared in case he hurt me, but he simply stood next to his family and smiled whilst Saniah and Arya grinned. 'Thank you for making me realise my mistakes. I had no idea what was happening to me.'

There was no sign of darkness in Bulzaar. He appeared to be in good health; his eyes were permanently brown and his face was no longer distorted. He was tall and towered over everyone. Saniah and Arya were in good spirits and were happy to have Bulzaar back to normal.

'You did it, Heera,' Saniah said.

'Thank for setting me free, Heera,' Arya said.

I didn't know how to respond and there was an awkward silence. Did they not realise that Lena was gone? How could I go back to the human world after what'd happened? I didn't care for their 'well dones' and 'thank you's.'

'Heera!' a voice said. I glanced at the door and this time my heart leapt. It was Jack, alive and well. Jack still had bruises and scratches on his pale face and some of the bruises were as black as his wavy hair. His brown eyes lit up when he saw me and he smiled from ear to ear. He stood with his arms folded and he was dressed in a simple black T-Shirt and blue jeans.

Kal was furious. I knew he hated Jack.

'Jack, sorry I didn't come and rescue you,' I said rather glumly.

'You must be going mad, Heera. It's because of you Bulzaar didn't get a chance to turn me into a Fire Blade... no offence, Bulzaar,' Jack grinned at Bulzaar. 'Agatha and her army stormed the castle and rescued me.'

Bulzaar grinned back.

'I think Heera needs to rest,' Kal said, rather abruptly.

'Heera, I'll see you once you've had some rest... alone,' Jack said and smiled at Kal. Kal clenched his fists and didn't return the smile. I didn't know what I was going to do with the both of them.

'Let's give her some time, she's tired,' Hosemee said, and slowly the room began to empty.

'Mrs Oak, Hosemee and Kal, please can you stay with me,' I said as everyone else left.

Kal lifted Hosemee onto the bed and I couldn't help the tears flooding down my cheeks. 'She's gone, Nerrah took her, and it's all my fault,' I sobbed.

'It's not your fault and Lena will come back again. Agatha and Hosemee said she will,' Kal said.

'Really? But how and when?' I asked, wiping my tears away while waiting for Hosemee and Mrs Oak to answer me. Mrs Oak was apprehensive at first and Hosemee shook his head.

'Yes, she will come back, but whether it's our Lena, we'll have to wait and see,' Mrs Oak said.

'What do you mean, Agatha?' Kal asked, clearly on the verge of breaking down himself.

'Nerrah is going to use Lena to bring Raven back. He'll break her down because Lena has been taken against her own will, and he will use her to his own advantage. Raven's power, in many ways, is stronger than Amunah's because he does not share it like his older brother.

'Lena will turn into our worst nightmare if Raven gets his way. She won't know any boundaries and she won't care for her friends or family. Bulzaar was defeated because you were able to break him down. I'm afraid with Lena it won't be so easy.'

'So you both knew there was another way for Raven to return but you never told us how?' I asked both Hosemee and Mrs Oak.

'Heera, now is not the time to discuss this,' Mrs Oak replied.

'How do we get her back?' I asked, pressing for answers.

'It's impossible,' Hosemee simply said. I knew he was lying because he said it so quickly and looked the other way.

'There has to be a way,' I said.

'Did you really meet, Amunah?' Kal asked and Hosemee clutched his heart. Mrs Oak gasped.

'Yes, I saw him in the temple. He was the one who told me where I should put the crystals.'

'Will he come back?' Hosemee asked hopefully.

'I don't know, Hosemee. I need to speak to him again and find a way to get Lena back.'

'WE have to get Lena back,' Kal said.

'No, you've both done enough, and you need to go back to your parents and live normal lives,' Hosemee said.

'What about Lena's parents? As for living a normal life, well for how long?' I asked. 'Raven will return and there will be nothing left, and he has his eyes set on the human world too. I need to save Lena from him.'

Hosemee became silent.

'How're, Fergal and Ruby?' I asked.

'They're back at the tree house,' Hosemee said. 'They really wanted to come when they heard what'd happened, but I felt it was best that they stay behind in my absence and take care of the others.'

'Heera, your work here is done and it's time for you to leave this world. I will take you back,' Mrs Oak said.

'I can't go, Mrs Oak! Don't you understand anything? I have to go get Lena,' I said.

'And how exactly are you going to do that Heera? Do you even know the danger you'll be dealing with?' Mrs Oak said.

'Agatha's right, Heera, you have to go home,' Hosemee said. I was crestfallen at their reactions, but in a way Mrs Oak was right. I had to prepare myself to fight Raven. Surely, the Elders would know what to do which reminded me of Landon.

'Mrs Oak, Landon Tomkins was the traitor!' I said.

She smiled and continued, 'Yes, we found out. He's been locked away in the Caves of Arya. We found out he was the culprit, the day after he left Kendolen. We found his walking stick in Gentley Woods, and when we searched his house, we found his magical mirror. We trained hard and ventured out of Kendolen with our army to face Bulzaar ourselves. He wouldn't expect us to bring the fight to him, and this of course, gave him the element of surprise.'

'What happened to the Fire Blades?' I asked.

'They've changed back to their normal selves,' Hosemee replied. 'Their power dwindled as did Bulzaar's, and thanks to you, hundreds of humans who were soldiers will again live side by side with witches, warlocks and other creatures in the kingdom. Amunah's wish of having a kingdom where all creatures and humans live in peace as equals has come true once again.'

'Won't the humans die? I mean to say, they're not magical and they can't live for hundreds of years,' I asked.

'They can in Fallowmere, Heera. Amunah made sure of that,' Hosemee said.

'How did Bulzaar's power drain so quickly?' I asked.

'Your battle with him drained him of the majority of the power he had, and after realising his mistakes and spending time with his family, the remaining power left him,' Mrs Oak explained.

'The portal's ready, Agatha,' Parmona said at the door. 'Heera, come, it's time to go,' the Elder said.

I really didn't know how to take Parmona. She was blunt and yet she'd come to help me on the mountain. I didn't react to the way she spoke to me because maybe that was just her character.

'Thank you,' I said, getting out of bed.

'I found your rucksack, Heera. You left it outside the temple,' Kal said.

I took the bag and found my sword and shield at the foot of the bed. I found it incredibly weird that this was how my time here was going to end. It didn't seem right.

Mrs Oak, Kal, Hosemee and Parmona led me down a corridor. Once we reached the grand staircase, I realised I was in Cranwell Castle. Bulzaar's whole family were waiting at the foot of the staircase, and I saw Kal's father, but there was no sign of Lena's parents.

Mrs Oak led me down the stairs and towards the black door, which I'd used to get to the tower. I didn't want to go home, and it must've shown on my face because each and every one was waiting to console me. They simply didn't understand that everything felt meaningless to me without Lena.

'Heera, wait!' I heard a voice say. I turned to find Tallon running towards me. He threw his arms over me and wouldn't let go. 'You set me free... I knew you could do it!'

'Thanks, Tallon,' I said.

Mrs Oak tapped her wand on the door and it shook violently; bright light filtered through the keyhole for a few moments before the door became still.

'OK, it's time,' Mrs Oak said.

'Agatha wait, before Heera goes, there's something I want to say,' Bulzaar said, stepping forward. 'I have no words to describe what you've done for me, Heera, and I can never repay you enough, but thank you very much.'

'You're welcome,' I said.

'Heera, this is your home too, and you are just as much part of this Kingdom as we are. Please don't forget us,' Zara said, giving me a tight hug. It was weird to see her as a young girl, yet she was still as gentle and loving as she had been when I'd first met her. Sebastian followed with a gentle hug.

'Are you actually leaving without saying goodbye, Heera Watson?' Jack asked. I hadn't seen him waiting patiently at the back of the crowd.

'Sorry, Jack. I didn't see you and yes, I'm going home now,' I said, blushing as he came forwards to hug me. The first thing I noticed was the strength in his arms. They were as strong as ever and I felt completely safe. I felt his breath on my ear and I panicked and pushed him away. Jack didn't think anything of it and smiled.

'You will be back though, won't you?' Jack asked. 'The whole coven has come out of hiding, and we're all moving back to Kendolen, and it would be good to... you know... see you again, or I'll have to make a trip to your world. Promise me, we'll see each other soon.'

'I promise,' I smiled.

'I'm sorry about what happened to Lena. She seemed like a nice girl,' Jack said.

Hearing Jack talk about Lena made me well up. Mrs Oak saved the day by interrupting, 'Heera, come on, it's time to leave.'

'Bye everyone,' I said, my eyes searching for Kal, who was standing with his dad.

Kal came forward and gave me a hug, his grey eyes brimming with tears, and he whispered in my ear, 'Bye for now, Heera. We'll get her back, regardless of what everyone says. I'm going to find out as much as possible because this lot are hiding something, and once I know what's going on, I'll come and find you.'

I smiled through my tears. Eventually, everyone moved back and with one last glance, Mrs Oak opened the door and pulled me into the smoke, which was erupting from the other side of the portal. I closed my eyes at the intensity of the lights flickering in the smoke. This portal was making my head spin and I felt nauseous. I heard another door open and Mrs Oak pulled me out of the smoke. When I opened my eyes, I was in my bedroom.

'I've tidied up and everything should be as it was,' Mrs Oak said. 'Your parents and brothers are in their rooms asleep. When I wake them up, they'll think the whole family has come down with flu. You've been absent for three whole days at school, not including Saturday and Sunday. Today's Sunday, and you can rest and return to school tomorrow.'

'Only three days? I've been away for almost two weeks in Fallowmere,' I said.

'I told you, Heera… time works differently in Fallowmere,' Mrs Oak laughed. 'You have to pretend you've been ill, and it's best if you never tell your parents or anyone here what happened to you, Heera. It's for their own good.'

'I won't tell anyone,' I said. Even if I did, my parents wouldn't believe me. I was just happy my family were safe.

'There is something I want to ask you but don't take it the wrong way, Heera. Do you want me to erase your memories because I have the power to do so?'

'No, Mrs Oak, how could you even ask me that?' I said, rather sharply.

'It's for your own good,' Mrs Oak said, kindly.

'No, I want to keep my memories and I will get Lena back somehow, regardless of what you say or think,' I said.

'That's exactly what I expected from you, Heera. If only your family knew what you've been through, they'd be so very proud of you,' Mrs Oak said. She hugged me before leaving me in my room to check on my parents and brothers.

I closed the door to my bedroom, put my bag down on my bed and hid my sword and shield at the very back of my cupboard. I had to find another hiding place for these, I thought to myself. Imagine trying to explain to my parents what a sword and shield were doing in the house.

As I turned towards my bed, I felt my pendant throb and an image came into my mind. I felt a sharp pain at the back of my head as if someone had hit me with something hard.

I fell to the ground.

A dark room came into view. I couldn't see anyone.

'Where is she?' a stony, callous male voice spoke, sending shivers down my spine.

'Bring her in!' a woman barked.

'GET OFF ME!' I heard Lena scream. She came into focus and she was being handled by two hooded creatures. I couldn't see their full faces, but they snapped their jaws at her, baring their sharp black teeth next to her face to scare her. Lena screamed again and shut her eyes, 'Let me go please! Amunah, please help me!'

The creatures let go of her and she stood shaking, pleading with Nerrah, who came into view out of the darkness. 'I'm sorry, Nerrah, please forgive me. Let me go back to my parents.'

'Oh my sweet girl, who says I'm angry at you. There is someone I want you to meet... he will be your new God and you owe your allegiance to him,' Nerrah said very sweetly while putting her arm around Lena and bringing her forwards to the corner of the room.

Lena shrieked out loud when she looked up into the corner, and she fainted and fell to the ground. Nerrah laughed and the cold voice sniggered. 'She's perfect,' Raven said.

Just as the vision had come, it went in an instant. I managed to stand and I took a hold of my pendant. Where was Amunah? Didn't he know Lena was gone? Why wasn't he giving me any solutions as to how to help find her? I was angry and confused. I'd find a way myself. I owed that to Lena and her parents. The house phone rang; I reluctantly answered the handset in my room.

'Heera, you best not be lying to me about being ill just to get out of coming to the Christmas party,' Emma said. 'Laura Foster and her gang have been talking about you behind your back because they expected you to do the science project for them, and they can't get a hold of you.'

'Ems, I'll be in school on Monday and Laura Foster's time as a bully is up. She won't know what's hit her. As for her gang, once their leader's powerless... well... they will be too. Things are going to change with me and for the better. I will be attending the Christmas party with you, and not to prove a point to Laura, but because I promised you I'd come.'

'Ummm, is this Heera and if not, what have you done with her?' Emma said, shocked at hearing me talk about Laura like this.

'Let's say I've been on quite a journey… see you tomorrow!' I said, putting the phone down.

I knocked on my parents' bedroom door.

'Come in!' I heard from the other side and at the same time, the door to my brothers' room opened and they both came running out and headed straight into my parents' room.

Mrs Oak was no longer here.

I entered the room with relief and a smile at seeing them all together. I could hardly believe it had taken a journey filled with so many challenges and dangers for me to understand how much my family meant to me.

The hardest part would be to return to normality knowing I had a deep dark secret. I only hoped Kal would do as he said. He was right about one thing in that Mrs Oak and the others were hiding something, and I was going to make sure I found out exactly what it was.

I laughed and smiled with my family, trying to forget, for the time being, about Fallowmere, Kal and Lena. It was not easy; my hand was restless for my sword and my pendant beat against my chest.

When the time came to rescue Lena, I knew I had to be ready to fight with all my strength, all my resolve, and all my courage.

THE END

Acknowledgements

I would like to thank my family and my close friends for helping me to become who I am today.

My thanks also to James Essinger for believing in me and in Heera, and to Francesca Garratt for her excellent editing.

Finally, I would like to thank Charlotte Mouncey for her brilliant design skills on the cover of the book.